CW00950249

BEC MCMASTER

THE MECH
WHO
LOVED ME

LONDON STEAMPUNK
THE BLUE BLOOD CONSPIRACY

ALSO AVAILABLE BY BEC MCMASTER

LONDON STEAMPUNK SERIES
Kiss Of Steel
Heart Of Iron
My Lady Quicksilver
Forged By Desire
Of Silk And Steam
Novellas in the same series:
Tarnished Knight
The Curious Case Of The Clockwork Menace

LONDON STEAMPUNK: THE BLUE BLOOD CONSPIRACY SERIES
Mission: Improper
The Mech Who Loved Me

DARK ARTS SERIES
Shadowbound
Hexbound
Soulbound

BURNED LAND SERIES
Nobody's Hero
The Last True Hero
The Hero Within

LEGENDS OF THE STORM
Heart of Fire

OTHER
The Many Lives Of Hadley Monroe

Kiss Of Steel – Georgia RWA Maggies Best
Paranormal Romance 2013

Heart Of Iron – One of Library Journal's Best
Romances 2013

Forged By Desire – RITA Finalist Paranormal
Romance 2015

Of Silk And Steam – RT Reviews Best Steampunk
Romance 2016 and Best Steam-Powered Mechanical
Costume Award from SFR Galaxy Awards

Mission: Improper – #1 Amazon Steampunk
Bestseller, Finalist for 2016 PRISM Award Best
Steampunk

Hexbound – Winner of the 2016 PRISM Award for
Historical Fantasy

CHAPTER ONE

THE BRIDE WAS resplendent, the groom was nervous, the drawing room decked out in enough flowers to make a florist envious, and someone had seen to it there was enough blud-wein to satisfy even the most ravenous blue blood. Ava McLaren stood at the back of the room as the man she'd once thought she loved married the woman of his dreams.

And she wasn't quite certain how she felt about that.

Happy, of course. They were her dearest friends. But there was also a lonely little feeling in her chest—a feeling that wondered if *she'd* ever be the one standing there stating her vows with a man she loved.

"I now pronounce you man and wife," the celebrant called, and Caleb Byrnes captured Ingrid's face in his hands as he leaned down to kiss her. All of Ava's wistful feelings swept away. It was a beautiful moment shared between two people she loved, and if she took herself out of the equation, then she was genuinely happy to be here.

And then of course, *he* appeared.

The storm clouds to her sunshine. The bah humbug

to her Christmas.

A warm presence brushed against her bare elbow. Deliberately, she was certain. Kincaid knew what sort of effect he had upon her. Ava clapped her gloved hands as the groom kissed his bride, all of her senses locked onto that one imposing figure behind her. The faint hint of mechanical oil contrasted sharply with his lemon verbena aftershave. He was an enormous man who towered over her, and it always felt like some internal furnace threw heat out from his body like some sort of aura. Or perhaps that was simply the fact he was human, when she was a blue blood, and therefore had a lower temperature.

"Well, there goes fifty quid," Kincaid muttered in her ear. "Thought Byrnes would see sense in the end."

Ava's spine stiffened.

"Then you're a fool," she whispered, half craning her head toward him, even as her hands continued clapping. She caught a glimpse of a smooth jaw—at least he'd shaved for the occasion, even if his jaw would bear dark stubble by this afternoon. "Byrnes loves Ingrid. And he's a lucky man to have a woman like her by his side. Anyone who knew how much they've been through in the past couple of months would see this is the happiest day they've had in a long time."

"Easy, kitten." Kincaid breathed out an amused laugh, the faint lines at the corners of those devastatingly blue eyes creasing. His fingertips rested against the small of her back. "With such fervency, you'll scare off the local bachelors."

A swift retort died on the tip of her tongue. All she could feel were those warm fingers against her back.

Kincaid seemed to sense her hesitation. He looked down just as she looked up, and suddenly it felt as though all sound drained out of the room.

He rarely touched her.

Or at least he hadn't in recent weeks.

Ever since that night she'd gotten lost in the gardens of a pleasure house, and Kincaid found her. Ava had been suffering one of her hysteria fits, and somehow he'd calmed her down. By the time she'd realized they were alone and his coat was around her shoulders, the predator within her had roused.

At first she'd thought she wanted his blood. Her affliction with the craving virus had forced her to endure many moments like that over the years. But the second he touched her, something in her body had shifted, and suddenly she wasn't thinking about his blood at all.

And he'd known it.

Damn him.

"The only bachelors in this room are Charlie and yourself," she said, finally finding her voice. "Charlie's barely a man grown, and you... well you're entirely unsuitable. If you feel the need to flee then please don't hesitate. The rest of us are here to celebrate a wedding."

That hand splayed across her lower back, his palm caressing her spinal muscles. *Good heavens.* Ava's mind went vacant for a moment.

She swiftly tugged out of her reticule the small flask of protein solution she'd been using to keep the craving at bay. Ava unscrewed the cap, tipping it to her lips. It tasted vile and it barely assuaged her thirst, but it seemed her body was surviving on this last batch better than any of the others she'd concocted. It kept the crawling itch in her throat to a tolerable level, and stopped her vision from slipping into the sharp black-and-white-tinted relief that heralded the rise of her bloodlust.

"Tempting," Kincaid murmured, "but Byrnes has promised me the finest bottle of brandy he could get his hands on. He owes me for the broken nose." A nose which had healed slightly wrong, giving Kincaid a somewhat rakish look. Ava's lips thinned as she glanced away from his face. "So there's no other reason you're here at this moment? Not a single reason?"

"I was still holding the carriage to Calais out front," he jested.

Or at least, she hoped it was a jest. "Too late now. They're married and about to start the rest of their lives together."

"It's never too late."

"Why are you so cynical?" she demanded in a hoarse whisper, still trying to keep her voice low enough so none of the others would hear.

"Why are you such a dreamer?"

Touché. Ava glanced back at the bride and groom as guests greeted them. Ingrid glowed with happiness. "Because this world can be a horrible place," she said softly, "and it's moments like this that remind me there can be joy and happiness sometimes too. This moment is a lovely one, and I shall cherish it for as long as I live. My friends are happy. They're married. They're about to step into a long, blessed future. It's perfect."

She felt that knowledge fill her from within, softening all the lonely little hollows that lay tucked in her heart. On the darkest night, in the worst moments of her nightmares, she could look back on this moment now and it would fill her with hope.

"It's a fairy tale," Kincaid murmured, and he too was watching the bride and groom, almost as if he saw something she didn't. "And how long does the fairy tale last? Nobody ever thinks about what happens to Cinderella after she marries the prince. Maybe her life is not all hope and dreams, as she spends the rest of her days with a man who couldn't even recognize her. I'm not a cynic. I'm a realist."

Ava punched him lightly in the arm.

He looked down in surprise.

"Stop ruining my moment. Take your scowling elsewhere. Cinderella lives happily ever after and I will not accept a different conclusion."

"You like weddings," he accused, his dark brows drawing together as if he'd only just realized this fact.

It wasn't as though she was ever going to have one herself, so she might as well enjoy others. "Yes, I like weddings."

"You want to be married," he said, and Ava's insides went cold.

"Blood and steel," she hissed. "Who doesn't? Surely everyone dreams of a loving lifetime with—"

"Marriage doesn't mean one enjoys a happy life. I've known plenty of unhappy marriages."

"You're impossible."

"At least I tell the bloody truth," he snapped back at her.

Ingrid gave the crowd her back, and moved her arm. Ava shot Kincaid a fierce glower. "Well, you're the only man who thinks—"

Something came at her. Fast.

Ava threw up her hands, catching whatever it was, and found herself in possession of a bunch of flowers.

The room stopped dead. Heads turned, people moved, and suddenly Ava found herself the center of attention.

She and Kincaid.

Who finally jerked his hand off her back, the wretch.

"Best of luck, Ava," Ingrid called, blowing her a kiss.

The room erupted. Clapping echoed and Ava froze.

Then the rest of the guests were moving on to the wedding toast, finally letting her fade back into obscurity.

She could almost *feel* his eyes on her.

"Do. Not. Say a word," she ground out through gritted teeth.

"I—"

"I mean it." Slapping the bouquet against his chest, she pushed away from him. "The flowers are all yours."

Then she left Kincaid with Ingrid's bouquet, gathered her skirts, and slipped from the room.

"They're about to serve the wedding breakfast," said a low feminine voice behind her. "Are you coming in?"

Perry. She was one of Ava's best friends. They'd worked together for years at the Nighthawks—a guild of thief catchers and hunters—and shared a common history. Perry was also the only person who might see straight through her.

Ava took a deep breath, putting another smile in place as she turned away from the gardens. "Oh, are they? I just wanted some fresh air and it's been so long since we had a sunny day like this." Being alone also made her feel like she didn't have to keep the charade in place. It was oddly restful to let her smile fade.

Perry shot her an odd look, but leaned on the balustrade beside her as they looked out over the gardens. "You're upset."

Damn it. Ava's shoulders slumped. "No. I'm happy for them, truly I am."

"You cared for Byrnes."

"I also care for Ingrid. She suits him. And... I guess seeing them together makes me realize what Byrnes and I never had."

Perry's mouth pursed thoughtfully, but she didn't prod. It was one of the reasons Ava liked her so much.

"I had this idea of how my life was going to work out," Ava continued. "After Doctor Hague kidnapped me and destroyed my life, it took me such a long time to find my place at the Nighthawks. The work in the laboratories fascinates me and I'm perfectly suited for it, but... I wanted more. I keep trying to find my footing, to find a place where I belong, and I thought Byrnes was it. I like him. He makes me feel safe and normal, and he never looks at me as though he can't wait to escape me when I prattle on about odd things like autopsies, or a new species of orchid, or... all of the things ladies shouldn't speak of in polite circumstances. He was a friend when I needed one very, very much, and I kept thinking he would probably be the only man who might marry me." She looked down at her clasped hands. That dream was well and truly dashed, but she couldn't find it in herself to begrudge Ingrid her happiness. When Ingrid walked into Byrnes's life, all she'd ever done was open Ava's eyes to the truth: Byrnes was one of her dearest friends.

And that was all.

"After Hague, it took me a long time to find my place in the world too," Perry said softly, staring out over the gardens.

They both fell silent.

Nothing more needed to be said in regard to Hague. The scientist had been obsessed with creating the perfect biomechanical heart to implant in people. Unfortunately, he'd needed to experiment on real humans to perfect his transplant process, and he'd chosen young women whom he'd kidnapped right off the streets. Not all of them survived.

Perry was the one who got away years before Ava was ever taken, but they both shared the same nightmares. Ava had been one of his later victims, one of only two who survived the process. Six months of hell. She closed her eyes, taking in a shallow breath.

He was dead now.

Perry's husband, Garrett, had killed him, finally setting Perry free from the nightmares that haunted her. But Ava sometimes felt as though he would always exist in her own life, a dark cloud hovering on her every horizon. "I just... I don't know where my life is heading. I enjoy my work. It's challenging and I have value here. But I feel like I want more, and it's difficult to watch others who've found that *more*. And it's so horribly selfish of me to begrudge—"

"It's not selfish," Perry corrected, patting Ava's hand. "It's human. And it's honest. Why shouldn't you want more? And I know you don't wish Ingrid and Byrnes ill, you're simply focusing on what you *don't* have when you look at them. You'll find someone, Ava. I promise you."

She sighed. "You make it sound easy."

"It is easy, in the end. I never dared admit what Garrett meant to me. I never dared hope for marriage, or children, or even love, because I knew until Hague was dead, I would never get that chance. Don't stop believing, Ava. There's someone out there for you. Someone who will love you exactly the way you are, autopsies, rare plant obsession, and all."

"Well, I wish he would make himself known sometime soon," Ava said. "I'm nearly thirty, and the closest I've come to a kiss is my ex-fiancé, which was more of a swift peck against the cheek. I shall, however, draw the line if I'm nearly forty and still in the same dire straits."

Sunlight gleamed in Perry's golden hair as the other woman laughed. She'd stopped dying it black after Hague died and her true identity was revealed. Marriage and babies had softened her in other ways, and though she was the daughter of an earl, she'd decided to stay on at the Nighthawks. She was no longer the quiet, insulated hunter she'd once been, but nor had she returned to ranks of the aristocratic Echelon. Instead it seemed as though Perry had found some sort of middle ground, and flourished there.

Ava longed for that kind of self-acceptance. "I don't know where my place is anymore. Or where my future might lie. I just feel lost, Perry, and it's more than merely wanting a happy future for myself. Every day just seems the same."

"Then maybe you need to change something in your life? It seems from what you've said marriage is a goal. Not specifically marriage to Byrnes."

Ava paused. "I guess I cannot see anyone else wanting to marry me."

Paul's face flashed into her mind. He'd been her childhood friend growing up, and had promised many things when he'd proposed to her. Three days later, Hague kidnapped her out of her carriage on her way to Paul's house for a dinner.

Nightmares aside, by the time she escaped from Hague, all she'd wanted to do was return to her normal, small little life.

Except it wasn't the same.

Paul had been downright shocked to see her again. Especially since he was betrothed to someone else. Ava had never felt smaller than she did in that moment, and she'd wished them well, and meant it, but... he could have waited just a little longer. It hadn't even been a year.

"Mmm." She curled a frond of the nearest fern around her finger, letting the feathery tip caress her skin. "I think I am going to bury my desire for marriage. I just don't think it's ever going to happen."

After all, if Byrnes didn't want me, then who would?

"Don't lock yourself away," Perry warned.

"I won't." This time her smile at the other woman was genuine. "I have too many good friends who won't allow me to do so."

"I'm sure there's someone out there who is looking for a woman, one just like you."

"You have to say that. You're my friend. But the only gentlemen I know are those I work with." Ava screwed up her nose. "Yes, none of the Nighthawks are squeamish, but none of them interest me even vaguely."

"What about that big fellow inside? He kept looking at you today—at least often enough I noticed it."

A frown drew her brows down. Big fellow? The ceremony had been small, the guests a carefully picked handful of Nighthawks Byrnes knew, the Company of Rogues of course, and Ingrid's adopted family. Who else could look at her like—? "Kincaid," she suddenly blurted.

"Tall, savage-looking mech?"

"Have you had too many wedding toasts?" Ava blurted.

"He's handsome," Perry pointed out. "Clearly knows his way around women, and he couldn't take his eyes off you."

"I'm probably the only woman in there who's not married. He is the worst sort of rake! And he doesn't like me. We work together. We—"

"A physically fine specimen, however."

Heat filled Ava's cheeks. "While I cannot deny that, there is one crucial flaw with your thinking. Kincaid despises blue bloods." She gestured to herself. "*I* am a blue blood. He also has a distinct dislike for virgins and no interest in marriage. Indeed, a significant aversion to such a state. This morning he told Byrnes if the groom wanted to flee across the Channel, there was still time and he'd stall the wedding party."

Perry crossed her arms over her bosom. "You don't have to *marry* him."

"*What?*" She wasn't certain she'd heard Perry correctly.

"And if he is opposed to your state of virginity, then he could rectify that quite swiftly."

Please, garden, swallow me whole....

"If you cannot find someone who fits your ideal as a husband, and you feel like you're missing out, then why not explore your options? Consider it an experiment. Do you really want a husband? Are you simply lonely? Curious? Or is it something else?"

Ava stared at her. The very idea... was not as outlandish as it first seemed.

"Ah, I thought I heard your voice out here." With that, Perry's husband Garrett appeared. He slid a hand over the small of her back, and the two of them looked into each other's eyes. "Were you looking for me? I heard you mention a 'physically fine specimen.'"

Perry rolled her eyes. "This is none of your business. Go back inside."

"Who do I have to kill?" he asked promptly.

"No one. I was referring to a gentleman for Ava. Not one I had *my* eye upon."

Garrett's blue eyes twinkled teasingly as he glanced at Ava. "Good. It's bad taste to shed blood at a wedding. Who are we hunting?"

Oh, God. Ava groaned. "We are not hunting anyone. *I* am not hunting anyone. Perry has this mad scheme."

"You always have the best schemes," he told his wife. "What's the scheme?"

Perry fiddled with the buttons on his coat, setting him

to rights again. "You're not going to like it."

"You don't know that," he protested.

"I told Ava she didn't need a husband. What she needs is... to experience passion."

Garrett looked blank. Then his cheeks reddened. "No. That's enough." He held his hands in the air. "I positively don't need to know anything more about this scheme. Do not listen to Perry. You're a young, unmarried woman—"

"A state that doesn't seem to have any prospect of changing anytime soon," Ava argued. "And I'm six-and-twenty, Garrett. Hardly a debutante."

"You also didn't seem to have those compunctions when you were chasing me." Perry crossed her arms over her chest.

"That was different."

"Oh?" One perfect blonde brow arched.

"It was different because it was me, and I knew what my intentions toward you were," he countered. "What you're encouraging is—"

"An experiment," Ava said, warming up to the idea. Not a husband, but a lover.

"Possible future heartbreak." Garrett hesitated before patting her shoulder. "I don't want to see you hurt, Ava. You know...."

What you've been through, remained unsaid.

It flavored every encounter she had with the Nighthawks. They all knew. They'd all been there, and seen her slow recovery. Physically she'd been fine, but emotionally.... That was a different story.

It was one of the reasons she'd accepted the Duke of Malloryn's offer to become the Company of Rogues' crime scene investigator. She'd desperately needed to get out of the Nighthawks guild, even for a little while.

Ava's shoulder wilted under his touch. Garrett was like

an older brother; the one she'd never had. But sometimes his presence seemed stifling.

"And what *you're* suggesting," Perry added quietly, "is Ava never gets a chance to spread her wings. Sometimes concern can seem like a cage, Garrett. I've been there. It's a horrible thing to feel lonely, even when you have a dozen people watching over you. Especially then."

Garrett opened his mouth to say something, and then shut it. "A wise man realizes when the odds are against him."

"I haven't said I'm going to do such a thing." Ava hurried to fill the sudden awkwardness. "I'm just... contemplating options. At this moment I cannot see marriage in my future, and as Perry says, it's a lonely feeling."

"Fine," he growled. "It's your choice, Ava. It always is. Just be careful. I should hate to have to murder someone because they broke your heart. It's not very becoming for the master of London's law enforcement to have blood all over his hands."

"I'll be fine." A sudden kerfuffle drew her attention inside, to the appearance of a liveried footman wearing dark red and silver. Whose House colors were those? She wasn't familiar with the aristocratic Echelon who'd once ruled the city, beyond a peripheral awareness.

But Perry stiffened. As the Earl of Langford's daughter, she had been raised within the Echelon and trained to recognize such things. "Sir Gideon Scott's footman, by the look of it. But why would he be interrupting the wedding of two people he barely knows?"

Sir Gideon was an official representative of the Council of Dukes who ruled the city, and it was rumored he had the queen's ear. A powerful man.

"Here," Garrett called, gesturing the fellow through

the glass doors onto the patio. "You look lost. Can we help?"

The footman seemed breathless. "Is the duke inside?"

"More specifics, man," Garrett said. "At last count we had two of them."

Lynch, the Duke of Bleight, and—

"Malloryn," the footman replied.

The Duke of Malloryn was the head of the Company of Rogues, the group of spies and assassins Ava had been asked to join. "I'll fetch him. Why not sit and rest? You look like you've been running."

"It's rather urgent."

Perry and Garrett exchanged a look. "We'll keep the bridal party distracted," Perry said, slipping her hand over the crook of her husband's elbow.

"And I'll find the duke," Ava promised, though she had no intention of leaving it at that.

With thoughts of Perry's mad scheme plaguing her, she didn't plan on remaining for the rest of the wedding breakfast. Especially not with Kincaid in the room.

How on earth was she going to ever look him in the eye again?

CHAPTER TWO

THE DUKE RETURNED with a placating smile for the party.

Kincaid watched Malloryn swim through the crowd, murmuring platitudes. Malloryn reminded him of a shark. All white teeth, smooth glide, and hunting eyes. And something was up. With the way Ava had suddenly reappeared and commandeered Malloryn's attention, he knew it had something to do with the work Kincaid undertook for the Company of Rogues.

It was about bloody time something happened.

The Sons of Gilead, a terrorist group they'd been hunting six weeks ago, had vanished off the face of the earth, and there'd been not a single sighting of the *dhampir* who'd been working with them either. The Company of Rogues had become restless, none more so than Kincaid.

He'd worked damned hard during the revolution to overthrow the corrupt prince consort and his bloodthirsty pack of blue blood aristocrats. The last thing he intended was seeing the blue bloods that had lost their rank at the top of the food chain ever regain it.

Speaking of blue bloods, the Duke of Malloryn crooked a finger at him. "Meet me in the study in five minutes."

Then he moved on.

Kincaid glanced around the room, handing his empty glass of champagne to a passing footman. Finally. Some action. He slipped away from the room, leaving Byrnes and Ingrid behind with the guests in the parlor of Malloryn's ducal manor.

What had roused Malloryn's ire? The icy duke kept all emotion off his face, but Kincaid had begun to learn his tells—the faint flicker of a muscle in the man's jaw, the thinning of his lips.... Something had the duke's drawers in a right knot, and as much as he would usually enjoy watching Malloryn squirm, it also meant danger might be afoot.

He asked for directions from the footman, then made his way upstairs.

Kincaid pushed through the doors to the study, startling someone who was sitting at Malloryn's desk.

Ava gave a small squeak, standing in a sudden flounce of lacy skirts. "What are you doing in here?"

"Waiting for Malloryn, as requested," he replied, easing the door shut behind him. "I do work for him, remember?"

"How can one forget?" Ava smoothed her skirts, studiously avoiding his gaze. The duck-egg blue of her overjacket washed out her pale skin, but drew his attention to the gilded highlights in her dark blonde curls. Every inch of her from the throat down was hidden, from her gloved hands to the tips of her pointed ankle boots. There were so many ruffles on her skirts he could barely make out her figure beneath it.

A pity.

She was beautiful in her own way, though firmly on his do-not-touch list. Even if he'd wanted to flout his own set of rules and poach a virgin, Byrnes had threatened him with dismemberment if Kincaid even looked at her. He wasn't scared of Byrnes, but Byrnes had a rather large advantage in any fight: he was now married to a verwulfen woman with a fiery temper, who happened to quite like Ava. Byrnes probably wouldn't even have to lift a finger. Nobody in their right mind crossed verwulfen. Their berserker rages were legendary, and even a blue blood would have a hard time taking one down.

Hell, Kincaid had seen Ingrid dismantle a vampire piece by piece, and that was possibly the only thing scarier than her.

Still... nothing was quite as tempting as a woman you couldn't have. Kincaid crossed his arms over his chest. Ava hadn't asked what he'd done with the blasted flowers. Indeed, she'd barely looked at him as he entered, though her cheeks bore a trace of color. "What's going on?"

"I don't know. A messenger arrived with something urgent for His Grace."

"You didn't listen in?" She had superior hearing after all, thanks to her cursed blue blood nature.

"Of course not. It was private."

"And at least one of you knows what that word means," Malloryn said, entering the study as silently as a ghost, with Isabella Rouchard, his right-hand woman—and mistress, Kincaid suspected—on his heels.

Gemma Townsend and Charlie Todd entered behind them. Together with Byrnes, Ingrid, Ava, and himself, they made up the Company of Rogues, Malloryn's hand-picked team. Gemma, both seductress and assassin, looked ravishing in red silk, and Charlie was a man just over the threshold of adulthood. Both were blue bloods.

In fact, he was currently surrounded by them, which always made him a little uneasy.

The duke locked the door. There was a file under Malloryn's arm, and Kincaid's gaze went directly to it. He'd been out of action for over a month while his broken nose healed, and he needed to get back to work.

"You put together a company of spies," he pointed out. "Don't be so surprised if we want to know everything that goes on 'round here."

Malloryn shot him a chilling smile. "Keeping you in the dark, Kincaid, gives me no small amount of enjoyment."

Bastard. His temper roused, but he fought to restrain it to just the muscle jumping in his cheek. Malloryn knew Kincaid didn't like him, and seemed to take perverse pleasure in pushing that fact in his face. If the prick didn't have access to something he desperately wanted, then he'd have pushed on from this whole scenario weeks ago.

Maybe.

There was the small matter of the Sons of Gilead and their intention to destroy the newfound peace in London; a peace Kincaid had worked hard for, three years ago, during the revolution. There was also the fact he needed the coin—and there was nowhere else he could earn this kind of living, doing violent reckless things, which was precisely his forte.

Destruction is your gift, after all. Kincaid rubbed his knuckles, trying to force his brother's words deep into the dark recesses of his memory. "Please tell me you've got something interesting for me."

"Something for all of you," Malloryn replied, slapping the file down.

That... was not quite what he'd planned. Kincaid glanced at Ava beneath his lashes. "I wasn't aware Miss

McLaren was to be working in the field."

"Not usually, no," Isabella broke in. If Gemma was a seductress, then Isabella was a cool goddess, warming only when Malloryn looked at her. "But Miss McLaren's specialty is crime scene investigation and... other things of which this case has particular need."

"We have a crime scene?" Ava blurted.

"A fresh one," the duke replied, sliding the file toward her, which she grabbed with eager hands.

"*Dhampir*?" It had been over a month since the mysterious group of evolved blue bloods had revealed themselves as their opponents. Kincaid still couldn't quite come to terms with it. Blue bloods were bad enough, what with most of the aristocracy infected with the craving virus that made them what they were. Then there were vampires, who were a nightmare out of any old story, but they were bloodthirsty monsters, devolving to an entirely predatory existence. Terrifying and extremely difficult to kill, but driven purely by the thirst for blood.

Dhampir... were something else.

Kincaid crossed his arms subconsciously, his nose aching in remembrance. A blue blood's one fatal flaw was the fact that as the craving virus colonized them over time, they began to devolve into a vampire. However, two months ago the Rogues had discovered there was one other option available for those devolving blue bloods if they used an *elixir vitae* to control their transformation. Instead of dying during the last stages of the Fade and being reborn as a vampire, those blue bloods transformed into the *dhampir*. They bore the same strengths of a vampire— faster, stronger, almost impossible to kill—but they retained the rational instincts of a blue blood.

It scared the shit out of him.

"I don't know. There's been no sign of the Sons of

Gilead, or this mysterious group of *dhampir* that are working against us." Malloryn handed over a photograph. "Until now. We know there was a power struggle within the Sons of Gilead and Lord Ulbricht won. He now leads the SOG, and their mission is to return the blue bloods and the Echelon to power. Ulbricht was spotted in Brighton two days ago, an agent of mine informs me. Whatever he's planning, I want to know about it. Gemma, fancy a little trip?"

The vivacious young woman snatched up the photograph, smiling down at the sneering face of Lord Ulbricht. "It would be a pleasure. Do you want him dead or alive?"

"Alive, preferably. I want to know everything he knows," the duke replied. "Take a dirigible to Brighton, and—" His gaze slid over them, making Kincaid stiffen, before the duke's eyes narrowed on Charlie Todd. "Take Charlie with you."

"To protect her?" Charlie asked.

Both Gemma and Malloryn snorted. Even Isabella succumbed to a faint smile.

"He's such a sweet boy," Gemma said, patting Charlie's cheek. "There are at least twelve ways I could kill you, Charlie, despite the fact you're a blue blood. For a human, there's at least a hundred. No, Malloryn wants to send you as a distraction for Ulbricht."

"I could do it," Kincaid said.

Isabella rolled her eyes. "Unfortunately, Kincaid, you're not quite the right sort of distraction."

He shot an incredulous look at Charlie, who'd crossed his arms over his chest. The lad was dangerous—all blue bloods were—but he was barely in his early twenties. "I—"

"You would terrify Ulbricht," Gemma hastened to add, as she slid an arm around Charlie's neck. "Charlie is young, handsome, intelligent, and—"

"Exactly Ulbricht's type," Malloryn concluded.

Both Kincaid and Charlie shot him a sharp look.

"I thought Ulbricht had a mistress," Charlie blurted, flushing bright red.

"He did," Malloryn said. "Zero, a young, beautiful blonde *dhampir* who was very dangerous. Ulbricht likes fair-haired youths of either gender. He also likes his bed play a little dangerous. Gemma will brief you on the flight."

"I am *not* seducing Lord Ulbricht!" Charlie looked horrified.

Kincaid scratched at his jaw. "There's no need, I'm sure. I doubt even Malloryn would send you off to be some blue blood lord's catamite. A little flirtation, and if you're lucky, you can lure him somewhere isolated where Gemma can truss him up and return him to face the duke's tender mercies. Am I correct?"

"I don't know that I would use the words 'tender' or 'mercy,' but something like that, yes." Malloryn's smile died. "Ulbricht knows I want his head. He's bound to be well guarded by his fellow members of the SOG. Be careful."

"I could do this in my sleep, Your Grace," Gemma replied.

"And me?" Kincaid demanded. Surely there had to be something for him to do? Malloryn wouldn't have called him or Ava up here just to listen.

Malloryn shot him a look. "A crime scene just came in. It has nothing to do with our work, but the Nighthawks have requested Ava's assistance, as she used to work for them. It's the fifth death in a fortnight.... I think Master Reed said they were referring to it as the Black Vein."

"Black Vein?" Ava murmured.

All of them turned to look at her, as though startled to find she'd spoken. Kincaid examined them from beneath sleepy eyelids. Sometimes she faded into the wallpaper—or perhaps that was purposeful—but he seemed to be the only one who always saw her.

Malloryn waved a dismissive hand. "Some sort of disease afflicting blue bloods, and now a human by the look of it. Kincaid can make sure you're safe."

Bodyguard work. He slid his hands into his pockets... and didn't say a damned thing.

"But blue bloods *cannot* succumb to illness," Ava protested. "That's impossible. The craving virus is a jealous mistress—it will tolerate no other diseases in its host while it sets about colonizing them. It heals all wounds, and there's been no way to even cure it."

"Well something is killing blue bloods," Malloryn said, "and considering your interest in the craving virus, it was thought you would be the perfect candidate to proceed with the investigation. Just be quick about it. The second Gemma and Charlie have Ulbricht in hand, I plan on setting things in motion very swiftly. I want to crush the SOG before they can cause further chaos to England, and then we still have those *dhampir* to find. Whatever is killing blue bloods is important, but it pales in comparison to the real threat to the empire." He gained his feet. "Report to Isabella in my absence. She'll keep me apprised of any of the goings-on. And make sure you keep your actions quiet. The last thing London needs is mention of a disease running rampant."

"Will do," Kincaid muttered.

Ava blinked, and Kincaid *willed* her to look at him.

Seemed they were going to be spending more time together than anticipated.

He could hardly wait.

CHAPTER THREE

SHOUTS ECHOED THROUGH the narrow streets.

"What on earth is that sound?" Ava demanded, as the steam carriage came to a halt. "Are we going to make it to the crime scene?"

"Hopefully." Kincaid helped Ava down from the steam carriage, a scowl furrowing his brow. The traffic had been thick in the last few minutes, but he'd been distracted by Ava's absorption in the notes she'd been writing. He hadn't been paying attention to what was going on around them. This was his home territory—the borough he'd been born in, and had spent most of his formative years within. Sheets flapped from laundry lines slung between narrow alleys; windows were boarded over; and the usual assortment of flower girls were out with their baskets of posies, trying to beg a sale.

But something was wrong. There was a tension in the air he hadn't seen for at least three years, almost like a thunderstorm on the horizon. And the streets were far less crowded than usual.

"Five shillings," said the hackney driver nervously, his

hand sliding over the stick shift of the steam hack.

Kincaid paused with his hand on the pouch. He couldn't hear anything anymore, but there were hints of smoke in the air. Across the street a man hurried his wife and child down a small lane, glancing back over his shoulder. The butcher in the store opposite them locked his door and then pulled down the blind.

"I've got another hire," the hack driver muttered, as if to hurry him along, and Kincaid made his decision.

"Are we going?" Ava called.

There were Nighthawks holding the scene of the latest Black Vein death, Malloryn had said. A ruckus was clearly going on nearby, but it wasn't unmanageable. And Kincaid was armed if necessary. Handing over the coin, he helped Ava onto the footpath and out of the way as the hack driver pulled out into the traffic.

"How unusual," Ava muttered, staring after the hack. "He couldn't wait to be rid of us."

"Expect trouble," he told her, tucking her hand through the crook of his arm. "I don't know what's goin' on precisely, but something's brewing."

"The disease?"

"Perhaps." The body they were going to investigate was certainly in the direction of all the noise. "Can you hear any—"

"Get back!" someone called. The sound of cries suddenly echoed ahead of them.

Kincaid stopped dead in his tracks. A pack of street children ran past, thin leather shoes slapping on the cobbles. A pair of dogs galloped at their heels, tails tucked between their legs. Kincaid captured Ava's hand beneath his, stepping between her and the rumble of brewing noise.

"What is it?" Ava asked, trying to peer over his shoulder.

She took a step toward the noise—which matched the address of their crime scene—and he suddenly realized what was happening.

"Bloody cravers! Taking our blood! Our jobs!"

Something smashed around the corner from them.

Flames whooshed, as though oil or something flammable was thrown on a small fire, its orange glow licking over the rooftops ahead of him. Kincaid took a step back, nerves firing to life down his spine. *Shit.*

"Take back what's ours!"

"Should've killed them all!"

Somewhere ahead of them glass sprayed with a tinkling sound across cobbles. A cheer went up and it sounded as though a dozen men slipped their leashes, their excitement tumbling all over the crowd as they egged each other on.

He'd heard that sound before. Trouble.

"Stay here," he urged, shoving Ava into a nearby alley. "Have you got a pistol? Or a weapon?"

Ava flourished her parasol. He'd seen some of her defensive designs in action, and knew that hidden within the lace was a shield, and possibly worse. The last one she'd designed had a hidden bayonet at the tip she could trigger with a twitch of her finger. "Not a weapon, precisely, but it will do. What are you doing?"

"Let me check it out first." He could feel the blood rushing through his veins, preparing him to fight—or flee. "It sounds like a riot's about to happen."

"A *riot*?" She'd know what that meant just as much as he did—once upon a time it had been the only weapon the human classes and mechs had owned against the powerful aristocratic Echelon.

"Just keep your head down. It's not as though the Echelon sends out its Trojan cavalry to crush a mob anymore." Once upon a time, the automaton cavalry rampaged through the streets upon the Echelon's bidding, crushing any and all who stood in their path. You'd hear the horns blaring, and it would be every man for himself as he fought to clear the streets. Those days were long gone, thank all the gods. "I'll be back before you know it."

"You can't go by yourself," she protested.

"Ava." Kincaid looked down at the small hand on his sleeve. "I'm human. You're not. And from the sounds of it, you're precisely what this mob wants to get its hands on." He could still hear them bellowing about "death to the cravers." "Stay here, and keep out of the way. I'll be back shortly. I need to see how big this is getting, and where it's spreading."

As she let him go, he strode through the crowd that was gathering. Some fled—the more sensible perhaps. But others seemed drawn to the vortex of violence ahead of him, as though hungry to see what was happening.

How many years of peace had there been since the last time London went up in flames? Once, a riot was the only thing the corrupt prince consort and his Council of Dukes feared. But ever since humans reclaimed their rights to live freely, there'd been only one riot, and that had ended when the queen made a plea for clemency.

Kincaid shoved his way through the growing spectators. He and Ava had a crime scene to investigate, but he certainly wasn't bringing her to the address until he knew what lay in wait for them. This wasn't his first riot. He'd grown up in streets like this, and had brought ruin to dozens of blue blood businesses and houses in his time—back when they were the monsters everyone feared, and there was no other recourse for people like him.

"Down with the cravers!" someone screamed, and a queer sort of shiver went through him.

Those words had been in his mouth many a time. The feeling of rage ignited along his skin, taking him back into the past, when he'd stood at the head of a mob like this. Emotion would be contagious, and he felt it stirring within him even though he worked on the other side now.

A thousand slights against him. Watching those he loved die at the hands of blue bloods. Working his fingers to the bone just to get a fucking scrap of something out of life.

"Serves them right!" another shout echoed. "All blue bloods should die!"

Once upon a time he might have shared the same sentiment. He'd spent years in the blistering heat of the mech enclaves, his freedom sold to the blue bloods who ran them in exchange for the mechanical hand they'd fitted him with. His mech debt—the years of service he owed for the hand—stretched to fifteen years, and until the revolution started brewing, he'd despaired of ever tasting freedom again.

And then he'd been asked to join the Company of Rogues, which was formed almost solely of blue bloods. The hatred hadn't died; it still smoldered in his gut, even though he considered some of the other Rogues to be allies, perhaps even friends.

But it was Ava who'd forced him to rethink his position all blue bloods should be guillotined, like the French had done to their blue blood aristocracy. Ava, with her big green eyes, her revulsion for blood, and the way her cheeks burned whenever he flirted with her, or made a crude joke. Ava was a kitten, not a predator, no matter what virus ran through her blood.

And if *she* could be innocent, despite her affliction, then how could he categorize the rest of them? He didn't entirely know what to think anymore. And it fucking bothered him sometimes.

"Burn them!"

Ahead of him he could see the crime scene address, and the Nighthawks standing in a sharp line in front of the building, nervously trying to hold the crowd at bay. Kincaid didn't even know why he'd come. He'd taken the measure of the crowd already—this was going to turn violent.

"Stand back!" one of the Nighthawks called to the mob. "There's already been one death today, and we don't want any—"

"You're cravers! Just like them as killed our sons and daughters!" A bottle launched from where the voice was coming from.

"Nobody's killing your families," said a sharp voice through a speaking trumpet. "The revolution was three years ago. We all have the same rights now—"

Another missile was launched at the fellow. "Burn the blue bloods out!"

The cry went up, and Kincaid's gut locked tight as he sensed the tide turning. Torches flared across the mob and Kincaid found himself buffeted from all sides. There was no point in pushing ahead to deal with the crime scene. The world was about to burn.

"Jaysus." *Ava.* He had to get back to her.

Before anyone realized what she was.

"Burn them!" The crowd chanted. "Burn them out!"

Greasy smoke stained the air. "Get out of my way!" Kincaid growled, fighting his way back the way he'd come.

"Burn them!" a man in front of him yelled, his eyes wild and a makeshift torch in his hands.

Kincaid punched him in the face, dropping him like a stone, and the crowd around him gasped, clearing a small space for him. He snatched up the torch as the fellow sputtered, and plunged it into a puddle of sludgy water in the nearest gutter.

"You'll set someone alight, you barmy bastard," he snarled, and those nearest him—who might have taken exception to his opposition—nodded as if it made sense.

Whistles blew and heads turned all across the square. Nighthawks reinforcements. It was about bloody time.

Behind him glass smashed. All it would take would be one hint of opposition—he almost felt sorry for the poor Nighthawks—and this entire scene would go up as though someone set a spark to a puddle of oil.

"Disperse peacefully!" came a voice through the speaking trumpet. "Or we will be forced to use the water cannon. Lives are at risk, and nobody wishes a fire in these close quarters!"

"Burn them!" someone bellowed. "Burn them all!"

"Kill the cravers!"

And the noise behind him roared to a crescendo.

What had bloody set them off like this? As far as he knew, the last few months had been peaceful.

Kincaid started running. Blue bloods could be hard to spot. Any man or woman with a pale face was suspect, though they could be merely someone who kept out of the sun, which meant virtually half of London. In this crowd, people wouldn't check before they bludgeoned someone to death.

Real fear began to curdle in his gut. He skidded around the corner where he'd left her. There was no sign of her. "Ava!" He kept calling, ducking back into the streets.

People fled from the mob. Kincaid was knocked aside by a man drawing his tweed coat tight around his wife. No sign of a blonde head anywhere. Where the bloody hell was she? He'd told her to stay there, damn her.

"Kincaid!"

There.

He found her in an alley a hundred feet down from where he'd left her. She trembled, her skin even paler than usual. "I-I had to move. A man demanded to know what I was doing there, and I...."

"Smart choice," he muttered, grabbing her by the upper arm, not unkindly. "Can you run?"

"What's going on?" He caught a glimpse of that upturned face. "I can hear them yelling about killing cravers."

"The Nighthawks just arrived. This whole borough's about to go up like dry tinder, and we need to get out of here. Now."

"What about the Black Vein victim?"

"He's not getting any deader." *You, however....* He kept that little tidbit to himself.

"Hey!" a man declared, shoving Kincaid in the shoulder and glaring at Ava. "Is she a craver?"

Kincaid stepped between them, his lip curling back off his teeth in a snarl. "Did you just fuckin' push me?"

Doubt appeared on the fellow's face, but he tipped his chin up. "Your lady friend's got awfully pale skin. We don't like that sort here."

"If you're referring to my *wife*," he stated coldly, "then I'm going to take exception to your tone. And it's bloody England, man. Everyone's got pale skin."

A vial appeared in the man's hand and he threw it at Ava, even as Kincaid shoved him back a step. *What the hell?* He snatched a handful of the man's collar, shooting a look at her. "Ava?"

There was blood spattered all over the front of her coat. Her mouth fell open in shock but her eyes flashed black with the craving as the predator within her roused, and Kincaid knew they were in trouble.

It all happened in an instant. The man's eyes lit up.

"Got one—!"

Kincaid drove his mech fist into the man's throat, crushing the sound of the words before they could draw any attention. "You son of a bitch."

The bastard dropped, clutching at his throat and making some sort of gurgling sound.

"Did you just...." Ava trembled, one hand to her lips.

"No time for manners, kitten." Kincaid grabbed her by the hand. A cry went up behind them. They'd been spotted. "Let's see how fast you can run!"

They ran for several blocks, his hand wrapped around hers. Blue bloods were faster than humans, but Ava was gasping for breath within two hundred feet, one hand clasped to her chest. For some mysterious reason, she was struggling, and with his health conditions, the fact he was outrunning her was a surprise.

"There they are!" someone screamed.

And Kincaid made a decision. "We're going up."

"Up?"

He turned and caught her around the waist, lifting her in the air. "Lean on my shoulder."

"What are you *doing*?"

"Put your foot in my hand."

"Kincaid!" He ignored her cry and grabbed hold of her foot. The second he had a firm grip, he launched her into the air.

She landed on the roof, scrabbling for purchase on the tiles. Kincaid eyed the narrow alley they'd ducked into, then ran at the opposite wall, leaped onto a rain barrel, and shoved off the wall. He twisted in midair, catching hold of the gutter behind him near Ava's foot, and then used brute strength to haul himself up beside her. His legs might threaten to buckle beneath him occasionally, but he still had an enormous amount of strength in his upper body.

"Keep going, we're not out of danger yet," he said, finding his feet and helping her onto hers. The skirts were going to be a problem. Kincaid grabbed hold of her arm again, aware he was probably bruising her, but unable to slow down. Ava would survive a tight grip or two right now.

If that mob got their hands on her though, then he didn't like her chances.

"Come on," he said, hurrying across the rooftop and helping her scramble over the gable. Chimneys dotted the rooftops, but the only smoke was coming from behind them. The sun had showed its face this morning for the wedding, but dark clouds seemed to have come from nowhere, and it was getting hard to see. "Let's get out of this mess."

"But where?" Ava bit her lip, glancing back toward the screams and the smoke.

Only one place to take her. He cursed under his breath, hating the thought of the intrusion into his private life, but he couldn't risk her safety. Not in these streets.

"My uncle lives nearby. We can take shelter there until this blows over."

Ava gently put her hand in his.

CHAPTER FOUR

BANG. BANG. Kincaid rapped on the door to a small house in Fitzrovia, then reached up under the thatch and lifted a key down. He opened the door, ushering her inside. "Ian? Orla? It's just me."

Silence echoed through the small house. It smelled musty, and... there was some odor Ava didn't like. Like liniment, and tonics, and sickness. Trying to catch her breath after that mad dash across the rooftops of London, she was helpless to do anything but stumble inside after the big mech. The heart that ticked in her chest was made of biomech pieces—a literal clockwork heart—and she'd been warned against too much exertion, as the atrial pump might not be able to handle the flow pace.

Nobody truly knew the limits of her heart, and she wasn't interested in testing it.

Sweat clung to Kincaid's back. He'd lost his coat somewhere along the way, using it to lower her down into the streets once they'd lost the crowd chasing them. He should have looked unruly, but she couldn't deny there was something vital about him in this moment, something very masculine. He was everything she'd never been drawn to before, towering over her first fiancé, Paul, and even Byrnes. *Brute* was possibly the term she'd first thought when she caught sight of him, and yet there was also something comforting about his size and height, especially today.

His stride was long and firm, his manner brusque and competent. She'd been so scared, and having him there at her side was the only thing that kept her from being overcome with fright.

"Are you all right?" he demanded, setting her leather satchel on the table.

"This is your... uncle's home?" Ava hovered in the kitchen he'd led them into, not quite daring to take another step.

Kincaid didn't look happy to have her here, and his manner had become curt on the way. Irritation and nervousness about the riot? Or was it something else? She couldn't quite read him.

"Aye." He captured her fingertips, looking down at her from beneath those dark lashes that made his eyes so very blue. "I didn't hurt you, did I?"

Hurt her? "Pardon?"

"I wasn't very gentle," he admitted, and brushed the backs of his fingers against her upper arm.

She'd probably sport a bruise or two in the morning, but that mattered little. "You saved my life," she blurted. "I thought that man's friends were going to set me on fire."

Coldness burned in his eyes. "Like hell. Not while I'm there."

She'd seen the look in the man's eyes when he threw that vial of blood all over her. The shock of it—the smell, the splatter against her face—had ignited the craving within her and it had taken her precious moments to get herself under control. Suddenly it made her feel sick. Ava tugged at the buttons on her coat, and started stripping it down over her arms. She wanted it off. "He looked at me like he hated me. He looked at me like I was a monster. Get this off me...."

The damned sleeve was caught on her wrist. She tugged and pulled, but to no avail.

Firm hands caught her arms, helping her with the sleeve. "Ava, you're not a monster."

No? She had to get the blood off her. The craving virus roused through her, bringing a rush of blood through her veins. "I've never felt that way before. I've never done a damned thing wrong, and yet—"

"Hey, now." His voice lowered, and he rubbed her arms even as she threw her coat on the floor.

She never wanted to see it again.

A sob caught in her throat. *I never asked for this.* But before she had time to try and choke it down, she found her face buried in Kincaid's chest, those strong arms wrapping around her, one hand cupping the base of her skull.

"You're not a monster," Kincaid said, gently stroking the back of her neck. "That man wasn't thinking clearly. He was seeing what he wanted to see—an enemy, someone to blame for the hellish way his life has probably turned out. And it's easier to see your pale skin and blame you than it is for him to take some responsibility for his own damned bad luck."

"How do you know that?"

"Because that man was me several years back."

Ava looked up, meeting his eyes. There was so much she didn't know about this man, though his body bore scars of a rough life. He hated blue bloods. Hated them. And people just didn't hate for no reason—even that man in the street had a reason for the rage that filled him the instant he realized what she was. Empathy filled her, and she realized her thumb was rubbing against Kincaid's side. Back and forth. Back and forth. The brush of his shirt was almost hypnotic.

"Careful, kitten," Kincaid whispered, his lashes lowering almost sleepily.

She didn't want to be careful.

She... she didn't know what she wanted. But something hollow ached within her. And he was so warm, so virile and full of life.

Frustrating, yes. Impossible, yes. But safe too, in a way she wasn't sure she wanted to explore. It was like having a tiger in her chambers, and wondering if she dared pet it.

"If you keep looking at me like that, then I'm going to have a hard time pretending to be a gentleman," Kincaid warned.

"You *are* a gentleman," she protested, for despite his roguish demeanor, he was very careful with her at times.

"I'm really not," he insisted, and his head lowered toward her, just the faintest of fractions.

Ava sucked in a short breath.

As she filled her lungs, the scent of him stole through her. Sweat and cologne, and everything *male*. Her vision went dark, the predator within her surging to the surface. *Yes*, it whispered, and her mouth watered as the stupidest urge filled her, one that wanted her to rub her face against that chest, to lick his throat and perhaps sink her teeth into the vein there.

Ava panicked, and shoved away from him. "I'm sorry."

Kincaid staggered, one eyebrow arching at her strength. They stared at each other and Ava swallowed, trying to lower her no-doubt-black eyes. The kitchen suddenly seemed far too small. What was she doing? What was she thinking? This was *Kincaid*. The man who despised blue bloods. The one who thought marriage was a trap, and who seemed to know every young woman in the neighborhood.

The one who roused that shiver of heat deep within her abdomen every damned time she looked at him.

"It's all right, kitten." His voice sounded like honeyed gravel. Amused. "Neither of us was thinking straight. And you've had a hard time, what with that man throwing blood at you, rousing the—"

"I wasn't thinking about...." She couldn't say it.

"Blood?" He scraped a hand through his unruly black hair. "I know."

The words jolted her. The craving virus unleashed so many foreign feelings within her, including a desire for blood or for... other things. Things that involved the heated stroke of his hand on her body, the trace of his lips against her skin.... "You do?"

"I told you. I'm not a gentleman. I know what was going through your head right then."

There was a wealth of meaning in those words, but before she had a chance to process them, footsteps echoed above and they both looked up.

All the heat seemed to evaporate off Kincaid, and tension rode through his shoulders. "There she is." He raised his voice. "Orla, do you need a hand?"

Ava's hearing was exceptional, but she couldn't tell whether it was a man or woman. A slight crinkle drew between her brows.

"Liam? Is that you?" a woman called.

"Aye. Don't worry about fetching your pistol."

Liam? Ava silently mouthed the word, looking at him for confirmation. He'd never mentioned a first name. He scowled back at her, then lifted his voice, "Want me to put the kettle on?"

"Oh, that'd be dear." Whoever she was, she sounded tired. Soft murmurs echoed. "There's a pot of soup in the icebox. Could you set that to heat too? Ian's ready for lunch."

"Aye." He moved around the place as though he knew it well, gathering a teapot and setting it on the stove, then locating the icebox.

"Liam?" she repeated quietly.

Kincaid knelt in front of the heavy ceramic stove and stoked it. "Could we please pretend none of what you hear while you're in this house is going to make it to the ears of the rest of the Rogues?"

"It's just... I've only ever known you as Kincaid." She frowned. "Doesn't anybody else know your name?"

"No. And I'd like to keep it that way."

She folded her hands in her lap. "It's a lovely name—"

"Ava." A growl.

"I don't know why it bothers you so much, but I promise I won't reveal your *dirty* little secret."

"I've got dirtier ones than that, luv."

Heat thrilled through her. Ava swallowed. "I'll bet."

There was that look again. The one he often graced her with when he let his guard down, as if he forgot to remember he was supposed to stay away from her. Then it faded as rapid footsteps started down the stairs. "In fact, whatever you see or hear here, please don't repeat it. To anyone."

Ava had never been the overtly curious sort. She respected people's rights to their secrets—after all, she had her fair share—but the way he was acting set off her instincts.

Kincaid was hiding something, and that had to be the

reason behind his tension on the way over here, and the stillness that lingered in his shoulders as he stirred the soup.

"I'll keep your secrets," she said quietly, reaching over and resting her hand on his forearm—the real one.

Kincaid looked down at that touch, then their eyes met, and something passed there that she hadn't felt since that night they shared in the Gardens of Eden six weeks ago, when she'd almost kissed him. Lust was one thing— she knew she was attracted to him. But there'd been something between them that night, a gentle sort of tenderness in his words and his touch, and now she was the one offering that to *him*.

He looked away. "You make hating blue bloods hard, did you know that?"

"Don't tell me I'm corrupting you to our side?"

There was a swish of skirts, and a breathless gasp as a young woman emerged from the stairwell. "Well, don't you look grand? Give us a look at you, Liam!"

"Orla." His expression and tone brightened, and he crossed to drag the small redhead into his arms, planting a kiss on her cheek. "It hasn't been that long."

"Two weeks."

"I've been busy," he protested, and the two of them shared a look that made Ava feel a little uncomfortable.

Whoever she was, this woman knew Kincaid in a way she didn't.

"Busy with what?" the woman demanded, and those gray eyes narrowed on Ava.

"Orla, this is my friend and associate, Miss Ava McLaren. Come on over here. Orla won't bite." When Ava complied, he tucked her hand in the crook of his elbow. "Ava, luv, this is my cousin, Orla Kincaid."

Cousin. She didn't know why that word eased the uncomfortable feeling within her. "A pleasure."

Orla turned back to Kincaid and arched a brow accusingly. "A blue blood? You've got to be kidding me."

Was it painted across her forehead?

His smile died. "Ava's a friend."

"Aye. I've met your *friends* before."

"That's enough." The abruptness of his tone shocked both of them. "It's not like that. Not at all. And I won't tolerate your rudeness to someone who ain't earned it."

Orla blinked, then turned to look at Ava again, as though seeing her for the first time. "I apologize. It's been a trying day."

"Oh, there's no need for apologies," Ava replied, though she didn't take her hand off Kincaid's arm. The animosity was something she'd seen happen to other blue bloods, but never experienced firsthand.

At least not until today. Today had been a day of firsts, she thought sadly.

"How is he?" Kincaid let her hand go, and returned to the soup.

"The same," Orla replied.

"Ava, have a seat," he said, and gestured toward the scarred kitchen table. Dozens of copper pots hung over it, and someone had been chopping parsley. "I'll fetch you some tea as soon as the kettle's boiled."

"*Tea?*" Orla stated, as though she couldn't help herself.

"Ava doesn't drink blood," he replied, that heat turning his blue eyes stormy again. The cousins glared at each other. "She's created a protein solution that seems to be able to sustain her." His hands kept moving, stirring the soup, and then setting out bowls, as though the everyday tasks came naturally to him. "She's the laboratory assistant for the company I work for."

"And which company was that again?"

"Malloryn Enterprises," he lied blandly, ladling soup

into a bowl. "Does Ian want bread with it?"

Orla grew curiously quiet. "He's not got the stomach for it anymore. The soup will be fine."

Kincaid handed her the tray, and Orla gave a curt nod in Ava's direction before she ascended the stairs.

Something was very wrong here.

"Is your uncle unwell?" she asked quietly.

Kincaid startled, then turned back to the boiling teapot. Every movement was carefully measured as he poured the fragrant brown liquid into chipped porcelain cups. They looked expensive and were clearly cherished, though Ava's father would have turned his nose up at the setting. "He's dying."

Dying. The word loomed in the small, cozy room. "Is he... Orla's father?"

"Yes."

"Oh, I'm so sorry." No wonder the other woman looked tired.

Kincaid brought the tea setting over, handing her the pink cup with its dancing shepherdess painted on the side. "Forgive her the sharp words. She's forced to care for him day in and out, and it ain't a kind death."

"What's wrong with him?"

"His... his heart's getting weaker." Kincaid's nostrils flared. He must have been close with his uncle. "I don't really want to talk about it if I don't have to."

Ava sipped her tea, searching for a new topic of conversation. "How long should we hole up here while we wait for the riot to be shut down?"

That seemed to ease him. He sank onto the stool opposite her. "It will blow over within an hour or two. I'll go out and check if it's safe or not, before we head home."

"Back to Malloryn's safe house?"

He looked up. "Where did you want to go?"

"Well, if it was safe, then I wanted a look at that body," Ava protested. "The more time that ticks by, the less information I'll be able to gather from it."

"You do realize Malloryn's throwing us a bone here. This is a distraction. Nothing more. Just something to get the pair of us out of the house after so long trapped within."

"Well, *I* want a look at that body. It's the fifth one in two weeks. Whether the duke thinks it a diversion or not, he's granted me leave to look into it."

And damned if she wasn't going to do the best job she could.

Maybe it was just a disease that afflicted blue bloods, but Ava couldn't help feeling as though there was something more to it than that.

After all, blue bloods didn't succumb to disease. The craving virus was far too ambitious to allow something else to kill its host. They could heal from anything short of decapitation, burning, or a mortal blow to the heart, damn it.

What could be killing them?

Kincaid sighed. "You're not going to let it be, are you?"

This was the first case Malloryn had allowed her to lead. Ava tipped her chin up stubbornly. "Would you?"

"It's not as though we've got any other leads at the moment—only that sighting Gemma and Charlie are looking into."

"And don't you find that unusual too? After plaguing us for weeks, Lord Ulbricht and his SOG suddenly vanish into London's depths, never to be seen again? They're aristocrats. There's no possibility they'd be content in hiding, without their fancy manors. They have to be up to something."

"They will be." He looked unconcerned. "That's Gemma and Charlie's problem right now."

"They tried to kill Byrnes! They *nearly* killed Ingrid. And they were working with a *dhampir* woman who had vampires on a leash. I think that is cause for more than a little alarm!"

Kincaid leaned back in his chair, folding his arms. "And does your outrage at the matter have to do with Ingrid, the vampires... or Byrnes?"

Ava drew back abruptly, feeling like he'd slapped her. "He's my friend."

"Friend?"

"He is." She hid behind her teacup, the saucer rattling as she jerked the cup to her lips. "It's not.... It's never been more than that."

A cool, scrutinizing gaze locked on her. "Maybe not for him."

And there was the crux of the matter. Ava squeezed her eyes shut. "Can we not speak of this?"

"Just trying to figure out where you stand on the matter."

I don't know where I stand. I thought— *I* hoped.... "The last few years have been a little unkind to me. You don't know what it's like to have the rug pulled out from under your feet." She'd never told any of the other Rogues what she'd been through, and Byrnes was the only one who knew her story. "The one constant in all of that was Byrnes. He was my sense of safety when I felt adrift. He was kind when I very much needed kindness. And he... he never judged me. I never felt lacking when I was with him."

"Why would you feel lacking?"

"You might have noticed the distinct lack of suitors at my door," she said dryly. "I spend my days surrounded by dead bodies, laboratory equipment, and my orchid samples.

I can practically see men's eyes glaze over when I get excited about the things that fascinate me. Who wants to hear about the latest advances to my protein solution? Or a test I've been trialing for a more accurate way to test a blue blood's stage of genesis? We have means to assess the craving virus levels in their blood, but what stage of metamorphosis are they at? With the *dhampir*, Zero, revealing that...." The words trickled to a halt. Damn it. She was doing it again. "You see? I'm physically incapable of holding a socially acceptable conversation."

"Well, we could discuss the weather if you wanted," he pointed out, with a slightly amused smile. "But I'll let you in on a little secret. Most men don't really give a damn about that either."

Ava groaned, slumping her head into her hands. "You're lying if you claim you'd rather listen to me rattle on about CV levels."

"True."

She gestured to him in despair. "And thus I have few redeeming social attributes. I am going to die a virgin, and—" Kincaid suddenly looked like he wanted to spray his mouthful of tea across the table. "Oh my goodness. I cannot believe I said that. I think the stress of the riot has gone to my head. My brain's not working anymore."

Kincaid succumbed to a coughing fit, shoving his teacup away from him. "Jaysus." His face went red, his eyes wild.

"Forget I said it. I'm not— I'm not going to die a virgin, I mean... I probably will, but I don't want to, and— I'm so sorry!" Ava slammed a hand over her mouth. *Stop talking, you fool.*

Kincaid had buried his face in his hands and his shoulders were shaking.

Ava stared at him, physically holding the words inside

her. It was possible she'd been this mortified before, though she couldn't remember a specific occasion.

Finally he erupted into a bark of laughter, lowering his hands. "Jaysus Christ, you're going to kill me one of these days."

"Stop it!" she said. "Stop laughing at me."

That set him off again. "I'm not laughing at *you*."

"You are!" A little frisson of hurt worked its way through her, and he must have heard it in her voice.

Kincaid looked up, his eyes still crinkled with humor and shining with half-shed tears. Ava sat very still. It wasn't as though she'd thought them friends, but as she'd tended to his injuries in the last month he'd become not so gruff, a little teasing at times. And the more comfortable she found herself in his presence, the more her mouth started to run away with her.

She had the sudden, striking realization Kincaid was possibly the only other man—besides Byrnes—who made her relax to the point where she forgot to censor herself.

"Ava," he said, his voice lowering as he reached over and cupped her hand.

"I can't help myself sometimes."

"Please don't ever change, Ava. *I* find you intriguing, conversational gaffes and all," he admitted, though the admission might as well have been pulled from him. Almost grumbling under his breath, he added, "You're not like any other woman I've ever met."

Ava threw her hands in the air. "You see?" *Hopeless*. She might as well condemn herself to a nunnery.

Footsteps hammered down the stairs. "What's all that noise?" Orla called. "Ian nearly choked on his soup."

Ava sat back with a sigh. Kincaid looked like he was digesting a particularly troublesome meal.

"Just a rather lively discussion," Kincaid told her, that

twinkle back in his eye.

Don't you dare breathe a word of it. Ava glared at him.

He crooked a brow, as if to say, *Would I do that?*

"Do you want to see him?" Orla's gaze remained cool.

Kincaid let go of a huge breath Ava hadn't realized he'd been holding. "I probably ought to."

He pushed away from the table. "Be nice to Ava, brat."

"Always," Orla said, and then turned that unblinking stare on her.

"Oh, and Ava?" Kincaid paused.

"Yes?"

"What I said before?" He headed for the stairs, glancing over his shoulder. "That was a compliment."

About...? Ava stared after him, before it struck her. *You're not like any other woman I've ever met....*

Suddenly her cheeks felt hot again.

"Orla tells me... you brought a girl... home," Ian rasped, his lungs catching at the effort, though he smiled.

Aye. And she's plaguing my mind. "Didn't have much of a choice. There was a riot."

All the laughter and cheer Ava brought into his life vanished. Kincaid refused to look at his uncle's withered legs where they lay under the blankets. The Ian he could remember was a monster of a man, hale and hearty, with a laugh that could shatter your eardrums. He used to throw Kincaid up in the air as a child, until he was shrieking with laughter, and he'd been the father Kincaid never had, after his own abandoned his mother a year after his birth.

It was hard to look at him like this. Harder to imagine what his uncle was going through. All alone in here, trapped in his bed, with his body dying inch by inch and Orla forced to clean up his messes, to feed him, to turn him, to bathe him....

"I'm sorry," he said bluntly. "I haven't been avoiding you."

Ian fumbled for his hand, his thin forearm barely able to lift off the coverlet. Kincaid caught his uncle's straining grasp, his fingers brushing against paper-thin skin.

"I know, you... daft fool." Ian tried to squeeze, but the effort was lackluster at best.

And it hurt to look at him. Hurt to sit here and listen to Ian's lungs slowly forcing themselves to work, even as the muscles that surrounded them resisted. It was some sort of palsy, the doctors said. A slow degenerative swan dive that stole his uncle bit by bit, and ran in the family.

Heat seared his eyes.

"Here, now," Ian scolded. "No tears, Liam. Tell me... about this girl. This... pretty girl you brought home."

And so he told him about Ava. It wasn't as though he made her out to be something she was not, but he let himself open up in a way he rarely did, if only to give his uncle some hope. And it was difficult not to notice his voice warm at the words, a warmth that seemed to flood through him whenever she was around.

Trouble. Kincaid stared at the patterns on the coverlet, seeing the heat in her cheeks when she'd blurted out the fact she thought she was going to die a virgin.

He'd been half ready to offer to help her out with that prospect, but she... she wasn't like the usual sort of women he seduced. And he couldn't offer her anything else. Perhaps they shared an attraction, but they came from different worlds, and they were travelling to different places. Maybe he could show her she wasn't undesirable, or even difficult to be around, but he'd only break her heart in the end, and he wasn't bastard enough to start them down that road.

And so he only told his uncle half the truth.

"She sounds... lovely," Ian rasped.

"She is." He paused. "She's a blue blood."

"A leech?"

"She's not like that." He leaned back in his chair, clasping his hands behind his head, the muscles in his chest stretching. "I'm earning good coin at the moment." The change in topic made Ian's eyes narrow, but Kincaid pushed on. "I've got enough saved up... to see you with a nurse, or even to admit you to—"

"No."

"Or what about renting another house?" he continued, despite the expected resistance. "We could get one with bedrooms on the ground floor, and I could design a steam-powered wheeled chair that could give you some independence—"

"*No.*"

"Why not?" He leaned forward, the front two feet of the chair hitting the timber floor. "Why do you have to be so bloody stubborn?"

"I'll not see... you into debt for—"

"So you can enjoy what's left? Or so it's easier on Orla? I'd care for you if I could, but we can't afford for me to lose this job!" Kincaid shoved to his feet, unable to sit still any longer. "The Duke of Malloryn's offered me the assistance of the Royal College of Physicians. They're working on this disorder, and I could insist upon having a doctor to call upon you. After all, a blue blood's saliva can heal wounds, and the craving virus can heal *anything*, so there's a chance they could extract the healing components of the virus from a blue blood and—"

"Malloryn? The duke?"

"He's pleased with the work I'm doing and so—"

"No!" This time his uncle twisted in the sheets, a flinch of frustration that was all his body would allow. "I'm done, boy. You're the only one... who won't accept... it."

"Can't."

"*Won't.*" Ian gurgled deep in his throat. "I'm content. Just leave me... be. I've accepted my lot. The only thing that could hurt me at this... stage is false hope."

"There's no saying it's false, until we explore all of our options."

"I don't... want to explore... them! I don't want... to hope!" Tears gleamed in his uncle's eyes. "Just let me die, Liam."

"Maybe it's to give *me* some hope then?" he shot back, and Ian froze.

Their eyes met.

Kincaid cursed under his breath. "Forget I said it." He turned and paced to the window, lifting the lower pane of glass so fresh air flooded the stale room. Being in here made him sick to his stomach. And what kind of coward was he? To condemn Orla to this fate when he himself couldn't handle it?

Keep telling yourself it's the prospect of work that keeps you away.

He lowered his head, knowing Ian was watching him. Knowing his uncle could read his mind.

"I'll let you die," he whispered, "though I can't watch it. I *can't.*" *Not again.* He'd seen men die a hundred times over in the enclaves and he wasn't certain what was better—a sudden, brutal accident, or this long, slow decline.

First his brother, then his uncle on his mother's side. The Kincaid men laughed at the Kincaid curse in a show of bravado, but it was only when he was alone his laughter turned bitter and hollow.

"I won't ask you to," Ian said gently, and that was even worse, because it should have been him comforting his uncle—not the other way around. "I know what it cost you to hear of William's death."

Will's face flashed into mind, pale and gasping for lack of breath, his dark eyes pleading. Kincaid hadn't been able to say goodbye, as the enclaves had only granted him one day of leave to visit his brother before the end—and the end came shortly after, Will slipping away before Kincaid even knew about it.

It was a kind death. A merciful one, Orla said. But he felt the weight of it on his soul every damned day.

"You should find some joy with your girl," Ian said breathlessly. "It's a long, lonely life, Liam—"

"Or a short one," he said brutally, shaking his head. "And I find joy on a regular basis."

"An anonymous roll in the hay's all well and good... but that's not—"

"It's the sort of thing that doesn't destroy people's lives. I provide a widow or two with a bit of fun on a lonely night, and I don't make promises I don't intend to keep. It works for all of us. But Ava's not... not like the others. She's the type of girl who wants things I can't offer."

"Like love?"

"Like a husband, a home, and a family," he said bluntly.

"You could give her all three."

"It would be better if the bloody curse died with me, so let it. I promised myself no children."

"It's only... a bit of bad luck," Ian said, with a cough. "No such thing as curs... curses—" He broke into a hacking cough.

Kincaid hastily reached for the glass of water on the

side table, and helped his uncle sit up just enough to sip it. Ian spluttered until the fit finally subsided.

Lowering him back down, he tucked the blankets up under Ian's chin.

"Curse or not, I can't offer her a future." Pressing a kiss to his uncle's forehead, he pushed away from the bed. "I'll fetch Orla for you." Then he strode from the room, and nearly flattened poor Orla.

"What are you arguing with him about?" she demanded.

"Nothing."

"If you've set him off again—"

"He's fine." Kincaid shoved his hands into his pockets, shuttering the sorrow that punched inside his chest like a fist trying to hammer its way out. His voice softened and he barely got the words out. "I agreed to let him die."

"Oh, Liam."

He shook her off and tugged his money pouch out of his pocket. Orla started to protest, as he'd expected. "Shut up and take it. He's my blood too. And you need to pay the rent."

Ignoring the suspicious gleam in her eyes—Orla never cried—he folded her fingers around the coins he poured into her palm, and forced her to accept them.

"You're a good man, Liam Kincaid, and don't ever let anyone else tell you otherwise," she said.

He tugged on the end of her braid with a sad smile, hoping she didn't see through him. "Stop ruining my reputation. I'm a devil, and the ladies love me for it."

That earned him a narrowed look. He'd grown up with her, and they could read each other like books.

"What?" he demanded, opening up a new script, one that was easier to deal with than the other one.

"And does herself downstairs love you for it?"

Bloody hell. Not Orla too. He should never have brought Ava here. "It's not like that." He scrubbed a hand over the back of his neck. "We work together—"

"She's pretty."

"Is she?"

That earned him a snort. "Not your usual sort at all—"

"What gave it away? The craving virus?"

"The intelligent, well-articulated and clearly educated conversation. The frills. The lace. The way she looks at you—"

"She's completely innocent. I don't trouble myself with virgins. And she's not looking at me like that." Which was a blatant lie that would have earned a slap to the back of his head from his mother, God rest her soul.

Ava looked. She lingered too sometimes, and he was rake enough to know tumbling her into bed might require a little bit of effort, but not a lot. Someone was curious.

And hurt. He was wise enough to understand Byrnes's recent marriage had something to do with Ava's sudden lingering looks.

Orla crossed her arms over her chest, eyeing him with an evil look. "I know you, Liam Anthony Kincaid. You want to trouble yourself with her, virgin or not."

"It's complicated."

"I assure you it's not. You've told me many times it's simply a matter of inserting your cock into—"

Kincaid clapped his human hand over her mouth. "Jaysus, woman. That's enough. She might be able to hear you."

Orla's eyes were expressive enough that he grinned, and let her go. With a sigh, she reached up on her toes and brushed a kiss against his cheek.

"Don't break her heart," she whispered softly, as he

turned for the stairs.

"I don't intend to."

"Don't let her break *your* heart then."

A flinch went through him. "No fear of that, Orla-luv."

"No?" Her words haunted him as he started down the stairs. "If you weren't worried about it, then you'd have had her twice over already."

He paused halfway down the staircase and looked up at her. "She's not the sort of woman you tumble."

"She's the marrying sort?"

He nodded.

Orla's eyes turned big and soft with sorrow. "Oh. Maybe you should tell her then. Let her make her own decisions?"

Not a chance. Kincaid turned his back on her before she could see what was on his face. Thank Christ Orla understood why he couldn't ever touch Ava, even if Ian did not.

CHAPTER FIVE

"YOU'RE QUIET," AVA murmured as she examined the body.

The riot had disbursed by the time they left Kincaid's uncle's house, leaving the streets oddly bare, though its echoes remained. Rubbish lay strewn in the gutters, glass was smashed in several shop fronts, and a smoky pall hung over everything. There'd been a full dozen Nighthawks holding the scene for her—three times as many as usual for something like this—and they'd been tense as she and Kincaid arrived.

"Got anything?" Kincaid clearly didn't want to discuss the odd scene at his uncle's house, and the way he'd barreled them out of there with barely a goodbye to his cousin.

And then, of course, there was that half-muffled argument she'd tried desperately not to listen to, humming under her breath as voices rose.

"I'm not certain." Ava looked down at the deceased blue blood on the examiner's gurney. She'd been lucky Dr. Gibson, the Nighthawk who managed the mortuary at the guild, had been rostered on when this came in.

"Apart from his name...." Kincaid glanced at the notes the Nighthawks had given them. "Mr. David Thomas. Unfortunate cause of a riot. I wonder if they'll put that on his headstone?"

"Mr. Thomas had nothing to do with the riot," she protested, stroking a gloved finger gently over the deceased man's face. Black veins traced their way through his skin, making him look half-mottled and violent. That was unusual, and clearly where the "disease" had gotten its name. "There was obviously malcontent in this borough with blue bloods, and when he died—revealing his true nature—it set off his neighbors."

They'd heard it all as they entered through the throng of neighbors: *such a nice man; never knew he was one of* them*; a craver living right here on the doorstep; where was he getting his blood from, I demand to know....*

Unusual that nobody had ever suspected him. Mr. Thomas's pale skin and preference for night should have given it away, though perhaps—with the response his death and subsequent coming out had achieved—there'd been good reason to keep his true nature under wraps.

It had been a long time since she'd felt uncomfortable with what she was. Or more to the point, uncomfortably aware other people thought her ilk monsters. London had been at peace for three years, damn it.

Ava sighed, and slid her magnifying goggles up on top of her head. "I've taken samples of Mr. Thomas's blood and the froth at his mouth to make sure there's no sign of chemical interference." Not that poison had much of an effect on a blue blood, despite the fact hemlock paralyzed them for several minutes until the virus burned through it. "But something tells me I won't find anything. Gibson would have tested the other victims' blood work. He wouldn't miss something like poison. This fellow appears to have suffered some sort of apoplectic fit, and bitten half his tongue off. The veins disturb me, however, and I think this needs further investigation." What had made them stand out like that? They looked black, and his irises were violently dark, as though the darker side of the craving virus had roused in him before he died.

Blue bloods had darker blood than humans—an almost bluish-red which gave them their name—but that didn't account for the blackness.

There was limited sign of livor mortis too, as though barely any blood had pooled in the corpse's back and legs.

Internal bleeding?

The only time she'd seen something similar was when Malloryn found Zero's body slumped in the cells last month, with no sign of a break-in. Malloryn had intended to question Zero about the whereabouts of her fellow *dhampir*, and just precisely what they were up to, but she'd been dead.

And *dhampir* were just one step along in the evolution chain for a blue blood. Ava paused. The black veins looked very similar, though Zero's capillaries had all burst, and she'd bled internally. Though the craving virus should have healed her, especially with the CV levels Zero had, for some odd reason it hadn't.

Something stopped her body from healing, even as it caused her to bleed.

Was this the same? Was it some sort of disease? A malady that killed only blue bloods and their evolved brethren, the *dhampir*?

Or something else?

"You think there's more to the death than there seems?" Kincaid asked.

"I'm just wondering.... Zero had black veins just like

this when she died," she replied vaguely, peeling the blue blood's lip up to see if there was anything in his mouth that might have caused this.

"If Malloryn thought this had anything to do with Zero's death then he wouldn't have sent *us*. He'd have been here himself, probably with Byrnes and Ingrid, despite their wedding."

"You think I'm conjuring a link between the two deaths?"

"Six deaths," he pointed out. "There's been five blue bloods go down with whatever this is."

Ava quietly gathered her skirts around her and stood, fussing with her gloves as she pried them off. "But you think I *want* this to be connected?"

Kincaid's mercurial gaze settled upon her, and he crossed his arms. "I know you want a case—"

She threw her gloves on the floor. "That is not true, damn it. Or yes, it's true—I want a case. But I'm not simply trying to conjure a link because I want this to connect back to the missing *dhampir*, or even Ulbricht. I've been taught to assess facts, not find a conspiracy. And the facts state this man died in mysterious circumstances, and his symptoms are familiar in some ways—though not all—with the mysterious death of our *dhampir* captive. Even you have to admit the black veins are conspicuously similar."

His gaze remained flat. "If this does lead back to the *dhampir*, then perhaps it would be best to bring in the others."

"What are you saying?"

"That neither of us is equipped to deal with those monsters. I'm human, and you're...." He suddenly seemed to realize she was glaring at him.

"I'm *what*?" Ava practically dared him to say it.

After all, she'd heard it all before. She had hysterical

attacks at times; she'd panicked the one time she'd tried to shoot a pistol at a man who'd tried to kill her; and she felt both a little ill and excited at the sight of blood, which was ironic in itself considering the craving virus. What sort of blue blood disliked the idea of drinking blood?

She was not Gemma, femme fatale and dangerous spy.

She was not Ingrid, whose Amazonian build and verwulfen temper frightened even the boldest of men.

She was Ava. Quiet conqueror of the laboratory, the woman most men overlooked in favor of others, and awkward enough in company she generally sought to avoid it these days.

A muscle in Kincaid's jaw ticked. "You... are no match for a *dhampir*."

Ava threw her hands in the air. *Coward*. "Who *is* a match for a *dhampir*? One of them took down both Byrnes and you without breaking a sweat."

"That's not the point," he said, his voice heating.

"Or should I say... by breaking a nose?"

Kincaid winced, and she focused on the slight hook to his nasal column. "The point is neither of us is suited for a confrontation with a creature that could rip our throats out without even blinking. If there is a link between Mr. Thomas's death and Zero's, then we're calling in Malloryn and the others, and gratefully handing this case on."

"Fine. *If* this leads to the *dhampir*, then we wash our hands of it." She didn't have to like it. This case was *hers*. "I'll go with Mr. Thomas to the morgue at the guild and see if I can sit in on the autopsy. I want to see if he's bleeding internally, as Zero was."

"You'll be careful?"

Ava looked up sharply.

"This is the fifth blue blood that has died like this," he pointed out. "What if it *is* some disease? I'm fairly safe, but who knows if you could become ill?"

"If it is a disease, then it's not very contagious." At his blank look, she continued. "It was compulsory for unapproved blue bloods to be listed before the revolution overturned the process. I checked the blue blood registry before we came, and there are certain boroughs of London that were approved for blue blood housing. This borough was a hot spot, which means there are quite a few blue bloods living in the area—probably the cause of the rumblings of discontent we ran into. Last year's census showed over thirty in this borough alone. If the disease were contagious, you'd expect more cases. This is the only one in this district. Clerkenwell's the only borough with more than one death within it."

"We don't know what's causing this. So promise me you'll be careful. Just in case."

Ava sighed. "I promise. I'll wear a mask during the autopsy, and I'll make sure I don't get any blood on my skin."

"There is one other way it might be transmitted... if it *is* a disease."

There was? Ava looked up.

"Something that might, ah, control the spread of the disease. It depends how they caught it, after all." Kincaid's face grew curiously flat. "Similar to the French pox."

Oh. She understood what he was trying to say. "All of the victims have been male."

"Women were never allowed to be infected with the craving virus, so that doesn't mean it applies only to men."

"Nor were any men who didn't have aristocratic blood flowing through their veins, but accidents happen," she said dryly, gesturing to herself. "And there are more female blue bloods out there than you'd think. A few cases have come out of the woodwork now it's no longer so strictly controlled. But I see your point. It could be only men who've been stricken down because there are more male blue bloods by a factor of a thousand, or it could be... because they're more prone to sharing certain bodily fluids. But where is the index patient? Something like syphilis is easily spread. We'd see more cases among the blue blood population if this disease was spread by sexual contact." She thought about it. "Unless we're catching this early. Maybe there was a... a lady in common. Or they've all visited the same brothel? Maybe it kills them before they've had a chance to spread this? Or perhaps humans don't develop the disease, but only carry it?"

Maybe it didn't have anything to do with Zero and the *dhampir*? Her shoulders slumped a little. It wasn't as though she wanted to come face-to-face with the terrorists, but this case.... She'd thought it might be her break. Her first chance to really prove herself for the Company of Rogues.

Anyone could do the lab work.

Kincaid knelt and picked up her discarded gloves, tucking them behind his belt so she wouldn't have to touch them. "Might not even be a disease."

"Then they're ingesting something, but poison doesn't affect a blue blood. Not permanently. There's no mark upon him, nothing to suggest a needle, or a cut. Not even under his lips."

"Could've healed. And you haven't checked everywhere yet."

Ava growled. "Maybe, maybe, could have, and possibly.... This is utterly perplexing. I'd hoped we'd have more to go on."

"Wait for the autopsy," he said, with a shrug. "You'll know more then."

Including what—precisely—had killed David Thomas.

"Internal bleeding," Dr. Gibson confirmed the following afternoon, pushing his goggles up on top of his head, and removing his gloves with the kind of pristine care a cat used to groom itself. "Myocardial rupture. Ruptured spleen. Bleeding in the liver, the kidneys, and the gallbladder."

Exactly as suspected. Ava frowned. "What caused it? He's a blue blood, after all."

She hadn't been able to isolate the agent.

Gibson sighed and tossed his gloves toward the medical waste bin. "Your guess is as good as mine, lass. Something caused the late Mr. Thomas to bleed out internally, and destroyed his organs. Something stopped his body from healing the ruptured veins and capillaries. No sign of poison in his blood work, but then the craving virus is rabid at detecting threats and removing them, so that's no guarantee. Only those odd-shaped blood cells that keep popping up here and there, but then is that a response to whatever happened to him? Or the cause?"

Ava peered through the microscope, and those odd-shaped cells came into sharp view. She'd been staring at them for nearly an hour, and neither she nor Gibson had any sort of clue where they'd come from. Except.... "Do you have the autopsy results on the *dhampir* I brought in two months ago?" Gibson didn't know precisely where she was working these days, nor what she was working upon, but she'd insisted upon him performing the autopsy. Gibson was an expert. "I examined them afterward, but I seem to recall fairly inconclusive results. As in, something killed her, and we don't know what."

Malloryn suspected Zero had been assassinated by her brethren, and the safe house breached. There'd been such a mad flurry as they were transferred elsewhere and locked down, and she'd been busy dealing with Byrnes, who'd been forcibly given the *elixir vitae* that transformed a blue blood into a *dhampir*.

They hadn't thought he'd survive, and Ava had pored over the diary of Dr. Erasmus Cremorne, the man who'd first created the elixir many years ago. Zero's results had been a minor note in her life, and by the time she had a chance to review them, it had been over a month later.

Gibson stroked his mustache. "It was inconclusive, yes, but I seem to recall a myocardial rupture only, and her capillaries and veins disintegrated. She died from mass internal bleeding, and the heart attack, but there was none of this other damage. Mr. Thomas's internals look like pulp. Zero's were fine, apart from the disintegration of her superior vena cava and the pulmonary artery."

"A *dhampir* is stronger than a blue blood, with presumably better healing qualities, though we haven't had a chance to test this theory. But Byrnes said a cut on Zero's skin healed in moments, where it would take a blue blood a few minutes for the wound to seal. So if the same agent killed both Zero and David Thomas, then perhaps her body fought the agent better." Ava tapped her lips. "This is a mystery. Did you test his CV levels?"

"Twelve percent." Gibson looked insulted. It was probably the first thing he'd done.

"Twelve? Why, he's barely a blue blood. Mr. Thomas must have been newly infected. He shouldn't even be showing any signs of the craving yet." Which made her wonder... "How did his neighbors know he was a blue blood? He would only just be starting to feel the stir of the hunger."

"I think you'd need to question his neighbors first," Gibson shrugged.

The thought made nervousness stir through her. The

sudden shout of fury from the riot echoed in her ears. "I'm not certain that's a good idea. They weren't very receptive to blue bloods. However...." Kincaid sprang to mind. "I know someone who might be able to coax the information out of them."

For if it wasn't a disease, then someone had killed Mr. Thomas, and with so much outcry today, it was more about narrowing down a suspect pool than trying to find someone with the motivation to murder.

CHAPTER SIX

"HERE IS A list of questions," Ava told Kincaid, handing over a sheet of paper. "I want you to ask around Mr. Thomas's neighbors, and discover how his blue blood status became known. He was barely into the first thirst, so he can't have been infected with the craving virus for long. Maybe a month. Maybe two. He might not have even known he was infected until recently."

"And you?"

She looked at him, and he saw the hesitation in her eyes, as if she still saw that vile man throwing blood over her. "I think it best if I stayed here at the guild and discussed the findings of the other deaths with Dr. Gibson, to acquaint myself with the case. The riot's barely settled. Evening's falling. The last thing the residents of Fitzrovia want to see is my pale face."

Kincaid shrugged, examining the list of questions she'd given him. "They're the ones missing out." There was a long moment of silence, and he looked up, realizing her eyes were upon him, a hesitant expression upon her pretty heart-shaped face. "What?"

"Nothing."

He lowered the list. "I'm fairly certain that wasn't 'nothing.' You're the worst liar I've ever encountered." Every hint of thought shifted across her expression with startling clarity. She should never play cards for money.

"No... I just.... Was that a compliment?"

The fact she had to ask made him feel a little angry on her behalf. "Of course it was a compliment. You're beautiful, and kind, and any man should be pleased to see you."

Ava smiled thinly, hurt gleaming in her big, green eyes. "Sometimes it's hard for me to tell, especially when it comes from you, because you're so flippant. And... men generally pay me few compliments. Except for Byrnes," she finished in an exasperated tone, "but one generally takes what he says as a somewhat brutal truth, rather than flirtation, and he was always focused on how clever I was."

"You have feelings for him still."

"I don't even know what I feel," Ava admitted, a considering frown on her face as though she was dissecting the facts of a case, rather than her feelings. "I like Ingrid. And I care for Byrnes. And when I look at the pair of them, I can see how well suited they are. I get this lump in my throat, because seeing how in love they are makes me happy for them...."

"But?"

Ava glanced up from beneath her blonde lashes. "There is also a part of me that aches, and asks 'when is it my turn?' Something horrible happened to me several years ago, and when I escaped, Byrnes was kind to me, and Byrnes is rarely kind to anyone. He accepted me for who I am, and I never felt as though I had to pretend to be someone else with him. But I realized what I feel when he looks at me is safe. And when he looks at Ingrid I see something else, and suddenly I don't know if 'safe' is a big enough word for what I want."

Jaysus. "You want to fall in love."

That right there ought to stop this strange fascination with her. Virgins were forbidden territory. Bluestockings had never caught his attention. But women who were looking to fall in love had to be avoided like the plague.

And yet....

And yet.

Curse her. His eyes narrowed, and he slid his hands into his pockets. Ava was the least foolish woman he'd ever met, despite her fascination with fairy tales. She was everything wrong. Against all his self-imposed rules.

"Ava, far be it from me to comment on your situation, but hopin' to find a man who tolerates your eccentricities ain't bloody good enough. You deserve better than that. You deserve a man who loves you *because* you babble on about bloody plants, not despite the fact you do. You deserve someone who thinks you hung the moon in the sky, and looks forward—every day—to coming home to you."

Her eyes were wide. "Thank you."

Kincaid looked away, across the foyer of the guild. "Byrnes didn't deserve you."

And now it was her turn to sound uncomfortable. "I know."

He shot her a sharp look.

"He had four years to notice what was beneath his nose. He didn't. Clearly he wasn't the right man for me. I'm starting to see that now. Maybe... maybe it was a good thing?" Her words became a little firmer. "His friendship—and Ingrid's—is important to me. But you're right—you've always been right. I deserve more. I deserve better. I deserve someone who is going to love me for everything I am."

"You'll find him," Kincaid replied, and damn him, but he felt a hot surge of... something flood up inside him.

"In the meantime, I am considering other options," she admitted.

He didn't like those words at all.

"Other options?" he ground out.

"Well, it's no secret the state of my... ah, experience, is significantly limited. And I was talking to Perry at the wedding about the sad status of my life. She proposed an experiment."

"An *experiment*?" Was she suggesting what he thought she was?

"Are you all right?" Ava peered up at him curiously. "You keep repeating everything I say."

Kincaid stared at her; all those layers of muslin skirts, the way her hair drooped in its chignon, the mass of curls barely tamed by her pins. Trussed up like a porcelain doll, and a thought went through his head: Ava was a pretty pigeon, ripe for plucking.

And some man would take advantage of her.

"Just what, precisely, are you proposin' to set about? An experiment in what?"

Despite her confession of gentlemen avoiding her like the plague, there were men out there who'd not hesitate to snatch her up. Men who'd lie through their teeth just to get her in bed, who'd not take the care she needed, and break her heart without a second thought.

Men who didn't deserve a woman like Ava.

"Well, you don't have to get angry," she said, looking startled. "I'm hardly going to ruin myself. I'm just... curious. I'm a virgin and a spinster, and I think I would like to relieve myself of one of those titles—"

It was exactly what he'd expected. "Are you *out of your*

mind?"

Ava stiffened. "Well, that's somewhat hypocritical coming from a man like you. Need I point out you were escorting a rather imposing young woman in the gardens at the back of a house of pleasure when you came upon me suffering a... a hysterical moment? You might think I was born yesterday, but I know exactly what you intended with her that night."

"Is this because of the wedding?" he asked incredulously.

Now it was her turn to get angry. "It's not *because* of the wedding in the way you're thinking. But it made me consider where my life is heading. And do you know what the answer to that question is? *Nowhere.* My life is heading nowhere. All I can see ahead of me are endless years in a laboratory—which is intellectually stimulating, don't get me wrong—but somewhat lacking in warmth. Do you know how long it's been since someone touched me? Do you know how many years have passed since my last kiss? Which, needless to say was disappointing, to say the least. I want love. I want *something else.* And if I cannot find love, then why not settle for passion?"

Jaysus. Kincaid stared at her, the vein in his temple throbbing in time to the heated pulse in his cock. He'd always liked Ava, but to see her temper aroused lit everything inside him on fire. He wanted to kiss her.

Right here.

Right now.

Despite the fact they were standing in the middle of the guild.

"Do you have some objection?" Ava demanded, tilting that pointed chin up.

Not an objection, no. Not to exploring her curiosity, and learning what passion felt like. The problem was...

where would she look for it? "How do you even know you could trust a stranger? What if the bloodlust overcame you and you went for his throat? And he wasn't expecting it?"

Ava's lips thinned, pinkness creeping into her cheeks. "I haven't given the idea a great deal of thought, I'll admit, but... in my brief experience with men, I've found one type of lust precludes the other."

"And what is your brief experience?"

She stared at him.

And suddenly he knew exactly what she was thinking about. That night in the Garden of Eden lingered between them. His breath exploded out of him. "Me. You were thinking of me, and what happened that night."

"Nothing *did* happen."

Kincaid ground his teeth together and crossed his arms over his chest. "Deny it all you want. There was a moment that night when I was tempted to kiss you, a moment where you touched me, and you were thinking about it too. And let's be honest. Ever since then you've not been shy in staring at me when you think I'm not looking. Pretend all you like, kitten. I know you shiver when I touch you. I know you blush every time I look at you. I know you think wicked thoughts whenever I flirt with you. It's written all over your face, in the catch of your breath, the way your cheeks flush with heat." He reached out and caressed said cheek. "The way they've pinkened now."

Ava broke free from beneath his touch, taking several paces away from him with her arms wrapped around her middle as she sucked in an enormous breath. It wasn't a rejection. He turned to watch her, and she suddenly spun around, looking like a startled doe. Her eyes were black, a sure sign she felt the press of the hunger rise within her. Animal passions, she'd called it once. Bloodlust. Or just plain lust. He'd slowly learned the difference.

Do not do it.

Do not say it.

"If you want to lose your virginity," Kincaid snarled, his cock giving a tempting stir behind the flap of his trousers as he took a step closer to her, the distance between them evaporating into a heated space. "Then you don't need a stranger. I'm right here."

Ava's eyes widened. "*What?*"

"I'll give you time to think about it," he snapped, despite the thought this was a terrible idea. Kincaid waved the list of questions at her, feeling both utterly furious and aroused. "If you want passion, then I can give you passion, and you won't have to worry about what a stranger might do to you. It's a perfectly logical, rational decision, therefore it should appeal perfectly."

Then he turned and stormed out before he saw the answer on her face.

"If you want to lose your virginity, then you don't need a stranger. I'm right here."

Oh, God. What had she done? What had she said? Ava slammed Dr. Erasmus Cremorne's diaries closed, unable to concentrate on them or the task at hand. She'd used them to research the transformation from blue blood to *dhampir* when Byrnes's life hung in the balance, and only her ability to create the *elixir vitae* herself and give him the next doses had been able to save him. She'd wanted to find if there was any mention of something that might affect the *dhampir* in a Black Vein way, but Kincaid's words kept ringing in her ears.

A perfectly logical, rational decision? Ha! What was

logical about this incessant ache? She could barely think. She'd read the same page several times over, until the words all blended into each other.

Who did he think he was?

Ava pressed her fingers to her temples. He'd given her time to think about it, and so that was what she was going to do. She wanted Kincaid. He was correct in that assumption. She'd wanted him in some sort of physical way ever since he'd looked at her that night and told her to touch him. But what about... all the problems that might arise if she let him be her lover?

They were working a case together.

She'd see him every day, regardless of how this ended.

What if there was some argument? Some unpleasantness? She could not escape him if there was, and she liked her new job working for Malloryn. It gave her purpose, and a sense of excitement.

And speaking of Malloryn, he certainly wouldn't approve.

Ava sighed, going to make herself another pot of tea. She needed to weigh up the advantages and disadvantages of the situation.

Lust was not always enough.

Though it was a very, very convincing argument.

"Here's something," Kincaid said, striding into the laboratory at Malloryn's safe house and finding Ava curled up in an armchair, asleep, with a cold cup of tea sitting beside her. He'd spent six hours questioning Mr. Thomas's neighbors, though he had to admit he'd been distracted.

Who wouldn't be when the one woman who got under his skin professed a sudden desire to lose her virginity?

He paused as he stared down at her.

She'd tucked her feet up underneath her skirts, and her head rested on her outflung arm, a diary of sorts in her lap. It looked terribly uncomfortable, but for a moment, looking down into her heart-shaped face, he had a feeling of... something. And it vexed him to not know what that something was.

"Ava?" He shook her gently.

It was like watching the sun dawn on the horizon; a flicker of her lashes, her eyes blinking sleepily as awareness came back into her face. The faintest of smiles when she saw him. "Kincaid?"

"Sleeping Beauty," he murmured, caught for a moment in the spell of seeing her like this.

"Pardon?" She was swiftly rousing, and his statement clearly flummoxed her enough to get that clever little mind working. "Are you speaking of fairy tales?"

"It seemed to suit the situation," he replied with a soft smile as he sank into the armchair opposite her. "All it needed was one kiss to truly wake her. And I know how much you like the idea of them."

Ava blinked at him, and just like magic, her cheeks turned rosy.

Kincaid waited for her to refer to their earlier argument—and his proclamation. It was written all over her, but she swallowed, and then cleared her throat. "Did you... did you question the neighbors?"

Ah, business then. He smiled at her, unfooled by her redirection. She hadn't said no, and she needed time to think about it.

He could be patient.

"I did."

"And?"

"A curious thing," he said. "Mr. Thomas only discovered three days ago he was stricken with the craving virus. It's a very interesting tale. He was most shocked, hence why the woman who did his washing knew."

"Shocked?"

He could understand the question. With a single drop of blood able to transmit the craving virus, most people who developed it knew they were at risk, or at least suspected. There was usually an altercation. Or a man or woman was paid for blood, or sex, or sometimes both. "With good reason," he said, passing her a small piece of paper. "This is the vaccination certificate for Mr. David Thomas, who attended the clinic on St. Paul's Street. Six weeks ago, he received a vaccination *for* the craving virus. He was rabidly anti-blue blood. A humanist through and through."

Ava sat up abruptly, peering at the certificate. "But that's.... Then how did he get the craving? The vaccination is quite safe. It's been thoroughly tested. And we've had no evidence of anyone coming down with the craving post-vaccination."

Kincaid scratched at his jaw. "Did he have the craving before he received the vaccination?"

She started pacing, her skirts dragging behind her, and a lovely little frown drawn between her pale brows. Those stockinged toes sank into the carpets. "Now you've mentioned it, I cannot help but recall seeing something about a vaccination somewhere. Dr. Gibson showed me the files on the other victims, and I swear there was a note in there. I'll have another look for it. They're in my rooms."

"Are you certain?" She looked exhausted, despite the fact it was night, and therefore a blue blood's "day."

Ava waved him off, already turning back toward the autopsy rooms. "I'm certain. There's no use in me seeking my bed tonight, not with all these questions circling through my head. I'll be awake all night, staring at the ceiling. Might as well have a look. I'll see you on the morrow."

Then she was gone, leaving him alone in the armchair with an unanswered question in the forefront of his mind.

CHAPTER SEVEN

"FOUND IT!" AVA declared, holding the folder up high as she hunted Kincaid down the following afternoon. She could hear him moving around inside his bedchamber at the secret house, and rapped swiftly on the door.

"Come in," he called.

"I was right. There is more to this than expected," she said excitedly, slipping inside his bedchamber. "Two of the other victims recently received vaccinations! One of them was a staunch humanist and the other—" Ava staggered to an abrupt halt, losing track of what precisely she'd been saying.

For there he was.

Half naked.

And everything she'd been trying to forget rushed back in. *"Pretend all you like, kitten. I know you shiver when I touch you."*

Kincaid's braces hung from his waist as he stared into his mirror, and the top button of his trousers was undone in the reflection. There was a towel around his bulky neck, barely covering the heavy slabs of his pectoral muscles, and a froth of shaving cream covered his cheeks. She wasn't a complete innocent; she'd seen half the Nighthawks at the guild in various states of undress as they fought and sparred in the weapons room, but Kincaid was... different.

For one thing, he was an absolute brute of a man, layered with thick, heavy muscle, his left hand constructed purely of steel spars and hydraulics. The posterior triangle of trapezius muscle flexed in his back like a pugilist's, and his deltoids rippled... both drawing her attention and making her mouth a little dry.

For another, Kincaid was the only man who got to her like this. Every time their eyes met, she couldn't stop herself from blushing. There was just something about the look in them.

If I were a worldly woman, I'd diagnose you with a severe case of lust.

Antidote: either pretend it's not happening, or... submit to it. Get it out of your system.

"What are you doing?" she squeaked. This was not helping her levels of distraction.

Which was probably exactly what he'd intended when he told her to come in.

"What does it look like?" A black lock of hair fell over his forehead, highlighting the blue of his eyes in the reflection. "A man has to shave."

"Yes... but...." Ava gestured to his chest, and didn't quite have the words to continue. He had a thick pelt of black hair on his chest, and a trail of it led suggestively from his navel down into his—

She jerked her gaze elsewhere, feeling flushed and bothered. There was some sort of steel contraption circling his waist under his waistband, but his trousers were tight enough for her to see prime example of an exquisite gluteus maximus and she forgot what she'd been thinking about.

Kincaid smiled smugly when he saw where her attention had gone. "Are you tempted, Ava? Are you thinking about my proposition?"

My goodness. Her cheeks heated, and she abruptly gave him her back, squeezing her eyes shut. There was no help for it: the image of him was imprinted behind her eyelids. How horrifically embarrassing. "I am trying to concentrate on this case."

"Ah, the case. So... two other blue bloods visited the vaccination clinics recently and ended up dead with Black Vein," he mused, and the sound of the scrape of his razor over his skin made her nipples harden. "I'm no investigator, but that sounds like a connection."

Ava stared at the wall, the folder curled against her chest. *Concentrate, damn you.* "Uh, yes. Francis Jenkins was the second victim, and Marcus Long was the fourth. Both had been vaccinated around a month before they died." There was a pause. Water dripped, and she could only imagine it gleaming on Kincaid's smooth cheeks... sliding down his hairy chest in rivulets. "Could you please put some clothes on?"

"Why?" That suggestive lilt was back in his voice as fabric rustled. A towel, perhaps. "Does it bother you?"

"*Yes.*"

"Keep your voice down," he murmured, setting something aside with a clank. His razor, she suspected. "We're surrounded by people with exceptionally fine hearing."

"What's wrong? We're not speaking of anything untoward, are we? You're not embarrassed by your suggestion?"

"I value my balls where they are, thank you very much, and several Rogues have made quite complicated threats to their well-being, should I even look at you twice."

Her cheeks had to rival a sunset right about now. The other members of the Company of Rogues had threatened him? Wait... what? "That makes no sense. It's not as though I have to beat my suitors away with a stick. I would have thought Gemma a more likely candidate for seduction?"

The femme fatale gave new meaning to the word alluring. Sometimes Ava just liked to sit and watch Gemma in action when she was flirting. The other woman always had a witty comeback, a saucy double entendre. Sometimes Ava wished she too had the same confidence and easy manner, but she might as well be wishing for the moon.

"You underestimate your attractions, especially to a man like me. Gemma's the one warning me away. She smiled very sweetly as she offered to poison my tea with a severe emetic. Then there's Malloryn, of course, who was most put out to find Ingrid and Byrnes in a dalliance. He wouldn't approve. You're you and I'm me, and never the twain shall meet. That sort of thing."

Never the twain shall meet? "That's not what you were proposing last night."

"Oh, were you thinking of accepting?"

Ava caught her breath. "I haven't decided, but I will thank the lot of them to keep their noses out of my affairs."

"They're just protecting you."

"I can make my *own* decisions, thank you very much. I am not a child. I am not a weak-willed woman. And if I want to indulge in an affair, then that is my business and no one else's."

"Perhaps Gemma thinks I have a bad reputation?"

"You do." She'd seen women eye him appreciably, and Kincaid had often given them a wink in return. That utterly wicked smile spoke more than words ever could. "Now... are you dressed? We have to work out why there are five dead blue bloods."

"Yes, I'm dressed." Fabric rustled once again. "Your poor innocent eyes should be safe if you turn around. So what's the diagnosis? Disease? Murder?"

"I don't know. But don't you find it interesting this Black Vein rears its head at this particular time—right when Lord Ulbricht and the *dhampir* group have shown themselves committed to causing civil unrest in London? Right when one of the *dhampir* themselves died in the same way? As much as I dislike leaping to conclusions, as you said, that sounds like a connection."

She chanced a look at him, only to find him doing up the buttons on his shirt. *A pity.*

Ava pinched herself. *Not a pity. It is* not *a pity.* She needed to forget he'd ever put his hands on her at the Garden of Eden. It was too distracting, too close to home. There was nothing between her and Kincaid.

You're lying to yourself. You find Kincaid physically compatible.

If one were looking at a list of faults and strengths, then she had to admit she found him attractive in a visceral, somewhat barbaric way. He was no gentleman, and sometimes it looked like his shoulders threatened to tear through his shirt and coat.

Ava belatedly realized he was staring at her, and he'd said something, and— "Pardon?"

"We don't even know they're working together," he clearly repeated, looking younger with such smooth cheeks. "Ulbricht was Zero's puppet. There may be no connection between him and the remaining *dhampir*, now she's dead."

She forced herself to focus. "But their cause is the same. Civil unrest, chaos, the queen off the throne, and in Ulbricht's case, the Echelon back in control."

"I'll concede that point, but what makes you think our little mystery is even connected to them? It sounds like there's something wrong with the vaccination, a side effect or a... vulnerability. Something causing this Black Vein, since you're not convinced this is a disease."

"Perhaps there's a bad batch of vaccine? The science behind it is accurate—I remember reading about it in the medical monthlies when Sir Artemus Todd published it posthumously, but I confess I simply haven't had the time to research the science in more depth." The black veins in Mr. Thomas's pale dead face sprang to mind again. Ava frowned. "The vaccine works because the craving virus cells they inject have been made inert. So if it were a bad batch, then you could perhaps say Francis Jenkins, Marcus Long, and David Thomas might then become blue bloods—which is what happened. But... there's no reason to suspect it would do anything other than afflict them with the craving. No black veins. No side effects, barring perhaps a fever. I've been speaking to Dr. Gibson, and the entire time the craving virus has been known in England, there's never been a single case of something like this happening to a blue blood. This Black Vein looks like... like something ravaged Mr. Thomas's body, rupturing all his veins and capillaries and making a mess of his inner organs. The craving virus simply couldn't heal all that damage in time. But I would like to attend some of the clinics today, just to see what their procedures are like, and whether Jenkins, Long, and Thomas are isolated instances."

"Sounds more like connected instances to me," he said. "We just happen to have three dead bodies, who were all recently vaccinated, and all just happened to come down with this Black Vein?"

Ava released a slow breath. "I've been taught not to believe in coincidence and not to make judgment until we have solid evidence. If you lock your mind into a position, then it's very easy to convince yourself with the merest fragment of proof."

"Still, it's a damned good thing I haven't received a vaccination," Kincaid muttered, rubbing his arm.

"You were thinking of getting the vaccination?" Of course he was. He despised blue bloods, and the worst thing any humanist could imagine would be to become infected. "What stopped you?"

After all, it had become common practice among those who were rabidly humanist as soon as the vaccine was made widely available.

Kincaid shrugged. "I don't like needles."

Ava felt a smile curve her lips.

"What?" he demanded.

"Nothing."

His eyes narrowed. "You're trying not to laugh at me."

She couldn't help herself. It erupted from her in a loud snort. "It's just the thought of you, Liam I'm-too-brash-for-my-own-good Kincaid, shuddering at the thought of a needle." The mere image of it set her off again. "Mr. I don't need laudanum for my broken nose because I'm far too brave for that."

Kincaid very carefully crossed his arms over his chest, scowling down at her with menacing form. "*Miss* McLaren, I'm a man. I *am* brave."

"You're a fool," she said, rolling her eyes. "It's not as though I thought any better of you for denying yourself pain relief for your nose. That's not courage. That's obstinacy."

"Well, I was flirting with you. I hardly wanted to look like I had the pain tolerance of a child."

"While you had a broken nose?" she demanded. "You were not!"

"I assure you, I was."

Kincaid would flirt with her dead grandmother. Ava turned away with a scowl of her own. She didn't know why that thought bothered her so much. "I shouldn't believe a word that comes out of your mouth."

But a little part of her was still wondering....

Disadvantages: he is arrogant, he hates blue bloods, and he drives me insane.

Advantages: he thinks I'm not like other women. In a good *way. And he called me beautiful.*

There was silence.

"What?" she demanded.

"Nothing."

But she could tell it was something all right. He had that thoughtful expression that made her feel a little wary at times.

"Spit it out. It's not as though we've ever kept secrets from each other." Indeed, the blunt way he spoke his mind often made her feel relaxed—she had a terrible habit of blurting whatever came to her mind, after all, and it was nice to know she could do that with him.

Kincaid grabbed his coat, slinging his arms through it. The metal spars of his mech hand caught in the fabric, and he worked them free. "You may think the worst of me, Ava, but the truth is, you also think the worst of yourself. The very idea a man might be flirting with you or find you attractive doesn't even occur to you, does it?"

She was trapped between him and the door, and the sudden lack of space between them made her nervous. Ava dashed a blonde curl behind her ear. "What... what do you mean?"

Kincaid pressed a hand against the door beside her head, leaning closer. The scent of his cologne did wicked things to her, and the hunger within her awoke, whispering naughty thoughts inside her head.

"I mean... if you weren't off-limits, then I'd have had you in my bed a dozen times over already." His gaze slid down her body in an intimate caress, and Ava froze, feeling that look on her skin. "You're beautiful, and intelligent, and a part of me wonders exactly what you're hiding beneath all those ruffles and lace. You think you're not the sort of woman that men look at, but you're dead wrong. I've been looking."

"You'd say that to any woman," she retorted, flushing hot.

He made it sound like she was highly desirable. *Me, Ava McLaren. With my stuttering awkwardness, and my logical assessments, and my slender, pale body....*

"No." Kincaid leaned closer, his mouth a bare inch from her ear. "I'm not going to let you tarnish me with a lie, nor yourself with doubt. I've never been a saint, Ava. I never will be, perhaps. But there's something about you that takes my breath." He lifted his mech hand, those steel fingers almost, but not quite, brushing against the spill of lace at her throat. "I think together, you and I would be explosive. I sometimes see you looking at me, and there's some part of you that wants to be utterly wicked. And I want to help you unleash her. I want to be wicked with you, see if we're just as good together as I suspect we'd be."

He pushed away from the door, gesturing her through it with a particularly scorching look that lit her toes on fire, almost as if he was challenging her. "But I guess we'll never know, will we? Unless you make a choice."

Ava practically fled.

CHAPTER EIGHT

AVA MCLAREN WAS ridiculously easy to flummox.

Kincaid stretched his arms across the back of the seat as their hired steam cab took them to the vaccination clinic listed on Mr. Thomas's certificate, watching as she tried to pretend what had happened in his rooms hadn't happened. "I think you've read the file several times. Or that particular page, at least."

Big green eyes locked on him, and for a second he tensed, for she looked ready to flee. Perhaps he'd pushed her too far?

The very idea a man might be flirting with you or find you attractive doesn't even occur to you, does it? He didn't even know why he'd said it, but he disliked the idea she saw herself as beneath the notice of a man's attention.

"I'm merely familiarizing myself with the details," she blurted, refusing to take the bait. "I don't want to fail. Not with this case."

"Why is this case so important?"

"It's my first one, working as the lead. I just... I want to be something more than a laboratory assistant. Gemma and Ingrid are—"

"Stop comparing yourself to others," he snapped. "You're you, and you should be proud of that fact. There's a million women like Gemma in the world, thousands of women that can flirt, and seduce, and steal a man's secrets. Not so many with Ingrid's fighting skills, no, but anyone can hit something. But you? There are only a few who have anywhere near your intellect, and even fewer still who retain your sense of empathy."

Ava nibbled at her fingernail. "To feel empathy is easy—"

"In this world? To keep it after seeing so many bloody horrible things.... You have no idea how rare you are. You're the kind of woman who can make a man like me—a man twisted with hate—start to think, maybe he's wrong? Maybe there is goodness in the world? In blue bloods? Maybe there is hope for a lasting peace between humans and cravers?"

"I'll thank you not to use that word, please. I don't like it."

And he was becoming rather helpless against her wishes. "Sorry. I'll try not to... if you promise to stop wishing you were someone else."

"I'll... try." Green eyes danced to him then back to the window. "You're a rather complex man. I sometimes cannot figure you out. When you first started with the Rogues, you were terribly unkind to everybody."

"I was never unkind to you."

"True." She laced her fingers in her lap, her head bowed. "But you've softened toward the others. You barely even snap at Gemma anymore."

"And Gemma doesn't provoke me as much as she used to." He sighed. "Maybe I'm not as big and bad as I pretend to be?"

That earned him a shy smile.

Maybe I am? Because right now, he wanted to be very, very bad, and damn the consequences.

"Maybe," she said, swaying as the carriage pulled up. "But sometimes I think I'm not the only one who pretends to be something they're not?"

The steam cab idled at the curb, and Kincaid glanced out the window. Saved by their arrival. He twitched a brow at her, then opened the door and stepped out. A shadow rippled over them, and he looked up to find a dirigible passing overhead. London was taking to the skies, gathering steam with the rest of Europe. About bloody time. France apparently had fields of airships, and if not for the heavy English dreadnoughts that patrolled the channel, they'd have sent their fleet north a dozen times.

"The vaccination clinic." Ava's gaze slid past him as he helped her down. In the sunlight, her skin seemed creamy and glowing with excitement. "Hopefully we can find some answers here."

He loved the way the thought of an answer to her questions made her flush with life. Only Ava would be practically dancing on her toes at the idea of getting her hands on the vaccine clinics. Kincaid paid the driver, and then headed for the door. "How are we going to play this?"

She withdrew something from within her reticule. "I still have my Nighthawks credentials. They'll have to answer my questions."

"And what do you want me to do?"

"Perhaps try to look broody and menacing," she threw over her shoulder. "It shouldn't be difficult. That's what some of the other Nighthawks do."

Bloody woman. He smiled.

Kincaid tucked the collar up on his shirt. Being intimidating came naturally to him, but sometimes he wished there was something else he could do. He had no book smarts, like Ava did, but when it came to working with his hands and creating a mech device, that was where his talents shone.

Not quite talents required for a spy. Sometimes he wondered what Malloryn had been thinking when the duke had offered him the job.

Ava entered the clinic, the bell above the door tinkling, and there was nothing for it but to follow. The foyer was stark and decorated with painted timber signs advertising what the vaccine did, and carefully printed pamphlets on the small tables. *Protect your family from the craving virus.* The clinics were government owned, which made people a little wary of them, but with the virus easily transmitted by blood, and no longer a province of the Echelon, it was easier than ever to be infected.

Once upon a time, only aristocratic families were allowed to be made into blue bloods, with each noble son going through the Blood Rites at the age of fifteen to see whether he'd be "worthy" of receiving such an elitist boon. Women had been strictly forbidden from receiving it, which made him wonder about Ava's past, but then accidents occurred.

But where had she come into contact with a blue blood? She was clearly a virgin, so it wasn't as though she'd served as some rich lord's blood thrall. A flash of something hot went through him at the thought—the idea of Ava giving up either her flesh or blood rights to a nobleman in exchange for protection and a rich life made him want to punch something.

"Good afternoon," Ava greeted the receptionist, flashing a small leather badge with a striking hawk embossed upon it in steel. "I'm Miss Ava McLaren of the Nighthawks. I'm here to ask some questions about a crime

I'm investigating with my partner, Mr. Kincaid."

The receptionist blanched, her arms half-slung through her cardigan. "A crime? I'm not quite certain how we can help but—"

"Is the clinic doctor on duty?"

"Aye, ma'am. We were both just finishing up for the day. I can see if he's—"

"Tell him we'd like to talk to him," Kincaid interrupted, leaning on the counter and staring at the older woman. "It's official business."

Ava rapped her fingers on the counter as the woman scurried off, and then picked up one of the pamphlets on the vaccine. "Side effects," she read, "include a fever, a rash, sensitivity to light, and a headache. Please see a doctor if symptoms persist beyond a few days."

"No black veins?" It would be too easy.

"No internal bleeding." Ava put the pamphlet back.

The door opened. "This way, sir. Miss. Dr. Harricks has a few minutes to see you." The receptionist ushered them through into the clinic, then raised her voice. "Cheerio, Dr. Harricks. I'll see you tomorrow."

She closed the door behind herself.

The examining room was private and painted a relaxing blue. A gentleman dressed in a tweed suit cleaned his glasses in the corner, his hair neatly combed. "Good afternoon," he said politely, his gaze sweeping over them, then doubling back to Ava with a hint of male appreciation. "I'm Dr. Harricks, the clinic specialist. How may I help you?"

A service automaton swept patiently in the corner, steam hissing from its vents as it worked its way around the room. Needed servicing by the look of it.

"A Mr. David Thomas was a patient of this clinic six weeks ago," Ava started, as Kincaid strolled around the room, glancing at the clean counters and meticulous files. She flipped through her folder. "He was found two days ago, dead in his parlor from internal bleeding and ruptured internal organs. The preliminary autopsy showed he was several weeks into the metamorphosis stage of the craving virus, with CV levels of 12 percent. I wanted to confirm whether Mr. Thomas received a vaccination here."

Dr. Harricks looked surprised, and then he turned to one of his cabinets. "Thomas... Thomas.... It sounds familiar, though I cannot recall a face. I receive dozens of patients through here each day."

"The vaccine is popular?" Kincaid asked, as Harricks flicked through his files and withdrew a slim folder.

"Increasingly," the doctor replied absently. "I'm booked out two months in advance these days. With more and more blue bloods swimming through the general population, people fear for their children."

"The craving virus is becoming more prevalent in the general population?" Ava asked.

"I'm not quite certain whether it's spreading now the legislation against unapproved infections has been lifted," the doctor admitted, "or whether blue bloods have always been there. They were put on a register when the prince consort was in power, and some were hunted and executed, depending upon how they became infected—it was supposed to be restricted to the Echelon, yes? But some slipped beneath notice, and I suspect in the last few years, now the law against casual infection has been changed, they're not hiding as much as they used to. Or at least, they weren't."

"You think that's going to change?" Kincaid frowned.

Harricks seemed to have found the file he wanted. "I expect it will. There's been a push for more vaccinations in the last two or so months, ever since the blood taxes were lowered to two pints per year for each human adult, and the humanists started stirring up trouble again." He hesitated. "It's... well, some of my clients seem angry these days. They're tired of being forced to give their blood so the Echelon can survive. Anti-blue blood sentiment is becoming rife. I thought we'd done away with all that since the revolution, but there's definitely a ripple of dissatisfaction brewing. One only has to look at the recent riots to see that."

"You found it?" Ava gestured toward the file.

"Ah, yes. Mr. David Thomas was vaccinated on the twenty-first. I tested his CV levels beforehand, and his results were conclusive: no factor of the craving virus present in his blood at all. He was 100 percent human when he received his vaccination." The doctor looked at his file again. "That doesn't make sense, unless the brass spectrometer I'm using is uncalibrated. It means the vaccine didn't work, and we've never had anything like that happen before."

Ava went into a line of questioning about how the vaccine was stored, and the science behind it. Kincaid found his attention drifting.

"Do you have a sample of the vaccine?" Ava asked.

There was an icebox in the corner, and the good doctor fetched them a tray of small vials.

"May I?" she asked, gesturing to Dr. Harricks's microscope.

Kincaid nudged the servant drone. It was stuck in the corner, bumping repeatedly against the wall. The sensor must be stuck. "Want me to have a look at your drone unit?" he threw over his shoulder. "I used to work the enclaves."

The doctor waved a hand in his direction with a "Yes, yes," but his attention remained on what Ava was doing.

Kincaid pulled his small lockpick set out of his pocket. There was a three-inch-long screwdriver in there, as well as various other tools. He knelt beside the drone and reached beneath it for the Off switch. It hummed to a stop, an exhale of steam warming his calves. Kincaid placed a hand against the steel barrel body of the drone. Hot. But not excessively so, considering the boiler had been going for a while by the look of it. The bloody things could run on a pint of water a day. He deftly undid the screws in the electrical panel, watching Ava as she reared back from the microscope.

"What is it?" Dr. Harricks demanded of her, drawing Kincaid's attention.

Ava looked perplexed, and adjusted some knob on the microscope. "This batch of vaccine looks like it's been untreated. The virus is alive, not inert."

Harricks pushed her out of the way, pressing his face to the microscope in horror. "That's impossible. I've been meticulous with my testing." He drew back, clearly confused. "You're right."

The good doctor snatched up a vial, reading the labels on it. Kincaid returned to his task, prying the back panel off the servant drone. Wasn't much he could do to help right now. This was Ava's area, not his. And sometimes it didn't hurt to vanish into the background and watch a suspect's body language—not that Harricks was a suspect. Yet.

"Hold on," Harricks burst out, examining the vial she was testing. "This vial label is missing its category number."

Ava leaned closer to look. "Do you think it's been tampered with? Or replaced?"

Kincaid watched for a second, hands setting the panel out of the way as he peered inside.

An 1864 service model. He winced. Jaysus. Didn't the

queen provide better funds for her clinics? No wonder the drone was struggling. It was over twenty years old, and he knew from past experience the '64s often had a fault in the wiring of their electrical circuit. He'd fixed enough of them in his first two years at the Southwark Enclave before he transferred to the King Street Enclave, once his talent with mech-work was noticed and he was set to work on war machines.

One of the wires was missing from the circuit board. Without a light, he couldn't see much else, but that was easily the problem. Watching as Ava and the doctor had a spirited discussion about the vaccine's manufacturer, he reached inside and brushed the wire gently out of the way with a wooden tongue depressor he'd found in the doctor's supplies, pausing as he heard a faint click—

Tick, tick, tick....

Kincaid jerked his fingers out of the drone and peered inside. *What in the devil's name?* There was a small clip attached to one of the wires—a pressure sensor by the look of it. And a luminescent clock face leered up at him from the bowels of the drone, the second hand ticking steadily toward twelve. Anchored to the clock were an explosive device, two sticks of dynamite, and a few wires.

"Ava!" he yelled, launching to his feet and sprinting toward her.

Kincaid caught a startled flash of her expression, the doctor's shocked, "*What on earth?*" and then he dove toward her and the doctor, sending all three of them flying through the window.

His shoulder hit it first, and glass shattered. They landed in the back alley, sharp shards stabbing into his back. Ava bounced in his arms, and the doctor rolled free, tumbling over the top of him.

"Get down!" he bellowed at Harricks, lurching to his

feet with Ava tucked under one arm, throwing them both behind a moveable waste receptacle in the alley.

The doctor held his hands up to protect his head, looking utterly perplexed. "What is the meaning of—"

The explosion lifted him off his feet, flinging him back into the opposite wall. Ava screamed, and Kincaid slammed her into the wall, using his body to protect her from the rubble as bricks, glass, and steel flew past them.

A waft of heat roared over them, thick with black smoke, and his ears rang. Ava squirmed against him, clapping her hands over her ears. It seemed to last forever. But finally, finally the intensity of the heat died down, and Kincaid lifted his head, feeling Ava gasp and collapse against his chest.

The alley was a ruin. The clinic blackened and charred, it's wall half-standing.

Flames crackled. Black smoke spilled from the bowels of the ruined clinic. Kincaid slowly lowered his arm from his face, his bare forearm blistered from the heat, and his head aching where he'd been slammed against the wall. "Harricks?" he yelled.

The doctor was buried beneath a mound of rubble. His boots kicked frantically.

"Ava? Are you unhurt?" Kincaid demanded.

"*What?*" she asked loudly.

Her acute hearing would have suffered more than his. He cupped her chin, checked her over, finding no trace of injury, before he urged her to stay there and hurried to the doctor's side.

Harricks, mercifully, looked like he'd sustained a broken wrist, and little else other than bruises.

"What happened?" the doctor kept gasping, staring at his burning clinic like a banked fish.

Kincaid helped him to his feet. "Someone planted a

bomb inside your service drone. There was a pressure sensor attached to one of the wires, and the second I touched it, I activated the bomb."

"But why?" Ava came out of the shadows, her face sooty and her dress streaked with dirt and burn marks.

He'd never forget how close she'd come to dying. Kincaid glared at the clinic. "Probably to cover their tracks. I think someone tampered with the vaccine vials, replacing some of the vaccine with live samples, from what I could gather. I'd assume the same person planted a bomb in the drone. It had a remote detonation charge upon it, so I'd guess they meant to return one night—or day—and set it off, except I got to it first."

"But why blow up the clinic?" Harricks still looked shocked.

"Why tamper with the vaccine?"

Ava met his gaze, rubbing at the skin in front of her left ear. "It sounds like someone wanted to make people scared of the vaccination clinics."

"Sounds like someone we know," he told her pointedly.

Because both Ulbricht and the *dhampir* had been trying to cause chaos last month. Maybe this wasn't connected—Ava would demand proof—but he had a gut feeling it was.

They found the same circumstances at two of the other clinics.

Tampered vials of vaccine. And another automaton drone that smelled like Nobel's blasting powder, according to one Nighthawk. The clinics were cleared and locked down, the Nighthawks sent to examine the remaining four clinics within the city, and a message sent to the Council of

Dukes. Reporters lingered at each clinic, shouting questions, but Ava kept her head down and tried not to make eye contact as she directed the Nighthawks to remove the vaccine vials carefully and transport them to Dr. Gibson's lab at the guild.

She found Kincaid carefully removing the back panel of the automaton drone in the alley outside, where he pronounced this particular model to be free of explosive devices. Several Nighthawks breathed sighs of relief, and took it into custody to examine further.

"We're finished here," she finally announced, stepping in front of Kincaid and forcing him to come to an abrupt halt. "Which means it's past time for me to have a look at that arm."

"It's nothing—"

"Don't you give me that nonsense." She gestured to the evacuated clinic. "Sit. And roll up your sleeve!"

To her surprise, Kincaid gave her a wry smile, and then collapsed into a chair. Smoke stained his face, and runnels of sweat had made tracks in it. This only served to highlight the intensity of his eyes. "As you wish."

Ava unwrapped the linen bandages she'd applied earlier, when they'd been in a rush. The sight of his blistered skin made her wince. She'd washed it thoroughly under cold water earlier, and the extent of the damage wasn't too bad. Fairly minimal in fact. But his skin was reddened, and hot to the touch, and there was one blister she didn't like the look of. He'd borne most of the heat wave when the clinic exploded, protecting her with his body.

"This is going to be a little disgusting," she said, spitting into her handkerchief, "but a blue blood's saliva can heal most wounds. Could you please not look?"

He obediently looked away as she pressed her saliva

against his skin. "Can't infect me, can it?"

"The craving virus is blood-borne. And I would never risk that if it wasn't." Still, the fact he'd asked bothered her a little.

"I trust you," he muttered, wincing a little.

"Thank you," Ava said quietly, as she used the clinic's bandages to redress his arm once she'd checked it. The redness was already fading, but she hated seeing him hurt like this. "I think you saved my life today."

Kincaid shrugged. "It happened quickly."

Ava slowly looked up from beneath her lashes. "You don't like it when I praise you."

He graced her with another careless smile. "I'm not a hero, angel—"

"I beg to differ," she said, "considering both Dr. Harricks and I most likely owe our lives to your quick thinking."

He had such astonishingly blue eyes. Ava blushed. "Thank you." Straightening out of her crouch, she pressed a swift kiss to his cheek, the smoothness of his freshly shaved skin like silk beneath her lips. "For everything."

Kincaid inhaled slowly, and his fingers caught in her skirts, trapping her. Heat darkened his eyes, and Ava was suddenly aware of how a simple turn of his head might result in her mouth meeting his. She reluctantly lowered her hand from his shoulder and turned away, flushing a little. The kiss had been instinctive. A tender thank-you.

But it wasn't tenderness she saw blazing in the sapphire blue of his eyes. It wasn't tenderness that made his fist clench in her skirts.

"Are you going to let me go?" she whispered, not certain whether she truly wanted him to.

Kincaid looked up from beneath thick black lashes, his fist flexing a little in the fabric of her skirts. "Should I?"

The words stole her breath. She didn't know how to answer him. And maybe he saw it in her face, for he released her, stretching back in his chair and running both hands—human and mech—through his thick, dark hair. "Go, Ava. Give me a minute alone."

"Thank you," she whispered, stepping back out of reach.

She'd thought his flirtations meaningless, and had brushed them aside until now, but as Ava headed for the alley outside to catch her breath, she suddenly realized he wasn't just flirting with her because she was a woman, and that was what Kincaid did. Those heated looks he sent her were specific. The offer he'd made her was centered purely on *her*. It was Ava he was imagining in his bed in those moments, Ava he visualized whenever he gave her that wicked smile.

And it had been for a while.

"Oh." Ava paused, pressing her back to the wall and sucking in a huge breath. Goodness. Liam Kincaid was flirting with *her*, Ava McLaren, owner of enough fichus to sink an airship, and the lady most likely to end her days as a spinster, surrounded by a dozen cats.

And he meant every single thing he was silently telling her when their eyes met.

Including his proposition.

There was no sign of Malloryn when they returned to the safe house, but the woman he'd left in charge in his absence, Isabella Rouchard—or the baroness, as Ava referred to her—was there, and in Malloryn's absence, she was the person they reported to.

"Someone's tampering with the vaccination clinics?"

Isabella echoed, once Ava finished giving her report. "I can scarcely believe this. People stricken with the craving virus after receiving a vaccination, this Black Vein, bombs.... What on earth does it all mean?"

Ava exchanged a look with Kincaid. "We have no proof, my lady, but... it has to be connected."

"These riots aren't coming from nowhere," Kincaid added. "I haven't heard much from my mech friends, but the good doctor mentioned unrest among the population. Perhaps that has something to do with it? Maybe someone's got a grudge against the vaccination clinics."

"Or... it could be something more sinister," Ava pointed out.

"You think this has something to do with the *dhampir* or Ulbricht?" Isabella demanded.

At this Ava hesitated. She wanted the suspect to be their mysterious enemy, but.... "It could be anyone with humanist sympathies who can't forgive the blue bloods, despite the revolution. It might be some of the humanist contingents that were left over from the revolution. It might be the *dhampir*. We don't know."

Isabella paced the rug in front of Malloryn's ornate desk, her hands clasped behind her back. The woman ran the Rogues in Malloryn's absence, but Ava had had little to do with her in their time together. Gemma could stir the blood in a dead man's veins, but Isabella Rouchard intimidated her on an entirely different level. The baroness was frighteningly beautiful, with sharp black-winged brows, and hair the color of a raven's wings. "I'll mention it to Malloryn. He's busy with his forthcoming wedding at the moment, but I know he'll want word of this. In the meantime...." The woman tapped her ruby lips, staring into the distance. "Keep digging. We need to know who is behind this. If the unrest in the human population grows any worse, it could threaten our peace, and even the crown. We cannot tolerate that."

Ava curtsied politely, and began backing away. "Yes, my lady."

"Ava?" the baroness called.

She paused, her shoulder brushing Kincaid's. "Yes?"

The baroness tipped her head in a polite nod. "You've done very well with this case, but be careful how far you step. Our enemies unleashed vampires on London last month without even a thought to the carnage that might have occurred. If they *are* the ones behind this, then they won't hesitate to remove you from the situation. If I had the option I'd replace you with Gemma or Charlie, purely because they're more capable of protecting themselves, but they're still not back, so... be careful. "

A chill ran through her.

But Kincaid rested his hand on the small of her back. "If someone wants to hurt Ava, they'll have to go through me first."

And somehow, Ava felt perfectly safe, in a way she hadn't since before Dr. Hague got his hands on her.

CHAPTER NINE

SHE COULDN'T BREATHE.

That was the first thought that struck her. Ava froze, trying to drag her hand to her face. There was something there. Over her mouth. And her skin felt warm and wet, as though some sort of liquid surrounded her. Metal under her touch. The brass filtration device over her mouth and nose, with a tube leading back to an oxygen canister.

She felt the beginning of that old panic. She knew this place. Knew where she was, how she'd been trapped.

Naked limbs. Naked all over. Her only decoration was the enormous scar up the center of her chest, where Hague had cut her heart out and replaced it with his own clockwork version.

Ava screamed, bubbles slipping from the breathing mask over her face, rippling over her delicate cheeks and shooting toward the top of the small tank she floated in.

Hague's healing tank, he'd told her.

She pressed her hands against the glass, her vision blurry through the water. Ava pounded her fists against it, but it would not break. She'd tried, a thousand times before, ever since she'd woken up here in Hague's dark laboratory. She was trapped in here, trapped forever, unable to ever escape—

"Ava! Ava!" Hands caught her shoulders.

She fought him, trying to push Hague away, but then he said the one word that stayed her fury. "Damn it, kitten. You're going to give me a black eye."

Kitten?

Only one man ever called her that. Ava caught Kincaid's wrists and gasped. Cool metal met her left hand, the bare spars fused into flesh with exquisite workmanship. Suddenly she could see again. Recognize where she was. Kincaid knelt on the edge of her bed, his palms cupped around her shoulders. He loomed over her, but there was a lantern in the corner and its golden light backlit him, revealing just how quickly he'd rushed in here. She caught a vague glimpse of naked skin, but the darkness threatened to suck her under again.

"Here." Warm arms enveloped her even as she sucked in a sharp breath. "I've got you. You're safe. You're with me. I've got you."

Ava burrowed her face against Kincaid's throat. The first sob took her by surprise, a spasm ripping through her chest as she tried to suppress it. She might be safe, but she'd never be entirely free of Hague and the shadow he cast over her life.

Kincaid held her for a long time as she struggled to fight back the tearless sobs. His human hand stroked her hair, catching in tangles of it, and then gradually easing them free. It was that which brought her back to the present. The patient, slow way in which he finger combed her hair. Not a single question, or a demand she fight her way through her panic-fueled nightmares, but just letting her find her way back when she was ready.

He'd done the same to her in the Garden of Eden when she'd suffered her hysteria attack—whatever else this man might be, he was patient when he needed to be. And surprisingly gentle. She'd have never expected it of him, with his brutish body, the sparse steel of his mech hand, and the fierce expression he so frequently wore.

Ava turned her head, pressing her lips to his throat and breathing in the scent of him. She couldn't stop herself from darting her tongue against his skin and tasting the salt there. The kick of his pulse against her tongue made the shadows rise again. But this time they were different shadows. The craving ignited inside her as the predator within her raised its head, scenting blood. She could hear his pulse in her ears, feel it flickering against her lips, just daring her.... So near she could almost taste it—

"That's enough," Ava said, pushing him away with a gasp.

Kincaid reared back onto his knees on the bed. He wore trousers, at least, but the sight of his light-touched skin drew her gaze, and made her uncomfortably aware of how quiet the night was.

How they were possibly the only two people in the house right now.

"What are you doing in here?" she whispered, sitting up and dragging the sheets under her chin.

Kincaid arched one of those dark brows. "Rescuing you from an assassin. Someone screamed the house half down. Thought you were being murdered. Turns out you were fighting off your sheets instead."

Of course. She felt like the worst sort of fool. If the ground opened up to swallow her whole right now, she would pray to any god. "Did anyone else hear?"

"Apart from Herbert, I'm the only one here, princess. Our resident inventor, Jack, had mysterious business in the city. Viscount business, I suspect. And the baroness was up to no good. Looked like she was heading out to a ball. If she doesn't come home with at least a dozen hearts in her pocket, I'll be disappointed."

A joke, for the baroness was cold and reserved, except for when Isabella looked at Malloryn.

Apart from Herbert, the butler née assassin, Ava realized she was all alone in the house with a half naked man who was a physically fine specimen of male anatomy indeed.

Kincaid resettled himself on the edge of the bed, shirtless, and with the buttons on his trousers half undone. Ava blushed. Hair trailed from his navel down into his pants, and a generous dusting of it shadowed his chest. He was nothing like Paul, her ex-fiancé. Side-by-side he'd dwarf poor Paul, and he felt... threatening in a way Paul never had.

Because you want him. Because there's danger inside this man, and you're not quite certain how to handle him.

"I'm sorry. For dragging you out of bed."

"Don't be sorry." He scratched at the faint scar on his chin. "Happen often?"

"Sometimes," she said noncommittally.

"Something bad happened to you once."

She didn't deny it.

"It's written all over you, luv." Those wicked eyes narrowed, but more in consideration than anything else. "You don't have to tell me."

Ava drew her knees to her chest. Suddenly Hague was back, trailing ghostly fingertips down her spine. She pressed the heels of her palms to her closed eyes. "I don't really want to talk about it. But yes, something bad happened to me once. Something that gives me nightmares, something I can never escape."

A soft sigh escaped him. When she lowered her hands, she found Kincaid sprawling across her bed, looking utterly relaxed, his fingertips brushing against her calf through the sheets.

"We all have fears," he finally said.

"Even you?" *The mighty behemoth?*

He cradled his mech hand behind his head, his abdominal muscles flexing. "Jaysus. I've had more than my fair share."

"But you're...."

"I'm...?"

"So powerful," she blurted, gesturing to his body. "And cocky. And rash. I cannot imagine anything could ever frighten you." The past swam up between them, when she'd tended to his broken nose, and Kincaid had snapped at her to get it healed so he could rejoin the hunt in time. "You wanted to hunt a vampire, when the very thought made my blood curdle."

Shadows darkened his eyes. "Vampires don't really scare me. It would be a quick death. A fairly clean one—"

"You've got to be jesting me," she broke in. "I cannot possibly imagine death by vampire to be quick, or particularly merciful."

"It is compared to the fate of others." His voice roughened. "Over in an instant of fierce terror and pain, rather than the long drawn-out spiral downward of something degenerative where you stare your death in the face every day, wondering when the time will come where your body fails you. Wondering how many days you can spend trapped within your body before you go mad."

"Well, I couldn't think of anything worse than a vampire."

"Really? Not a single thing? Not even whatever causes your nightmares?"

Ava opened her mouth to reply, but an image of Hague sprang to mind, strapping her to his examination table and shining the harsh light in her eyes as she screamed and tried to escape—to no avail. A chill ran down her spine. Kincaid was right. Death by vampire might be considered a blessing in some circumstances.

Or was it...?

She'd lived after all. She'd survived the unsurvivable as Hague infected her with the craving virus and then cut her heart out of her chest while she swayed in and out of ether dreams. It was a horrible nightmare—six months of torture and misery and hopelessness—until Perry and Garrett had appeared, bringing light and hope back into her world. Bringing freedom. Maybe Ava would never escape the past, but she was here and now, and there was a whole life stretching out in front of her, filled with all the things she'd never done.

Perhaps the idea wasn't to forget the nightmares, but to accept them. She'd spent years trying to pretend she'd put all the pieces of herself back together. To hide her screams at night, to make sure nobody knew how much it sometimes scared her to leave the house and walk the streets. To pretend she was confident and had her wits about her at all times, when but one sharp noise might send her crashing down like a cracked porcelain vase given a shove.

"You're right. There can be worse things than vampires. And you, sir," she pointed out, before he could interrupt, "have initiated a rather macabre turn of conversation."

Kincaid scraped his hand over his face, sighing as he rolled onto his side. "Maybe it's macabre, but maybe... it's easy to talk to you about the fears a man has." One blue eye locked on her as he drew his hand away. "You're very easy to talk to, Ava."

She blushed. Nobody said that about her, especially not men. Usually they were searching about them for some means of escaping her. "When I'm not babbling about autopsies or the craving virus, do you mean?"

"What's wrong with hearing you speak of dismembering cadavers? I think all those others who disdain you simply have weak stomachs." His smile faded. "I didn't realize how long it's been since... I could actually talk to someone."

He didn't look happy about this realization.

"What's wrong?" she whispered. "You sound like that's a horrible thing." Every person needed a friend— someone who could hear their inner thoughts without flinching.

"It's not." He toyed with her blankets again, looking so much younger in this moment. "It just makes me miss my brother. He was the only other person I could speak to like this."

Oh. "He's...?"

"Dead," Kincaid muttered. "His heart gave out on him three years ago, a month before I finally escaped the enclaves. There's irony for you. I never got to see him again. I spent ten years in that hell, and his heart couldn't bloody wait one more damned month."

Ava slid her hand over his, a pulse of sympathy sliding through her, but Kincaid shook it off. "Sorry, luv," he said, shooting her an insincere smile as he sat up. "There's things a man can speak of, but I draw the line at being pitied."

"I wasn't pitying you."

"No?"

"No. I was seeking to... to offer comfort."

This time, the look he gave her was hot and slow. Kincaid finally sighed. "It would be almost too easy."

"What do you mean?"

"Nothing." Kincaid rolled onto his knees. "Don't ever change," he murmured in her ear, before pressing a gentle kiss to her cheek. The heat of his breath ghosted across her jaw, and a shiver ran through her.

His face lingered there, and Ava turned wide eyes toward him, holding her breath. It would be terribly easy to remove the distance between them, but she was suddenly shy again.

He backed away, as if he knew precisely what was going through her mind. Ava cleared her throat, feeling awash in an unknown wave of heat. Good lord. He'd barely even brushed his lips against her cheek. *Yes, but he's practically naked.* And suddenly her mind was taking her down dark avenues she'd never truly explored. "I won't change. I don't think I'd even know how."

"It's part of your charm."

"Charm," she scoffed. "Now I know you're jesting—"

Kincaid captured her jaw, forcing her to meet his suddenly steely gaze. "There can be charm in honesty, Ava. Charm in a woman who is so blatantly unaware of her own enticements. Charm in an innocently curious gaze."

And she was blushing again, for he'd noticed where she was looking. "I'm a scientist. I cannot help feeling curious."

"So I've noticed. But if you were truly scientific, then you'd be more interested in putting a theory into practice."

Those eyes twinkled with mischief. Daring her.

Ava looked down. To the thumb just brushing against the pulse at the inside of her wrist. She swallowed.

"You know what I'm talking about, Ava."

"I thought you refused to have anything to do with virgins." Somehow she managed to meet his gaze, though her cheeks burned. "You told me that once. So how can I consider your proposition to be a serious one?"

"There's a part of me that is reevaluating that rule. Every damned time I look at you, lately. My rules are simple: don't play with virgins. Don't break hearts. Make the rules clear from the start. But—"

"But?" she dared, the sensation in her chest expanding, leaving her slightly dizzy.

"Ava," he warned. "Don't start a game you won't finish. I will play along. To a certain point. But I don't like being trifled with."

Ava couldn't help thinking about her earlier realization that although she'd survived and put her life back together, there were quite a few things she hadn't experienced.

A proper kiss, for example.

Her gaze slid to Kincaid's mouth. Paul—her ex-fiancé's—kisses had been dutiful, and she'd seen Perry and Garrett steal enough kisses in the Nighthawks guild to know when she was missing out. Those types of kisses did not seem anything like the chaste caress Paul pressed upon her once upon a time.

"Why are you looking at me like that?" Kincaid breathed.

She crossed her arms over her nightgown. It was strange how safe she felt with him in her room, at night, when she wore little more than thin cotton. Kincaid gave the devil a run for his money when it came to mischief, but he obeyed a peculiar set of rules he'd set himself.

Maybe I could use him to test out some of my theories? a little voice whispered. *Maybe we could both give each other pleasure?* He wanted her, after all, and she was very curious about what, exactly, he would do to her.

Suddenly she felt like she had an answer to his proposition.

Nobody would get hurt. She knew what she was

entering into. An experiment. A purely physical one. Exactly what Perry had recommended she do.

She couldn't deny she was attracted to Kincaid in a physical way, but she also quite liked him. The craving virus roused the primal side of one's nature, but she couldn't entirely blame this... this lust upon it. She wanted those strong hands on her bare skin. She wanted to touch Kincaid, to lick him, to taste those devilish lips, in a way she'd never felt before.

None of this made any sense at all, except for the demanding pulse of the ache between her thighs.

"What if I *do* intend to finish it?" She was tired of living within the rules—tired of being polite, and letting her own desires go unanswered. Perry's suggestion had only exacerbated the sense of frustration.

And the more she thought about it, the more Kincaid seemed to be the perfect answer to her problems.

Even if her words wiped the smile off his face.

"Are you sure you know what you're asking for?" he asked, pushing away from the bed and pacing across the room, the bulky form of the mechanical brace that girdled his hips and thighs bulging beneath his trousers. She wished she knew why he wore it.

Ava sat up on her knees, leaving her a little chilled as her blankets fell away. "Yes, I do. I trust you. And this attraction doesn't seem to be going away, so why not?"

"I know women. You're not the sort to enjoy an affair if your heart is not involved. And I'm not offerin' a future, Ava. I need you to understand that."

"Pfft." She waved the thought away, determined now she'd made up her mind. "You might have a good deal of experience with women, but you forget something. I am not like most women. I'm a scientist, Mr. Kincaid. You said yourself, this makes sense in a logical, rational way. And you present a very intriguing dilemma for me. I have never felt so curious about... about a man's body before. When you are in the same room with me, I am—" She searched for the means to say it. "—overcome with purely physical desires. I cannot stop thinking about it, and it's quite vexing. Usually when I am interested in a man, it is because I find him charming, or he is nice to me, or I admire his manners, or—"

"Or in the case of Byrnes, you found him comfortable to be around." Kincaid crossed his arms over his chest as he faced her.

"Ye-es," she said carefully. "He was easy to be around because he accepted me as I was, without seeking to change me or disapproving of the way I think. You don't know how rare that is." Again, she thought of Paul, the man who hadn't entirely approved of her. She didn't blame him for moving on when he thought she was dead, after Hague kidnapped her, but at the time the loss had hurt her.

It didn't anymore.

Kincaid's eyes narrowed. "Did you ever want to kiss Byrnes?"

"Well," she sputtered. "Of course I did. He was very kind to me, and I cared for him, and—"

"Kind?" The way he drawled the word made her feel like he knew something she did not.

"Byrnes has no concept of charm, but he *can* be kind. I know you probably can't imagine it, but—"

"I thought there was something between the pair of you, but if there was, then you wouldn't be thinking of him as *kind*. That's the very last word anyone would ever use to describe that smug bastard."

"Whatever does that mean?" she asked suspiciously.

Kincaid rubbed his mouth. "Ava, do you have any idea what it is like to bed a man?"

"Of course I do. I've seen—"

"Outside of what you've seen in books."

They stared at each other, and she felt like they were having two different conversations. "No," she admitted. "Only what I've read, or what I've seen in diagrams."

"I see."

"I'm not completely sheltered. There were farm animals at my father's country manor. And I saw the shadow show at the Garden of Eden." He looked unconvinced. "I studied anatomy, for heaven's sake. I know how things fit."

Kincaid growled under his breath, scraping his hands over his face as he muttered, "*Why me?*"

"I can hear you. Enhanced hearing, if you'll recall? And if you want an answer to that, then here it is. I don't love you. You don't love me. There's no risk here for me. But I like you—enough to trust you with my body—and I... I think you like me. Or you would, if I weren't a blue blood, but—"

"I do like you," he admitted gruffly. "Blue blood notwithstanding."

Something warmed with her. "And the truth is, I'm not certain I've been *living* my life. I needed time to put myself back together after what happened to me, and I think I'm nearly there. But the last few years have been... controlled. Full of routine, and me trying to pretend everything is fine, and dusk to dawn spent in a laboratory, or traipsing through crime scenes, and while that is all well and good and intellectually stimulating it has come to my attention it also makes me feel a little hollow. Or... lacking. Lacking something."

Those sleepy eyes turned dangerous. "You mentioned a taste of passion."

Passion. That was what had been missing. "Yes," she

breathed. "I want to experience something that sweeps me out of this ordinary life. I want a taste of everything I'm not supposed to want, and everything I've been suppressing for the last few years. Perry suggested I take a lover, but I think it's more than that. And I don't know precisely what that something is, but there's a hollow inside me, a yearning for... something. And maybe if I start with a lover, then I'll work out what that something is."

"Malloryn wouldn't approve. After Byrnes and Ingrid, he specifically demanded no more fraternization occur."

"I thought thumbing your nose at the duke was the highlight of your day? And who are you to speak of rules? You, who clearly likes to break them?" She could see the furrow on his brow still, the disapproving way he held himself, as though she'd suggested he rub mud all over his skin. "And if you won't help me, then I shall find someone who will."

"Like hell you *will*," he growled. "Christ, woman. Think of the risk."

"That's why I'm asking *you*. I know you wouldn't hurt me. I... I trust you with my body." And wasn't that a thought, for someone who'd been another man's captive. True, Hague had had no interest in her body sexually, but he'd still controlled every aspect of her. She'd been helpless for a long time, and unable to control even the slightest physical interaction.

But when she thought of giving herself to Kincaid, there was no fear there. Only... interest. A delicious urge to spread her wings and take what she wanted, for once in her life.

Kincaid eyed her with an evil look. "What was that thought?"

"I trust you with my body," she said gently, half in wonder. "I didn't understand why it had to be you, but I think that is the answer. I am both attracted to you, and feel safe with you. You don't know how rare it is to find a man who makes me feel like that."

He looked uncomfortable again. "Has a man ever hurt you, Ava?"

"Not... in the way you mean." She hated talking about it. It seemed wrong, in a way. *I survived, and the others didn't,* and sometimes that woke her more often than any nightmare she might suffer. What did she have to complain about? A little hysteria every now and then? An inability to leave the house when she was suffering the worst phases of her trauma? It could be worse. She could be buried in St. James's cemetery, like Evangeline, or in Harknell like Suzette. Or she might even be one of the girls that had vanished completely. Only Hague knew where those bodies went, and he was dead and never telling.

But Kincaid needed to know.

Just in case she panicked if he made a sudden move.

"Four years ago," she said quietly, rubbing the sheet between thumb and forefinger to help ground herself, "I was captured by a madman. He was a scientist who created clockwork and mechanical organs, and he needed humans to test his operations on."

"The Steel-Jaw case?"

It had been all through the papers at the time. No wonder he knew it. "I was one of the girls he experimented upon. He wanted to create a clockwork heart that could sustain a patient dying of heart failure. But the problem was he couldn't keep the girls he experimented upon alive throughout the process of removing... removing...."

Removing their hearts.

"Dr. Hague infected me with the craving virus, so I might survive," Ava whispered, unbuttoning her nightgown a little so he could see the top of her scar, and trying to ignore his paling face. "I was his first successful heart transplant patient. But not by choice. Byrnes, Perry, and Garrett... They rescued me from that vile laboratory, and though I have managed to resurrect some semblance of a life, it haunts me every day." She glanced up from beneath her lashes. His eyes were wide with horror. "I was one of only two girls who survived. I saw them die, Kincaid. And... and there was no way to escape. I had no hope left. Nothing but pain, and...." She gasped, her fingers contracting into a fist.

"Hush, kitten. It's all right." Kincaid slid onto the bed, curling a hand around the back of her head as he dragged her against his chest.

Ava released a shuddering breath. She wasn't going to allow Hague to intrude upon this moment. "I know what it's like to be unable to make choices in regards to your own body," she said, absorbing the heat of his body, "but I want to learn what it's like to give myself to a man. *I* make this decision. It's my body to give to someone else, and I choose you."

There was a long moment while Kincaid thought about this. He kissed the top of her head. "Hell, Ava, I had no idea."

She pressed her finger to his lips. "I don't want to talk about it. I want to talk about the future. About us. About... your proposition."

"Very well. An affair." He kissed her finger. "But if we agree to do this, then we do it on my terms. I want you to be very certain about this, so I don't intend to rush you. We take this one step at a time, and I decide when you're ready for the next step, considering how eager you are, and how much you don't know."

"Agreed."

Kincaid's eyes darkened. "Agreed."

Silence fell in the room, a hush of sensual awareness. The lantern light flickered.

"Aren't you going to kiss me?" Ava breathed.

Kincaid became very still. "What?"

"Sealed with a kiss," Ava said, her heart ticking quietly in her chest as a thrill of nervousness lit through her. "Isn't that the way it's done?"

CHAPTER TEN

THIS WAS THE worst decision Kincaid had ever made—he couldn't help thinking trouble would come of this, no matter how much he wanted it.

But hell if he could deny her, as Ava stared up at him with those eager eyes of hers.

If she were any other woman, you wouldn't say no, said a little voice, deep in his heart.

If she were any other woman, he wouldn't care if he said yes. A quick tumble in the blankets and then he'd be on his merry way, without another thought in her direction.

But this was Ava.

There are rules, damn it. Both his own, and the unspoken one among the Company of Rogues that said Ava had to be protected at all cost. Not a single one of them hadn't had blood on their hands at some stage. All of them wanted to protect their country, no matter what that took. None of them were angels, particularly not him, but...

Ava was the odd one out.

You couldn't look at her and not know she was innocent through and through. Somehow, despite the past events she'd mentioned—and wasn't that a fucking horror story—she still looked at the world with bright-eyed optimism. Not naïve. Never naïve. But she was somehow untarnished, unlike the rest of them, which was both miraculous and a tribute to her courage. And then, of course, there was Byrnes's recent marriage. He wasn't stupid. Ava had to be smarting from the loss of... whatever hopes she'd held in that direction, regardless of what she'd said.

She was also sitting there in her thin lawn nightgown with expectant eyes, and that fleshy lower lip caught between her teeth as she waited for him to take the first step. The mere sight of her stirred him in a way he'd never felt before.

His cock roused, throbbing behind the buttons of his breeches. He'd never been a hero. He'd never played the gallant champion. He'd never wanted to. He'd taken what he wanted in fleshly sins, drowned himself in drink to hide his demons, and told himself if he was going to die young, then at least he'd know what pleasure felt like.

Ava should be just one more conquest. Another night of lust and stolen kisses, and considerably more. But for some damned reason, he couldn't stop himself from offering her this one last chance.

Kincaid cupped her face in both hands. "One kiss," he told Ava, his voice hoarse. What the hell did she do to him? "Tonight all we're going to do is kiss. You need time to process this decision, and I don't intend to rush you through it."

She unexpectedly rolled her eyes. "All I do is think, Kincaid. My mind keeps going day and night. You have no idea what it feels like to stare at the ceiling all afternoon, when you're supposed to be sleeping. I *have* thought about this decision."

That was interesting. "That's an awful lot of thinking in so few days."

Ava froze, and then swiftly tucked a strand of hair behind her ear. "I—"

"You *were* thinking about this before I made the suggestion. Weren't you?"

"This is all your fault," she blurted. "I wasn't imagining anything of the like until the night we all went to the Garden of Eden, and I got lost in the garden, and you found me, and then unlaced my corset because I could barely breathe—"

"When you felt me up and stole my coat?" he asked, mildly amused.

"I didn't steal your coat!"

"You never gave it back," he pointed out. "I like how you're not denying you had your hands all over my chest."

"I had no choice. You were holding me there by the lapels of my coat—"

"*My* coat."

"Which I was wearing at the time," she said swiftly, her cheeks blazing with heat. Then— "You never asked for it back. And I forgot to return it."

"Then maybe *I* need time to think," he admitted. There was danger here. Not for her. She seemed remarkably clear-eyed about the entire process. But... though he'd said Ava was the weakest link on the team, he was also growing aware *she* was becoming the chink in his armor.

He remembered the night at the Garden of Eden. He'd been two seconds away from seducing a delicious little morsel who'd found him in the gardens, when Ava stumbled onto the scene, shivering like a wet kitten. Protective instincts he'd not felt in an age sprang from nowhere. He couldn't remember what he'd said to the other woman, but then she'd been gone, and he'd put his coat around Ava's shoulders as she fought to suppress her panic.

"I see," Ava replied, crossing her arms over her chest. "You've never once met a woman who you've refused, but suddenly you turn into a dainty miss with delicate feelings when I practically—"

"I am *not* suffering from delicate feelings."

"Of course not. You're just—"

That did it. Kincaid slid his hand through the thick mess of curls loosely gathered at her nape and captured the base of her skull. He dragged her closer, Ava's hands abruptly meeting the wall of his chest as her eyes widened. And then those maddening lips were beneath his, and his mouth captured hers, claiming it with a furious kiss.

Months of frustration, of trying to keep away from her, suddenly unleashed within him like a dam wall breaking. His tongue stabbed into her mouth, claiming her in some strange, utterly proprietary way that suddenly wasn't enough. He wanted to bite her throat; to rub his stubbled face across her pale, delicate skin until he saw the pinkness of his mark painted there; to kiss every last thought of every other man she'd ever seen out of her mind.

It was meant to be a kiss to make his point. A kiss to prove he wasn't protesting *too* damned much.

Instead it became a kiss that captured both of them within its grasp.

Somehow he tumbled her onto her back. Ava splayed on the blankets beneath him, stiff with shock for all of a second before she surrendered, his hips sinking between her parted thighs. His weight pressed her into the mattress, and Kincaid groaned as his heavy cock was crushed between them.

Damn, she truly was exquisite. Lantern light gilded the

soft gold strands in her hair, turned her skin to pure, molten honey, and for a second he couldn't believe she was real. That this was happening. He captured her mouth again, teasing her with his tongue, coaxing her to kiss him back when she hesitated, before she finally began to capture the rhythm of it.

Fuck. Kincaid eased the collar of her nightgown open, fisting his hand in her hair and turning her face to the side as his lips followed the smooth column of her throat down, down to the sweeping curve of her breasts. Breathing hard. Panting in fact, his hand sliding down to cup her breast—

"What are y-you doing?" Ava gasped.

And he realized where they were, and what he'd promised, and the fact she probably hadn't experienced anything like this before.

Damn it.

Somehow he pulled himself together. Kincaid looked down at her face, breathing hard. Her nightgown was bunched between them, barely clinging to the curves of her puckered nipples. The thin silvery scar rested between her small breasts, but he didn't have time to explore more. He had a nervous virgin on his hands, and he'd pushed too far. "I'm showing you what you asked for."

Her hands fluttered between them, then she hesitantly rested her palms on his bare chest. "I... see."

No, you don't, not truly. And the lie came undone in his mind as he realized everything he'd told himself in the last month was untrue. *She means nothing; you only want her because you can't have her; you're just bored and her innocence is appealing; she's not for you....* That last one, and only that, was the truth.

Ava McLaren was dangerous.

"May I touch you?" Ava whispered, and there went his mind into dark places.

Yes. He wanted to drag her hand lower and curl those

curious fingers around his cock.

Even as he knew she wasn't ready for that.

Kincaid caught her hand in his, and kissed her palm. She followed the movement with those expressive eyes, and when he licked the sensitive skin there, her eyes widened. God, she was so damned perfect. He wanted to see those eyes widen when he slid his cock inside her for the first time, to see the wonder in them. "I don't think touching me is a good idea right now."

Or else her experience with sex would be a very short, brief affair. The ache in his cock was almost excruciating.

Those glorious eyes shuttered. "But...?"

"Not tonight," he replied firmly. "Sleep on it. Be certain this is what you want. Because the next time we do this, I'm not going to stop."

"Oh." A soft, reverent sound. She was thinking again.

He had to get out of here. "Good night, Ava." Leaning forward, he kissed her again. Her mouth and thighs both parted with ease, and then he was groaning and trying to push away from her. Or at least, he intended to push away from her. His cock had other ideas. Kincaid's hips flexed, his erection pushing into her belly, and Ava gasped as she arched beneath him.

Jaysus.

He shoved to his feet abruptly, rearranging himself in his pants. Ava lay sprawled on the bed, looking utterly ravished. All those blonde curls splayed across her pillow. Why was he saying no again?

Right. He needed to find some control, and she needed to be certain this was what she wanted.

"Sweet dreams," he murmured as he turned around and strode toward the door.

Before he could change his mind and scrap all sense of honorable intentions.

Sweet dreams? Ava paced the bomb site at the clinic the following afternoon, her skirts seeming to irritate her sensitive legs. Ever since Kincaid left her in a heated mess on the middle of her bed last night, she'd been unable to concentrate. She'd never felt this way before.

Of course, she'd never had a man press his body so intimately against hers, especially in places that had never felt a man's touch before....

Ava groaned, trying to clear her mind. The Duke of Malloryn was due at any moment for a briefing. And Malloryn was the most perceptive man she'd ever met. If she even thought about carnal relations with Kincaid while Malloryn was in the building, she was certain the duke would notice.

Right on cue, a carriage rounded the corner, a team of matched blacks trotting along in front of it. Horses seemed an old-fashioned concept these days—an extravagance the Echelon still liked to display—what with steam power ruling the city. Most regular people were forced to make do with coal and steam power, which left a dirty pall hanging over London.

Not the Duke of Malloryn.

Malloryn's crest gleamed on the door of the carriage, and the footmen wore his livery. The silver griffins of the House of Malloryn leered at her.

"He's certainly not hiding who he is today," Kincaid muttered, appearing at her shoulder.

"Perhaps he's here on official business?" Malloryn liked cloaks, and shadows, and disguises. Sometimes he'd appear inside the safe house and she'd not have even noticed a door opening. It was like he sprang from nowhere.

Malloryn alighted from the carriage, wearing a black velvet coat with puffed shoulders, a loose white shirt, and leather trousers. He looked particularly dangerous today, and there was a rapier sheathed at the belt around his hips.

"Didn't know you'd turned pirate," Kincaid said, his eyes twinkling as he looked the duke up and down.

"Ha," Malloryn replied, without a trace of humor. "How droll you are this afternoon, Kincaid. Especially considering the city is under threat by unknown agents who have an enthusiasm for bombs. This is my court dress. I've been in meetings all morning."

"How civic-minded of you," Kincaid countered, and the duke shot him a withering glance.

"Ava." Malloryn tipped his head to her, dusting off his gloves as he looked around. "Perhaps you would care to show me around? I received the baroness's missive, but I'd like to hear it from both of you, if you would?"

"This way," Ava instructed, grabbing a handful of her skirts and pushing open the charred door to the front of the clinic. She wore dark blue today, a color that normally washed her out, but one which would survive better than yesterday's concoction of lace.

She led the duke through the building, staring at the wind-chilled sky that appeared overhead in the actual clinic as she ran through what happened. Malloryn picked his way through the rubble, leaning on an ebony-handled cane that bore his signet.

"What made you look inside the servant drone?" Malloryn finally asked, turning to Kincaid.

Kincaid knelt in the ruptured remains of the room, nudging a scrap of blistered metal. The paint had bubbled off it. "It wasn't working properly. Ava was busy talking incomprehensible scientific theories with Dr. Harricks, and

I have experience with such units. I offered to fix it."

"So pure chance?" Malloryn seemed surprised. "And you set the bomb off?"

"It had a remote detonation charge on it, but there was also a pressure sensor. I set the sensor off."

"I wonder when they planned to detonate it," Malloryn mused.

"Who knows? Maybe they intended to blow up all the clinics in the city at once? Maybe they simply planned to cover their tracks in case the vaccine tampering was discovered?"

"The question now is who," Malloryn murmured. "This is either the work of the humanists, or someone more sinister."

Ava's heart ticked a beat. "Do you think it has anything to do with the SOG?"

The three of them stared around at the blackened room. "The SOG work on creating chaos," Malloryn said slowly. "So I am very interested in this mystery all of a sudden."

The breath rushed out of her.

Malloryn sighed, and pulled out his pocket watch. "I have another meeting in half an hour, but speaking of Ulbricht, Gemma and Charlie returned an hour ago." Malloryn rested one hand on the remaining wall, and peered into the alley behind it. "No sign of Ulbricht in Brighton—but they managed to get their hands on a man who looks remarkably like him, who was being paid to parade around down there."

Kincaid scratched his jaw. "They wanted us to think Ulbricht was there."

"A distraction, yes." Malloryn's black boots crunched on blackened timber that crumbled into ash under his weight. "Did you know Lord Ulbricht has an investment in

Bayard Industries?"

"Bayard Industries?" Ava asked.

The duke graced her with a small smile. "An umbrella for the smaller company, Kestrel, that produces the vaccine. I've been busy too."

"He's involved with the vaccine tampering." All the hairs on her body stood on end. Her case was connected after all!

Malloryn held a finger to his lips. "Possibly. There certainly does seem to be a connection, and if Ulbricht's working to cover his tracks, then he's up to something."

"But why? I still don't quite understand why the SOG would tamper with the vaccine," Ava said, running her gloved fingers along the smoke-grimed steel workbench that had been warped in the blast. "*If* Ulbricht is behind this"—she had to keep saying "if," just in case she corrupted her chain of evidence—"then what purpose does it present for the SOG? I just cannot suspect a motive in all of this. They're blue bloods. Was the Echelon up in arms about developing a vaccine for the craving virus?"

"Quite the contrary," Malloryn admitted. "The Blood Rites were always meant to be an elitist privilege. The vaccine, therefore, played perfectly into Ulbricht's intentions of keeping the Echelon 'pure.'"

"It's not about the vaccine, or the Echelon," Kincaid said suddenly, startling both her and the duke. "It's about creating fear in the populace. He's striking at the humans, taking away their perceived safety. There's a great deal of humanist sympathy left over from the revolution. The staunch humanists were the first to line up for the vaccine when the clinics first opened, so they'd never have to fear an accidental infection turning them into... into what they consider to be monsters."

A pause. She was quite certain he'd mean to say

"turning them into monsters," and it made her feel a little hollow inside.

"Go on," Malloryn instructed.

"Last month Ulbricht was involved in the mass disappearance of people. The kidnappings and disappearances made people afraid, and they also just happened to help feed his mistress's vampires."

Ava shuddered. A truly horrific thought.

"But the people don't know that. Their friends and family vanished, and the Council of Dukes hushed it over and paid out in blood money. Those we rescued from Zero and her vampires were returned safely to their families, but... not all of them came home. It looks like the Echelon are up to their old tricks," Kincaid said, and Malloryn gestured for him to continue. "So Ulbricht takes away their vaccination clinics. Nobody's going to receive the vaccination if his or her friends are coming down with the craving virus after having it."

"For what purpose though?" Ava asked. "Ulbricht's cause was to see the Echelon back in power. How does this help his cause?"

"I agree. That's a great deal of maybe and perhaps," Malloryn said. "What does it gain him?"

"If I wanted to cause chaos in the city, then that's how I'd do it," Kincaid replied. "Stir up old resentment. Make people afraid of blue bloods again."

"But for what purpose?"

Kincaid shrugged. "As you said, we don't know for sure Ulbricht is behind any of this, and until we do, we can only guess what he intends."

Malloryn scratched at his jaw. "I've got all my spies out trying to track down any of the other members of the Sons of Gilead."

"Makes it easy, when they bloody tattoo themselves

with a rising sun," Kincaid muttered.

"Agreed." For once Malloryn seemed almost cordial when he tipped his head to the burly mech. "*If* such tattoos were in plain sight. Some of the SOG members think this a game, a lark. Ulbricht's been toying with the young sons of the Echelon, and playing to their sympathies with his tales of how things were better in the good old days. Half of his SOG are stupid young nobles who are fresh out of their Blood Rites and perfectly content to tattoo their allegiance on their wrists. It's not them I'm interested in. They're the sheep."

"The Echelon is still holding the rites?" Ava asked in surprise. Once the Blood Rites had been deemed a nobleman's rite of passage—the time when a young boy was first infected with the craving virus, provided his candidacy was approved, of course.

"It's tradition," Malloryn replied, "and there's nothing the Echelon likes more than to cling to outdated practices."

"You don't approve?" Kincaid looked at the duke as if he'd done something interesting.

"I'm not particularly fond of the old ways, or those blue blood relics who cling to them, like Ulbricht and his cronies. The Great Houses manipulating and assassinating their way to glory... it made for a rather wary childhood, if I'm being honest. You only have to have one servant try to cut your throat one morning to realize there are better ways of doing business." He shook his head. "No. I'm interested in progress. The revolution changed the empire, and I'm tired of dragging blue bloods kicking and screaming into a better future. However, when Ulbricht and his cronies start using the heirs of that future—that is when I am going to have to take a stance.

"I want Ulbricht's head, and the only way to find him is to find those SOG members who don't flaunt their tattoos. They're the ones in power, and they're the ones I would like to have a rather stern word with."

Ava exchanged a glance with Kincaid. Ulbricht deserved whatever Malloryn had in mind, she told herself.

"I'm sending Gemma and Charlie to investigate Bayard Industries," Malloryn said, "and the Nighthawks are all over Kestrel Laboratories."

Her heart fell. "But this is—"

The duke arched a brow.

—*my case.* Her shoulders fell when she saw the implacable cast of his shoulders. One didn't tell Malloryn what to do. Especially not when he was in this mood.

"There was a photograph of the clinic in the paper this morning, with you in the background, Ava," Malloryn said, resting both hands on his cane. "It was claimed you're with the Nighthawks, but if the right people were looking, then they'll have noticed your face. It's not personal. You've done very well so far. But nobody knows Gemma and Charlie work for me. You, however, have rather distinctive blonde curls."

She hadn't even realized the journalists baying outside had had a photographer with them. Damn it. All the excitement she'd felt crumbled to ash, much like the building around her.

Kincaid crossed his arms over his chest. "Then what do you want me and Ava to do?"

"Wait. The Nighthawks will be bringing back samples of the vaccine from Kestrel Labs, and I'm sure Dr. Gibson would welcome Ava's assistance in testing the vials to see if any of them have been tampered with at the laboratories— or whether they were affected *after* they'd been transported from the production facility."

"It was clearly tampered with at the clinic," Kincaid interrupted.

"Most likely. But I want to be certain. We have to work out whether the entire production needs to be dismantled, and how to control the outcry. And," Malloryn speared Ava with a stern look, "we still need to discover what this Black Vein is, and how it's killing blue bloods."

"I'm working on it." The problem was she had a dozen puzzle pieces, and no precise means of putting them all together yet. Black Vein seemed to be connected to those humans who'd received the tampered vaccine. She'd found nothing in the contaminated vaccine vials so far that might explain it, but perhaps the Nighthawks' samples would contain some clue.

"Keep me updated."

"As you wish, Your Grace," she said, swallowing down her disappointment. Years of experience with the Nighthawks had taught her to be patient. They had a suspect, they had a few clues. She could work this out.

"Excellent." Malloryn snapped his pocket watch shut, and headed for the door. "Keep me apprised of the situation. Or... keep the baroness apprised. She'll pass on what she deems relevant to me, and if Ulbricht does rear his pale head, I'll take over."

"You're not going to be overseeing the operation?" Last month, Malloryn had had his fingers in every pie.

Malloryn shot her a raised-brow look. "I forget how distracted you can be, Ava. Kincaid, what is happening in my personal life this month? Since you're all so terribly interested in it?"

"You're getting married, Your Grace," Kincaid replied. "Every single Rogue in the Company—excluding Ava—is wagering on whether you'll get the lucky bride to the altar or not."

"Correct. I would much rather be overseeing this case. But apparently I have flowers to peruse, and cakes to taste, and places to be seen...." Malloryn grimaced. "One month and then I can forget this ever happened, and return to my regularly scheduled duties."

Forget he was married? Ava blinked. She knew the duke and his fiancée were forging a marriage of convenience in the wake of a scandal where the duke had been caught in the gardens of some ball with Miss Hamilton, but she'd thought relations between them might have thawed by now. "Isn't it time to forgive Miss Hamilton?"

"*Forgive* her?" Malloryn shook his head. "Miss McLaren, I know you're a kind soul, but one doesn't forgive being trapped into marriage by a manipulative young woman. Ever."

"That sounds like a very sad state of affairs to me," she said quietly.

"Quite the opposite. Sadness indicates one cares. Marriage is going to be a formality, a distant affair Miss Hamilton and I shall navigate with the utmost ease. If I'm lucky, I doubt I'll see my wife more than once a week. If she's lucky, she won't protest this fact." Malloryn tipped his head to her, "And if we're quite finished here, I'd best be on my way. There's a garden party this afternoon, apparently. I'm the guest of honor. I can hardly wait."

"Good luck," Kincaid called as the duke exited the building. He glanced down at her, his hands in his pockets. "I'd make some pithy comment about enjoying the idea of Malloryn choking down samples of wedding cake, but you have that look in your eye."

"This proves nothing. Weddings are a happy event in most cases. Of course Malloryn *must* be the exception, but not all marriages are unhappy affairs."

"I beg to differ," Kincaid began. "I think this proves my point quite perfectly...."

But she wasn't truly listening to him. Carriage wheels turned, and she waited until the horses clopped away before kicking a pile of tumbled timbers.

"Damn it," she whispered. "He's taken my case away from me. I knew he'd do this the second Gemma and Charlie returned."

"He's merely getting the others to do the legwork. Be patient, Ava. Neither Gemma nor Charlie know how to examine the evidence, so let them fetch it like errand runners. You're the one who can draw the conclusions."

He was right. "Well, what are we going to do in the meantime? If I sit around at the safe house I'll go mad, and there's no point pacing the Nighthawks guild while I wait for them to confiscate all the vaccine samples."

A wicked, wicked smile dawned on Kincaid's lips. "Well, I have something we could do to pass the time."

Ava paused, the breath rushing out of her. He looked so devilishly assured all of a sudden. "You do?"

"We have an hour or two to spare. Come with me," he said, taking her hand and tucking it inside the crook of his elbow. "I can almost guarantee I can distract you."

She was quite certain he could too. "Where are we going?"

"I am considering how best to go about our compromise," he muttered, leading her out of the burned clinic. "You want me to bed you. But first, I want you to be aware of what, precisely, you are committing yourself to. Consider it a way to take your mind off the waiting for a few hours, at least...."

Ava swallowed.

CHAPTER ELEVEN

"THE HAMDEN GALLERY?" Ava demanded as she stared up the marble steps to the Corinthian entrance of a very subdued building. Only the brass plaque on the stone wall gave any hint to what was within. "I've never even heard of it."

"I daresay you haven't. It's not widely advertised, and it's not the sort of place innocent young ladies are aware of."

"I don't really appreciate art," Ava muttered, though she could admit she sometimes admired the skill it took. Art seemed a little drab and dull, from her limited experience.

"You'll appreciate this." He guided her up the stairs, his hand on the small of her back. "I can almost guarantee it."

"Mr. Kincaid, just what are you up to?"

Pushing open the door, he gestured her inside, then followed. Ava felt a hand press against her back, and suddenly she was flush against the door as he closed it, staring up at the pulse in his throat.

"It's called seduction, Ava." His breath whispered against her temples, and his thumb brushed beneath her jaw. "I told you I wanted you to be aware of what you should expect, of just what you're agreeing to. This is your last chance to say no."

She swallowed, uncertain what sort of thing might make her consider backing away from this bargain. She wanted it so very much, after all. "Just what sort of art gallery *is* this?"

Kincaid had the sort of smile that might have graced Lucifer himself. "I wouldn't want to spoil the surprise."

Without another word, he pushed away from her, greeting the red-liveried servant who was hovering circumspectly. Kincaid paid him, and then held out a hand toward her.

If you dare, his eyes seemed to say.

Ava stared across the sumptuous red carpets, taking in the gilt on the ceiling and the dark mahogany panels on the walls. Kincaid stood amongst it all, dressed in black, looking like some feudal warlord. He'd always had rough-hewn, somewhat savage features. The only thing lacking was an axe in his hands.

It felt a little like stepping into temptation itself, but she was curious. *One last chance to turn around....* Heart kicking a little in her chest—or perhaps skipping a gear—Ava swept toward him. She was tired of her sheltered existence. Tired of always being overlooked. Surely Kincaid wasn't leading her too far astray—she trusted him to look out for her.

Kincaid took her hand, staring down into her eyes. Not surprised, so much as viciously pleased with her decision. "Didn't think you'd do it."

"I'm a woman of my word."

"Yes, but we're skirting dangerous territory in your

eyes, Ava." His voice roughened. "You're the type of woman who likes to know what lies ahead, and in your worldview, we just stepped off the edges of the map. Here be dragons, kitten...."

Dragons. She almost smiled. "It's a good thing I'm a virgin then."

Startled blue eyes locked on hers, and then his smile dissolved into something smug. "Not for long, sweet Ava. Not if I have my way with you."

He handed her a guidebook, took her hand in his, and led her along the plush red carpets.

"What is this?" she whispered, for the front cover depicted a naked woman draped in red cloth, one who glanced over her shoulder at the viewer with a naughty expression.

"You've seen anatomical diagrams, yes? I thought we could at least start with something you had some experience with. The owner of the gallery is a man I know. I created a piece of artwork for him several years ago—a private, very wicked commission fused of metal. I've paid him for the hour. Nobody will disturb us. It's the sort of place that offers *exclusive* entertainment."

"Just how much did you pay him?" she whispered, glancing over her shoulder to find the servant. He'd vanished.

She was all alone with a man who intended to ravish her.

Ava couldn't wait. A burst of excitement flooded through her.

"You don't want to know." Kincaid pushed open a door and led her into a hallway.

Windows further along the hallway let in a wash of gray light, but the carpeted path was silent and empty. Candles flickered as Kincaid shut the door behind them—

and locked it.

"There's nothing here," she whispered, staring at the red velvet curtains on the walls.

Kincaid reached for the nearest velvet covering, and then hauled it away from a painting with a flourish.

It wasn't a diagram.

Ava sucked in a sharp breath as her mind made sense of what she was seeing. Rich dark colors splayed across the canvas, highlighting its main focus, and the frame was gilt.

There was a naked woman on her knees, the pale globes of her breasts luridly graphic. A man knelt behind her, one hand curled around the woman's hip and the other clenched in her hair, forcing her head back until the woman's spine arched in an almost obscene—

It all hit her at once. What the man was doing to the woman in the painting.

And every inch of her went still.

Every inch of her was hot and cold all at once.

Kincaid watched her, clearly digesting her every thought. Ava swallowed hard, gaze flickering from the painting to Kincaid, then back to the painting again.

It was *nothing* like her anatomical diagrams.

She stepped closer, her fingers running over the oil-roughened canvas. The man's lip curled, his hips thrusting forward as he filled the woman from behind with his... his *penis*.

Kincaid's legs brushed against her skirts as he stepped behind her. "Do you like it?" he breathed, one hand resting lightly against her waist.

She felt the shock of his touch as if she were naked. "Like it? He looks like he's hurting her."

"Does he?"

Ava's eyes found the painting again. The woman's pale skin proved a stark counterpoint to the man's olive body.

Her lips were parted, her eyes closed. An expression, not of horror, but... something else.

Ecstasy?

Warmth slithered through Ava's veins. She didn't quite understand the painting. But it made her feel something she'd never felt before in her life.

And Kincaid's hand was rubbing, just gently, against her hip.

Suddenly her focus wasn't on the image, but on the press of his body against hers. A wash of heat swept through her.

Suddenly she was *inside* the painting, on her hand and knees, and it was Kincaid behind her, buried to the hilt inside her. Every nerve in her body was suddenly alert.

"He's not hurting her," Kincaid whispered, his breath warm on the back of her neck. "Some women like to be controlled like that." His mech hand brushed from her nape the loose curls that had tumbled from her chignon, and swept them over her shoulder.

Ava shivered, and her nipples hardened. She clenched her fingers into a fist, almost desperate to touch herself there. Or no, to ask him to do it. But even as she thought it, she knew she couldn't say the words. Not quite that confident, not yet.

Kincaid's mouth brushed against her nape, and it was *everything*. Ava curled a hand over his, forcing his touch to harden against her waist. She couldn't stop herself from melting against him, until her back was pressed against every inch of his chest and abdomen, and her head tilted forward in subjugation, surrendering her nape to him.

"I think you're that type of woman," he whispered. "Do you want to be controlled, Ava?"

Hell if she knew. She nodded, her lips parting slightly. Right then she'd say yes to anything he asked.

"Do you feel wet?" he murmured, brushing his mouth against her ear. "Between your thighs?"

A pulse of illicit pleasure echoed through her abdomen. How could she answer a question like that? "I-I don't know what it feels like."

"You ache," he said gently, splaying a hand across her lower abdomen, "here. Don't you?"

Ava's knees trembled. It was as though he set off a chain reaction within her. "Please," she whispered, not quite certain what it was she asked for.

"Not yet. You've barely seen anything yet. I want you to know what you're committing yourself to, Ava. What I'll expect from you. Come." Taking her hand, he moved toward the next painting, and relieved it of its velvet cover.

Ava followed him in a hush of skirts. The oils in the painting were dark, yet lush. She'd never seen art like this before. There was something incredibly warm and inviting about it, something intimate.

And then she realized what she was looking at.

A woman lay sprawled across dark red velvet, staring out at the viewer with a knowing Mona Lisa smile, even as she slid a hand through the dark hair of the man bending over her. Ava froze. The man's face was buried between the woman's thighs, and she had no idea what he was doing to the woman, but... but she felt it, somewhere deep inside her.

Do you feel wet? Kincaid had asked her, and Ava knew now what he meant, for there was a delicious slickness between her thighs. "What is he doing to her?"

"He's pleasuring her, kitten." Kincaid stepped between her and the painting, and her gaze locked on the way the top button on his shirt was undone. Her vision dipped, turning the world to shadows around her, and then he was pushing her back, one hand clutching her fingers and the other on her midriff. "Fucking her with his tongue." He leaned toward her, brushing his lips against her ear and the sensitive skin in front of it. "Perhaps he's even nibbling on that sweet little button between her thighs. Have you ever touched yourself there, Ava? Do you know what I'm speaking of?"

"I know what the clitoris is," she whispered, arching in his arms as his teeth sank into her earlobe, shooting lightning through all her veins. "*Oh.*"

A rush of molten heat went through her, centering right between her thighs.

"You didn't answer the question." Kincaid's whisper held all manner of wickedness. "Tell me. Do you ever touch yourself, Ava? Do you fuck yourself with your fingers? Do you know what I'm talking about?"

She pushed away with a gasp, pressing her hands to her cheeks. "Yes."

But he wasn't done with her.

A hand captured hers, and he spun her back against him, breathing hard. Kincaid pressed her against the wall, and this time he held nothing back. The hard planes of his thighs melded against hers, until she found her own legs parting, just slightly, and then there was something else pressing against her quite intimately.

Something hard.

Something that hit her at exactly the right spot.

Ava caught his wrist, flinching as a shock of sensation ran through her. Her skirts were crushed between them, and her body at his mercy. It was overwhelming to know she had no control in this moment beyond her consent.

And thrilling in a peculiar, utterly breathtaking way.

"I'm not *kind*," Kincaid breathed in her ear. "And if you're still interested in having me relieve you of your virginity, then you need to know it won't be *sweet*, or *intriguing*, or *satisfying* to your sense of curiosity. That clever little mind of yours won't be taking down notes while we do this, kitten. It won't be an experiment."

She sucked in a sharp breath, but his hips thrust, and her eyes almost rolled back in her head as his erection pressed directly against that special spot again. "*Oh.*"

"Look at the painting, Ava." A whisper. A demand.

She complied, her nipples aching, and her eyes taking in the flash of pale breasts, and the man with his face between the woman's thighs.

"Do you want *that*?" Kincaid demanded hoarsely, and this time he bit her sharply. "Do you want me to fuck you? To lick your sweet little cunt until you scream? To consume you? Because that is the offer on the table."

Yes. Her hands curled into fists in his collar. She didn't even need to say the word, he saw it in her eyes.

And his own darkened, stormy seas of pure desire that set her aflame. "God damn you, you've the worst sense of self-preservation."

"Do your worst, Mr. Kincaid." She couldn't resist daring him. "I'm not afraid of what you could do to me."

"No?"

"No." She licked his jaw tentatively, feeling as though her body wanted to burst its seams. Her skin felt too tight. "You were right. I had no true understanding of what I was asking. But now I do. And I want it. I want *you.*"

I want pleasure, and abandon, and sensation. I want to feel like a woman, with a man who looks at her as though she steals his breath... even when that woman is just me.

She'd never be able to tell him what it felt like when he looked down at her as though she was the most beautiful woman in the world. Ava shivered, stroking his jaw.

The breath shuddered out of him. "You'll be the death

of me."

Why is he trying so hard to warn me away from this course of action? From him?

A kiss stole her breath, and then her wits. Ava pressed herself against him, draping her arms around his heavily muscled shoulders. The hunger reared within her, and somehow she knew her eyes were black, and her vision darkened, even with them closed. It didn't matter. All her senses became more acute as she gave herself over to her primal nature, reveling in the firm hands that slid up and down her waist. His thumbs brushed her breasts, and Ava moaned into his mouth, arching her back shamelessly, begging him for more.

But he needed one last hint of permission from her. Kincaid drew back breathlessly. "You won't be in control here, Ava. I am. Do you want that? Will you submit to me?"

She didn't know what was happening to her. All she knew was she wanted more of it. "*Yes.*"

Then her skirts were being dragged up out of the way in bunches. Kincaid pinned her wrists above her head with his mech hand, and she was strangely helpless, yet not in a way that roused the panic inside her. Their eyes met again.

"Spread your thighs," he told her.

His thumb brushed over the tops of her garters, and Ava flinched. She'd never been touched there before. Not by someone else. Heat spilled through her cheeks. Taking short, sharp breaths, she took a step to the side, parting her legs just enough.

"Wider." The look in his eyes dared her.

Her cheeks had to be crimson. Ava gasped in a short breath. *Yes.... No....* It felt dangerously exposing. And she... wanted to do it. Slowly she let her legs fall apart.

"*Wider,*" he whispered, brushing his mouth against her

lips in the faintest of caresses.

Cool air brushed against her inner thighs. With her skirts bunched between them, she was more exposed than she'd ever been in her life. That thumb stroked across her garters, exploring her stockings slowly as he gauged the expression in her eyes.

Then his touch was drifting higher.

Higher.

Ava stopped breathing as she felt her drawers shifting beneath his touch. Her hips gave an unconscious flex, and she finally looked away, turning her face to the side as two of his fingers found her through the slit in her drawers.

The touch sent a spear of sensation straight through her. Ava's spine bowed, her eyes shooting wide. Kincaid pressed his face against her throat, the rasp of his stubble shockingly sharp against her skin. But it was his touch below that anchored her entire being.

A slow, steady stroke through wet folds. So light she could barely feel it, and yet....

"There you are," he whispered, nuzzling her ear. "So wet, Ava. That's your body readying itself for me."

Her hips bucked again. She couldn't escape the sensation. Everything in her body felt on edge. Her vision blackened, the craving virus rearing within her, but this time she didn't feel like the predator. This time she didn't want blood. "Oh. *God.*"

"That's it. I know what you need, kitten." Fingers skated up her thigh, tracing small wet circles deep between them. She was shocked at how wet she was down there, and her thighs closed on his wrist, stopping him just before he could thrust them inside the very heart of her.

"Let me," Kincaid breathed against her sensitive mouth. "Let me fuck you with my fingers."

It was a conscious choice to part her thighs again. Ava

flung her head back as the tip of his thumb danced over *that* spot. A shiver of pure need went through her. Clitoris was such a sterile name, and yet the feeling of him touching her there was completely the opposite. She strained to tear free from his grasp on her wrists, but there was no escaping.

Pinned there. Open to his touch. Completely at his mercy.

"That's it. Open more. You'll like it. I promise."

Then something began to stretch her. A fascinatingly intimate experience, for she could feel his finger sliding deep within her. Ava stared at him with her mouth slightly parted.

"Don't tempt me."

"Tempt you?" She gasped a little as he thrust his finger inside her again. Then realized what he meant.

The painting opposite them showed a woman on her hands and knees, her face buried in the man's lap. Those painted lips stretched wide around the man's erection.

Ava felt the brush of his knuckle as he shoved his finger deep inside her, and there was a curious pressure within. She spasmed, her breasts thrust forward. *Please.* She didn't know what she was begging for.

But he did.

His thumb settled over that exquisite spot he'd touched before, and then he began to rub small circles there, even as he curled his finger inside her. A second joined it, opening her wider. Ava writhed, uncertain precisely what he'd done to her body. She felt caged in need, like a wild animal pacing the confines of a cell, feeling like she needed to burst out of her skin.

"One day I am going to have you on your knees," he said, his mech hand sliding down her forearms to brush the pearls at her throat. "And this is going to be the only thing you'll be wearing."

Oh, God. Somehow that made the wildness within her even more unbearable. "Kincaid," she breathed.

He fucked her with his fingers, slow, smooth strokes that seemed like the only thing she could concentrate on. "You're going to open that pretty little mouth, Ava, and you're going to lick every hard inch of my cock. And when you're done, I'm going to paint those pretty tits of yours with my cum."

It shocked her.

It also ratcheted the tension within her even tighter somehow. Suddenly she couldn't just see the painting over his shoulder, but she could imagine herself within it. An image of herself naked on red velvet drove all other thoughts out of her mind, and she could almost feel Kincaid's mouth between her legs.

Right where his thumb was transcribing irresistible torture.

Words tumbled from her lips. Words like, "*Yes, yes*," and "*More...*," and "*Oh, my God!*" She lost herself a little as his fingers worked her. All she could feel was the heat between her legs and the bite of her fingernails in the back of his shoulders. She hadn't even realized he'd let her hands go.

Instinct took over; Ava's mouth found his in the dark shadows of the gallery. Kincaid met her frenzied kiss with fierce abandon. He captured her mouth, his tongue stabbing into it, even as his fingers fucked harder into her body. A kiss sloppy and consuming, and made of everything.

It was so intense she couldn't breathe. Couldn't move. All she could do was throw her head back in surrender as her body hovered on the edge of that monumental cliff.

Ava shattered.

And the world obliterated around her as she screamed her pleasure against Kincaid's mouth.

He'd never been a patient man.

A fierce need drove through him, his cock aching with regret, but Kincaid forced himself to stand still as Ava collapsed in his arms with a startled sob.

All it would take would be one simple step: to thrust her skirts up, part her thighs around her hips, and drive his throbbing erection inside her.

But Ava deserved more.

Her body might be ready, but she herself wasn't.

And it was that thought that stopped him. Swallowing hard, he wrapped both arms around her, dragging her against his chest as she shuddered from the aftermath. The scent of her arousal filled the air as he withdrew his fingers. He couldn't resist licking her wetness from them, the taste of her testing his self-imposed limits once more.

"Oh, *God*," she rasped.

"Easy, luv," he whispered, feeling tremors work all the way through her.

Somehow he set her on her feet again. She leaned against the wall, still completely shocked. Or perhaps overwhelmed was a better word. Kincaid knelt at Ava's feet, his cock throbbing painfully as he set about straightening her skirts.

"That's it." He curved his hands around the backs of her calves, and looked up.

There was a blush on her pale cheeks as she looked him in the eye, and thank God, but she finally knew what she was asking of him.

"Not yet," he assured her, "but one day soon, I'm

going to fuck you, Ava. Just don't give me your heart, for this ends when the case does."

It had to.

CHAPTER TWELVE

THIS ENDS WHEN the case does.

The words echoed in her head as she spent the next twenty-four hours working with Dr. Gibson in the Nighthawks' laboratory, studying vial after vial of vaccine to discover if someone at Kestrel Laboratories was behind the tampering, or whether it occurred purely at the clinics themselves.

Ava felt raw and on edge, barely able to concentrate. It wasn't like her at all, and she kept watching the clock, counting down the hours until this thankless job was done.

Kincaid had opened her eyes to passion, and she felt like her body was in control now, demanding more of the enticing drug. The need for his body warred with her desire to complete the job. Rational impulses versus primal. It was probably a good thing he wasn't here, or she'd be virtually useless.

"Well, that's the last batch," Dr. Gibson said, dusting off his hands and looking tired. "Not a single tampered sample."

Kestrel Laboratories used glycerin to both conserve

the vaccine and make the virus inert, which took time and a low temperature. The vaccine vials were kept in the icebox at the clinics, so it wasn't as though someone could have injected a live specimen of the craving virus into the vaccine. The glycerin would have acted to damage the new viral cells. So the saboteur had to have replaced the vial, leaving out the glycerin or any antiviral agent. Ava capped the last vial she'd been checking, and placed it in the tray to be destroyed with the rest of them in the Nighthawks' incinerator. "Kestrel's innocent. All of their samples are perfect, and they claim the vaccine is transported under security from its facility to the clinics, following the picketing against the clinics that happened when they initially opened. So they don't think it happened on their end."

"So it's the clinics, lass," Gibson said, casting his apron aside. "Hell of a case."

Considering the bomb planted in the drones, she'd already concluded a break-in had occurred, but they had to be certain. "Thank you for your help. Let's hope it was only the one batch of vaccines that were sabotaged."

Gibson flicked through the roster of patient names one of the Nighthawks had collected from Dr. Harricks. "There were one hundred vials of vaccine ordered in the batch that contained Mr. Thomas's afflicted sample. Marcus Long was also one of the patients seen that week at the clinic, so that makes at least two out of a hundred who were stricken with the craving."

"Dr. Harrick's statement claimed the batch arrived on the nineteenth and he didn't unpack it until the clinic was closed, so it could only have been touched that night—or one of the following nights. He ordered a new batch on the twenty-third, as he was running low. If we presume that batch was the only one tampered with, then we have a four-day window during which someone broke in and sabotaged the vaccine."

"Both David Thomas and Marcus Long were seen on the twenty-first," Gibson pointed out.

"So a two-day window, and potentially a hundred patients who might have been stricken, if it happened the first night."

"I'll mention it to Garrett and he can see all of the patients are questioned."

Thank God. It was a monumental task, let alone the fact Francis Jenkins, the other vaccinated victim, had been a patient of the clinic on Church Street, in Marylebone, which significantly widened the victim pool. Ava rubbed her temples. "I have a headache just thinking about it."

"Then don't. Go home, get some rest. I'll handle this end of the investigation and let you know the results." Gibson leaned against the steel workbench. "I don't entirely know what this is all about," he said, "as Garrett's keeping the investigation into the bombing quiet, but you're not getting in over your head, are you? With this mysterious employer you've left me for?"

Ava patted his arm warmly. "You worry too much, Doctor. And my employer's offer was better than yours." A means to spread her wings outside this laboratory, and perhaps work a case of her own, one that might save London.

Gibson clamped a hand over his heart. "Aye, lass, you've a wounding tone. What could be better than working here with me?"

Ava's smile died. This room held its own ghosts for her. Once, she'd thought it a safe haven, but lately she'd begun to wonder if it was becoming a cage. "I need something more."

"I know you do," he said, kissing her on the forehead

in a grandfatherly fashion. "Just don't get yourself killed while you work out what that something more is."

"It's not as though I lead an exciting life, Doctor," she scoffed, heading for the door and her coat and scarf. "I'm a laboratory assistant, and a crime scene investigator. What on earth could hurt me?"

"Someone clearly didn't want it to be known the vaccine had been tampered with. And we don't know whom. Or why they did it."

She looped her scarf around her throat. "'*Yet,*' as you always say," she said, "Someone, somewhere has slipped up. I just have to work out how and where and when. Everybody leaves a trace, or a secret, or a witness. Leave no stone unturned, and whatnot."

Gibson couldn't help rolling his eyes. "Get out of here before it's too late. You're even starting to sound like me."

Ava smiled to herself as she exited the room. "Not an entirely bad thing, Doctor. You're efficient, if nothing else."

Something bothered Ava about the case.

Oh, not about the vaccine. That trail led to a dead end for the moment, but she couldn't help picturing Mr. Thomas's black-veined face.

If she put the facts together she could fill in enough gaps: Mr. Thomas, a staunch humanist, received his vaccine six weeks ago, not knowing the vial was tampered with.

He began to exhibit signs of the craving virus, though they'd likely have been minimal and he might not have even known until it was too late.

And then something killed him.

It wasn't the vaccine. But was it the virus someone had changed the vaccine with? Had he been infected with some sort of mutated craving virus? She'd never heard of any complications, but then... that didn't mean there were none.

Ava frowned, pacing the small laboratory she'd set up in Malloryn's safe house. "No," she whispered to herself, thinking about Zero, the *dhampir* woman who'd been found dead in her basement cell in Malloryn's hidden safe house, black veins streaking like obsidian lightning through her skin. There'd been an injection site on *her* body; evidence someone injected something into her, which killed her.

But what?

Poison? Hemlock was the only thing that had been discovered to have an effect on a blue blood, and that wore off in minutes, depending on how high the blue blood's CV levels were.

It couldn't be some rare mutated form of the craving virus, one that killed its host as it tried to transform them. Because it wasn't isolated solely to blue bloods.

True, *dhampir* were evolved from blue bloods, a step along the evolutionary chain, if one had read *The Origin of Species*, as she had. They required an *elixir vitae* to help with their ultimate transformation, but their blood work was just different enough to a blue blood's, and their bodies even more invulnerable to harm.

So she now knew *how* Mr. Thomas became a blue blood. She just didn't know what had killed him. Or Zero. Or the other four victims.

She felt like she was missing something... like a thought hovering at the edge of her mind, but the more she chased after it, the more it dissolved into nothing.

"Penny for your thoughts," said a deep voice from the doorway.

Ava spun with a gasp, all of her senses heightening when she saw Kincaid resting a shoulder against the doorway. She'd barely seen him since last night, after they parted ways when they returned to Malloryn's safe house— she to the guild, and he... to do whatever it was that kept him busy today.

"Sorry," he said, looking anything but apologetic. "I thought you'd have heard me, or smelled my cologne."

Little more than twenty-four hours ago, he'd pinned her to the wall of the art gallery and driven her to the point of orgasm. And she was clearly not the only one reminiscing, judging by the twinkle in his blue eyes.

When he smiled like that he stole her breath. The slightly crooked slant of his nose, the fullness of his mouth, and the faint dimple on the right side of his mouth stirred her in ways she couldn't quite comprehend. She could still taste that mouth on hers, and Ava swiftly looked away, trying to busy her hands before he noticed her fascination with him. They didn't have time to play games today, but he'd promised her the next time he kissed her, he didn't intend on stopping.

"Busy day?" she asked.

Kincaid stepped inside the room, taking it in. "I slept," he admitted, "since you had little use for me, and then I visited Orla and Ian this morning, and returned for lunch. I'm not much help with the laboratory work, I'm afraid."

She filled him in on what she and Dr. Gibson had found.

"Something is vexing me," she admitted, pushing thoughts of Kincaid's mouth and body out of her mind. "If someone killed Mr. Thomas, then that someone *knew* he was a blue blood. How? Was it someone watching the clinics? The same person who tampered with the vaccine and set the bombs? Did they tamper with all the vaccine vials and track every single victim down? The lack of bodies on the ground suggests otherwise, as there were at least ninety-eight other patients through the clinic during the time period we've nailed down, and there's been no outcry. We'd have noticed if people were finding more bodies. So why Mr. Thomas? Why Marcus Long? Why Francis Jenkins, John Redmond, or Quentin Longbow? What made these gentlemen stand out as men to die?"

"Can't help you, I'm afraid."

She sighed and lowered her head, resting her hands on one of her benches. There were no answers to that question, not yet. But if she kept asking questions, then maybe she'd jog loose whatever thought kept teasing her. "I'm missing something. I'm sure of it. There's something about this case I feel I should know."

His hands settled on her shoulders. "You've done an amazing job already. I'm in awe of your thought processes."

Awe? She swallowed a little, still feeling the weight of a thousand other rejections over the years. "It's nothing, really. Dr. Gibson helped me figure out most of it."

Kincaid turned her around, his black brows drawing together. "Ava, I've been at your side for most of this case. Dr. Gibson might be an accessory to the thought process, but you're the one in charge. You're the one who's putting this altogether." He arched a brow. "I feel fairly bloody useless, to be honest."

"You're not useless," she protested. "You saved my life at the clinic when the bomb detonated. I wouldn't be here—"

"It wouldn't have detonated if I hadn't opened the back panel."

"Yes, but then whoever set it could have triggered the detonation at any time they wished, and we'd know no better." She glared up at him. "I wouldn't have even made it to Mr. Thomas's house in the first place without getting caught in that riot."

"So I'm to provide some muscle, am I?"

"I'm sure you'll come in handy," she replied, not quite looking at the breadth of his chest.

"Aye, when someone needs a bunch of fives," he snorted.

"When *I* need you," she said quietly, and the night he'd put his coat around her shoulders at the Garden of Eden sprang to mind. "I couldn't do this without you. I grow hysterical sometimes, when I cannot even help it. Here, looking at vaccines, and evidence, and bodies, I'm in my element. It all makes sense to me, and I'm in control. Out there"—she gestured to the windows—"I'm fighting to keep my equilibrium. You know London like the back of your hand. You know its people and the way they think. I'm merely a bystander, plucking clues from what they leave behind. You're more important than you think."

The intensity of his gaze burned her. "You're my anchor," she whispered, "my link to a world I sometimes don't understand."

Kincaid twirled something in his fingers; a flash of color, quickly contained. "I'm not going to keep arguing over which one of us is more useful than the other. You win. You couldn't do without me."

A laugh escaped her, but he reached out, brushing the curl of hair that had escaped her chignon back behind her ear, and when he removed his hand, there was something else tucked there.

Ava tugged it free, catching a hint of its dark, sultry scent. Brilliant magenta petals draped lushly over her palm. "*Cattleya labiata*," she breathed. "Oh, my goodness, where did you get this?" Then horror dawned. "You *cut* the flower off the orchid?"

"I told you I was busy today. Do you like it?"

"Yes!" Even if he'd beheaded it. Ava cupped the

precious bloom in her palms. "This was the first orchid species Mr. William Swainson sent back from Brazil in 1818. I've seen it in books, but never...." Never in person.

She felt almost breathless. He'd picked a flower for her. No, he'd gone out of his way to find an orchid, because he knew she adored them, and had a fascination with plants. Ava looked up, a smile spreading across her face, and that's when the tickling knot at the back of her mind suddenly unraveled, almost as if she'd pulled a thread. Suddenly her mind made one of those leaps of intuition it sometimes did, and Ava's gaze drifted past Kincaid and settled on the bookshelf.

A bookshelf groaning beneath the weight of over a dozen books on rare plants from various parts of the worlds, some with healing properties, some poisonous....

"That's it," she whispered, and hurried toward the bookshelf, still cupping the orchid. Excitement bloomed. Where the devil was it?

"What's it?" Kincaid followed her, but Ava paid him no mind.

She let her fingers run over the leather-bound spines of the books, pulling them out and then discarding them on her desk until she had a pile. She was going to crush the orchid, so she tucked it back behind her ear, flipping through a book.

"I kept thinking it's not a disease that killed Mr. Thomas. There's no viral or bacterial interference, and no other agent can cause such destruction within a blue blood's body. It has to be a toxin or a poison, and I remember... there was something I read once...."

A poison, herb, or toxin that affected blue bloods and their evolved cousins the *dhampir* in a different way than it did humans?

Maybe her interest in obscure plants could be the

make-or-break lead this case needed? Ava tossed the book aside, and pulled down another.

"*Rare Plants from the Himalayas.*" Kincaid picked up a book and read the spine as she flicked through the pages of hers, before his words penetrated.

Ava stole the book from his grasp and turned to her reading desk in the window, rifling through the careworn pages. *Himalayas...* that rang a bell. "We're searching for a toxin," she told him, "one that strikes down blue bloods."

"Hemlock—"

"Paralyzes them. It does something to a blue blood's blood pressure and their muscles. I've looked into it, but I'm not quite certain what it does on a cellular level. Unfortunately, there aren't many blue bloods that will allow me to paralyze them momentarily while I take samples. And I clearly cannot use myself as a test subject. I tried once, but by the time the paralysis wore off my blood cells had returned to normal, though my CV levels were exacerbated. No,"—she traced her finger over the page, ticking off plant names mentally—"hemlock has nothing to do with this. But I do recall something.... A plant that came from the Himalaya region I was warned never to use against a blue blood. I was researching a toxin, or a weapon, something to take down the *dhampir* with. It was just a throwaway line in a book I flagged as interesting, but didn't get time to pursue. Everything with Zero happened so quickly."

"A plant that could destroy one of the *dhampir*?"

"Maybe." Ava's finger paused on a pair of words, excitement flooding through her. "Caterpillar mushroom. That's it! It's grown above an elevation of three or four thousand feet in the Himalayas, and I always thought it an unusual plant, as the lower part is a caterpillar, and the upper part is a fungus. Basically, the fungus spores land on the caterpillar and as it grows the caterpillar dies.

"It has tonic properties, I believe. Or the Chinese certainly believe so. I read transcripts of a Tibetan medical text by Zurkhar Nyamnyi Dorje about its aphrodisiac properties. They call it Yartsa gunbu. And that," she said, snapping the book closed, "is the limit of my knowledge. Beyond, do not touch if one is a blue blood."

"Interesting."

Ava couldn't quite read the tone of that one word. "What do you mean? You keep looking at me with that strange expression on your face."

"I'm just... you're frightfully intelligent, did you know?"

Her heart thudded in her chest. "Frightfully?"

He looked at her, his eyes narrowing as if he saw right through her. "Poor choice of words. You're astoundingly intelligent."

It still made her feel a little discomforted. Her ex-fiancé, Paul, had been wary of her thought processes, until she'd learned to censor herself and not delve into such topics that interested her.

Kincaid leaned toward her, bringing his lips close to her ear, "Your great, big intellect makes me want to do naughty things to you, Miss McLaren."

This man was clearly not a small-minded man like Paul. Ava caught her breath.

He continued, "Maybe one day you can spout all of these big words at me while I run my hands beneath your skirts, and—"

"Kincaid!" she gasped, and he burst into laughter.

Ava slapped him on the arm, her face burning. She had the sudden urge to kiss him again, just to see if her memories of last night's events were quite as overwhelming as they'd seemed, or whether she'd simply been caught up in the moment of her first assisted orgasm.

"Has no one ever flirted with you before?"

Ava snapped the book shut, and set it aside. "Of course they have. I was engaged once. There was flirtation, though... decidedly more mild than your so-called attempt."

"*So-called attempt?* I see I'm not succeeding very well. Perhaps I should press my endeavors?" He stepped closer, backing her against the desk and trailing his fingers down over the lace that covered her breasts. "I keep thinking about these pretty tits."

Ava's breath caught. "You're so vulgar."

"You're entirely too innocent. And," his voice dropped, "you *have no idea.*"

He'd startled her again. What was it about this man that made her enjoy his flirtation so much? She knew they were all kinds of wrong for each other, but she simply couldn't help herself.

Ava gave him a sidelong glance. "Perhaps, Mr. Kincaid, I *could* imagine."

Kincaid's smile grew soft and heated as he rested his knuckles on either side of her hips. "That's the spirit. Now tell me... engaged? I didn't know that."

"It was a long time ago. Before Hague kidnapped me. Actually," she amended, "Hague's kidnapping is the reason my engagement ended." Storm clouds brewed in her heart, an old hurt she'd never quite gotten over. "By the time I returned home to see my family, they'd moved on. Paul thought I was dead, and he'd already become engaged to someone else." Only six months missing, and she'd been replaced, as easily as if she didn't matter.

"He's a fool then."

Ava's shoulders relaxed. "Why do you always know the perfect thing to say?"

"Haven't you realized yet?" he drawled. "I'm the

perfect man."

"Perfectly ridiculous," she said, pushing at his chest. But she was smiling again, her woes forgotten. "Now stop distracting me. We have a case."

"And now we have a lead. So what's the next step? How do we find this caterpillar mushroom?"

Ava finally unleashed a smile. "I know just the place."

CHAPTER THIRTEEN

"HERE WE ARE," Kincaid said, pulling to the curb and thrusting one foot out to steady them.

Ava clung to him tightly, squeezing her eyes shut behind the goggles he'd provided her with. He'd insisted they ride his velococycle, a three-wheeled contraption one sat upon, which was going to be the most popular vehicle in London, he'd assured her. She sat sideways on the seat behind him, her breasts crushed to his back, and the throb of the growling steam engine in the velococycle quivering beneath her like some maddened beast.

Ava scrambled off the velococycle, clutching at a lamppost. "My God." Solid ground. She wanted to kiss it.

Kincaid shoved his goggles up on top of his head, scruffing up his black hair. He laughed at her as he tugged his leather riding gloves off, looking younger than she'd ever seen him. "Anyone would think you didn't trust me."

"It's not you I don't trust." She pointed at the velococycle's shiny black painted body. "There's a reason we ride in carriages. Because they are safe, and slow, and nobody is hurtled to a fiery death on the cobbles, which are barely *inches* beneath your feet, might I point out—"

"Ava." He slid off the velococycle, the flaps of his long leather coat slapping against the backs of his thighs as he captured her upper arms in his hands. "Breathe. I would never put you at risk. I'm an expert driver. I helped build the bloody machine after all, and was on the enclave team that came up with the concept. Surely it was just a little bit enjoyable?"

She stared up at him. Now she had her feet under her again, she felt infinitely better. She'd pinned the enormous mass of her hair back tightly, but loose curls escaped it, and if she were being honest, she couldn't deny there'd been a slight thrill. "Just the littlest bit."

Their eyes met, and then Kincaid's smile grew. "Spread your wings, Ava."

"But," she said, stepping away from him and smoothing her skirts as she set eyes on Winthrop's Emporium, "I still might walk home, thank you very much. Now let's go find my caterpillar mushroom."

Ava pushed open the door to the shop, the bell over it ringing as she entered. Kincaid's body was a warm presence at her back.

"Hello?" she called. "Is there anybody here?"

The small store smelled musty. Books lined the walls in mahogany shelves that groaned under their weight. Maps of the globe splayed over the bare inches of actual wall that remained, highlighting exotic countries with names like Afghanistan, and Nepal, and Bhutan. Little baskets of herbs sat on every flat surface, some bundled up into little sacks, and others spilling from the baskets. Incense burned, and the smoke hovered just below the stained ceiling like some watchful cloud.

Movement drew her attention to the back. A handsome gentleman appeared, wiping his hands on a clean rag, his mustache neatly trimmed in an almost militaristic style, and his boots polished within an inch of their life. He was a big man with proud bearing, but she couldn't help thinking beside Kincaid, he seemed... small. "Ah, what prosperous day brings such a lovely young flower into my midst?"

He was talking to her. "Good afternoon," she replied, taking a moment to gather herself. "My name is Miss Ava McLaren, and this is my—"

"Fiancé," Kincaid interrupted, taking her hand and resting it on the crook of his arm with a painted-on smile. "Liam Kincaid."

Ava didn't quite look at him, though her lips twitched. *Fiancé?* What the devil was he about?

The stranger eyed them both for a second, and then gave her a broad smile. "Of course. You're a lucky man, Mr. Kincaid. I'm Major Tom Winthrop, formerly of the East India Company."

The pair of them shook hands, and Winthrop's gaze dropped to Kincaid's mech hand, though he didn't say anything. A company man, one who'd left London during the prince consort's reign, no doubt, when mechs were deemed less than human, and akin to the dirt beneath a blue blood's heel.

Ava bristled in Kincaid's defense, but kept all trace of it out of her voice. "You've travelled through the Orient?"

Winthrop's smile widened, and he showed them the maps pinned to his walls. "Widely. I spent a great deal of time investigating opportunities for the Company in Lhasa, until things turned a little... well, frankly, it was a bit of a hotspot of political interest with the Emirate of Afghanistan sniffing at the door, and the bloody Russo's looking on hungrily, not to mention the White Court of China. After I left the Company, I guided an exhibition for the Duke of Vickers, which searched for the hidden city of Shambhala."

"Shambhala?"

"A hidden land," Winthrop breathed, and she realized he was a natural storyteller, light gleaming in his eyes as if he could see such a thing himself, spread before him. "They say there is a hidden *beyul*—or valley—hidden high in the Kunlun Mountains, ruled by a mysterious people who are not entirely human. The Land of the Living Gods." Winthrop smiled down at her, his voice taking on a lilting quality. "The people there are almost immortal, and age very slowly, almost not at all, it seems. And they have pale, pale skins, though they worship the sun-chariot."

"Pale skins?" *And immortal?*

Winthrop's smile widened, his mustache twitching. "They say it's the birthplace of the craving virus."

How fascinating. "I thought the birthplace of the craving virus was in the lands of the White Court?"

"Technically, Tibet has been claimed by them, yes." Winthrop waved a dismissive hand, leaning toward her. "Hundreds of years ago a traveler allegedly found Shambhala and returned to the White Court with the craving. The rulers of the White Court insisted he share this 'gift' of immortality with them, and then they cut off his head so they alone became gods. Only a member of the Imperial family can be given the gift."

"Sounds rather like the aristocratic Echelon," she replied, "and the Blood Rites. Why is it nobles always seek to control such a thing?"

"Power," Winthrop said, ghosting through the bookcases and luring her back into the shadowy bookshelves. "Money. Might. The craving virus makes one faster and stronger, and almost impervious to death. What ruler doesn't want to be semi-immortal?"

"All very interesting," Kincaid drawled, "but we're here searching for a mysterious book, aren't we, Ava darling? Or do you want to hear tales of a mythic city, and the origins of the craving virus?"

Nothing interested her quite as much as esoteric information. And a hidden city, which might be the birthplace of the craving virus? There was an almost fairy-tale quality to such a story. "You're right. *Darling*." She turned to the major with an almost apologetic smile. "I'm researching a herbal remedy I've heard about. One of the ingredients comes from the Himalayas, and we were directed here. A pharmacist in Marylebone said you were the leading expert on matters of that part of the world."

The major puffed up. "Aye, I am." He gestured to his shop. "I have books, maps, articles of clothing, painted scrolls.... And I stock ancient Oriental herbs and medicines. There's a rich trade for certain things like powdered rhinoceros horn or tiger... ah, tiger parts," he hurried on, as though realizing to whom he spoke, "and herbs like ginseng, or dried mushroom like *Boletus lucidus*—"

"*Boletus*... this is a mushroom, yes?"

"Spirit mushroom—"

"Speaking of mushrooms," she said hurriedly, "one of the ingredients I'm most interested in *is* a mushroom. A caterpillar mushroom. Do you know of it?"

"Yartsa gunbu," he muttered. "I've heard of it, yes. Grows out of the head of a caterpillar in Tibet somewhere."

"Do you have any of it?" Ava held her breath.

The major shook his head abruptly. "No, can't say I have. I have a book on rare plants in the Himalayas, however, if you'd like to look at it?" His smile returned. "I have several books on the Himalayas." He grabbed one off the shelf, and Ava exchanged a frustrated glance with

Kincaid.

Another dead end.

"Do you know anyone else in London who might have some of this caterpillar mushroom?" she asked. "The remedy I mean to create was quite specific."

"No, no. Haven't heard of anyone. Here," Major Winthrop said, pressing a book into her hands. "It was written by a traveler who collected stories. There's a section on Shambhala. You should read it. Consider it a gift, from one curious mind to another."

"Oh, I couldn't, Major. This is a beautiful book. It must be expensive." And the sort of thing that sounded quite rare. She patted her reticule, looking for her purse.

"I insist," Major Winthrop said, not quite quirking a brow at her. "Consider it... an engagement present."

"Ah, thank you." Ava tugged one of her calling cards free, and passed it to him in exchange. "And if you do hear of the caterpillar mushroom, please let me know. I'd be very grateful."

"That man was lying," Kincaid said, as soon as they were out of earshot of the shop.

Ava tore her attention away from the book. "Major Winthrop? Lying? Why ever would you think that?"

"Because the second you asked him about it, his entire manner changed, and he became curt and couldn't wait to get you out of his shop. He knows more about this caterpillar mushroom than he's claiming."

Based on what evidence? Ava gave an exasperated sigh. "You just didn't like him from the start. You were practically bristling."

"That's because he was eyeing you like some tasty little

morsel he wanted to sink his teeth into."

"He was not," she protested. "He's a man with a shared interest. I know what it feels like to find someone who shares your passion. It's exhilarating. And, I'm fairly certain you're describing the way *you* look at me sometimes. Not Major Winthrop."

"That's different."

"Oh?"

"He's a stranger who gave you a rare book he could have sold for a princely sum, for Chrissakes," Kincaid muttered, "even though I introduced myself as your fiancé."

He did have a point. "Maybe he was being kind...." Her words trickled to a halt as she replayed the conversation in her head, and saw the way Winthrop smiled at her. He'd virtually ignored Kincaid. "Oh."

Storm clouds brewed on Kincaid's expression. "You are utterly oblivious, did you know that?"

"Well, men generally don't fall at my feet."

"Or maybe you just don't notice when they do," he muttered.

She shot him a long, steady look. "You're behaving not at all like yourself, did you know? One would almost think you were...."

"Yes?"

"*Jealous*," she said carefully, though the word sounded ridiculous in her mouth. Liam Kincaid jealous? Over her?

Kincaid's lips thinned, and he looked around. She barely noticed the opening of an alley beside them, before he dragged her into it, his broad body shielding her from street view. "Of course I'm jealous." His hands gripped her shoulders, the look in his eyes naked with unrestrained need. "I want you. And while I'm willing to wait until you're ready, I'm also very aware we made a deal, and I want to fulfill it. I can be patient, Ava, but there's a limit to my patience, and that limit is reached when other men try to charm you."

He captured her chin, one thumb pressing into her lower lip. "You're mine, Ava. Not his. *Mine*."

Their lips met, and Ava threw her arms around his neck. She'd never been the sort of woman who considered a masculine conquest intriguing, but she understood it now. What it felt like to have a man claim you, a rather barbaric declaration, and it sent a thrill through her. *Mine*. She kissed him hungrily, not holding back this time, now she knew what she was doing. The fit of his body against hers felt so right. Kincaid lifted her off her toes, one hand splaying over her bottom as he grabbed a handful of her bustle, driving her body against him until she felt something hard press against her belly. It was not his belt buckle.

Desire bloomed to life within her, pure, primal need roaring along her nerve endings. "Kincaid," she whispered, arching her throat as he kissed her chin, then bit her gently.

"Liam," he told her, and she lost herself in that moment. Surrendered completely.

"*Liam*."

The steel of his erection was defiantly insistent. And the rest of the art in the gallery sprang to mind; a woman's hand curled around a tumescent purple erection, her lips lowering to wrap around that bulbous head.

Is it...? Ava slid her hand lower, drawing back from the kiss to stare into his eyes as her palm brushed over a firm, heated length.

Kincaid's eyes grew glazed, his mouth parting. "Jaysus." He captured her hand, shaking his head. "As much as I'd love to let you finish that thought... this isn't the place. Or the time."

"Sorry," she said.

And he smiled his slightly crooked smile, the one that stole her breath. "Don't be sorry, Ava. I'm postponing the gesture. Not rebuffing it. Later."

"Later." She kissed him as he set her down, and then groaned when he captured her face and gently pushed away from her. "We have to stop doing this," she said breathlessly, licking her lips as she staggered a little without his body to support her.

Kincaid reared back as if she'd struck him.

"No... I mean... not the kissing. The kissing is wonderful. But you dragging me into alleys? Kissing me in art galleries?" She flushed with heat. "What if somebody sees us?"

"Nobody here knows us. Your reputation is safe." He splayed his hand on the brick wall beside her. "Ava." Pure heat spilled through his eyes. He wanted her. She could see it.

"When?" she whispered.

"When your mind's not full of vaccines and rare mushrooms, and *dhampir,* and you can pay me some thought—"

This time, *she* put her finger to his lips. "You have no idea how distracting *you* are. Dr. Gibson asked me several times whether I was all right when I was helping him. It's not the case distracting me, Kincaid. It's you distracting me from the case."

Kincaid bit her finger, and a wave of pleasure swept through her, a soft gasp escaping her lips. Then he smiled. "Well, now. That's what a man wants to hear."

Pushing away from her, he captured her hand and tucked it in the crook of his arm. There was a cocky strut to his step, as if he'd staked his claim and been reassured.

She'd never have suspected he hid so much doubt. Ava brushed hair out of her face. "I've never wanted a man as much as I want you."

Kincaid paused. "Never?"

There was a question there, one that hinted at the issue between them. Byrnes. His wedding. And all the left-behind feelings she'd dealt with.

Had he been speaking of Winthrop when Kincaid told her she was his? Or was it someone else he pictured?

Ava forced herself to deliberately think of Byrnes. And for the first time, she realized it had been days since she'd given him thought. And perhaps she'd been *too* innocent, but the thoughts she had given Byrnes in past years had been different to those she felt now. *He smiled at me. He touched my hand.*

"Never," she admitted, and the word was as much concession for herself as it was for him.

For it was all Kincaid. And if she was quite honest, it had been ever since that interlude in the Garden of Eden when she stole his coat. She still had the bloody thing. She might have even sniffed at it once or twice, drinking in his scent in the privacy of her rooms where she couldn't be caught. Ava groaned. "You frustrate me intensely. But you're always interested in what I have to say. You never treat me with kid gloves. It's.... I feel freer with you than I've ever felt in my life. I don't quite know what to make of it. Of any of this." She gestured at the brick walls. "I just kissed you in an alley where anyone could see us!"

"You're in lust," he said, giving her that wicked smile.

"In lust," she repeated.

She wasn't entirely convinced of the idea. Her mind kept flashing to the orchid he'd tucked behind her ear. The way he'd draped his coat over her shoulders in the Garden of Eden, to keep her warm and make her feel safe.

I like him. A lot. Very much so.

I trust him.

And there was something else there, something she couldn't quite identify.

"What a fearsome frown," Kincaid said. "One would think you're not happy with the idea of being in lust?"

An omnibus blared past, and they broke apart with a start. The world started intruding. Ava caught a glimpse of a little boy glancing at her from the street, his hand in his governess's as they strolled past.

"It's not that." She cleared her throat. Later. Now was certainly not the time for this discussion. "See? You're doing it again. I should be thinking about how I'm going to get my hands on this caterpillar mushroom, but instead I'm thinking about...."

"About?"

Your soft mouth, and the way it tastes.... "Caterpillar mushroom!" she cried. "I am thinking about caterpillar mushroom, and where I can find it." Turning in a rush of skirts, Ava rubbed her arms. Good lord, what was wrong with her?

"Well, one doesn't sound half as interesting as the other," Kincaid teased, "but so be it. I'll make you a bet," he insisted. "Winthrop lied. I think he knows exactly what this caterpillar mushroom is, and I think he's even got some on hand. I want a look through the rest of his shop, to see just what sort of secrets Major Winthrop is hiding. We'll break in tonight—"

"*Break in?*" she squeaked.

"Well, he's hardly going to give us the guided tour." A thought clearly occurred—one he didn't like at all, judging by his sudden frown. "You, perhaps, but there's no chance in hell I'm letting you go back in there unescorted."

"Gemma would. She'd give him a smile and a wink, and Winthrop would be spilling his secrets before he even realized what she was doing."

Kincaid stopped in his tracks and shot her a dark look. "No."

"Well, she would."

"You're not Gemma. And that's not a bad thing. But it does mean you're vulnerable to attack, when she is not. She's a trained spy who knows how to kill a man. Aye." He caught her flicker of horror. "You admire her for her confidence, and her beauty, but you never considered the flip side of the coin. Gemma does whatever is necessary to get the results Malloryn desires. She leads a darker life than you do—and sometimes I see the toll of that in her eyes—so pray you never have to lead the life Gemma does.

"As for Winthrop, we know nothing about what sort of man he truly is, except for the fact he worked for the Company, and he imports black market items."

"Black market—?"

"Trust me," Kincaid said. "I know the sort. What if Winthrop's working with our enemy? What if he overwhelmed you, or even killed you? No. And that's final."

"And if I'm right?" she challenged. "If Major Winthrop has nothing to hide, what then?"

Kincaid leaned closer to her, smiling dangerously. "If Major Winthrop is innocent, then I will put a ring on your finger, and give you the wedding of your dreams."

"You sound very certain." The color drained from her face. "I'm not sure I want to be right."

"And if you're wrong, Ava...."

They shared a glance.

"If I'm wrong?" she whispered, breathing a little faster.

"Then you owe me a favor."

"What sort of favor?"

Far, far too easy to walk willingly into his trap. He buffed the back of his knuckles down her side, skimming the lace, and Ava shivered. "I want to see what you're hiding beneath all of this fabric."

She considered it for a long, breathless moment. "Deal. I guess we shall find out tonight. But I don't want you to marry me if you're wrong." The thought was ridiculous. Kincaid.... No. Panic swelled inside her at the thought. She wanted marriage, but she wanted her husband to love her. Not marry her because he enjoyed kissing her.

Or because he'd made a bet.

"No?"

Ava swallowed, feeling a nervous little flutter fill her. She hesitantly traced her gloved fingers down his waistcoat. "I want to see what *you're* hiding beneath all of this fabric."

The look on his face warmed her from the inside, and she knew she'd remember this moment for the rest of her life—the moment she learned to spread her wings.

Then she turned and walked away, before her nerves got the better of her.

CHAPTER FOURTEEN

IF YOU WANTED something done properly, then you had to do it yourself.

Ghost moved through the back of the shop like his namesake, listening to the major complain to the Tibetan girl he'd taken as mistress. Ghost silently cursed the *dhampir* initiate he'd sent to deal with Major Winthrop, who had returned empty-handed. Following the loss of Zero, he and three others were all that remained of the original *dhampir* Dr. Erasmus Cremorne had created, and the new group of blue bloods he'd carefully selected to go through the serum trials were a complete and utter failure so far.

"—place is filthy! What have you been doing all day? Sniffing incense and—"

Pausing for a moment to make sure the man and his assistant were alone, Ghost leared his throat.

"—and bloody hell!" Major Winthrop slapped a hand to his chest, turning around sharply as Ghost made himself visible. "Oh, it's you. Christ. Near gave me a heart attack, creeping around back there."

"It's a good thing you're a battle-hardened ex-

Company man," Ghost said dryly, "with nerves of steel."

Winthrop's mistress hid the faintest of smiles, and then she turned to scurry for the door to pull the blinds down. He tracked her movements. He didn't like witnesses, but her grasp of English extended only just enough to understand his sarcasm.

And she wouldn't be difficult to kill.

"I'm here for the supply," Ghost said, waiting until the room darkened before he stepped completely out of the shadows. He was born for moonlight, yet he'd been trained to live in the shadows. "Jameson told me you couldn't give it to him."

Jameson had not had a reason for this lack, and now he also only had one ear. He should have *listened* to his instructions.

Winthrop's eyebrow twitched. "Ah, righto. Well, I... I've got just the one bag left."

"One?" He needed more. "I thought you placed an order months ago."

"Aye, I did." Winthrop bustled behind his counter, reaching under it to produce a small bag. "But your man picked up three pounds of mushroom last week, and it's not exactly a swiftly replenished stock. Takes years to get to the point where you can harvest it. Have you gone through your supply already?"

"*My man?*"

Any sane person would quiver at the soft way he said the words—anyone who knew him well enough, anyway.

Winthrop merely tossed the bag on the counter, and reached for his pipe, packing the bowl of it with tobacco. "Aye. Lord What's-his-name. The one with the toffy accent and high opinion of himself." He seemed to read the lack of recognition on Ghost's face. "The one who came with your lady friend, Zero, several months back. Lord... Lord

Albright?"

It hit him like a punch of rage. "Ulbricht?"

The major lit his match, pressing the flame to his tobacco and puffing gently to get it smoldering. "Aye. That's the one. Said you had another job for him."

Ulbricht was becoming a problem. As Zero's little pet, the blue blood lord had made a nuisance of himself and drawn the attention of the Duke of Malloryn and his so-called Company of Rogues. Malloryn didn't scare him, but it had been a mess, and Ghost disliked messes.

In fact, he disliked them so much that when Zero disobeyed him, he made sure she received a dose of her own medicine—a dose of the deadly caterpillar mushroom.

In hindsight, he should have just flogged her, but he'd been... *angry*.

"And you gave Lord Ulbricht my mushroom?" Ghost asked quietly, just to make sure he had all the facts correct. Zero had dared to bring that bastard here?

Finally, some hint of self-preservation reared itself in the major's reptile brain. Winthrop paused. "He said... he was here on your command."

"What am I paying you to do?" Ghost took a stealthy step forward, fetching up in the major's face.

The man swallowed, his unattended pipe smoldering in his left hand. "You wanted me to find a means to import the rare caterpillar mushroom. You wanted me to provide you with enough of it, and not ask questions. To make sure nobody else asked questions."

"And yet," Ghost said coldly, tugging off the fingers of his leather gloves, one by one, "you gave my mushroom to a man you've never seen in my company—a man who used *my* name to steal from me?"

The Tibetan girl froze in the corner. She at least had the sense to fear him.

"Aye, well, sir, how was I to know—"

Ghost punched him in the throat, crushing the cartilage there. The girl screamed, and he smoothly withdrew his pistol from inside his coat pocket and put a bullet in her brain. Her body slammed into the wall, spraying blood across the bookcase, but her eyes were already vacant by the time she hit the floor.

Winthrop coughed and gurgled, clutching at his throat as he went down to his knees. His eyes rolled, showing far too much white. There was a plea in them.

Ghost knelt in front of the major, watching him slowly choke to death. "I could save your life," he purred, "but I have no real reason to do so. You betrayed me. You cost me a very substantial amount of a medicinal product I need. These events have repercussions. How am I meant to put my plans into place if the people I rely upon are so faithless? So fucking stupid?" Standing slowly, he put his foot against Winthrop's shoulder and kicked the struggling man onto his back. "And there are other dealers I could turn to."

Winthrop reached for the counter, dragging himself up and slumping against it. His face was turning purple, but he somehow managed to slam a hand on a pile of papers.

"No weapon will save you now," Ghost murmured, looking around. There was little left to salvage here. Winthrop wouldn't dare lie. He had only the one small bag of mushroom, which wasn't enough, and none of the other herbs or books interested Ghost.

Winthrop caught a small card and tried to shove it toward him. Ghost frowned, then bent and picked it up when it fluttered to the floor at his feet.

"What's this?" He scanned the calling card, a very familiar name catching his eye. "Miss Ava McLaren." One of Malloryn's little mice. "She was here?" When Winthrop didn't answer, he caught the man by the jaw and slammed him upon the counter, his fingers biting into the man's skin. "Why was Miss McLaren here? What did she want? Was she asking about the mushroom?"

Winthrop gurgled, but he managed to give a faint nod.

Ghost snapped the man's neck, leaving the room suddenly silent. He wiped the froth of Winthrop's drool off his hands—*could the man not even make a clean death?*—and then considered the note again. Blood and ashes. How the hell had Miss McLaren discovered the link between the *dhampir* and the mushroom?

Ulbricht. It had to be Ulbricht. That bastard had done something with the caterpillar mushroom, something that drew undue attention, right when Ghost needed to slip beneath Malloryn's notice.

And worse, it meant Malloryn might now hold information on the one substance that seemed deadly to both a blue blood and a *dhampir*.

Ghost strode out the back door, meeting his second's eyes. Obsidian had been born in fire, the way he had been—created in the asylum and laboratories of Dr. Erasmus Cremorne. But there were times when he wondered if his second was quite as hard as he needed to be.

Those dark eyes flickered toward the interior of the shop, where nothing but silence remained.

"I have a task for you," Ghost said, handing the other *dhampir* the calling card. "Ulbricht's double-crossed me. I want his head on a platter. No. Actually, bring him in alive. I'd like to do the honors of carving his heart out of his chest personally."

"And Miss McLaren?" Obsidian asked, no doubt having heard it all, thanks to his enhanced senses.

Miss McLaren, hmm.... "She's interested in our

caterpillar mushroom, it seems. I think we should show her firsthand precisely what it does to a blue blood. Send one of the new lads out to introduce her to it. Perhaps Corbyn? It can be an initiation for him—it's not as though she's a dangerous target, and he now knows the price of failure."

He'd made Corbyn hold Jameson down while he removed the lad's ear.

"He's not ready."

Your opinion, not mine. Ghost ground his teeth together. "Then put a bullet in him and send someone else. Just make sure she's dead before she can breathe a word of what she's found in Malloryn's ear. Oh, and clean up that mess inside."

When one needed to enter a building unannounced, one called in the experts.

So it was that barely six hours after Kincaid matter-of-factly told her they were going to break into Major Winthrop's shop, Ava found herself crouched in the small alley behind it. Her clockwork heart was pressure-driven, but it seemed to be running faster than usual, and she had the horrible feeling Major Winthrop was going to jump out at any moment and catch them.

"Relax," Kincaid murmured, drawing a black leather mask down over his face. "Nobody's here. Charlie's already checked, and I wouldn't be bringing you into a situation I thought was dangerous."

Charlie knelt in front of the door at the back of the shop and withdrew two slim picks. The lad had been born in the rookeries as far as she knew, so picking locks was second nature to him. He could do it in his sleep, he'd assured them.

"I am relaxing," she whispered back, then flinched. Was that a cat yowling in the distance?

A warm hand cupped her nape, rubbing the muscles there. Despite her tension, Ava melted into Kincaid's side, shamelessly arching under his touch. "Sure you are," he whispered, and she could hear the smile in his voice. "Shame we're not elsewhere."

Alone was what he meant. His hand slid down her spine, tracing the armored leather corset she'd borrowed from Gemma, and then lower, caressing the curve of her bottom. She wore split skirts, which were also Gemma's, and the sensation of having something rubbing like that between her legs—even fabric—made her feel a little different. A little dangerous.

He was always touching her these days, almost as if he couldn't resist. Or maybe it was just a seductive ploy? She searched his eyes—and the heated look in them—trying to find answers.

Her lips tingled, as if remembering the kiss they'd shared. Had it only been seven or eight hours ago? It seemed a lifetime.

"*You look delicious,*" Kincaid mouthed, very clearly, and Ava flushed and—

Charlie cleared his throat.

Kincaid jerked his hand away from her bottom as though burned. "What is it?" he murmured, crossing to Charlie's side.

Moonlight gilded the sharp lines of Charlie's face. "I can smell blood. And the door's not locked."

As if to prove his point, he turned the handle and the door opened with what seemed a terribly loud creak.

Kincaid drew his pistol and pressed his back against the side of the door. "Keep an eye on Ava."

Then he was gone, edging inside with the pistol held

low in front of him.

Ava swallowed. The faintest hint of copper hit her nose, making her nostrils flare and her mouth flood with saliva. That was definitely blood. "What's happening? What's going on?"

She could barely see Kincaid.

"He'll be all right," Charlie replied, correctly interpreting her nerves.

And when she looked at him, she realized he'd noticed the way Kincaid had been touching her in the shadows. Heat burned up her cheeks. "It's not like that. He's just— We're just—"

"It's none of my business." Charlie winked at her.

Ava relaxed at his side. The young man was barely in his twenties, and yet the look in his eyes could be so mature at times. "I wish everybody thought the same way. They treat me like a child."

"Maybe it's because there's a darkness in all of those who work for Malloryn, and yet none of it stains your soul. We can all see it," Charlie said quietly. "It makes you something to treasure, Ava. It makes you someone to protect. The light within you brings hope to a dark world, and reminds people like me, Gemma, and Byrnes—even Kincaid—there is something worth fighting for."

"You're far too young to think yourself full of darkness."

Charlie smiled, but there was little warmth in it. "Age is a relative thing. I've seen children who grew up on the streets who have the eyes of old men or women." He paused. "And we all have ghosts riding our shoulders, whispering in our dreams."

For the first time since she'd joined the Company, she actually felt like she belonged. "Thank you, Charlie."

The shadows lifted from his expression. "For what?"

"For not making judgment upon what's happening between Kincaid and me. For treating me like someone who has a right to her own choices."

This time the smile was real. "Well, I've had time to get used to the idea. I'm fairly certain something happened between the two of you that night we all went out drinking at the Garden of Eden."

A very perceptive man. One who knew how to keep secrets.

She smiled.

And then Kincaid appeared out of the shadows within, looking large and menacing in black. "It's clear."

Charlie followed her inside, and she was aware she had two dangerous men guarding her—one in front, and one behind—and for the first time in over a month she didn't feel the lesser for it. The truth was, she wasn't a capable fighter, nor was she prone to a clear head in frightening situations. She was just Ava, laboratory expert, repository of utterly useless and esoteric facts, and someone who could trip over her own feet if she were distracted enough.

"What do you think happened?" Ava whispered as they entered the back of the shop and found themselves in the same room they'd been in earlier that day.

There was no blood. No sign of anything untoward.

But she could smell it.

And other things.

Ava wrinkled her nose up, but Charlie beat her to it. "Smells like someone shit themselves."

"Someone died," she said, suddenly certain. "And the body voided itself."

"I can't smell a bloody thing," Kincaid muttered.

"Be grateful you're human," she replied, running a finger along the counter and then rubbing forefinger and thumb together. Just as she suspected. "Can we shine a small light over here? The counter's been cleaned since this afternoon."

Which meant someone was trying to hide something.

And if someone had died, then someone had cleaned up afterwards. She'd been to enough crime scenes to know that.

Charlie shook something, and a luminescent green glow filled the room. A phosphorescent glimmer ball. He held it over the counter.

"This place was messy today," she said. "Winthrop had books and maps shoved everywhere, and there was dust upon the counter, and baskets of herbs beneath it."

All of them still there. Her senses started tingling. Poor Major Winthrop. She had a horrible feeling in the pit of her stomach.

"Do you think it was Winthrop who died?" Charlie asked.

"Want to check upstairs?" Kincaid suggested. "I'm fairly certain he kept rooms up there."

Charlie gave her the glimmer ball and then vanished.

"What are you thinking?" Kincaid murmured, leaning on the counter. She could feel his eyes upon her.

"Don't you think it's odd we came looking for a rare mushroom, and several hours later, someone kills the major?" A horrible thought struck her. "What if both events are connected? What if we lured a killer here?"

"I haven't seen anyone tracking us."

"Doesn't mean they're not there. I think this is our murder weapon. I think this caterpillar mushroom can kill a blue blood, and it's the reason behind David Thomas's death, and all the others. I also think—" She swallowed a little. "—it's the same thing someone injected into Zero." She turned, and stared in the direction of the guild. "I want to look at David Thomas's body again."

An hour after Ava pulled David Thomas's cold body out of storage at the guild, she found the injection site.

"It was in his hair," she said, pulling off her gloves and throwing them in the rubbish bin as Dr. Gibson slid the gurney containing Mr. Thomas back inside the chiller. Kincaid was waiting outside, quite content to leave this part of the investigation to her. If she wasn't mistaken he'd looked a little green around the gills when she suggested he could sit in on the second examination.

"I didn't even notice it." Gibson looked distressed.

"We weren't sure what was wrong with him," she pointed out. "When we were doing the initial autopsy we thought Mr. Thomas had been stricken by some disease, so we were looking for signs of that. Instead he was murdered—injected with a mysterious substance that kills blue bloods."

She'd neglected to mention the fact she suspected what had killed him. Caterpillar mushroom. Or Yartsa gunbu. A rare substance that came all the way from Tibet, which meant someone must have paid substantial money for it. Someone who knew the effect it had upon blue bloods.

And *dhampir*.

What precisely did it do? Did it rupture veins? And turn a blue blood's bluish blood even darker? It must also affect the craving virus, and its ability to heal a blue blood almost instantly. What a horrifying thought.

Gathering her reticule, she bid Gibson goodbye, and found Kincaid in the guild's foyer peering behind a curtain. "Hmm, did I hear a little mouse?"

What on earth was he doing? Ava paused and watched

him from the shadows, hearing a small giggle.

"There it is again," he said, as though he couldn't see a pair of little shoes hiding behind the curtain.

Then a little girl darted out from behind the drapes, her coppery curls gleaming in the light as she ran across the foyer.

"Why, it's a big mouse," he said, as one of Garrett's twin daughters turned and rushed back the other way.

"I'm not a mouse!" she cried, her whole face crinkling up in glee.

Ivy, by the look of her curls. Grace's hair was a little straighter, and she was quieter than her sister. The twins were a regular feature in the guild, and often came down to see Ava in the laboratory, as she showed them how her instruments and microscope worked. They'd been born blue bloods, as Perry was infected with the craving, and trying to wrangle a pair of super-fast, very agile toddlers had been a lesson in patience for the Nighthawks.

Kincaid knelt on the carpet, waggling his fingers in front of his cheeks like whiskers. "You've an awfully squeaky voice," he said, "like a mouse. And such little ears, and a little nose...."

The thought struck her: he was good with children, trying to make himself smaller so he wasn't quite so intimidating. The smile on his face lit him from within, and the little girl waved her fingers like whiskers too, and then shrieked with laughter.

Ava's heart melted.

"There you are, Ivy," Garrett announced, striding down the stairs and catching sight of his daughter. "I've been looking all over for you!"

Kincaid handed her over, his smile softening. "Someone made her escape?"

"I can handle a half dozen miscreants in the London

streets," Garrett drawled, kissing his daughter on the cheek, "but the second my back is turned, one of the twins takes it upon herself to flee. You look away for one second...."

"Aye." Kincaid scrubbed at the beginnings of his beard. "I've got many a cousin like that."

The two men locked gazes, and though they knew each other, they'd never officially met. Garrett extended a hand. "Garrett Reed. You're Ava's... companion." The hesitation was so minor it might as well not have been there, but Ava scowled at her guild master. He was no fool, and could probably smell her perfume.

Garrett was also devilishly perceptive. If anyone could spot any telltale signs of a flirtation, it would be him.

"Liam Kincaid. And aye, I'm working with Ava, though she's doing most of the work at the moment."

Garrett's gaze locked on her, and he winked, clearly aware of her presence all along. "Speaking of the devil... Ava, what are you doing hiding back there?"

Very subtle, Garrett. She rolled her eyes at him, and then painted a sweet expression on her face when Kincaid turned to look for her, as though she'd done no such thing. "I've just had another look at Mr. Thomas."

"Any luck?" Kincaid was suddenly all business.

"There's an injection site up under his hair, in that fatty roll of muscle where his scalp meets his neck. We have a murder." And now she knew what had done it. "It's not a disease. I knew it! He was poisoned."

"Mr. Thomas?" Garrett frowned. "Isn't that one of the Black Vein victims?"

"Yes," she enthused.

"Then we have five murder victims," Garrett said grimly, rubbing a hand down his daughter's back as she sleepily rested her head on his shoulder. "Not just one. And they're all blue bloods."

She heard the question in his voice. Garrett was frightfully intelligent, but until Malloryn gave her the go-ahead, she wasn't certain she should be mentioning the caterpillar mushroom to anyone. "We're not entirely certain what the agent is yet."

Kincaid's jaw flexed, but he didn't quite look at her.

If word of something like that got out, then blue bloods would be dropping like flies all over London. Too many people had grievances against the old Echelon, and some of them were blinded enough by hate to see any blue blood as a threat.

"I guess we have some investigating to do," she said brightly. "I'll keep you apprised of anything Mr. Kincaid and I find."

And Kincaid, thank goodness, kept his mouth shut.

"Thought Garrett was a friend," Kincaid said as they strolled down the street toward Malloryn's secret house.

He'd kept his suspicions to himself on the tram ride back, but he couldn't help voicing them now. Just why was Ava keeping secrets from the Nighthawks?

"He is," she said glumly, her arms wrapped around herself. It wasn't cold, but she often did that when she was lost in thought. Or troubled by those thoughts. "You understand what this means?"

"Someone's killing blue bloods?"

"Someone has found a blue blood's mortal weakness," she all but breathed. "Kincaid, this changes everything. Blue bloods have always been impervious to sickness or grave wounds. The craving virus heals everything, short of decapitation or removal of the heart. Or so we always thought. If the wrong hands get hold of this information...."

"There's a lot of people who'd kill to have that power." The thought of it stirred through him like a breath of fresh air. He'd been ground beneath the Echelon's heel once upon a time, forced to slave away in the enclaves with no hope of anything better in his life. Humans couldn't stand against blue bloods, not and hope to survive.

They were faster, stronger, and, as Ava said, impervious to mortal harm for the most part.

This leveled the playing field.

"You cannot breathe a word of it," she stated.

"Jaysus, Ava. Think what could be done with this information? The Echelon's still hovering over London like vultures! The revolution put power in the queen's hands, but all those blue bloods who looked the other way when the worst of them cut a girl's throat and drained her dry, they're still there. All those blue bloods who paraded their blood whores and thralls around on leashes, or killed people in the streets because they could! The queen might have changed some of the laws, but there's an awful lot of bloody predators still mincin' around in fucking silk with blood on their hands. With this information, they're no longer top of the food chain, Ava." His older sister, Agatha, flashed to mind, her feet so very pale as she dangled from the ceiling. "No one would have to worry when their sister doesn't come home at night, or—"

"So you'd kill them? Murder them?"

He drew back as if slapped. She didn't understand. "Do you know what it feels like to lose someone you love, because the Echelon thought it was a joke to serve her up at a *fucking dinner party* as the main meal, where they all shared her around as a blood whore? Do you know the shame a woman feels after that? What she's capable of doing—"

"Do you know what it feels like to have someone look at you as though you're a monster," Ava cried, "even though you cannot help your diet? I understand where you're coming from, I do, but I've never—"

"Diet?" His voice rose. "For fuck's sake, Ava, I know you can't help being what you are, but every man and woman in London still sees the draining factories pumping coal in the East End, and they're the ones as bring their children to the blood-letting stations, so they can pay their fucking taxes!"

Her face paled. "Without the blood taxes, you'd have a whole nation of predators forced to feed themselves by whatever means are necessary."

"Predators? Exactly!"

"The queen was right not to close the draining factories, or get rid of the blood taxes entirely," she said firmly. "The taxes are no longer dangerously high—"

"It's not just the blue bloods, it's the whole bloody system they create. People used to kidnap others off the streets and sell their blood!" he yelled, flinging his arms wide. "There were entire slasher gangs in the East End who killed, just for the price of what was in a man's veins."

"Then what about the Nighthawks?" she demanded, her eyes flashing fire. "They're all rogue blue bloods to a man—or woman. Denied the Blood Rites, but infected by chance, and yet they're the reason you're standing here today and weren't guillotined during the revolution. If you put this weapon in the wrong hands, Kincaid, then you cannot tell me innocent people won't die, and *that's* what I'm afraid of."

"Maybe it's worth it," he said, feeling utterly shaken. "Innocent people died in the revolution. People I considered friends, my cousins, my men. Humans, all of them. So why draw that line now when it's the blue bloods who will suffer?"

She looked taken aback. "You don't believe that."

He didn't know what he believed. Kincaid raked his hands through his hair, letting out an explosive breath. "I'm not going to breathe a word of this, I'm not, but Jaysus, if you only knew...." He laughed then. "Just mentioning a religious name would have earned me fifty lashes four years ago! Is that the world you can defend so vigorously? We could have overthrown them completely. We could have changed the world."

"I *am* them!" Ava drew back from him, her eyes wide. "We did change the world. And just so you know, I fought for the revolution too. I marched on the Ivory Tower with the Nighthawks and did what I could to help pull down the corrupt prince consort. This was never a human problem. It affected all of us. And you can't just stand there and insist on murdering an entire race as a solution, because if you do, then you're no better than them!"

"I'm not talking about killing them *all*."

"But you can't control which ones die," she snarled, and then turned in a whirl of skirts. "I cannot believe you can even stand there and speak of this to me."

"Ava!"

She fled down the narrow alleyway that led to a secret passage into the COR secret house.

"Ava, wait." He followed, but she was already gone, leaving him with an ugly knot in his abdomen.

Damn her. It wasn't an easy matter to say which was right or wrong. Was it? Had he truly lost so much of himself he could consider murder as a solution?

Pressing his mech hand against the bricks she'd vanished behind, he cursed again. Yes. He had lost enough of himself. He'd lost everything, one slow piece of himself at a time. First his sister's suicide, then his brother's death, his friends, his hope.

He wasn't a good man. And he wasn't certain what he was going to do with the information—for a part of him knew what those rioters the other day had felt like.

Angry. There was enough anger in him to burn the world to ashes if he let the leash slip through his fingers. And only the hurt in Ava's eyes stopped him from running out to the nearest sector of humanists who'd slipped back into the population and telling them about it. This needed careful thought. He needed to be able to control the danger of this weapon before he could ever dare use it.

But think of the opportunity! The thought made him breathless. No more Echelon. No more... of the bad blue bloods. If he could control the poison, then he could control who died. Couldn't he?

Kincaid pushed away from the hidden door in the brickwork, cursing under his breath, for there was little chance she'd welcome him tonight. He needed to think and clear his head. He needed a drink.

And so he didn't notice the pale man on the rooftops who watched him.

CHAPTER FIFTEEN

"COR BLIMEY, IF it isn't Liam Kincaid, back from the dead!" a voice bellowed as Kincaid strode inside the White Hart pub.

Half a dozen heads turned, and Kincaid found himself swamped by big, burly men who clapped him on the back and ruffled his hair.

He mock punched Willie Lewes, a young mech who'd been under his command in the enclaves, and made his way through the crowd of men he'd once known—those who'd shared the same sentence he had. John Hayes, Jem Stanton, Michael Hargreaves.

And... Xander McGraw.

His friend rested both elbows on the bar and watched him come. There was a twinkle in Xander's green eyes, but he also looked like he had a bone to pick.

"Back from the dead?" They clasped hands, and Kincaid thumped Xander on the back, squeezing his friend against his chest.

"Well, who'd have known otherwise?" the loud Scot demanded, shoving him in the chest. "Haven't seen your ugly face in months."

"Been busy." He slumped on the bar, raking a hand through his hair and looking around. He'd missed this life—these men. He was a different person here, sure of himself in ways he wasn't when he served the Company of Rogues.

"Too busy to come to my fucking wedding?" Xander asked, snagging a tankard of ale and glaring at him over the top of it. "Thought you were a friend, Kincaid."

Then Xander strolled away, leaving him standing there alone at the bar.

"Ignore him," said a cool, feminine voice. "He'll cool down."

"Wise words." Kincaid shot a smile toward the owner of the voice.

Maggie Doyle, the woman who'd helped him run the enclave with an iron fist, wiped down the bar, regarding him with a steady expression. She'd seen both the best and worst of him over the years, and there were few souls he could trust as much as her. "Long time, Kincaid."

"You look well. Marriage agrees with you."

Maggie found Xander in the crowd, and the faintest of smiles curved her lips. She'd softened since the revolution, he thought. She wouldn't have smiled before it. "Surprisingly, yes. Though I fought him to the bitter end."

Across the tavern Xander threw his head back and laughed.

The pair of them shared a smile. "He doesn't know what the word 'no' means," Kincaid said gruffly.

"He thinks it means 'try harder,'" she said, and poured Kincaid a shot of whiskey. "He wore me down with his courting. But he's angry you weren't at the wedding." Maggie lifted her snifter of whiskey. "Planned to have you stand up there with him."

Kincaid tapped his own whiskey against hers. "I was dodging vampires, if you'd believe. Heard it went well."

They both threw the whiskey back.

"Dodging vampires?" she asked, the second she got her breath back. "Real actual vampires?"

"Have I ever lied to you, Maggie Doyle?"

"Maggie McGraw," Xander corrected, slipping around the bar and slinging an arm over her shoulders. "And you won't like the answer to that, Kincaid."

Maggie rolled her eyes. "Behave—the pair of you." Grabbing a tray, she set four tankards of ale on it, then made her way around the bar with one last incinerating look at the pair of them. "If you destroy my bar, I'll make both your lives hell."

Then she was gone.

"You keep your eyes off my wife," Xander said with a smile, but his eyes were cool.

"You've got nothing to worry about. Maggie always was too smart to fall for my charms," Kincaid replied, pouring a second shot of whiskey.

"Aye, well. Would have said the same, until recently."

They clinked glasses together. Xander owned the word "brash," but there was an undercurrent of doubt beneath his dazzling smile. Kincaid frowned. "She wouldn't have married you if she didn't love you. You know that, right?"

"Took an awful lot of convincing," Xander grumbled. "She always liked you."

"Maggie...." He almost said, *was a sister when I needed one*, but that only dredged up memories of Agatha, and he was already awash with guilt. "Maggie knew me too well."

"So when you said vampires...."

"I meant vampires," he replied, and shuddered. "Sort of thing gives a man nightmares."

"But where have you been?" Xander demanded. "I

asked Orla, but she's not been sayin', and there's word you were working a mechanical job over in Southwark, but by the look of that nose it's seen some recent action, and... vampires?"

"It's complicated," he replied quietly, "and I don't have leave to discuss it."

"I'm your best friend, K."

"With anyone," he said softly, and Xander's lips thinned.

"Aye, well fuck you too."

This was what he hated about this line of work. "I can't talk about it, but if I could, you'd be the first to know. I just wanted a night away from it to clear my head, a night spent in the cups with some old friends."

"What can you tell me then?" Xander challenged.

"There's a woman," he said bluntly, "and she's getting under my skin."

"Well, there's a first. Can you talk about *her*?"

"Aye," he said, exhaling sharply, before words about Ava started spilling from his mouth, almost as if he'd needed someone to confess to. He was babbling, and he couldn't help himself. "She's smart, beautiful, shy, and bookish. But she's kind too. The type of woman who rescues abandoned kittens. And utterly oblivious to her own qualities. There was a man today who was flirting with her, and she had no idea." He shook his head. "Not a fucking clue."

"Sounds like she's got you wrapped around her little finger. Though she doesn't seem like your usual sort."

You have no idea.

Xander, wisely, poured him a whiskey. "So what's the problem?"

"She's never been with a man, she's in love with someone else, and she's a romantic through and through.

She sees me as an experiment, I think. A no-risk affair." And while the idea had seemed perfect at first—something uncomplicated—it was bothering him now.

He had to keep reminding himself he had no future. Nothing to offer her. Keep it nice and uncomplicated, and have a little fun. That was the plan.

The plan had failed.

"I like her," he admitted. "Too much."

Xander snorted. "If you tell me you're falling in love with her, I will gladly punch some sense into you."

Kincaid shot him a look.

"Shit," Xander said, snagging the whiskey bottle and drinking straight out of it. He wiped his mouth, and then handed the bottle to Kincaid. "All yours, old son. You clearly need it more than me."

Kincaid glared at the three-quarters-full bottle, and then sighed and tipped it up. "I'm *not* falling in love with her."

A look.

"I'm not," he repeated. "I know where this ends—no, I know it *has* an end." He scraped his hand over his face, looking down at his mech fingers drumming on the counter. Sometimes he could still almost feel the actual hand. "I'm the next victim of the Kincaid curse, whether you believe in it or not, and she... she's got her whole life ahead of her."

Years and years. He'd almost started to forget what she truly was, but this brought it into perspective. Ava wasn't immortal—no blue blood was—but sometimes it seemed like it. Some of the older blue bloods were over a century and a half old, still wearing their powdered wigs and rouged faces from the Georgian era. He'd seen them from a distance, and while they were slowly aging, they still looked barely old enough to be his father.

Ava had a good century ahead of her. He had a dozen years at most. Maybe more, maybe less. And they weren't going to be kind years.

"Have you told her?" Xander asked, and then sighed. "Of course you haven't. That's why you're here."

"It's got nothing to do with it," he growled. "We argued. I needed some time to clear my head."

"What did you argue about?"

"Nothing." Nothing he could mention here anyway. Kincaid rubbed the bridge of his nose. "No more talk of Ava. Tell me all your news. What have you been up to? What mischief have the lads been causing?"

Xander's gaze shifted, raking over the crowd as he leaned closer. "Heard there's something brewing on the winds."

Kincaid nursed his whiskey bottle. "Something specific?"

"Something... bloody."

Damn it. "The revolution's over, Xander. Don't get yourself killed." His gaze flicked to Maggie. "Not when you just got handed the world on a platter."

Xander eyed her too. "Some things are worth fighting for. Maggie's one of them. But so's a man's right to live his life freely, and to see his children grow without threat of a leash around their necks—"

"We earned our peace," he countered. "The human queen sits on the throne now, and this"—he held up his mech hand and waggled its fingers—"no longer denies me even basic human rights."

"The same queen who signed off on the Blood Tax bill?" Xander demanded. "The same queen who saw the Packenham riot crushed in favor of her blue blood friends?"

The same arguments he'd used. Kincaid shook his

head. Funny how now he was the voice of reason. "It was never going to be easy, damn you. Three races living side by side.... It will take time to understand how that works."

"Well, maybe there should be one race left standing? The human one."

Kincaid grabbed him by the shirt and hauled him close. "Tell me you haven't been joining those riots."

Xander brushed him off with a careless gesture. "You might have forgotten what you are, K, but me and the rest of the lads haven't." Unlacing his shirt cuff, he revealed the small tattoo on the inside of his wrist, the same one Kincaid wore on his hip. A branded H. "Humanists through and through, and we signed on to crush those pasty-faced cravers, no matter what it took."

"I'm working for them," he blurted.

"What?" Xander froze.

"I told you, it's complicated. But there's a threat to the alliance between our three races, and I got dragged into it to help keep the peace."

Xander swore under his breath, looking stunned. "What happened to you, K? Working for the blue bloods? Who are you? They're poison."

He scrubbed a hand over the back of his neck. Xander had a point. Who was he now? What was he fighting for? At first the only reason he'd joined the COR was because there was a threat to everything he'd fought for, and also because Malloryn could give him a fighting chance at avoiding the Kincaid curse, but now...?

It was different now he knew a few blue bloods as actual people. Christ, Byrnes was smug and arrogant, but had saved his life; Charlie didn't have a mean bone in him; Gemma gave new meaning to the word seductress, but she was dangerously protective of Ava; and Ava, well, she was the hardest one to categorize.

"Do you know what it feels like to have someone look at you as though you're a monster?"

Ava was the gentlest soul he'd ever known.

"They ain't all bad," he said gruffly, and Xander cuffed him over the back of the head.

"Maggie," he bellowed, "my man needs another drink! He's speaking in fuckin' riddles."

It took a moment, but suddenly there was an ale in his hand, and Maggie peering at him worriedly.

"Kincaid's gotten in with the blue bloods," Xander snarled, urging him to drink up. "The man's lost his mind."

"Keep your voice down," Maggie warned Xander. An announcement like that in there might just get Kincaid's head punched in. "And don't be stupid. Kincaid was the one who dragged us out of that hell, the one who found a way for us to fight. If he's working with them, then I'll bet my right hand it's for good reason."

"Thanks," he muttered, draining the tankard. "You've not been getting caught up in any of the riots, have you, Maggie?"

She gave him a long, slow look.

"Don't," he warned her. "There's something brewing behind the scenes—someone pulling strings who's trying to stir up trouble. Whoever it is, they don't give a damn about us humans. They're just using you to tilt at windmills."

"What have you heard?" she asked quietly, refilling his tankard.

"Can't really say." But something else was bothering him. And maybe it was the reason he was truly here. "What would you do if there was a way to get rid of the blue blood scourge forever?"

Maggie froze. So did Xander. Loud laughter and noise spilled over their trio, but he knew he had his answer.

"What do you mean?" Xander's charm slid off him in

an instant, his expression turning hard. "What do you know?"

And instantly he knew it was a mistake. "Nothing. It's nothing. I'm just speaking theoretically: if you had a way to kill blue bloods, what would you do?"

"Well, I'd get my hands on it," Xander said, a little louder, and Maggie instantly hushed her husband.

She was looking at him, her dark eyes reading the nuances Xander clearly didn't see. "For years we've been crushed under the heel of the Echelon, Kincaid. We never had a way to defeat them, because we're human, and they're not. They're almost impossible to kill, which is why we built the Cyclops. Only an automaton could survive a blue blood. If you know of something that could kill them, then you should speak up."

"And where do we stop? How do we control it?" he asked quietly. "The Nighthawks are all rogue blue bloods. Without them, we would never have had a chance to kill the prince consort. We'd still be sitting in that enclave and rotting. They were our allies."

Xander shrugged. "We don't have to kill the Nighthawks, unless they get in our way."

It was Maggie, once again, who saw the problem. "The needs of many outweigh the sacrifice of a few, K. You're the one who told me that seven years ago."

And he'd believed it then, when he ruled the enclaves and the only way out was to overthrow the mad prince consort. Did he believe it now? He'd yelled the exact same fucking thing at Ava, but it was only now, when his friends repeated the same views, he could see the dangers.

"Ava's a blue blood," he said, and Xander nearly spit out his drink.

"Fuckin' Jaysus," Xander said, and then coughed. "Are you mad?"

He scrubbed his weary face again. "I told you. They ain't all bad. Maggie's got more murderous impulses in her little finger than Ava has in her entire body. It's... opened my eyes a little."

"Here," Maggie said, exchanging a glance with Xander as she poured them all another round. "No more talk of killing blue bloods. Not now. Let's just have a moment to clear our heads and think about the repercussions. We'll have another ale and reminisce about old times."

Xander clapped him on the back. "I think K needs to swim in a vat of beer. He's spouting utter nonsense."

But Maggie looked at him, and he could tell she knew he wasn't speaking nonsense.

His head swayed.

Kincaid staggered up against a door, blinking when his nose met wood. He rapped loudly, cursing under his breath, which stank of ale.

"Hold up!" someone called from inside.

He rapped again, trying to hold himself upright. Christ Jaysus. Couldn't go back to Malloryn's. Not like this.

Orla answered the door, blinking in surprise. "Jesus, Liam. What gin joint did you drag yourself through?"

He staggered inside and collapsed on the small sofa in the parlor just off the kitchen. The room was spinning, and he pressed the heels of his palms to his closed eyes to try and stop it. "Not gin. Ale. Bloody... bloody McGraw."

Soft hands tucked a blanket over the top of him. "Aye, I can smell it now. Did you bathe in it, or simply drink the entire barrel by yourself?"

"Mebbe... bit of both. Needed to clear me... head."

"Oh, I'm sure you did that."

He winced at the strident sound of her voice. "Orla, d'you ever wonder what life would have been like if Agatha never went out that night?"

Orla knelt on the sofa beside his hip. "Oh, you've had a rare gutful, haven't you? There's no point in stirring up the past. Agatha's free of her demons now." She patted his hand. "You're the one still carrying them for her."

He dragged his hands lower, making out her shadowy form in the darkness. His voice was very quiet. "I like her, Orla."

"Like... who? Oh." Orla's hand softened on him. "Then you should be telling Ava that. Not me."

"I can't." He stared at the roof, as if he could see straight through it. His uncle would be sleeping now. "How long... does he 'ave?"

"The doctor says maybe a few months."

Tears suddenly blurred his vision. "I should visit more."

"He knows why you don't."

"Aye." Kincaid scraped them out of his eyes. "But what's that say for me? 'E deserves more. He practically fuckin' raised me." He had the sudden horrific thought of what it would feel like, trapped in a bed, with nothing to do, no one visiting. "I just can't bear it, Orla. All I see is Ian. All I see is my f-future. All alone."

"Oh, Liam." Orla slid into his arms, resting her head on his shoulder. "You know I'll be there for you."

And maybe that was worse, because she'd already given up so much of her own life to care for Will, and her father. He squeezed her tight, his voice roughening, "I won't do that to you."

"It's not your choice," she said simply, and kissed his cheek. "Go to sleep. You're drunk and feelin' the weight of the world tonight. You should talk to Dad about it tomorrow. There's still hope for you, Li. You said yourself your pasty-faced duke asked the Royal College of physicians to look into your case, and threw funding at the place to do it. You're barely past the first symptoms."

He turned his face into her hair, those old nightmares flashing through his vision again: the horror he'd felt the first time his legs went out from under him. A muscle spasm. That was all, he'd told himself. But he'd known then it wasn't. "Aye," Kincaid said softly, still staring at the ceiling. "They'll find a cure," he whispered, though he silently vowed if there was no cure, then he'd never burden Orla with another body to slowly bury.

Just as he'd never condemn Ava to the same fate.

CHAPTER SIXTEEN

WORD HAD GOTTEN round. Ava made sure of it, and when most of the Rogues were gathered in Malloryn's study the following afternoon, she handed out the small information leaflets she'd spent the night creating. The second the Duke of Malloryn arrived, she was starting this meeting.

With or without Liam Kincaid.

"Caterpillar mushroom?" Gemma asked, looking at Ava's neat notes with the expression of a woman who'd spent too many hours hearing about ferns and orchids. "This sounds fascinating, Ava. I can hardly wait."

Charlie nudged her. "Don't worry, the interesting part comes when Ava tells you what it does to a blue blood."

Suddenly Ava became the focus of every set of eyes in the room; Jack, the baroness, Herbert, and Gemma. Charlie shot her a wink.

The baroness cleared her throat. She'd already turned over the page, and was miles ahead of the others. "Blood and ashes, Ava. Are you certain?"

Ava shook her head. "Not until I get my hands upon

some of the caterpillar mushroom and test it myself, but... fairly certain. We think it's poisonous to blue bloods and *dhampir*."

And just as she dropped that explosive revelation, the door burst open. Kincaid strode inside, scowling over the top of a good day's growth of black beard, his blue eyes bloodshot, and wincing at the afternoon light that filtered through the window. He saw them all and swayed. "Jaysus. Thought you wanted me, Ava?"

Truer words had never been spoken. Or at least they had, if he wasn't planning on murdering blue bloods, and reeking of ale.

Where the hell has he been? She'd spent five minutes knocking on his bedroom door this morning.

Had he even spent the night there? The argument echoed loudly in her ears, but she couldn't ask him what he'd done after she stormed off.

What if he'd gone to another woman? He'd been so angry, and so had she.

"I thought we all needed an update," Ava said primly, pointing to a chair near the window. "How on earth did you manage to imbibe so much between now and last night?"

Kincaid sank into the chair, scrubbing his hands over his face. "I'm not drunk anymore, but could you keep that particularly strident note out of your voice?"

Strident? Her temper blazed.

"I believe this is the aftereffect of imbibing," Gemma noted, with no small amount of smugness. "I must note I've seen livelier-looking statues, Kincaid. You smell like a brewery—and a woman's perfume, if I dare to breathe a little deeper."

A woman's perfume? Ava froze. She could only smell liquor.

Kincaid shot Gemma his darkest scowl. "Seem to recall a morning when I *didn't* mention what time you staggered in—considering it was well after dawn, and you were last seen in the company of—"

"Truce?" Gemma broke in.

Kincaid gave her that particularly evil smile. "I was pulling my punches too. But agreed. Wouldn't want to corrupt innocent ears." This, with a glance at Ava. "And the perfume you smell is probably my cousin's."

Ava shoved one of her handwritten information pamphlets at him.

If she heard the word "innocent" *one more time....*

And now she took a delicate sniff; there was definitely perfume lingering on his skin. Orla's?

He wouldn't lie. He never had. It was one of the things she liked so much about him, but logic was failing her today. There was a visceral surge of pure fury lighting through her veins. She wanted to yell at him again, and there was no damned reason for it beyond.... Ava blinked. Was she jealous?

The duke finally arrived, handing his top hat and coat to Herbert. "I trust this is important," Malloryn said, and suddenly Ava felt a little overwhelmed.

What if it wasn't? What if she was only conjuring a case, putting a theory to a handful of innocuous clues....

"It's important," Kincaid said, clasping his hands behind his head and exhaling. "But I think Ava should be the one to do the honors. It was her discovery."

Carefully, she tucked a strand of hair behind her ear. Few people championed her, and despite their argument last night, she shot him an undecided look, and then cleared her throat. "If you'll examine the information I wrote for all of you," she said, and then continued to fill them in on everything she and Kincaid had found.

When she'd finished, you could have heard a pin drop in the room. Ava cleared her throat, trying to read Malloryn's reaction.

"This is what killed Zero?" Gemma whispered, looking ill.

The duke finally lowered his pamphlet and met Ava's eyes. "You're right. This is important." Then he was on his feet, taking over the room. "Who else knows of this?"

"Dr. Gibson," she replied. "From the Nighthawks. He was the one who performed the initial autopsy. He knows it's some sort of serum or elixir that was injected into Mr. Thomas, but that's all. Garrett is aware something is killing blue bloods, and I'm sure a few other Nighthawks suspect there's a problem. They're not stupid."

The duke shot Kincaid a hard look, and he shook his head sharply.

He hadn't mentioned it. Yet.

"Then we keep it that way." Malloryn included them all in a heated look. "If what Ava says is true, then this information has dire repercussions for the entire country. This could mean civil war, or at worst, a bloodbath."

"And who's behind the murders of Mr. Thomas and the others?" Gemma asked. "Someone clearly murdered the major, but who? Are the two cases connected? Are they aware we're onto them? Were they watching the major? Or were they following Ava and Kincaid? Was it simply coincidence?"

"Surely it's not Ulbricht," the baroness protested. "He wouldn't be so stupid as to dabble in a poison that could kill blue bloods! If the humanists get their hands on this, they'll murder the Echelon. Ulbricht lives and breathes the Echelon!"

"We have peace now," Gemma interrupted. "The humanists wouldn't dare use this—"

"They would," Kincaid said sharply, and all voices died off. "They wouldn't hesitate. You only have to look at the recent riots to know there's still malcontent among the general population. They wanted the draining factories gone, and the blood tax abolished, and they're not happy both issues remain."

"Without the blood taxes, the streets would be awash in blood," Malloryn retorted.

Kincaid held his hands up. "*I* know that. Doesn't mean I like it, but I know that. Others... are not as inclined to be logical."

Ava cleared her throat again. "We can argue as much as we like about the potential repercussions, but I think we need a plan of attack. Clearly, someone knows what this caterpillar mushroom does, and they're using it to murder blue blood members of the population. Considering Zero was potentially murdered using this same substance, we can include the *dhampir* on our lists of suspects."

"Kincaid and Ava, I think it wise if you both return to the major's store and search it thoroughly. Major Winthrop might have contacts among the black market trade of rare herbs. We need to track down everyone who is remotely connected to bringing this substance into the country, and lock them down until we know how many people are aware of what this product does. Contact the Nighthawks and have them assist you in closing down the scene—tell the locals it's a murder investigation if you must, but nothing else. Charlie, you can go with them," Malloryn said.

He was taking control of her investigation. Ava bit her lip, but nodded. At least she was still included.

"Gemma, I want you to make a move on the information I gave you yesterday," Malloryn instructed obliquely. "We've got a lead on Ulbricht, and I want him found."

"You have a lead?" Ava blurted.

Gemma gathered herself, looking pale. "One of Malloryn's other spies got his hands on one of the Sons of Gilead. We need to question him, but he might know Ulbricht's whereabouts, or at least he'll know how to get in touch with his SOG contact."

"Report to the baroness. She can contact me if necessary." Malloryn turned to fetch his hat and coat from Herbert. "I need to call an emergency meeting with the Council of Dukes and the queen."

They sent Charlie ahead to the Nighthawks guild, as he could move faster than they could, then set out for Major Winthrop's shop. Ava wanted to lock down the scene before anyone else could contaminate it.

Ava kept her manner purely professional when they arrived, checking the locks on the shop doors and waiting for the Nighthawks to arrive to set up a perimeter before she allowed herself to examine the shop. She didn't like their chances of finding anything. Whoever cleaned up after the bodies yesterday had done a meticulous job.

The Nighthawks finally arrived, and as predicted, there wasn't much evidence left within the major's emporium. Ava worked mechanically, her heart feeling a little heavy in her chest, though her peripheral senses were desperately aware of Kincaid.

"Are you going to speak to me?" Kincaid finally demanded, when the silence clearly grew too much for him.

"I don't particularly have much to say."

"Ava."

She turned, brushing a curl off her face. "Yes?"

Kincaid stared down at her with an uneasy expression.

"I'm sorry. You were right. It's a more complicated situation than I imagined. I wouldn't tell anyone about Black Vein."

Ava swallowed. "But do you see how that felt for me to hear those things from your lips?"

Hands cupped her cheeks and he lifted her chin until their eyes met. The dark scowl on his face was back. "I'm an utter shite, Ava. All those things I said about blue bloods. I didn't mean to hurt you. All I could see in the moment was everything I've suffered over the years, everything I've seen destroy the people I love—"

"It's all right," she said. "I know you have your own demons, and you couldn't have known."

"But I shouldn't have taken them out on you." Kincaid sighed. "And I know everything you went through; you didn't choose this. But you've made the best you could of the situation, and a part of me is in awe of that. I'm sorry."

"Apology accepted."

He leaned forward and kissed her forehead, and it was a strange moment, for she didn't know why.

"Truce?" she asked, curling her hands around his wrists.

They stood there like that for a long moment. "Truce," Kincaid replied gruffly.

"Then let us finish cataloguing Major Winthrop's belongings, so we can send anything we think might be evidence on to the guild."

For while she might have accepted his apology, her heart still felt a little battered and bruised.

He'd apologized. They'd called a truce, but something hot gnawed at Kincaid's gut as they finally finished up, and sent Charlie back to Malloryn's while the Nighthawks dispersed.

Ava locked up the Emporium, her head bowed and her manner still quiet. He hated seeing her like this. She was guarding herself, and he knew he was to blame and—

"Penny for your thoughts?" he asked, knowing she'd recognize the phrase.

"No thoughts. I'm just tired."

"And hurt."

A flash of green glanced in his direction, and he realized he'd hit the nail on the head. Ava looked down. "I just keep thinking, where is this going?"

Hopefully someplace private, for the look in her eyes scared him. That look was asking questions, and doubting the answers. "Nothing's changed."

"I know," she whispered, and then looked up guiltily. "But I like you. I do."

"I like you too. Very much so."

And yet he felt like he'd said the wrong thing, for she looked down, nibbling on her bottom lip.

If they weren't standing in the middle of the street then he might have taken steps to chase away that doubt.

Kincaid looked around. Nobody was looking, but it didn't mean they wouldn't draw attention. Capturing her wrist, he drew her into an alley. "Ava." He clasped her hand. "What are you thinking?"

Ava looked up. "That I want you to kiss me."

Normally he wouldn't hesitate. But there was her recent heartbreak over Byrnes's marriage to consider, and her innocence. There were doubts inside him, doubts that grew the more he came to care for her. And maybe they needed to talk right now more than they needed to kiss. Because she was clearly hiding something, and hell, so was he. "Why?"

"*Why?* Perhaps because when you kiss me, it chases away all the doubts. Perhaps because we argued, and I'm not certain where we stand right now."

"Nothing's changed," he repeated. "But the question is, why me? What doubts? Do you think I don't feel them too? Jaysus, Ava, you decided you wanted to lose your virginity, and I was the first person you saw when you turned around. Do you think that doesn't play on my mind? There's a part of me that wonders if I'm being used to scratch an itch just because you're suddenly curious, or because the man you thought you loved married someone else."

Tell me why you want me. Me, damn you, and not just a man to kiss. Not just any man.

Ava sucked in a sharp breath. "That's not what this is."

"No?" he challenged. "Then what is it? You were in love with another man." He wasn't going to let her sidestep the question.

"In love?" she blurted. "I didn't even know what love meant!"

"And you do now?"

Ava's pretty rosebud mouth opened and shut, her eyes darting to and fro. And something inside him squeezed, a horrified, breathless feeling. No. *No.* It was safer to keep her at arm's length and guard his heart against her. Safer to say her heart belonged to another, and he would never get his chance at it.

Because then he would never lose it.

Then he could never break hers.

"I don't know," she whispered, as if the realization of what stood between them physically hurt her. "I wanted something that didn't exist, and now I'm staring back at it, and wondering what it all meant. Because my feelings for Byrnes... are very confusing right now."

"Confusing?"

"I don't know what I felt for him!" she suddenly cried. "Because if that was love, then what is this? For this feels... like something more. Like something else. This feels like you're dragging me to the edge of a cliff and asking me to trust you when you push me off it, and it feels like you're taking a blindfold off my eyes and pushing me out into a wondrous world I never even knew was there, and you're there at my side every step of the way, a port of call, my shelter in any storm. It's... a maelstrom of emotions I do not know how to process. It makes me feel both safe, and yet so, so uncertain." She tucked a curl behind her ear, looking at him earnestly. "It scares me. It really scares me, because I don't know if I'm the only one who feels this way. And I keep telling myself to be careful, and not go any further along this path, because *this ends when the case does*."

Jaysus. Kincaid's heart kicked in his chest. He'd wanted a sign she'd chosen him, and then she'd kicked his feet out from under him.

Ava turned and paced, pressing her fingers to her temples. "I sorry. I shouldn't have said that—"

"It was exactly what I needed to hear." He stepped forward and caught her wrist, drawing her into his arms, kissing her, clutching her so tightly her spine arched and he felt her weight fall into his arms as he lifted her off her feet—

Ava gasped. Then both hands met his chest. And she was rather stronger than he'd expected, for he slammed back against the nearest brick wall, his arms flung wide and the breath leaving him. Heat curled through his lower abdomen. *Hell.* Those emerald eyes of hers were gleaming with determination, and he found himself facing down a tempest in muslin. A hand met his chest, and when she took a forceful step forward, he found himself looking down at her. Acres of skirts hemmed him in, and Kincaid stopped breathing.

Practical, stubborn, and quiet-natured, every now and then he caught a glimmer of the passion within her—most often when they argued—and it made him want to keep pushing her, to see just how far that passion extended.

But Ava in a temper?

That was temptation indeed.

"Kiss me," he told her.

And she didn't hesitate. Grabbing him by the coat collar, she stretched up on her toes and claimed his mouth, her tongue dancing against his. Kincaid's arms wrapped around her, and he lifted her off her feet again, drinking in the taste of her. A desperate, furious storm of passion engulfed them both.

To know he was the first one to show her this made him a little feral with need. But they hadn't finished the conversation. And he'd kissed her deliberately, to steer her away from demanding his feelings, but that wasn't fair.

Kincaid forced himself to draw a line in the sand. One to keep them on firm ground, before he lost his head and did something he'd regret.

Like press her up against the bricks in this alley and go to his knees in front of her, sliding his hands up her silken stockings, and wrapping them around the backs of her calves—

He drew back with a groan. Ava's eyes were so very wide, her body trembling against him. She licked her lips, almost as if tasting the warmth of his mouth, but he pressed his finger against those lips, forestalling her from reaching for him again.

Because maybe he wouldn't have the strength of will

to do this again.

"If I'm being honest, then neither of us is where we were when we set out to do this," he said hoarsely. "I like you, Ava. A lot. And you're not the only one who keeps telling yourself this has a beginning and an ending. And yet here we are." He looked down into eyes so very green he felt like he was falling into them.

"Here we are," Ava whispered, and her gaze dropped to his mouth.

"I can't stay away from you. And I don't know if I want to. But there are things you need to know. I *do* know there is an ending in front of us. There has to be, but it's not for the reason you think."

Ava slowly looked up, and he caressed her face.

"Ava, I can't give you a future. Not won't. But can't." His breath caught. "If I could... then maybe... maybe I would. Maybe I'd be that man."

Ava wrapped her arms around herself as she drew back, shaking her head slowly, as if she'd finally realized what he was telling her. "What do you mean?"

"What's the one thing I don't like talking about?"

The color was slowly beginning to drain from her face. "Why do you wear leg braces? Why the girdle around your waist? What's going on?"

And she deserved to know.

"It's a muscular disorder," he told her softly, steeling himself. "My brother had it, my uncle... and now me." He caught his breath, seeing Will's grave. "I thought I was safe. My brother began to show the signs when he was thirteen. Ian began at one-and-twenty, and I was almost six-and-twenty the first time my legs went out from beneath me. You keep thinking: did I just trip? Was I clumsy? Or is it something more sinister? But I can't deny it any longer. I'm the last victim of the Kincaid curse."

Ava's face was so very, very pale. "You said your brother died."

"He did." Kincaid forced himself to look her in the eye. "The same way my uncle will. His heart gave out. Like I said, it's a degenerative muscular disorder, and the heart is a muscle."

Ava dragged her hands over her mouth. "*No.*"

"Yes." His voice sounded cool and rational, but his heart was beating like a racehorse's in his chest. "I don't know how many years I have ahead of me. Ian's lasted years beyond Will. And it's early. My legs are weakening, I can feel it, but the braces keep me upright for now. One day I'll be in a wheeled chair. One day I'll be unable to get out of bed. And one day...."

He couldn't say it.

"Is there no cure?"

"Malloryn's instructed the Royal College of Physicians to try and find one, but... I don't hold much hope."

Ava was frozen, looking absolutely horrified. "What about the craving virus?"

"*No.*"

"It can heal virtually anything."

"You think that's any better? To become a—" He remembered to whom he was talking.

"A monster?" she whispered, looking even paler.

"Ava."

"Do you think me a monster?"

"No!" He held his hands up in a placating manner. "But what if it doesn't stop my illness? There are some illnesses, some tumors, the craving virus hasn't been able to help. I don't know if I could dare hope. And it goes against everything I've ever believed."

"You're being stubborn," she snapped, "because of your prejudices. If you'd just accept—"

"What? You want to lecture me? Why don't we discuss the way you accept *your* nature?"

Ava froze.

"Aye," he said deliberately. "You keep saying I'm the one with prejudices, and I should risk all in the hopes the craving virus will heal me, but you're the one who can't abide blood. You're the one who keeps working on this mysterious 'formula,' so you can pretend to be what you aren't—"

"That's not fair. And I won't take offense at it. You're afraid.... And—"

"Of course I'm bloody afraid." He rasped his hand over his mouth, reining himself back in. He didn't want to hurt her, but couldn't she see how difficult this was for him? "You live in a world of 'maybe,' Ava. And it's part of what draws me to you. Despite everything, you still have hope in your eyes, and it makes you more beautiful than you will ever know. But for me there is no maybe. All I can see is the end. I am going to die. Maybe not tomorrow, but in a few years. I'm sorry, sweetheart. I am. But as I said, fairy tales don't exist. Not in real life. And I'll live every day between now and then as if it were my last, but I won't drag you down with me."

"Is that *your* choice?" Her eyes were shining, but there were no tears. "It feels like you're not even giving me a decision in this."

"Because I know what that decision would be. Your most beautiful trait is the empathy you can't hide. I won't be pitied. I won't ruin your life because you think you need to nurse me into the grave." He could see everything she felt flickering over her face. "You want marriage, and you want children, and I will *not* inflict this on a child. I can't." His voice broke. "This bloody curse can die with me."

Kincaid nodded to her curtly, his insides twisted in

knots. "I just wanted you to know. And if you choose not to go forward with our agreement, then I'll understand. This is becoming emotionally tangled for both of us, and that's not fair on you. I'm sorry. I should have told you earlier."

But I wanted to touch you just once, and I couldn't deny myself.

Then he turned and stormed out of the alley, unable to bear the look in her eyes any longer.

CHAPTER SEVENTEEN

KINCAID CIRCLED CHARLIE. The young lad was lean and Kincaid dwarfed him, but the bastard was a craver through and through. Which meant he was faster than Kincaid, stronger, and recovered quicker.

If Kincaid didn't have a biomech hand that could punch its way through walls, then he'd be seriously outclassed.

He didn't care if he was outclassed right now. A part of him wanted to be punished, and maybe if he let the physical pain of a fight overwhelm him, then it wouldn't hurt so much inside.

He hadn't seen Ava since last night, when he dropped her home at the safe house and then went and got blind roaring drunk with Xander, ignoring the way his friend kept looking at him as if he knew something was wrong.

And there'd been a note this morning, a quiet one full of unspoken hurt, where she'd told him she'd knocked on his door and waited for him, but she needed to see to something at the guild and could no longer wait.

It was better this way. Wasn't it?

"Are you sure you want to do this?" Charlie asked.

"Just hit me already."

Charlie sighed, and then came at him in a blur of fists. Knuckles slammed into his side, and Kincaid retaliated with a sharp elbow, following up with a left hook that almost connected with the lad's nose.

He'd extended too far. Pain exploded through his cheekbone as Charlie planted him with a fistful of fives.

"Sorry," Charlie said, dropping his fists from a pugilist stance as Kincaid staggered back.

"Don't be sorry," Kincaid growled, and drove at him, desperately needing to drive the horrible feeling inside him away.

They punched, and wrestled, and slammed each other into walls. Blows turned his vision white, and he was soon limping, his body fatigued and bruised, while Charlie looked fresh as a daisy.

It rankled. He'd been worse than useless the night Zero attacked him and Byrnes and broke his nose. How could a human fight something that moved faster than he could even track? Surviving was the best he could manage, which often left him wondering precisely why the Duke of Malloryn had ever asked him to join the Company of Rogues.

He wasn't useless, and he wouldn't let this disease steal his sense of worth from him.

He was a good man in a fight, and he was tired of being taken for the weakest link on the team.

Kincaid went on the attack. Charlie danced around him, anticipating the next blow, and then answering with a right uppercut that slipped beneath Kincaid's guard.

His ears rang, his feet went out from under him, and then he was staring up at the ceiling, rolling his tongue around his mouth to check for broken teeth. *Fuck.*

"Jesus, are you all right?" An earnest head peered down at him, and that only pissed him off more. "I didn't mean to hit you so hard."

Grabbing the lad's hand, Kincaid hauled himself to his feet. "If you don't hit me hard in training, then the *dhampir* will when it counts. I need to learn to take those hits."

There was blood in his mouth. He spat through the open window and rinsed his mouth out, just in time to see Malloryn prance into the room.

"You're not enjoying this half enough," Malloryn told Charlie, who arched a brow dubiously.

"I don't enjoy hurting my friends," the lad replied. His fists were low, and he had a determined look on his face, as though he was going to refuse to go any further with this. "I'm done. You've got a death wish this morning, and you're not even protecting yourself."

Malloryn's calculating gaze slid toward Kincaid. "Trouble?"

"Nothing you need to know about."

Sometimes he didn't know why he was there. He was human, half-mech, and a lot of his principles didn't align with Malloryn's. The only thing they shared was the past. Both of them had fought to tear down the corrupt prince consort, though sometimes Kincaid wondered why Malloryn had lifted a finger.

Power?

He'd already been on the ruling Council of Dukes.

And he liked to glide through the shadows, even now. No. Malloryn's motives were completely opaque, and Kincaid wasn't sure if he wanted to know why the man did what he did.

"You," he said, pointing a finger at the duke and tilting his head toward the mats, "and me. Let's go."

Malloryn stilled. "I don't think that's a good idea."

Kincaid couldn't stop a grin. "Why?" He rolled his shoulders. "Think I'm going to spray those pretty teeth all over the room?"

"He's got one hell of a punch on him," Charlie warned Malloryn.

"Or do you save all those suave moves for a waltz at court?" Kincaid taunted.

Malloryn's eyes narrowed to thin slits. "If you think you're going to bait me into a match by referring to my conceit, then I'm afraid I'll have to disappoint you. I've been called many things in my time. Coward isn't something that riles me."

"Pretty boy?" Kincaid suggested, and if possible, those eyes narrowed even further.

"It's probably not a bad idea," Charlie said, his eyes meeting Kincaid's in a brief flash of conspiracy. "If we're attacked, Your Grace, then you'll need to know how to defend yourself."

"I know how to defend myself." Malloryn sounded irritated. "And if you call me 'pretty' one more time, I'll have to assume you're courting me. I've already got someone warming my bed."

"As well as a fiancée," Charlie pointed out, and Malloryn's scowl darkened.

"No interest in courting," Kincaid said. "Though I'll give you a love tap or two."

The pair of them circled him, and Malloryn's gaze swung between them. Charlie bounced on the balls of his feet, eyes alight in anticipation, "I promise I won't tell anyone if he beats you."

"Fine. Let's do this then. Once." Malloryn pointed at Kincaid. "You, on the mats." Shrugging out of his jacket, he turned that cool look on Charlie. "And to make this even, you can join him. If the two of you can take me down, then I'll forward you an extra month's worth of wages." Malloryn tossed his coat toward a chair and started unbuttoning his sleeves and rolling them up.

Charlie crowed, but Kincaid paused. In his experience, it was rare for a man of Malloryn's arrogance to walk willingly into a trap.

Which made him wonder about Malloryn's fighting ability.

He'd never seen the duke fight, though he knew Malloryn was devilishly handy with a pistol. He'd proved that when they all rode to rescue Byrnes last month.

Malloryn wasn't the sort to set himself up for embarrassment. No. He was the sort to set a trap, and as he caught Kincaid's eye, he smiled faintly.

Son of a bitch.

This was going to hurt, he suspected.

The pair of them danced around the duke as he limbered up. Malloryn had stripped to his trousers, like they had, and the duke was surprisingly muscular for a man Kincaid hadn't seen actually do much.

"Anytime the pair of you are ready," Malloryn said, shooting Kincaid a mocking little smile.

He went in, hammering a blow toward Malloryn's weaker side, but the duke was suddenly not there, striking up with a chop of his hand that slammed into Kincaid's throat.

He hit the mats, feeling like he couldn't breathe, and knowing Malloryn pulled the blow. Fuck. Charlie was dancing around, faring a little better, and Kincaid swallowed hard, before kicking the duke's feet out from under him.

Malloryn wasn't down for long. He arched his back and flipped onto his feet, turning to keep them both in his line of sight. He looked mildly discomposed.

And Kincaid suddenly wanted to take the bastard down.

"Work as a team," Kincaid told Charlie, lumbering to his feet, his braces holding him upright as he settled into a more defensive stance.

They moved together, trying to take Malloryn unawares. Punches hammered toward the duke, but he was simply never there. A hand caught Kincaid's wrist, heaving him in a wrestler's throw, and he somehow managed to flip over Malloryn's back, landing on his feet. Charlie stepped in, trying to distract the duke, and Kincaid decided the only way to do this was to throw all his cards in.

He took the duke down in a dive, Malloryn twisting like a cut cat in his arms. An elbow slammed into his solar plexus, and then his jaw, and Kincaid saw stars as the duke rolled over him and landed a sweeping kick to Charlie's chest.

"Jesus." Charlie hit the mats.

Kincaid tried to lift himself off them. This was not working the way he'd planned. Everything hurt.

"Where... the fuck... did you learn to fight like that?" Kincaid panted, hands on his knees, as he waited for Charlie to get to his feet.

"I was one of the heirs of a Great House." Malloryn was at least breathing hard. "The first time someone tried to kill me, I was six, for the only way to become head of one of the Echelon Houses is to either assassinate your way to the top, or present a duel to the death. My father was ambitious. I started playing with knives when I was two."

"Well," Gemma drawled from the doorway. "I hate to interrupt the sweat session, however, there's been a note, and it says it's urgent."

Malloryn lowered his hands from their defensive stance. "Had enough?"

Kincaid lifted his head from his slumped pose, then exhaled and nodded. "Yeah. You win."

Gemma clucked her tongue. "Which one of you two was foolish enough to challenge him?"

Kincaid raised a hand, then reached out to offer Charlie a lift to his feet.

"In Kincaid's defense"—Charlie threw the words over his shoulder—"I was right there with him. Didn't know His Grace could handle himself."

"Perhaps next time we can oil all three of you up, and let you have at it?" A sudden innocent smile decorated her full mouth, and her gaze slid over the three of them lasciviously. "But only if I get to let the rest of the ladies watch."

Charlie flushed pink and scrabbled for his shirt. Both Kincaid and Malloryn eyed each other. The duke's smile had faded, and he was once again reverting back to his controlled persona.

Pity. For a second, Kincaid had almost liked the bastard. Even if he was mercilessly beating the pair of them.

"You used to be more fun, Auvry," Gemma murmured, crossing her arms over her chest.

Malloryn sighed, and dragged his shirt on, buttoning it up to his chin. "I used to be naïve too. Yes, even me. What have you got for me?"

Gemma held up a small envelope. "I don't know. It's addressed to you, and I didn't think you'd appreciate it if I opened it."

"That's never stopped you in the past," Malloryn pointed out, snatching up the letter, and examining it. "You used to slide a hot knife under the seal, then re-melt the wax to seal it."

"Perhaps I learned my lesson?" There was something

sad about her smile. "Maybe I'm not as fun as I used to be either?"

Malloryn met her eyes, and Kincaid felt like an observer in some intimate dilemma. He knew there was history between the two of them, though he doubted it was romantic. Gemma had failed Malloryn once, though that was the extent of what Kincaid had heard.

"Or perhaps that's what you want me to think." Malloryn snorted, and it broke the tension, even as he slid his thumbnail beneath the wax seal.

"You're getting cynical in your old age," Gemma retorted.

"That's what happens when one of your spies bugs your study with a recording device, and the rest of them have a betting pool on whether you're going to get your fiancée to the altar or not."

Kincaid grinned. "Well, some of *us* still know how to have fun."

"So far you're in front, Your Grace," Charlie said promptly. "Though if the bride cries off, do let me know. I've got fifty quid riding on it."

"Miss Hamilton's not going to cry off," Gemma said. "She trapped Malloryn into a betrothal, so she's hardly likely to...."

Kincaid's attention shifted away from the argument between Charlie and Gemma. The duke had opened the envelope, and he saw the sudden tension in Malloryn's body.

"What is it?" he barked, cutting through Gemma and Charlie's conversation.

Malloryn's gaze cut to his. "Where's Ava?"

Something about the way the duke said it made Kincaid's insides turn to ice. "She wanted to discuss something with her mentor, Dr. Gibson, at the Nighthawks guild. Why? What does it say?"

Malloryn tugged a piece of blonde hair from the envelope. "It says, 'You should keep a closer eye on your operatives.'"

Kincaid's heart kicked in his chest.

"Sure you're all right, lass?" Gibson asked, pouring her a cup of tea.

Not really. No matter what she tried, she couldn't focus this morning, and poor Dr. Gibson had noticed.

I am going to die. Maybe not tomorrow, but in a few years. I'm sorry, sweetheart. I am. But as I said, fairy tales don't exist.

Ava moodily drew her synthetic protein solution out of her reticule. She rubbed at her arms. The smell made her feel a little ill, but she felt decidedly unbalanced today. She'd spent all night sobbing tearlessly to herself, alone in her room with her heart breaking in her chest, and all she could think was that she needed to find a cure. Something. Anything. Even if the answer was to convince Kincaid to risk the craving.

...the way you accept your *nature....*

Damn it.

"What do you know of degenerative muscular diseases?" she whispered.

Gibson looked up sharply, handing her the cup and saucer. "Not a great deal, I'm afraid. Why?"

"No reason." And no hope there.

Gibson went to put the blood back in its melting ice bath, but Ava suddenly reached out, stilling her hand. "May I?"

"Are you certain, lass? You've been off blood for a long time."

Too long maybe. She nodded, and laced her own tea. Blood spilled through the diluted water, like a reddened cloud in the bottom of her teacup. Ava stirred it even as heat spilled through her veins and the predator within her awoke. It felt like something alien took over her body. She was sharper, more alert, her vision suddenly catapulting forward in intensity until she could pick out the fine hairs on Gibson's cheek, and the network of capillaries beneath the good doctor's pale skin.

If she couldn't accept her own nature, then how on earth could she convince Kincaid to even consider the idea?

"Bottoms up," she said nervously, and gulped a large mouthful of her tea.

The taste of it exploded through her mouth like a supernova, slamming through her veins until her head spun and the world suddenly seemed warmer and brighter, and slightly more wonderful. A drug of pure bliss for her poor, starved body, and Ava swayed, grabbing hold of the armchair to steady herself.

She'd forgotten how wonderful this felt.

Hague had taken away her choice by infecting her. She'd always felt like abstaining from blood gave her some kind of control over the situation. It made her feel like it was her choice, and not his.

But in doing so, she let his ghost haunt her future.

Every action she made was because of that monster. Every time she denied herself what her body wanted, it was because *he* lingered there in the background.

And damn him, but she was tired of listening to his ghost. She had more important things to think about than a man who'd been rotting for over four years.

"Any reason for this sudden change?" Gibson asked, watching her carefully.

"No." *Yes.* She sighed. "Kincaid told me he has a degenerative disease. There's no cure for it."

Gibson added a cube of sugar to his tea. "That's the fellow who's been working with you? And this bothers you, because...."

"I have feelings there," she admitted quietly, taking another sip of tea. "He hates blue bloods, but he likes me. And I suggested the craving might heal him, but... he rejected the idea."

"Do his feelings extend to match yours?"

"I don't know." She dwelled on everything Kincaid had told her yesterday. "He said if he wasn't ill, then he'd... consider being with me. But he doesn't want me to watch him slowly die, and he doesn't want to pass on his illness to any children." All her secret hopes and dreams were the antithesis of Kincaid's.

"Sometimes it just doesn't work, lass."

She nodded sadly, her throat tightening, before she ruthlessly drained her tea. "Sometimes it doesn't." But she had to try. And she'd be damned if she'd let either Kincaid's or her own pride ruin their burgeoning romance. "I'd best be going. He'll be back at Malloryn's by now, and I think best when I can bounce ideas off him."

She set her cup and saucer aside.

"Be careful, Ava." Gibson gave her the folder containing all his notes on the case so far. "You deserve more than a broken heart."

It might be a little too late for that.

Fickle light trickled in through the steam cab's window as Ava tried to transcribe the notes she'd made after talking to Dr. Gibson.

The streets were quiet, all her leads drying up. She needed a dash of inspiration to break this case.

Rewinding the ECHO recording device Fitz—the Nighthawks mechanical genius—had created several years ago, she pressed Play and heard her own voice fill the carriage. "...*is it the SOG or the dhampir group behind all of this... Zero's death argues for dhampir involvement, but—*"

The cab hit a bump, and Ava's thumb slid off the button as she jolted. Her paperwork slid forward on her lap, and she hastily snatched it up. If the hackney driver thought he was going to charge her full rate for this ride, she'd be reminding him of the rough journey.

Ava pressed the button again. "...*who killed Winthrop? Why? Did they know we were there? Were they watching the shop? Or... were they watching us?*"

Another jolt. Ava looked up from the recorder, scowling a little. "Is everything all right out there?"

The steam carriage's boilers suddenly hissed, and then she was flung back in the seat as the carriage lurched forward.

"Hello?" she called, her clockwork heart beating steadily in her chest even as her head swam with a sudden surge of fright. The worst thing about her replacement heart was its monotone beat. Her body might be preparing itself to flee, but her heart ground inexorably on at its regular pace, and denied her the rush of blood she sometimes needed in these situations.

They veered to the right and Ava slammed up against the carriage door, crumpling the blinds, which revealed a searing flash of a green park rushing past the window, surprised faces turning to the carriage as it went by.

Something wasn't right.

The boiler was hissing at a frightful pitch. Ava shoved the blinds up, gasping as she saw the London streets rushing by. What on earth had happened to the driver? She wound the windowpane down, poking her head through the opening. The flap of a man's black split-tail coat was the only thing she could see of the driver.

"Excuse me!" she cried, gripping the windowsill in both hands. "Are you all right? What's going on? Why are we rushing—"

A gloved hand reached out, and as she watched, slid the carriage into a higher gear.

A thrill of nervousness lit through her.

He had to have heard her, but why would he be ignoring her? Or pushing the carriage to its utmost limits in these busy streets? This was madness. Someone was going to get hurt.

"Hey!" a man yelled—as if to prove her point—leaping out of the way.

"Stop!" Ava screamed. "You're going to run someone over!"

Or worse. What happened if they struck a building, or an omnibus? There were still horse-drawn trams in this section of London, weren't there?

Ava's breath caught. She couldn't help remembering the last time she'd been trapped in a carriage like this, her father's horses dancing in their traces as a man stepped out of the shadows and shot her driver off the seat. For a second she saw Hague's face superimposed over the driver in front of her as he glanced behind him. "Not *now*," she whispered grimly.

Hague was dead. This was an entirely new set of circumstances, and the last thing she needed was to lose herself when she was the only person who might be able to stop the carriage.

The driver gathered his feet beneath him, and then launched himself into the foggy afternoon.

Ava screamed as the carriage rocketed forward. He'd left her here! No. He'd deliberately locked the steering wheel, veering them directly toward a busy intersection ahead.

All the heat drained out of her face. Dozens of people looked up, pointing at the carriage. A child screamed, and his mother turned around frantically, looking for him in the sudden surge of a frightened crowd.

Shoving at the door, Ava found it locked, which should have been impossible. A swift glance down revealed a wrench thrust through the handle. She scrambled across the seat, only to find the same thing on the other side.

Trapped.

Please.... She hadn't survived a madman only to die now. Ava shook the door, slamming her shoulder against it. Would she even die in a crash? Or would the cursed craving virus resurrect her?

The window...

...was too narrow to fit her bustle through. Goddamned fashion.

Tugging out the lady's pistol Malloryn insisted she carry, she shot the lock off the door. The handle remained jammed shut. Ava leaned back on the seat and kicked it with her feet, forcing all her blue blood strength into the action.

The door jarred. Screams sounded through the open window. "Come on, damn you!" she kicked again, and this time part of the door panel broke free. Lace ripped along her sleeve as she forced the panel open, hammering at it with her heel one more time, and them scrambling across the seat to shove the door away.

It hit the cobbles, tumbling end over end, and leaving her free to remove the wrench. Grabbing her parasol from within, she hooked it over the top of the carriage roof and dragged herself up there somehow, clinging to the edges as her skirts choked her legs.

The intersection loomed. Someone honked a carriage horn furiously, its tinny squeal trying to clear the crossing. People scrambled out of the way, but there was far too much traffic clogged in the sudden panic.

She caught sight of a little girl crying, her pinafore stained with red lolly, and Ava forced herself to move.

The parasol was gone in the rush. Ava slithered along the roof, her hair whipping back in the wind as she tumbled forward onto the driver seat in front. Steam hissed past her from the boiler. The red arrow in the gauge trembled as it ticked dangerously into *Warning* territory.

It all happened so quickly. Ava tried to release the locked steering wheel, but the driver had jammed a bloody umbrella under it to hold it in place and the cursed thing was stuck. Lashing out with her foot, she broke it in two, then wrenched on the wheel just as they hit the intersection.

A carriage flashed past. The little girl's pinafore flapped in the wind and she cried out, the sound whipping into the distance. All Ava could see was a brick wall looming ahead of her, each brick carved out with precise mortar, as if her vision had sharpened, and she gasped in a breath and threw herself off the side—

The impact stole her breath.

Ava tumbled head over heels on the cobbles until she fetched up in a bruised mess against the gutter. A concussive explosion of sound forced her to fling her arms over her head as the carriage slammed into the brick wall. Screams echoed in the thoroughfare. Horns blared as a man on a steam-powered rickshaw tried to veer around the wreckage, and smashed into a gaslight. Her corset suddenly had steel teeth and they were closing around her lungs hungrily. It hurt to breathe. It hurt to move. The world was a mess of noise, and light, and people everywhere.

Then it was all over.

"Oh my goodness!" a woman blurted, staring at the wreck. "Oh my goodness."

The woman kept repeating herself, even as others came to her rescue.

"Are you all right, miss?" There was a gloved hand in front of Ava's face as she looked up into a man's face, or what she could see of it over the scarf wrapped around his throat. He was wearing a newsboy's cap covering his hair, and had pale blue eyes that seemed almost arctic in their intensity.

Her head spun.

Her shoulder ached from the impact, but there were other people in front of her who were hurt worse than she was. If there was one good thing about the craving affliction, it was the fact she could survive almost anything. Including a runaway carriage. "I'm fine," she said, sitting up and swaying slightly.

"That's a shame." Something sharp pricked her upper arm.

Ava blinked as she stared up into his face. What had he—? She felt the first faint chill down her arm, her body suddenly loose and weak as she sprawled back onto the cobbles. Nothing. Not a twitch in her limbs. Her steady, dependable heart kept ticking as if nothing was wrong, but she was screaming on the inside. She couldn't feel her feet or her hands, but her eyes still moved as the man loomed over her, peeling back one eyelid to stare down at her.

Trapped inside a body that no longer worked.

Hemlock. He'd used hemlock on her. The poison had an adverse reaction on a blue blood, paralyzing them for up to ten minutes, depending on the level of craving virus in the blood.

"That's better," he crooned softly. "Won't be long now, Miss McLaren."

McLaren? Her throat tightened. What was going on? First her driver tried to kill her, and now.... That was when she saw the split tail of his coat.

He'd been the one who locked the steering wheel on the carriage and tried to force her off the road.

What had happened to the driver she'd first hired?

He saw it in her eyes. "Nothing personal, you see. Just doing what I'm told." Rubbing at his cap, he dislodged it just enough for her to see his hair, and suddenly it all made a horrid sort of sense.

His extremely pale skin.

His icy blue eyes, so translucent they looked like a glacier.

His hair, a shock of white that resembled the down of a swan.

The scarf, gloves, hat, and coat, which covered as much of his sun-sensitive skin as possible.

For the last month they'd been searching for one of the *dhampir* that conspired against them, and here one was, right in front of her.

"Hey," another man said. "Do you need help? What's happened?"

"She's all right," the *dhampir* said, swinging Ava up into his arms, where she had no choice but to flop as though she'd come down with the vapors. "My wife was feeling poorly this morning, and I guess she's taken ill from the shock. I'll get her home and tuck her up in bed. She'll come round soon enough."

"Aye, good luck to you." The stranger surveyed the scene helplessly, even as sirens began to peal somewhere nearby. "What a mess. Good luck with your wife."

"Thanks."

Ava made a choking sound in her throat as the *dhampir* carried her away from the carnage, though she couldn't so much as cry out for help.

"Let's get you someplace private," the *dhampir* murmured, "where we can have a little chat."

CHAPTER EIGHTEEN

"WHERE IS SHE?" Kincaid demanded, leaping from the carriage almost before it had finished moving. Gemma and Charlie had made a mad dash for the guild, but he and Malloryn were using Malloryn's tracking device.

"Give me a moment," the duke replied tersely. Malloryn had insisted when they first started working with him that a tracking beacon be implanted beneath their skin at the back of their hairlines. It was some sort of gadget the Nighthawks had come up with. The compass hand spun, heading directly to the south. "There."

They both looked to the south.

Some sort of crowd gathered, hovering around the crossroads ahead of him. A chill ran down Kincaid's spine. They were too late. He just knew it.

Slamming past people, he shoved through the crowd. A carriage was smashed against a wall, the under-carriage snapped in two with the force of the impact, flames licking around the boiler.

"What happened?" Kincaid demanded, and a young girl beside him babbled about a runaway carriage, and a woman on top who'd steered it into the wall.

"What did she look like?" He grabbed her by the shoulders, and only refrained from shaking her when she began babbling in fear.

"I don't know! A lady. Dressed in green—"

"Pale green?" That was what Ava had been wearing when she left the house that morning.

The girl nodded in fright.

"Where is she now?"

"I didn't see what happened to her," the girl blurted.

"Leave her be," the duke commanded, turning this way and that through the crowd. "She's not here. She went this way." Malloryn started running.

Why would she leave the scene of the crime? Kincaid sprinted after the duke, his coattails flapping. "It's unlike her to leave injured people behind."

"Agreed." The duke paused in the next intersection. The arrow spun. "This way."

Left. Down a smaller street, then across another. "You think she's been taken?"

"Possibly," Malloryn called, sliding to a panting halt as he stared up at a small house across the street from them. "Unless she was injured and the craving virus overtook her. Then she might have sought privacy, away from any potential victims."

That made sense too.

Malloryn's head tilted sharply. His face paled. "I can hear her. She's in there." Kincaid shoved past him, and the duke caught him at the gate to a small Georgian townhouse.

"Have you got your pistol?" he demanded.

"Do I need it?" Kincaid replied.

"I don't know." Malloryn pushed on ahead of him, snapping the tracking device shut. "But I can hear Ava screaming. Be ready for anything."

The oddest thoughts kept running through Ava's head as she tried to still her panic. CV levels: 23 percent. And seven minutes of paralysis... possibly more. Seven and a half? Ava groggily forced herself to count. Curse her confounded desire to not drink blood. If she had, then perhaps her CV levels would be higher, and she might have begun to pull out of this already.

As it was, 23 percent CV levels meant at least eight minutes' worth of paralysis via hemlock, she deduced, as the stranger used his shoulder to push through a door into a small house, and what was clearly a kitchen. Every blue blood reacted to hemlock differently, depending upon how far gone they were with the craving and what their CV levels were.

A teakettle hissed on the stove, and sirens wailed in the distance. Ava was nothing but a passenger, a witness in her own body, unable to control a single thing about her destiny. The last time she'd felt like this was when Hague kidnapped her.

"Bloody thing," the *dhampir* muttered, wincing at the kettle's high-pitched whistle, and then looking up as the stairs creaked beneath the weight of someone.

Don't come down, Ava wanted to scream, but nothing was working, least of all her throat muscles. She could barely even breathe.

"Aye, aye," a woman's voice called down the stairs, "I'll put the bloody cat out, you old fool. It's the least—"

The woman's voice cut off. Ava couldn't see what happened, but she heard the gasp.

"Here now! What are you doing in here? What have

243

you done to that poor girl—"

The *dhampir* smoothly drew his pistol and it retorted with a sharp bark.

No! A choked noise came from Ava's throat. His body had turned just enough for her to see the little old lady go down like a puppet with its strings cut, tumbling down the last three steps, and Ava's fingers twitched.

"Shit," the *dhampir* muttered, slinging Ava into a chair and propping her there, before he crossed to the corpse and scraped a hand over his mouth. "Shit, shit, shit."

"Geraldine?" a man's voice called from upstairs. "What happened? I thought I heard a bump? Did that blasted cat trip you up?"

Nine minutes.

She was starting to come round. She could feel her feet at least. Ava flopped and wiggled, throwing her body to the side as much as possible. The chair tipped on two legs... then went over with a bang, sending her sprawling onto the floor where she hit her head and split her lip.

She ignored the pain. *Please, please let the old man have heard me....*

The *dhampir* took the stairs two at a time, his pistol held against his thigh. No. *No!* An almost moan came from her lips.

"Here now—"

Three gunshot retorts echoed and Ava gasped hopelessly as something heavy hit the floor above.

She had to get out of here.

The *dhampir* seemed unlike the Zero they'd all spoken of last month. "*Zero moved almost faster than I could see,*" Kincaid had muttered when Ava fixed up his nose.

"*Took down Byrnes, and he's good,*" Ingrid had added.

This fellow seemed young and inexperienced. Maybe he was freshly made? A new agent of the faceless enemy that worked against them. Maybe she could use that.

A cat hissed somewhere in the house, and more gunfire echoed. There was a furious animal snarl, and then a curse. Something smashed. The cat hissed again.

Come on. Ava swallowed, trying to make her fingers move again. The paralysis finally seemed to be wearing off, and there was a rush of heat through her veins as if the craving virus fought off the hemlock within her. She could smell blood. Geraldine's. The sudden surge of interest from the darker side of her locked on it, and Ava instinctively quashed it down, before realizing the craving could help her. In a heightened state of bloodlust, a blue blood was stronger, faster, even more deadly.

Possibly able to quell the hemlock in her veins faster.

Ava swallowed, thinking of blood. The thought left her both queasy and interested. *Not helping.* Damn it. Her natural reticence to drinking blood worked against her.

Think of... what? Was there anything about the bloodletting experience that excited her?

Kincaid. Her face flushed with heat, but now wasn't the time for missish delicacy. She'd been trying to forget the moment they'd shared in the gardens of a pleasure house a month ago. Now she forced the memory to mind. His hands on her upper arms, squeezing gently. His coat around her shoulders. The scent of him, all mechanical oil, cigars, bay rum, and something... something uniquely him. The scent of his skin, his sweat, his tooth cream, his arousal.... The way the vein in his throat suddenly seemed to pulse, as if it were calling out to her.

Heat flooded through her. Arousal. *Yes.* The color began draining from the room, which was precisely what she wanted.

Another crash echoed above. Her abductor was clearly wasting time looking for the cat.

She let her imagination roam, picturing what might have happened if she wasn't a lady, and if Kincaid wasn't disgusted by the bloodletting process. She could almost taste his skin beneath her lips, and what it would feel like to trace her tongue over the vein there....

"*He-pp.*" Ava licked the blood from her lips to wake the predator within her. Her tongue seemed heavy but she was once more in command of it, and it was getting easier to blink. Easier to twitch her fingers and toes. She was nearly there.

He must have heard the noise.

Footsteps paused above her, then turned unerringly toward the stairs. The cat kept making that horrible yowling sound in its throat, but the *dhampir* ignored it. His heels thundered on the staircase, and Ava forced herself to move, to crawl.

"Where do you think you're going, Miss McLaren?"

Too late.

Frustration tore through her. She was so close to burning the poison out of her blood, and her inner predator was definitely sitting just beneath the surface. The *dhampir* knelt in front of her and hauled her upright, taking in the jerky movement of her hand, and Ava's gaze locked on his throat. "I'm an idiot," he muttered, slinging her back into the chair, and then looking around, patting at his pockets.

No more hemlock, she guessed.

His eyes lit on a tea towel, which he tore into strips and used to bind her arms to the chair.

"That's better," he muttered.

Poor Geraldine stared sightlessly at the wall, a black-red flower of blood blooming in the middle of her forehead. Ava's vision kept coming in and out of color.

"Shit," her abductor swore again. "Ghost is not going

to appreciate this mess." He seemed to realize the water cart sirens outside were still wailing, and looked at her. "All right, let's do this." Reaching inside his waistcoat, he produced a small leather satchel and unrolled it on the kitchen counter.

Ava flinched back as far as she could.

"What... do you... want with me?" Or at least that's what she tried to say. Everything tingled. "What are you... doing?"

"I'm only obeying orders." The *dhampir* plunged a syringe into a wax-sealed vial, drawing up some sort of pale green liquid inside. "Relax, Miss McLaren. This won't hurt too much and then it will all be over."

No. *No.*

She twitched, forcing weak limbs to obey her.

The last time she'd been a prisoner of a man she'd been powerless too. And he'd hurt her, destroyed her life. Ava's vision dipped through shades of gray, the color bleaching from the world around her as some inner rage she'd never recognized rose like a snarling animal.

She'd felt the craving take her over before, when she'd smelled blood in the early days of her infection, or when emotion overtook her.

But this time she embraced it.

Feeling flooded along her limbs, along with the surge of blood. The killer looked at her, as if he'd sensed something different, and his lips thinned. "That's enough of that."

Stabbing the syringe into her neck, he pumped her full of a cold substance that burned through her veins.

Ava screamed, a gargle of sound that scraped her throat raw. A flash fire of arctic cold filled her body, flooding her vision with red. She could smell blood. Taste it in her mouth. Something cool slid down her cheek. Ava touched it, finding a tear of glistening black, that would probably be a bluish red if her vision was normal, and the irony bit her. She hadn't been able to shed a single tear since her infection, only this single bead of blood....

There was a coldness in her chest that made her lungs ache, but her clockwork heart ticked on, pumping blood through her system. It hurt. So much. But this was not the worst she'd ever endured. Pain was an old friend. Hague had hurt her worse than this *dhampir* could ever dream. Ava clenched her teeth, embracing the predator within her, and then slowly looked up.

The relief in the *dhampir's* expression wavered, his eyes darting to the syringe in his hand, then back to her face again. Whatever reaction he'd expected from her, this was not it.

Ava flexed her arms, a growl of rage filling her throat. Not again. Never again. Hague flashed into her vision, overriding the *dhampir's* face. One rope tore apart under the force of her arm, and then she turned and spun the chair against the wall, smashing it to bits, the other rope still dangling loosely from her wrist. The veins in the back of her hands were almost bruised, as though something was wrong with her blood, but her heart ticked on.

"How?" the *dhampir* barked, grabbing hold of her arms. "How are you doing this?"

Ava drove a piece of chair leg into his abdomen. A hand flashed up, smashing her across the face, and pain exploded through her jaw. She staggered back into the counter, and then he was there, grappling with her, the steel syringe clattering to the floor.

Red, red everywhere. It was all she could see. That and Hague, smiling down at her like a father as he cut the stitches out of her chest that last time. *"You're my finest creation, Miss McLaren."*

Ava kicked and fought, overwhelmed by only one desire: to kill.

"That," she snarled, stabbing him again, "is for that poor old lady!" Again. "And her husband!" Again. "And that little girl I nearly ran over—"

A hand caught her wrist and her suddenly nerveless fingers dropped the makeshift stake.

"Bitch." He caught her by the throat and kicked her feet out from under her. They both went down, Ava hampered by her skirts. His weight overpowered her, but she was fueled by something she'd never felt before.

She screamed a scream of pure rage, raking at his face and shoulders with her nails, wishing, *damn her*, she'd learned how to fight better when Byrnes taught her the basics. Pain bloomed through her hand.

"Stay down!" the *dhampir* hissed, but he looked frightened, as though he hadn't expected any of this. He clapped one hand over her mouth and nose, and the other over her throat. "The serum should have worked. What are you?"

She couldn't breathe.

But she hadn't been able to breathe a long time ago, and she'd survived that too.

"It should have stopped your heart," the *dhampir* yelled, and Ava suddenly understood.

Her cursed clockwork heart had just saved her life.

She rolled her head from side to side, trying to throw him off. No help for it. He was too strong. But... she caught a glimpse of the syringe in the corner of her eye, half an inch of milky green liquid inside it.

Pressure popped behind her eyes. Her lungs heaved. Color was starting to come back to the edges of the room, as though the craving was retreating, the predator silenced by lack of air.

Ava's groping hand reached for the syringe. *Nothing. Nothing.* Her vision swam. She didn't want it to end like this. There was too much she hadn't done, too much she hadn't seen. A life lived in a laboratory. Hiding in her books. Keeping her emotions and life strictly controlled. No blood. No Kincaid....

Her fingers closed over the syringe. Ava drove it into her assailant's side, pumping the rest of the dose into him.

His body arched instantly, a scream tearing from his lips. She could breathe again. Move. Ava shoved her way out from under him as he fell into convulsions on the floor, and then the door burst open, and—

Kincaid and Malloryn burst in, pistols drawn.

"Blood and steel," Malloryn muttered, lowering his pistol a little as the *dhampir* thrashed.

Ava groaned, rocking on her hands and knees. Something hurt deep inside. There was blood in her mouth, and the veins across the back of her hands pulsed, as if liquid mercury slid through them.

"Ava!" Kincaid sheathed his pistol, his face tight with concern. The color fled from his skin. "Jaysus, Ava!"

Malloryn kicked her attacker over onto his back, pointing the pistol warningly, but the *dhampir's* heels drummed on the floor, a bloodied froth forming at his mouth. Ava's mouth dropped open. That could have been her. It *should* have been her.

"What happened to him?" Malloryn barked.

"She's hurt." Kincaid knelt beside her, soothing a hand up her spine. "Jaysus, look at her face. Ava? Are you all right, sweetheart?"

The craving virus returned with force, the scent of Kincaid's body overwhelming her. All she wanted was to bury her blunt teeth in his throat, and drain him dry.

Not Kincaid. He'd never forgive her. "Leave me alone!"

She scrambled into the corner, her hands curled in claws and her body trembling as pain overtook her.

"Ava!" The cursed man came after her. "Ava, we're here. You're okay. We've got you." His rough voice thickened. "*I've* got you."

There was an unspoken message there she didn't have time to study. A sudden urge overtook her and Ava started coughing, blood spraying across her black-marbled hands.

Whatever the *dhampir* had injected her with, it hadn't finished wreaking havoc within her.

CHAPTER
NINETEEN

THERE WERE FEW things in Kincaid's life that had ever frightened him. Seeing Ava like this gutted him. Absolutely gutted him.

Especially when he considered their stupid fucking argument. He hadn't cared then if innocent people were hurt. All he'd thought about was bringing the blue bloods of the Echelon down, but Ava was right. Innocents would suffer, and until *she* was the one who'd nearly died, a part of him hadn't understood that.

Guilt ravaged him. She should have died. There was no reason for her to have survived. But somehow she had, and though he'd not prayed to any gods in years, he was praying now. *Please. Please let her survive this.*

She shuddered against his chest, her face streaked with blood and her skirts torn and ragged. Kincaid squeezed her gently. It was one thing to know the Company of Rogues agents walked into danger every time they faced these bastards—quite another to think of Ava in that same danger.

"I've got you," he muttered.

A shaky hand curled in his shirt, and Ava tilted her face up to his, her breath cool across his throat.

"What is it, sweetheart?"

She suddenly pushed him away, hiding her face in her hands, her shoulders shaking. Kincaid reached for her face, feeling sick to his gut. What had the bastard done to her? Had he touched her? Tortured her? Kincaid brushed some of her loose curls behind her ear. There was bluish blood all over her face, her lips. He wanted to kill the prick, but the truth was, she needed him at her side more than Kincaid needed to vent his feelings. "Are you hurt? Did I squeeze you too hard?"

A hand on his chest stayed him.

"She needs blood," Malloryn said, three simple words cutting like a scythe through the tremble in his heart.

Blood.

All of them knew his thoughts on the process of bloodletting. As much as he'd begun to accept the blue bloods he worked with, they took their blood in private, or out of a flask. He could handle that. It was the thought of one of them using a little razor on him—or someone else, right in front of him—that made the muscle in his jaw tic.

"No blood," Ava ground out, scrambling out of Kincaid's lap and tucking her knees up against her chest. She looked up, her eyes as black as pitch, and the breath went out of him. "Not right now. I can't control it."

Shit. Malloryn was right. The predator in her was right beneath the surface. Every vein in her face stood out as though black ink filled it, particularly under her eyes. She looked terrible.

She looked like the *dhampir* had, before he died.

Or like David Thomas.

Everything in Kincaid went cold. Everything. Hadn't she said it herself? *"If you put this weapon in the wrong hands,*

Kincaid, then you cannot tell me innocent people won't die...."

But he'd never thought Ava would be the one stricken down by Black Vein. He'd never... put a face to the nameless, faceless enemy in his mind when he thought of finally destroying the blue bloods with this weapon.

Why wasn't she dying? It felt like there was a hand around his chest, squeezing, squeezing....

"Where's my... my solution?" Ava patted at her skirts, hunting for any sign of the reticule she normally carried, even though it was nowhere to be found.

"I assume you lost it in the scuffle. The closest flask we know of is back at the house," Malloryn explained in the kind of tone one used on a child. "You're not yourself right now, Ava. We can't risk taking you out into the streets like this. All you'll see is prey when you look around you, and you've been resisting for so long you have no control when the bloodlust rises—"

"I *have* control," she snarled, and then froze, as if hearing the anger in her words. A twist of horror crossed her face. "He injected me with something. Said it would stop my heart, but of course it didn't, and now—"

Her clockwork heart.

"It's not your fault." Again Malloryn sounded exceedingly patient. "We can run tests on what he gave you back at the laboratory, but right now your bloodlust's been triggered. We need to deal with it first, and your injuries. You're bleeding internally."

"I'm fine." She coughed even as she said it, spraying blood across her cupped palm.

Malloryn looked at him, and that was when Kincaid knew what the duke was silently asking.

No. No way. He was nobody's blood whore.

Not even for Ava?

His stomach twisted. She was injured, and she needed

blood, but... all he could see was Agatha, swaying from the rafters of his house as he screamed and begged for her to come back.

Malloryn saw it on his face, and gave a little nod. "Here." The duke began unbuttoning his sleeve to reveal his wrist. "I'll do it."

And that was all shades of wrong. Kincaid's vision went white and he turned around, clasping both hands behind his head. The idea of Ava sucking on the duke's wrist made him want to punch something—though he had to admit the thought of her drinking blood wasn't the prime cause of that emotion.

Jealousy?

Shit. He shot her a look, finding her backing away from the duke, scrambling across the tiles, her gaze locked on the vein in Malloryn's wrist with a hunger she couldn't hide. *Yes* and *no* warred within her, and suddenly his hatred for bloodletting washed away. This was Ava he was thinking about. Not some leering blue blood lord who thought all humans were cattle. Not the bastards who'd used his sister like their own blood whore for the night, before casting her out into the streets.

Kincaid rubbed at his chest as Malloryn drew a small bloodletting blade from the kit in his pocket and placed the razor over the vein.

"My CV levels are in the high fifties, so the cut won't stay open for long," Malloryn warned. "You cannot fight through this, Ava, not without the predator taking over at some stage. Take a little blood to calm it down, and then we can return to the safe house and find your flask for you. Your body needs to heal too, judging by the look of you. You're very lucky."

"*Please*," Ava panted, but she couldn't look away from the razor. "Please, no. I can do this." She squeezed her eyes shut. "I don't want your blood."

Kincaid could see the lie on her face. "Malloryn's right," he said gruffly, surprised to hear himself say it. "A little blood from... from Malloryn, and then it will be safe to take you home and get your flask."

"Can you hold my hand?" she whispered.

His gut churned.

"I don't think that's safe," Malloryn interrupted, watching the pair of them. When Kincaid's gaze jerked to him, Malloryn shrugged. "You're human. Your blood smells and tastes better, and you won't be able to hold her off if she goes for your throat."

Another slap in the face. Another reminder of what she was. Hell, when had he stopped thinking of Ava as a blue blood?

But this was no easier for her than it was for him. *Can you hold my hand?* A plea, as if the thought of this hurt her too.

"I'll hold your hand if you need me to," he said, tilting his head toward the razor. "Distract her. And keep her off me if you need to."

Malloryn arched a brow, but turned back to Ava. "Ready?"

She swallowed. "Ready."

The razor pressed a white indentation along Malloryn's wrist, which instantly filled with bluish-red blood. Ava moaned, and Malloryn cupped the back of her head and put his wrist to her lips as though he'd done this a thousand times.

Kincaid knelt beside them, slipping his fingers through hers. He hated seeing her like this. Hated seeing Malloryn's wrist at her lips, in some vaguely primitive way that needed further investigation when he had time to himself to think, but this was about Ava now. "That's it, sweetheart." He stroked her hair, brushing it off her face and fingering one silky curl.

It wrapped around his finger, and he rubbed the end of it between thumb and forefinger, marveling at the sensation.

Ava's eyes lifted from where she clutched at Malloryn's hand, her lips around the duke's wrist. They were pure black, like a demon's, but something about the moment made his cock harden.

Malloryn looked away.

And Kincaid remembered the one thing he'd forgotten in all of this: a blue blood's saliva had chemicals in it that could incite ecstasy in their victims. It was the ultimate weapon for a predator like a blue blood, and though it affected people on different levels, it was the thing that had turned his sister, Agatha, from a girl with a promising future to a young woman who couldn't sleep, couldn't stop itching at her skin, craving the touch of a blue blood's mouth on her flesh.

Kincaid and Malloryn locked eyes. If the duke was finding pleasure in this moment then Kincaid was going to kill him.

Slowly.

But only once they got Ava to safety.

Evening fell.

Ava woke to find someone lighting the candles beside her bed. For a second she didn't know where she was, or who was in her room. Her heart leaped into her throat, and then she recognized the rough stubble along the man's jaw, and the brief flex of the pistons in his mech hand.

Kincaid.

Ava shivered a little, her body relaxing. Everything hurt, including her sprained wrist. Kincaid had bound it up earlier in a sling, but for a blue blood, the only thing to do was wait. She'd be fully healed in a day or two.

"Sorry. Didn't mean to frighten you." He blew on the end of the taper, extinguishing the small flame. "I know you don't like the dark."

And so he'd been making sure she wouldn't wake in it. His care toward her was almost... sweet, if one were trying to find the right word. *Sweet* and *Kincaid* were two words she would never have put together until now.

He dragged a stool closer to the bed, resting his elbows on the coverlet, though he watched her carefully. "How are you feeling?"

"I'm not going to attack you," she blurted, tucking the covers up under her chin.

He blinked. "I know."

"I just...."

His hand captured hers, warmth cocooning her. "I know," he repeated, and squeezed gently. "You were hurt and injured, and you needed blood. I'm starting to understand that. I wish I'd been able to donate. I wish...."

Ava squeezed her eyes shut, licking dry lips. The worst part of that morning's escapade was the fact now she wanted more of it. One taste and she craved hot, sweet blood. All these months she'd been telling herself her protein solution could sustain her, but it was nothing like the real thing. She felt like something dark had awoken inside her, and now it burned there, whispering seductive thoughts to her.

Like how close Kincaid sat, the scent of his cologne acting like an aphrodisiac. She wasn't certain whether she wanted to bite him—or kiss him. The urge rode through her body like a carpenter's file over her nerves. She couldn't help shifting, her thighs rubbing together temptingly. Wanting. Craving.

Blood and ashes. She was far too alive, far too aware, far too... hungry. For something, anything.

He was still talking. "...I'm so sorry, Ava. So sorry. You were right about the caterpillar mushroom. About using it as a weapon. Innocent people would die. *You* nearly died, and I would cut my own heart out before I ever let you get hurt."

"It's all right. I know you weren't thinking of the consequences—you saw only the possibilities, only the cause you sacrificed your life to."

He drew her hand to his lips, pressing a kiss to her fingers. "They took everything from me," he whispered hoarsely. "They killed my sister, turned her into something I didn't even recognize, and she couldn't live with that anymore. She killed herself. And I've hated blue bloods for so long, it's hard to realign my thinking. But seeing you like that today.... Jaysus. I couldn't do anything to help you. And you're lucky. So lucky your heart is made of clockwork."

She looked away, haunted by ghosts.

"I nearly lost you," Kincaid breathed, and curled her hand in both of his. "And I didn't realize until that moment how much you meant to me. How much losing you would hurt."

"It's okay," she whispered, stroking his hair from his brow. Her heart ticked inexorably on, but it felt like it should be racing. What did he mean by that? She felt like she stood on the precipice of a turning point, as though her future was suddenly very uncertain. "We had a lucky turn of events, and now we know what the caterpillar mushroom does to a blue blood."

"You were still coughing blood before you went to

sleep."

"I'm fine," she whispered. "I feel normal again."

Dark lashes obscured Kincaid's eyes as he glanced down, his thumb pausing right there on her vein. "I should have been the one to offer my blood."

What? She sat up a little straighter. Of all the things to say.... Couldn't he see how on edge she was? "*No.*"

"You don't *want* my blood?"

"No... I... Yes. Yes, of course." Plague him. "Who else is here?"

"Malloryn's returned home," he replied gently, "possibly to dwell on what you told us about the attack. Jack's in the basement I think, and I'm not sure if Charlie's around. He often goes out at night, and Malloryn wanted a report on what people are saying about the attack. Apart from that...." His expression suddenly froze, as if he'd finally caught the thread of where she was going with this line of questioning. Then he relaxed. "You're safe, Ava. I know you're not going to attack me, if that's what you're afraid of."

Safe? What a fool he was. She could still feel it brewing within her, a darkness full of hungry teeth. Maybe she had survived the caterpillar mushroom, but at what cost? For she didn't feel normal. She felt like all her safe trappings had been ripped away, and she was unmoored from her sanctuary.

She felt angry, and hungry, and not at all herself.

It was like living through those first horrible weeks when she'd been stricken with the craving and her body changed, flooding her with desires she'd never felt before. When lust became an all-consuming thought, and all she could think about was blood.

"Well, I *don't* know that!" Ava cried, feeling her vision drop from color to black-and-white shadows. She could hear his heart pounding. "If I let myself go for just one second... maybe I *would* be the monster you fear? Maybe I'd—"

Strong arms went around her. "You're not a monster, Ava. You just don't have it in you."

She fought against him for a second, but the warmth of his body was so damned sweet. Ava pressed her face into his shoulder. *Don't let me go. Please, don't ever let me go.* But beneath that sweetness was a restless ache. Ava cradled her sprained wrist carefully against him, breathing in his cologne. "I'm scared."

Today had terrified her, taking her straight back into the past. Being paralyzed was almost worse than anything Hague had done to her, for while she'd thought his chains and the straps tying her down made her helpless, she'd still been in some semblance of control of her body. "I couldn't move," she whispered. "I couldn't move my body. I couldn't even cry out."

"Hush, sweetheart." He kissed her cheek, his roughened stubble rasping against her. "You're safe now. You can move. Your body's your own."

But the fear remained. Ava grabbed a handful of Kincaid's hair, pressing her forehead against his. Her body was her own again. She was in control, and what she wanted was to make that clear—to herself.

She shoved him onto his back, and Kincaid hit the bed with a startled noise. He blinked up at her. "Ava, luv."

But she set both hands firmly on his chest and straddled him, her nightgown riding up around her thighs. Kincaid cursed under his breath, capturing her wrist with his human hand, his mech hand resting lightly on her thigh. "Ava, just what's going on?" Kincaid's whisper made the devil sound like a saint.

He knew, damn him.

"I'm tired of being treated like I'm made of porcelain," she whispered.

Thought shadowed his gaze, and it dropped to her lips. "You had a fright today—"

"Don't you dare!" she snapped.

The outburst startled both of them.

"I don't need to be wrapped in swaddling clothes, or treated as though I'm fragile." Maybe she had once, but she'd healed enough now. And that feeling of discontent brewed deep within her. She felt like she'd stayed in stasis for the past few years, and she was so damned tired of it she wanted to smash something. "You promised me an affair. You promised me experience, damn it, and to this point there's been far too much talking and not enough actually doing. And I haven't forgotten what you said yesterday, but right now, I *need* you. I need you."

"I don't want to take advantage of your emotions," Kincaid ground out, a flush of heat igniting along his cheekbones. His mech hand tickled her thigh, the smooth metal pads of his fingertips cool against her skin. "And if you want to pretend today didn't cost you something, then you can, but the black in your eyes reveals the lie of that. Today was the first time you've taken blood in months. Don't deny it didn't affect you."

"I'm not...." She pressed her lips firmly together. "I don't want blood now."

"Then why—"

"Because I want you! That's why my god-cursed eyes are black! Because I want you to touch me, and it hurts." Her hands clenched in her nightgown. "My skin feels like I'm wearing roughened hessian sackcloth over it. Everything aches. Everything. I want... I want you to bed me."

Kincaid looked taken aback.

She never raised her voice. She never yelled. "I'm sorry—"

The devil actually laughed, his entire body shaking. Ava glared down at him, feeling the darkness roll through her. "Stop it! Stop laughing at me!"

Kincaid reached up, grabbing hold of the back of her head as he rose. "I'm not laughing *at* you."

And then he kissed her.

Ava moaned into his mouth, her tongue darting over his, and her hands curling in his shirt, desperate for the feel of his body. The steel of his erection pressed against her inner thigh, and his arms captured her against his chest, her breasts pressing against the hard slab of his pectorals.

Then they were rolling, and Ava found herself beneath him, her thighs spreading as his weight pushed her into the mattress. Kincaid captured her mouth greedily, as if today had been just as frightening for him and he needed reaffirmation. Her body came alive, restless and driven by the primal hunger within her. Ava moaned, and sank her fists into his hair, silently demanding more.

"*Ava.*" Half-groan, half-surrender. "Merciful heavens, you're so fucking perfect."

His hand slid down to cup her hip, and then he thrust against her, and the shock of his hard cock pressing against her clitoris made her flinch.

Kincaid froze, as if he'd felt it.

"I'm sorry," she whispered, fingers splaying across his back to keep him there. "I didn't mean it. It was just... the surprise. The feeling of it."

She wanted more, but she didn't know how to ask for it.

"Don't apologize then. I want you to speak your mind when you're with me. And I think I'm starting to finally understand you," he rasped, looking down at her. "The past few years you've kept all your desires under lock and key, haven't you? No blood. No sex." He punctuated this statement with a taunting rock of his hips. Ava's mind went blank, and she clutched at his upper arms, desperate for him to push against her again. But he hadn't finished. Kincaid's stubble rasped against her jaw, and he bit her earlobe. "You said you wanted to experience passion, and I think it's more than that. I think something inside you chafes at the control. Everyone thinks you're sweetness and light, but I think there's something in there that's a little bit dark. I think some part of you wants to be naughty." He licked her ear, making her writhe. "It wants to unleash itself and do wicked, wicked things. I think there's a passionate woman inside you, and she's tired of being locked away. She's tired of being polite, and letting other people have their way while she sips her protein solution. She wants to yell at me, and dig her nails into my back while I kiss her, doesn't she?"

Ava shivered. He couldn't be right, could he? "It's dangerous to let myself lose control. You, of all people, should know that."

Kincaid reared up onto his hands and knees, staring down at her. She started to sit up in protest, but he pressed a hand flat between her breasts and pushed her back down. "Don't move," he told her, with a wicked gleam in his blue eyes.

A thrill ran through her. "What are you doing?"

"Maybe there's a way for you to experience passion, and still keep control?" Reaching out, he tugged gently on the little bow at her neckline, pulling each string loose.

And suddenly she was aware of just how little she was wearing.

Ava didn't dare say a thing. Her body was on edge, trembling just a little. Her wrists were pressed to the mattress in silent submission. She was terribly aware if she said something she might break the spell and then he'd stop, and she didn't want him to stop. Not at all.

"Did you know," he said, almost conversationally, "I'm the only person you ever yell at?"

"I'm so—"

His fingertip pressed against her lips, stilling the words. "No. Don't apologize for that, Ava. I like it when you get angry, because you let me see the real you. I'm not interested in a passionless automaton. I want *you*. I want the Ava that hides within, the Ava I see in your eyes whenever I say anything idiotic and you glare at me. And I want her, because nobody else ever gets to see her."

Slowly, he dragged his finger from her lips, down her throat and lower, parting her ravaged neckline and tickling across the silk-slick surface of the scar between her breasts.

He paused there, and Ava froze. She could almost feel his eyes locking on the heavy scar between her breasts. Hague's mark. Grabbing her nightgown, she tried to draw both edges together, but Kincaid caught her wrists and forced them back to the mattress.

"I said, don't move." This time his voice was smoke-roughened. It pulled at things *inside* her.

"I hate it."

He bent his head as if to examine the scar, and Ava turned her face away. "I don't," he whispered, and the hot flick of his tongue across her scar made her suck in a sharp breath. "If you didn't have a clockwork heart, then you would have died today. It's a part of you now, angel, and there's not a damned inch of you that's not perfect."

Ava sucked in a deep breath. His mouth parted and she could feel it pressing hot, open-mouthed kisses between her breasts.

"Kincaid." She grabbed his hair, and lifted his mouth

to hers. His body drove her down into the mattress again, but he captured her lips and suddenly she couldn't think.

It all felt so very, very good.

Ava ached, her nipples chafing beneath the press of her linen nightgown, her unbound breasts peculiarly heavy and... aware. Some part of her wanted to reach for his hand and place it there. To arch into his touch and beg for more. Ava slid her hands beneath the shirt he wore, drinking in the sensation of his bare skin beneath her palms. All her blood seemed to stampede into her head, leaving her light-headed and swaying against him. She kissed his jaw, her lips stinging with the scrape of his stubble, then lower, her tongue darting out to taste the beckoning kick of his pulse, and then—

More kisses.

More of those delightfully shiver-inducing caresses as his lips made their way down her neck.

More....

Unbidden, the images from the art gallery sprang to mind. A woman on her back, her thighs spread like a luxurious banquet as some man feasted between them. A woman on her hands and knees, a hand arching her head back as the swarthy figure behind her thrust his way between those thighs.

Heat filled her cheeks. The color in the room dropped away. And suddenly Ava was fighting against the dark nature of the predator within her, but this time it didn't want blood. This time it wanted flesh, wanted to submit beneath the rough steel and warm skin of this man's hands.

And this time, she wanted to let it rule her.

Ava sucked in a sharp breath. Kincaid's body aligned with hers so thoroughly she knew she was blushing again. There was something hard against her hip, his belt buckle digging into her belly. The sensation set off some sort of wild feeling within her, the craving surging through her veins. *Yes.* She bared her teeth, tilting her face away from him as urges she'd never felt before beat sharply in her heart.

"If I lose control, then stop me," she blurted.

She could feel him smile against the side of her breast. "I promise. You're safe here, Ava. You're the one who dictates how far this goes, but I'm in control."

Kincaid reared up on his knees, reaching over his head to drag his shirt off. He tossed it aside, revealing a massive chest sprinkled with dark hair. Scars marred his smooth skin here and there, and Ava lay back in pliant surrender as she looked her fill. She'd seen naked men before, but not like this. The reality of Kincaid in the flesh was quite shocking. She knew what his mech arm looked like, and the ragged, puckered scar where the limb had been taken didn't so much mar him as enhance the dangerous perfection of him. But it was the rest of him that made her eyes round.

He wasn't built like the men she knew, with narrow hips and broad shoulders that tapered to a V at the waist. He was huge, with hard knotted cords of muscle that raked his abdomen, and a deeply chiseled V at the hips that plunged into his trousers. The firm press of his erection left her slightly breathless. Hidden away, it still seemed enormous and vaguely threatening.

Ava swallowed.

All that stood between them was her flimsy nightgown and his trousers. And suddenly it wasn't enough.

"Nervous?" he whispered, leaning over her, one hand on either side of her head.

The bed dipped beneath her. "No."

"*Liar.*" A chuckle ripped through him as he leaned down, nuzzling at her jaw. "One of the things I like most about you, sweetheart, is the fact you can't hide a damned thing from me."

His kiss tickled. She shivered, her hands drawn up between them, hovering there indecisively.

She couldn't stop thinking of that image in the gallery, of the man's straining erection. Her cheeks burned.

"You're not ready," Kincaid murmured, his lips skating across her cheek, then her lips.

What? She most certainly was. "I—"

"So we'll play tonight," he continued, as if she hadn't spoken, "but I'm not taking you."

"You promised."

He lowered himself onto one elbow, pressing between her thighs again as he took her hand and opened her palm over his chest. "And we'll get there, gorgeous." His breath stirred the tiny hairs along the side of her ear. "But there's no rush. You wanted passion, not just to lose your maidenhead. So I'll give you passion, Ava." His mouth opened over her lips, his hand encouraging hers to explore the hard plane of his chest. "Tell me... what was your favorite painting?"

"Painting?"

"I know the answer," he whispered, capturing her mouth in a harsh kiss that stole her breath. Her hand was trapped between them, his chest pressing against her breasts. "You liked it... when he kissed her."

Kissed her? She couldn't remember seeing anything quite so innocent as that.

But Kincaid's other hand was moving, dragging her nightgown up, its hem skating over her sensitive thighs, and suddenly she knew what he was referring to.

Not a kiss on the mouth.

But there....

Her eyes shot wide and he was smiling down at her, looking so very, very wicked. "What's wrong, sweetheart?"

"Now?" she blurted.

"Now," he confirmed, and laced his fingers between hers, pressing her hand back onto the bed.

The time for exploring was over.

She'd barely even gotten the chance to touch him, but that didn't matter, for he was certainly interested in doing some touching of his own....

Ava arched her spine, alternatively shrinking beneath him and grinding against him as his hips flexed against her. That heavy weight was no longer pressed unthreateningly against her leg. It lined up right between her thighs, the insistent rub leaving her wide-open and vulnerable. There was another tug, and her nightgown slipped up and suddenly there was nothing but her drawers between her and the slick rasp of his buttons.

Blood and ashes. Ava didn't realize she was curling her fingers through his until pain bit through her wrist, and then she looked up and he was looking down at her, an intense look of focus in those eyes, as though he could see every flicker of need that crossed her face.

Kincaid bit her throat and it set every nerve in her body alight, his dull teeth driving into her bare skin. Ava cried out, halfway to destroyed. She didn't know what she wanted, but more... just more of it.

"That's it, kitten."

He brushed the neckline of her nightgown aside, revealing her breast. Ava's bare nipple ached. She'd never had a man's eyes on her, not like this. Kincaid captured the aching peak between his lips, and she cried out as his rough tongue circled her nipple.

Then he drew back.

His hips shifted, his cock riding over her clitoris, and suddenly she sobbed, so wound up she felt like she might erupt into a whirlwind of movement. "What are you doing?" The words tore from her lips.

She'd been so close to orgasm.

Her body jerked as he kissed her clavicle, his lips brushing against the lacy scalloped edge of her nightgown. His breath stirred her nipple and she writhed, her hand clenching his again.

She didn't want to let go of him. Somehow his fingers held her together when she was so frightened she'd fall apart.

"I want you under my tongue when you come, Ava," Kincaid ground out, and the words did something to her as his hot mouth closed over her other nipple, dampening the cotton of her nightgown.

She moaned, a desperate, begging kind of sound.

"I want to taste your sweet little cunt." A flinch of her hips at the word. Then he suckled her into his mouth, and her womb clenched with need.

"Please... *oh*."

"That's it, sweetheart."

Somehow her free hand tangled in his hair. Ava gasped and rocked as Kincaid made his way lower, pressing gentle kisses across her stomach, and then lower, dragging her drawers down her legs and spreading her thighs wide with one insistent push of his spare hand.

"Ava," he breathed, and just like that gooseflesh erupted all over her body.

She wanted to be taken. She wanted to be overwhelmed by him, to learn what this desperate ache within her meant and how it would feel to assuage it. She felt so empty, so hollow, and somehow he could take away that pain.

Then his mouth closed over the wet, slick ache between her legs, a devouring kiss that scraped along flesh that had never been touched before. Ava gasped, her hand clenching in his hair. *Oh my God.* His tongue rasped over her, drinking her down, suckling on that small bud between her thighs.

A cry escaped her.

Another.

She felt not at all herself. And maybe that was the point. Beneath his touch, Ava bloomed, like some exotic orchid he'd carelessly plucked for her. All she could see was that bloody painting, and suddenly it was *her* body she saw lying on those silken sheets, and Kincaid's dark head between her thighs, and it set off something within her she'd never known before. Some illicit wickedness that should have shocked her, but she couldn't quite find the breath to be so.

She couldn't escape the pleasure. It built within her like a tide, ready to come crashing down. She was exposed and raw, and somehow this moment would stay with her for the rest of her life. Kincaid nuzzled and licked, and the spring inside her wound tighter until—

Ava screamed.

She had one hand in his hair, the other locked around his hand. Every last lick of his tongue destroyed her, until she was grinding his face between her thighs, sobbing out her pleasure. On and on and on, until she broke. "No more! No more!"

It left her wracked and ruined. Writhing beneath him. Gasping, her back arching off the bed.

She had never in her entire life pictured anything like this. Finally there was relief. Kincaid's dark head lifted and he shuddered against her thigh, his mouth shockingly wet as he kissed her leg gently.

Wet from her body.

Wet from his ministrations.

And then it was over, Kincaid pressing a soft kiss to

her belly as he made his way back up her body.

He laughed under his breath as he dragged her onto her side, curling behind her. "Remind me to bring a gag the next time we do this. Let's hope nobody was home, or our secret's going to be out tomorrow."

Ava buried her face in the pillow as Kincaid slid into the hollow indentation behind her, his hand dragging her back against his body, where she fit, just so.

"I cannot believe you just did that," she whispered.

Kincaid tucked his face into the bare skin at her nape, nuzzling into her unbound hair. "I can't believe I *haven't* done that before with you."

And Ava pressed her hand to her flushed cheeks as he tugged her nightgown down over her bottom, leaving her with some protection from the press of his body.

"Feeling better?" he demanded smugly.

Her wrist hurt, a dull throbbing ache that had been blissfully absent throughout all of that. "Yes." She felt wonderful.

Tomorrow she might be able to look at him without blushing, but tonight was simply too much.

"Next time, you can return the favor," Kincaid whispered, and Ava moaned as an image of her kissing his cock sprang to mind.

CHAPTER TWENTY

BREAKFAST WAS AN ordeal.

"Pass the butter?" the baroness asked politely, and Ava shoved it down the table toward Isabella Rouchard, trying not to look anyone in the eye. Jack was absorbed in the newspaper, the baroness lifted the lid off the tureen to examine the coddled eggs, and there was no sign of Gemma, Charlie or Malloryn.

Probably a good thing. Not much bypassed the duke, and she was almost certain last night's escapades were written across her forehead in a big scarlet letter.

Ava cleared her throat. "Can someone pass the jam?"

Kincaid plucked up the small pot of strawberry jam. "What do you say?"

"Please," she added, then met his eyes, and knew he wasn't talking about jam. Everything inside her flushed with heat. Damn him.

"I like hearing that word on your lips," he said, and the inside joke made her squirm. He slid the little pot across the table toward her, as if he knew it was her favorite. "Sleep well?" he asked, sitting back in his chair and watching her with an entirely amused expression.

You know the answer to that, you devil. After all, he'd been there when she woke up, his body still curled around hers and his fingers toying with her nipple, until he slowly worked them down her abdomen, sinking them inside her and bringing her to another obliteration of the senses. He probably still had her teeth marks on his shoulder, where she'd bitten him to stifle her cries.

"Yes." Ava blushed, and swallowed far too much of her tea in a move that left her sputtering.

Skirts swished and then Gemma was there, elegant in green ruffles as she circled the table. "Feeling better?" Gemma murmured, leaning over her to press a kiss to her cheek.

It was almost exactly the same thing he'd asked her last night, after he'd... he'd....

"Much better," she croaked, her throat still convulsing with the need to cough.

And the bloody bastard simply watched her with amused blue eyes as Gemma patted her on the back and made cooing sounds of concern.

"Where's Malloryn?" Gemma asked, circling the table.

"*Rotting in hell for all I care*," came a mutter from Isabella.

Ava blinked, and so did Gemma, but the baroness merely pasted a smile on her face, lifting her teacup in both hands with dainty precision. She was usually cool and commanding, but watching the man she loved marry another woman had to be difficult for her.

Or perhaps Ava had missed some argument between them.

"So," said the baroness, pretending she'd never spoken. "Malloryn tells me we've had our first official sighting of the *dhampir.*"

Everyone was suddenly all attention.

Kincaid scowled. "One of them tried to kill Ava yesterday." He swiftly filled the baroness and Jack in on events. Gemma already knew, as she'd been to see Ava the night before, and she simply stirred blood into her tea, her eyes shuttered.

"I survived," Ava pointed out.

"But it was close," Kincaid said, and when he looked into her eyes he was no longer smiling.

Gemma cleared her throat. "What did Malloryn do with the body?"

"Which.... The *dhampir* who attacked me?"

Gemma nodded.

"He sent it to the guild," Kincaid replied. "I didn't think Ava would want to be the one who performed that particular autopsy, and Malloryn agreed."

That was thoughtful. "Did you tell Dr. Gibson about Black Vein?"

Kincaid scraped his hand over his newly shaven jaw. "I think Malloryn did. He needed to know what he's looking at."

Silence settled over the room. Ava buttered her toast, though a sudden flash of heat went through her as she added jam. She wanted blood. Not toast. Her fingers curled over the knife.

"Are you sure you're all right?" Gemma murmured, and Ava looked up to find the other woman watching her with narrowed eyes over the rim of a teacup.

"Of course," Ava stammered. "I just think I need a little more rest."

Scraping away from the table, she made her goodbyes, and fled.

A hand shoved him in the chest as he turned the corner on his way up to Ava's room, and then Gemma was there, slamming him back against the wall.

Kincaid let her, holding his hands up in surrender. Their gazes locked, and he saw the fury in her eyes. "Problem?"

Gemma's lips thinned. "Any reason Ava's unable to so much as look at you without blushing this morning?"

Kincaid said nothing.

Gemma growled, turning away with a filthy curse. She shot him a dark look. "You promised—"

"I didn't promise anything. And I tried to stay away from her," he snapped, shoving away from the wall. "It just happened."

"It *just happened?*" she mocked. "Christ, don't pretend you don't know exactly what you're doing when it comes to chasing skirt."

"Ava's different." When Gemma shot him another glare, he held his hands up to placate her. "Nothing happened. Nothing... permanent."

"And is it going to stay that way?"

He said nothing.

"Jesus, Kincaid. She's a bloody virgin—"

"She's tired of being one. She wants to know what passion feels like, and we've reached an agreement."

"An affair? You're going to seduce her and then... what? She's not the usual sort of woman you toy with, Kincaid. Ava's vulnerable. She's too kind, too sweet, too—"

"Have you ever thought she's six-and-twenty, and not a maid fresh off her father's farm? And she's more than sweetness, and kindness. She's a strong, determined woman who could outthink the lot of us," he growled.

"Have you ever thought she just watched the man she

loved marry? And now she wants to start an affair with you?"

He flinched. "I know she did. I know I'm not the one she wanted. But I can't stop her from making a decision like this, and I'll be damned if she goes searching for a remedy with someone who doesn't have her best interests at heart. I'm not going to hurt her, Gemma. Ava's.... You're right, she is too kind. She *is* vulnerable. There's a part of me that likes her a lot—" Those dark blue eyes locked on him. "Even knowing I can't give her what she truly wants, I'm still tempted. I can't marry her, or offer her a future, or...."

Or worse, children.

He wouldn't do that to a child. The curse ran in his blood, and he wouldn't. He couldn't.

"Can't?" Gemma asked softly. "Or won't?"

His nostrils flared. Jaysus. "*Can't*," he croaked.

"Kincaid—"

But he held his hand up to forestall her.

"It's possible I've seen the files Malloryn has on all of us," she continued, despite the gesture. Sympathy flashed through her eyes. "I know what he's asked the Royal College of Physicians to look into. I know your uncle is dying, that you were diagnosed only four years ago—"

"I told her," he rushed to say, scrubbing his hands through his hair. A sudden stab of panic made it hard to breathe. "I'm only just starting to display the symptoms. She doesn't understand. She wants to cure me."

And there was *no* cure for the muscular dystrophy that would eventually stop his heart.

A gentle hand pressed against his arm. Gemma tugged it down, sliding her hands into his, even the mech one. "Is that why you're doing this? Is that why it had to be you?"

He could barely breathe. Orla and Ian were the only ones who knew what he faced. He'd never spoken of it with anyone else. "I don't know. I just wanted her. Ava makes me feel like there's hope in my days. Have you ever looked at someone and felt like you know happiness for the first time in your life? I can't give her up, Gemma. I won't."

Something shifted in Gemma's eyes. "You stupid fool. You *love* her. How did I not see this?"

He pushed away from her, an odd note of panic echoing in his brief laugh. "Love? What's love to a man like me? Or a woman like you?"

"It's everything we ever secretly hoped for," Gemma whispered. "The type of thing people like us don't get to experience. Losing your heart is dangerous in this line of work. It deceives you as to whom the enemy actually is, and puts blinders on your vision, so you sometimes don't even see the world around you. Or the knife in the shadows. But the temptation always remains."

Now that was interesting. "You've been in love."

Gemma smiled sadly and looked down, the light filtering through the window and striking her black hair. "I *thought* I was in love. In truth I was living a lie, and I was the one telling it to myself. Malloryn's right. Emotions are dangerous. Love is dangerous."

There was a lump in his throat. "But it's also the one thing that gives a man hope and purpose. What happened?"

Gemma looked away. "It's an old story. A long story."

"Is he still alive?"

"No," she whispered, though she hesitated. "He was a foreign spy, Kincaid. He worked for one of Malloryn's enemies and I was supposed to seduce him, and pretend to be his lover. I succeeded," Gemma admitted. "Too well. It felt real, for the short time we had together. Dmitri and I...." She shrugged, giving a wry smile, as if to guard herself from the emotions she felt. "The truth was revealed, and he shot me, leaving me to plunge into an icy river.

"I don't remember much from that time. Pain. Cold. Trying to break back through the ice, and not being able to. Everything seemed to slow down. I was so scared I was going to die, and so I kept swimming downriver, trying to find a hole in the ice. That was where Malloryn hauled me out. I'd always thought him a pampered, spoiled bastard. Blue blood elite. But he dragged me out from under the ice, and used his own blood to heal me—and infect me. He sat on that frozen beach in wet clothes, rubbing heat back into my hands and feet, despite the fact my stupid feelings for an enemy agent ruined his entire plan and got all his men killed. It's the one reason I owe him my loyalty. He could have let me drown for my failures, but he smuggled me out of Russia and let me go unpunished while I tried to put the past to rest. And now he's giving me a second chance, when I don't really deserve one.

"Love will do that to you, Kincaid. Leave you broken and bleeding deep inside, where it never truly heals. For once in my life, I agree with Malloryn. It's not worth the risk, no matter how wonderful it feels at the time. It only breaks you, and especially in this line of work, leaves your friends vulnerable to the enemy."

"Ava believes it gives you strength in the darkest of moments."

"And that's why we love her. Because she reminds us of everything we've lost. That hope. Those dreams. But you're darkness, Kincaid. And so am I. And we're the type of people who ruin others. Don't do that to her."

"Truce?" he asked, releasing a shuddering breath. He felt like something had died a little inside him.

Gemma sighed. "Truce."

They stared at each other. He'd never liked her. Not the way he liked the others, despite their craving virus affliction. Gemma was too worldly, too guarded, too

279

callous. She reminded him too much of himself, in some ways, and perhaps that was why they butted heads.

"I didn't mean to say what I said about Byrnes," she apologized.

It still ached within him. "It's the truth," he stated flatly. "For whatever reason, Ava cared for him. She entertained hope there was something between them. But maybe... maybe we could be there for each other. Just for a month or two. Before we end it."

"Why did you insist I partner with Ava?" The thought had been frustrating Kincaid lately.

Malloryn glanced up from the desk. "Do you really want to know?"

"I wouldn't have asked otherwise."

Malloryn put his pen down and leaned back in the chair. "When you first joined the company, you hated every single one of us for what we are. It surprised me to realize you'd mellowed enough to consider a friendship with Byrnes and Charlie, though your prejudices still show at times—"

"So you thought you'd partner me with the least predatory blue blood you know." He tasted disgust. "I hate being manipulated."

"I know."

But it was working. Kincaid crossed his arms, squeezing his fists. "She's a kitten compared to you. I get it. I do. Not all blue bloods are the same. Not all blue bloods are bloodthirsty monsters. Not even you." He paused. "Why do you do this? I understand you're interested in progress, but it seems as though you expend a great deal of energy for a cause not your own. One could almost say you're driven by it."

Those icy gray eyes met his. "It's not the sort of thing I speak of to anyone."

"Yet you demand everyone else spill their fuckin' secrets. No, you insist. How can you ask for the trust of your agents if you won't give it in return?"

A long silence. "There was a girl. Back when I was young and foolish, and I got her killed. And that is the extent of what I'm willing to share. Anything else?" Malloryn's voice encouraged him to move on.

A girl? Malloryn? The man with no heart?

But then, the same could have been said of him.

"Why did you invite me to join COR?" Another question that had been plaguing him. "I can't physically match you or the others. I'm cannon fodder when it comes to the *dhampir*. You've got Jack in the basement, building your devices, so you don't need a mech. I just don't understand what I…" *bring to the group.* "What you want from me."

"You came highly recommended. The Duchess of Casavian told me you'd fight me every step of the way, but you were cunning, ruthless, and ingenious. You think in ways I don't, and you know the mech world, the humanist cause." Malloryn leaned forward, elbows on his desk. "You represent a part of the population I need to be able to read and reach out to."

"So it was all political?"

"Partly. I think you sell yourself short. You're a fighter, and you don't flinch in the face of danger—"

"I'm still the most likely to get my throat torn out."

Malloryn's gaze shuttered. "Your physical limitations bother you."

It cut right to the core of him. Was that why he'd been questioning his value so often this past month? Malloryn

281

couldn't know of the iceberg he touched upon—or he'd better bloody not—but maybe there was something to that train of thought?

"And?" he asked icily.

"Why don't you do something about it?" Malloryn suggested, leaning back again as if to dismiss the conversation. "Stop thinking about your weaknesses, Kincaid, and start thinking about your strengths and what you can bring to this team. Specifically that thing in the basement you've been playing with over the last month."

His mech-suit. Kincaid frowned, wondering how Malloryn found out about it. "It's something to do in my spare time."

"Is it?" Malloryn picked up his spring-pen again. "A curious choice of hobby for a man who derides his physical limits. Are you sure your mind's not trying to tell you something?"

Play to his strengths. He could do that.

After pacing the house for the next half hour, Kincaid found himself in the basement, or what they affectionately referred to as Dungeon II, after Malloryn moved them from the first compromised safe house. It was no enclave, but not too shabby in itself, with every tool he could possibly want. He couldn't stop thinking about what Malloryn had said. Jack blinked up at him through a set of goggles, as if wondering why he was there.

The other man wore a mask covering the lower half of his face, with a filtration device to purify the air he breathed. Scars disfigured his face, and Kincaid had heard Jack's lungs were affected too, but the man had the kind of hands that could build anything, and a voice like a circus ringmaster. "Here to finish your project?"

"I haven't had a chance to look at it in over a week," Kincaid said, crossing to the corner he'd taken for himself and ripping the sheet off his project. A full mech-suit gleamed in the bright lights Jack had installed.

It wasn't finished. He'd been hesitating to solder the final joints together, tinkering with the small steam-engine component that drove it, even though it was ready. A mechanical suit to reinforce a man's body, with pistons in the leg guards that could force a man's legs to work if they were feeble, and overlapping steel plates to protect his inner organs. He wasn't sure why he'd started making it. Or no... that wasn't strictly true.

His legs would fail, his muscles turning traitor on him at some stage. His leg braces kept him moving so far, but soon enough they wouldn't be strong enough to hold him up. Even now, he could feel the faint tremor in his calves, and stairs would one day be the bane of his existence. Kincaid ran the pads of his fingers over the chest piece. A suit like this meant an independent life for as long as he could strap himself into it.

But if one looked at it in another way, it was also a means to give a man mechanical strength his own body couldn't provide, as well as protection from injury. With this, Kincaid could leap off roofs, punch his way through a brick wall, and deflect any blow from a blue blood.

Jack slid his magnifying goggles atop his head and rubbed the bridge of his nose. "Are you going to finish it today?"

"Not much else to do." Malloryn had set his spies into action, and Ava needed rest. By himself, he couldn't work out the science behind Ava's assumptions. He needed her quicksilver mind and defiant focus. The Nighthawks were keeping an eye on the city, and they'd be contacted the moment another Black Vein case came up, but for now... he needed something mindless to do.

"I like it," Jack said, admiring his work. "Not a Cyclops—nowhere near as heavy, for example, but it will give you greater maneuverability, and the smaller size makes it more versatile. Are you thinking of getting a patent for it? I know a great many factories would see a use in making a single man as strong as an ox, and I'm sure those who work in law enforcement would appreciate the added protection and strength."

He hadn't thought so far ahead. Kincaid dragged on his gloves slowly. A patent on something like this and a means to manufacture it would provide enough money for Orla to pay for proper care for Ian—and give her a damned rest every now and then. There'd be risks involved—he hadn't a clue how to get started, but it was a spark of inspiration. "Now there's an idea."

"You'd need a partner." Jack circled the suit. "Someone mechanically minded."

"Anyone you know?" Kincaid slowly smiled. Jack had been one of the masterminds behind the Cyclops.

"Possibly." Jack's eyes creased in a smile the mask hid. "And a backer... preferably a rich one."

A grimace. "If you're suggesting I go talk to Malloryn—"

"He's got the funds, he's a duke, he has influence, and he's very likely uninterested in controlling a business something like this would need." Jack sucked in a slow breath through his mask. "My sister is married to a duke too. But there's certainly no harm in talking to Malloryn. He's quite forward-thinking, for a blue blood."

For a blue blood. It wasn't as though he was growing to like Malloryn, but... the duke wasn't as bad as he sometimes made out. None of the blue blood Rogues were.

Kincaid stared at the suit, then glanced at Jack. "You were a humanist once. What do you make of all of this?"

Jack's green eyes narrowed thoughtfully. "The mech-suit? Or the brewing war between blue bloods and humans?"

"You know what I'm talking about."

Jack sighed. "My sister's married to a blue blood, and while he can be a little stiff at times, he's a good man. Then there's Debney."

Jack's *friendship* with the viscount had not gone unnoticed. Kincaid said nothing, but he'd seen the pair of them slip away at Byrnes's wedding. In the past, men like that would have been executed, but it wasn't his place to say anything. Nor his place to judge.

"I feel like I'm standing on the edge of a storm," Kincaid admitted quietly. "I have friends. Humanist friends. I see their anger over the blood taxes and the draining factories still loom large in the East End. But I also understand it's not an easy solution.

"And we don't know who's working to stir up the general population—whether it's on Ulbricht's side, or the *dhampir*, or someone working behind the scenes—but a part of me is tired of war," he said. "I don't want to see any more humanists die. I don't want to see any of my blue blood friends die. But we're heading toward a collision. Any fucking fool can see that."

Jack sighed, rolling a coin over the back of his gloved hands—a habit he had sometimes. "All London needs is a spark, and it will go up in a fiery blaze, you mark my words."

Fuck. Kincaid rested his hip on the edge of a stool. Maybe he'd overtaxed his body recently, but he felt dull and weak today. Exhausted. "But what's the spark going to be? We can stamp out all the fires we see—these Black Vein murders, the vaccine clinics being sabotaged—but I just feel like there's something else out there. Something we're not seeing. I mean, one by one these Black Vein murders aren't going to tip this war over the edge. The humanists don't care about blue bloods dying, and the Echelon doesn't give a damn about rogue blue bloods. If it were one of their own, however...."

"I agree," Jack said, shrugging. "But I don't think the spark's going to come from the Echelon. This all feels like it's a stalking horse. Something to set the Echelon on edge, but they don't have the advantage anymore. Some of them still stockpile automaton troops, but if they step out of line? The queen and the Council of Dukes will use the Cyclops they confiscated during the revolution against them. It would require a mass effort from most of the Echelon aristocrats working together to start a war, and they'd have to topple the queen or the Council first."

It all made little sense. These riots were stirring, yes, but some people still liked the queen. She wasn't her husband, mad and dangerous. She was human, and she'd been their figurehead during the revolution. Disappointment reigned at the moment, thanks to the recent lowering of the Blood Tax bill, but it hadn't destroyed the people's confidence in her.

"To whip the humanists into a frenzy, they'd have to strike at something the humans consider important. Hell if I know what that will be." Kincaid pulled on his protective gear, then reached for the carbon arc welder and his carbon rods. "Guess we'll just have to be prepared for anything."

Jack turned away. "Have a think about what I said earlier. It's just conjecture at this point, but I think you have a marketable product."

Kincaid clipped each claw onto the positive and negative wires, and then dragged his face mask down. "Will do."

CHAPTER TWENTY-ONE

"ARE YOU AVOIDING me?" Ava's voice broke through Kincaid's solitude as he stared at the nearly finished mechsuit.

"Of course not." His words were brusque; he heard it himself.

"After last night, I thought you might have...."

"Might have?" *...slipped into her bed, and woken her.* He'd thought about it.

But Gemma's words kept hounding him.

Ava didn't reply. Blonde lashes swept down, obscuring her eyes, and his stomach dropped through his boots. "Ava." He picked up a screwdriver. "You were hurt. You needed sleep. I'm not avoiding you."

Liar.

Guilt scoured him. He didn't want to hurt her. And while there was passion between them, there was something else growing. Hell, he couldn't deny it. Last night she'd fallen asleep in his arms, and before he'd slipped from her bed this morning, there'd been a part of him that wanted to linger. Just to relax for a few more hours with

Ava curled up against him, all those messy, vibrant curls spread across his pillow. But he was fooling himself. Gemma said it herself this morning: he was no good for her.

They just needed a little space between them. A clearly marked line that said, *this is an affair, and it will end when we finish this case.* Then they could go their own separate ways, and even though a part of him would always look back in regret at what he'd let slip through his fingers, it would be better for her.

Until he looked at her and saw her face.

Shit.

Glancing around, Kincaid captured her cheeks in his hands, carefully wielding the screwdriver. "I didn't think we wanted anyone else to know."

"We don't."

Kincaid kissed her gently on the lips, his heart softening. "Then that's all it was. Should you even be out of bed?" He could still see it, the moment he'd seen her face and realized she'd been poisoned.

That he could lose her.

He wasn't coping very well with the idea, and Ava made a small sound as his grip on her face tightened.

Kincaid released a heavy breath and let her go.

"I'm fine," she said, frowning in confusion, as though she'd sensed some part of his inner turmoil. "My chest still aches a little, but every hour I can feel the weight in my lungs easing. At least there's one good thing about the craving virus... it heals very quickly."

One good thing.... He'd have never even thought it before, but he could admit it now. And he knew she was making a point to him, one he couldn't accept.

Can't you? He'd deliberately not vaccinated himself, after all, and though he'd told her it had to do with a fear of needles, he'd been lying.

"What have you been doing down here? What are you making?" Ava stepped around him, gaping at the steel mech-suit. "Is it a Cyclops?"

The enormous Cyclops had been used to thwart the mechanical army the prince consort used to protect himself during the revolution.

"Not a Cyclops," Kincaid muttered, swinging under the arm of the suit and prying open the electrical panel on the back. "Though it's inspired by one of them." He tugged a few wires loose, examining the circuit board. Something still wasn't right in the boiler, and he set his mind to the problem of working out what. "I call it the Achilles, an invincible exosuit I can fit inside. It's smaller than a Cyclops, and designed to protect a human's vulnerable points, while also packing power behind any movements. The idea is that wearing this means I can jump off a building and land without busting a kneecap, or punch my way through a brick wall. Jack's been working on it with me in his spare time."

There was a moment of silence.

He turned to find Ava peering at him with big eyes. "You'd be as strong as a blue blood," she said softly, seeing straight to the heart of the matter.

"Not as fast though," he muttered, finding the loose wire in the circuit that was currently thwarting him. Aha. "Not until I can get the pistons in the leg armor working better."

"You do realize Achilles had one major vulnerability?"

Kincaid knelt and patted the steel boots he'd fit his foot inside. "As you can see, no issues with the heel here."

"I didn't know you had an interest in mechanical... creations." Ava knelt beside him, stroking a curious finger down the slick spar that bound the thigh armor to the shin

289

guard.

"I spent ten years in the enclaves," he replied, looking down at her gilded blonde curls. Jaysus. If she turned her head, she'd catch an eyeful of his hardening cock. "That's what my sentence was to repay the cost of my hand."

"How'd you lose it?"

Ava looked up, and Kincaid had the sudden urge to grab a fistful of her hair and haul her toward his aching cock. He could suddenly picture her on her knees, her hands on his thighs as he undid his belt, her lips parting to swallow his cock whole....

Not going there. Not at this moment. Gemma's words had undone him. Kincaid scowled, and slammed the electrical panel shut, pinching his finger in the process. Thinking about his hand deflated his cock. He could almost feel his nonexistent fingers tingling. "I was an apprentice mech-maker when I was fifteen. The older lads thought it'd be funny to hold my hand close to a threshing machine and turn it on."

Her face drained of color. "It didn't—"

"It did." He stepped back from the mech-suit, wiping his hands clean on a rag. "Nearly killed me, what with the shock and blood loss, and then the surgeon removing what was left. My brother nursed me through the fever, then went to the enclaves to barter for a replacement." Kincaid looked down, clenching the rag in his fist. Bloody William. Always trying to play the knight in shining armor. "He served two years in that hellhole while I recovered and learned to use the bloody thing. Then I took over the debt, and took his place. His health wasn't.... He should never have been there."

"I'm so sorry. They say they were horrible places."

"Aye." No denying that. "But I'll be honest and admit I made something of myself there. I've got a gift for mechanics. Wires, and steel and cogs... it all makes a certain sort of sense to me. I've always been good with my hands and I worked my way up to overseer. Gave me a chance to get in on the action when the humanist cause first started rearing its head among the downtrodden classes. The Duchess of Casavian gave me the designs for the Cyclops, and the mechs in my enclave created them, right beneath the noses of the blue blood lords who owned shares in the place."

"What do you intend to do with the Achilles?" she murmured, glancing up at him from beneath her lashes.

"Punch a *dhampir* in the teeth," he told her, "and hopefully survive. I haven't tested it yet, but it's better than nothing."

"You think we're going to come face-to-face with the *dhampir* again?"

He exhaled slowly. "One of them tried to kill you. It happened for a reason, and I think that reason is because we've discovered their precious poison. So yes. I expect we'll see them again."

Ava shifted, and he realized she meant to stand. Reaching down, he caught her bare fingers and hauled her to her feet. Ava balanced on the tips of her toes, trying not to fall against him, but to no avail. When she tried to take her fingers back from him, he resisted.

He wanted her.

And she wanted him.

It was painted across her face, displayed in the slight catch of breath that swelled her breasts. Ava was a picture of restraint, as hesitant as a hunted doe, and yet the look she gave him betrayed her curiosity.

And fuck the future. Fuck, Gemma. Fuck all of them.

Every little flicker of thought that went through her mind displayed itself on her expressive face. It was one of the things that intrigued him about Ava. He could never resist teasing her, when it was so easy to see the results of his words. Maybe the same vivid pictures weren't running through her head as they were through his, but she was clearly aware of him as a man. Aware of how close they stood. Of how his shirt unbuttoned just low enough to reveal a hint of his chest. He could follow the path of her gaze—and her thoughts—as clearly as his own. He could almost taste her on his tongue, hear the sweet mewls she made as he made her come.

What a picture the pair of them would make. She in her buttoned-down gray serge, with a froth of lace at the throat, and he in his coveralls, streaks of oil marring his skin.

Kincaid cleared his throat and let her fingers go. "Sorry. Didn't mean to get grease all over you."

She stepped back as if suddenly realizing the impropriety of the moment herself, and examined her fingers. A mere smudge darkened her index finger. "No harm done."

He produced a handkerchief, and she gingerly cleaned it off.

"Well," she said, handing him back the piece of fabric. "Everyone's home tonight, so I guess... I'll be sleeping alone."

He shouldn't do this.

But he wanted to.

"Would you like to go for a walk?" he finally asked, staring at her.

"A walk?" she repeated, glancing toward the thin cellar window. "It's almost evening."

"I know." He started packing his welding gear away. "Give me time to wash up. I feel like I need to get out of here." Slowly he looked at her. "And I'd like it if you came with me."

A soft pink filled her cheeks. "Is there any particular reason you're trying to lure me somewhere private?"

Kincaid gave her a flash of his usual devil-may-care smile, capturing her fingers in his and dragging her hand down to cup the heated erection in his trousers. Jaysus. His balls tightened, blood flooding through his cock. "I need you to help me examine a crime scene."

"Has there been a crime?" she asked breathlessly.

"Yes." His voice turned guttural. "A certain gentleman made a promise he hasn't kept, and there are going to be dire consequences if he doesn't change that fact sometime soon."

She glanced up as the floorboards above her creaked. "You wash up," she said, removing her hand with one last lingering caress. "I'll go fetch my cloak."

"Ava," he called, as she turned to the stairs.

"Yes?" She rested one hand on the timber railing, and he almost smiled when he saw the look in her green eyes.

"Leave your drawers at home."

"Where are you taking me?" Ava demanded, her nerves on fire with anticipation. She'd expected a hotel, or some set of private rooms somewhere, but they were heading toward a section of the city she vaguely remembered, but couldn't quite place.

"Someplace you've been before," he said. "The place it all began."

The place it— She paused. "The Garden of Eden."

The place she'd stolen his coat. The place where he'd calmed her after her hysteria attack, and she'd thought about kissing him.

"Are you saying that's where *we* began?" she whispered.

Kincaid leaned back in the carriage lazily, his fingers laced with hers. "At least, it did for me. I thought you wanted my blood, but you were overcome with lust. You. Sweet Miss McLaren, who looked at me like she wanted to fuck me."

Ava shivered. "It was all your fault. You unlaced my corset."

"You were struggling to breathe—"

"And then you put your coat around me, and all I could smell was your cologne...."

He nuzzled against her throat. "You like my cologne. I've noticed you sniffing my shirt when you think I'm not paying attention."

Ava pressed her hands against her hot cheeks. "I do *not* sniff your shirt. I'm a blue blood. My senses are more acute. It's just... distracting."

Kincaid stole a kiss, and Ava was suddenly overcome—not by embarrassment, but by a heated curl of desire. She moaned into his mouth, kissing him back with ardent, barely restrained desire, until he captured her face and drew back, leaving a scant inch between them.

"I notice you don't deny you wanted to fuck me."

The words fell into the silence of the carriage. Kincaid slid a hand down her shoulder and cupped her breast in his palm. Ava caught her breath. *Yes.*

"That would be lying," she whispered in return, aching for him to extend the touch. "And I try not to lie if I can help it."

He'd told her to wear nothing beneath her skirts, and the sudden flush of heat between her thighs was slick.

The smile on his lips was positively decadent. His thumb found her nipple behind the thick fabric, rubbing a little, teasing her. Ava shifted on the carriage seat. "Was that the night it began," he whispered, her nipple hardening beneath his touch, "for you?"

She'd promised not to lie. "Do you remember the day you were helping me set up my laboratory? You were lifting all of the heavier items I had: the box with my microscope, and the brass spectrometer I use to test my CV levels... and it was a warmer day, and you took off your coat."

"I remember." That thumb said, *go on*. "It was two days before the Garden of Eden. You were wearing white. Layers upon layers of lace and muslin. You didn't realize I could make out the shape of your legs beneath your skirts when you stood in the doorway with the light behind you."

Ava shuddered, biting her lip as he deliberately pinched her nipple. "*Oh.*" She cupped her hand over his, forcing him to caress her entire breast. She wanted to touch herself between her legs, to rub her fingers there, the way she sometimes did when she was alone in bed. Her fingers curled into a fist. That wasn't something a lady admitted.

But he'd always challenged her to accept her sexuality.

He'd love it if she touched herself in front of him. Ava just knew it.

Opening her eyes, she stared into his. "The very moment I first saw you I was taken aback. You were so large." She stroked his shoulder, shifting onto her knees. "Intimidating. I was still a little uncertain of you when you helped me with my laboratory. And yet, that night, when I lay alone in bed...." She shuddered.

"Go on," he whispered.

And Ava slid into his lap, settling one thigh on either side of his hips, trying to manage her skirts, trying to find her balance. Kincaid caught her hips, dragging her closer until she couldn't help feeling the hard-muscled thighs beneath her, and the leather straps around his legs that were part of his leg braces.

"What did you do, Ava?" He stroked her thigh, making no attempt to avoid the areas that made her shiver.

"I touched myself," she whispered. "You'd rolled your sleeves up, and I kept thinking of the muscles in your arms, the blue of your eyes."

"Where?" Of course he wouldn't leave it at that.

Heat flooded her cheeks. "You know where."

"Show me."

"Please tell me you're not going to stop tonight," she whispered.

His thumb rasped along her inner thigh, breaking off just before he reached the very area where her fingers had been. "I'm not going to stop."

A flood of relief—and nervousness—swept through her. "Good. For I should be tempted to commit a crime of my own if you *even think about it* tonight."

"Someone sounds determined," he teased.

"I want you," she breathed, coaxing her hands over his chest and absorbing the sensation of his coat. "I've always wanted you. And it means a lot to me... to think of making love to you."

Kincaid grasped her hips, hauling her closer to him so her legs straddled his thighs. "Pull up your skirts. And then show me where you touched yourself."

"Here?" She glanced toward the window, but nobody could see her.

Kincaid's wicked smile sent a flush of heat through her. "Right here," he said. "I want to see if you obeyed me or not."

Ava grabbed a handful of her skirts, yanking them, inch by inch, out of the way. It bared her stockings to the cool night air, and his hands. She shivered as metal raked over her skin, his thumbs stroking up her inner thighs and catching beneath her garters.

"Wider," he whispered, kissing the line of her jaw as he shoved her knees further apart.

She'd never felt so exposed in her life.

"Now show me," he demanded, in a tone that brooked no denials.

Ava stared into his eyes as she slid her hand lower, searching for her clit beneath her skirts. Kincaid's eyes glittered, and his chest heaved in a breath. "That's it."

She felt the first tentative touch, and arched her head back, closing her eyes.

"Merciful heavens," he breathed, fluffing her skirts away so he could see. "Look at you, all pink and glistening."

He'd kissed her there, but it was one thing to remember that—quite another to have him staring at her so blatantly. Ava shuddered as she stroked herself. A sweet, familiar tension began to form. It always took longer than this, but there was something about the moment, about him watching her, that ignited the pleasure within her.

"That's it." He captured her wrist and drew her hand to his mouth, sucking her wet fingers. She felt the pull of his mouth all the way through her womb.

Ava stared, unable to look away. "Kincaid."

"Liam," he demanded, reaching between them and undoing the buttons on his breeches. "Now touch me, Ava. I want to feel your wet little pussy on my cock."

Touch him— Then his other hand caught her bottom, and pushed her against him.

Ava grabbed on to the seat behind him, her breasts in his face. *Oh my goodness!* A large, brutish instrument butted against her, sliding over her clit. She chanced a look down. She'd seen penises in books, and she'd felt his erection behind the safety of his trousers—a monstrous thing—but she'd never seen an aroused cock in the flesh.

Her wetness gleamed on the slick purple head of his cock, the slit weeping. "Ride me," Kincaid dared her. "Use my cock in place of your fingers. Show me what it felt like when you fucked yourself with your fingers, and thought of me."

It was wicked, and wet, and delicious, and so, so tempting.... Ava rose and fell against him, grinding her hips in a rhythm he coaxed from her, one hand on her bottom, the other on her waist. She could feel their breath heating the carriage space, sense need tightening within each of them. Her corset seemed too tight, her clothes confining. Heat bloomed all along her skin. Need, hot and fierce.

She just wanted him inside her.

Here.

Now.

She was all hot and shivery and so close to orgasm she had to grip the carriage seat behind him and bite her lip to stop herself.

Somehow their positioning changed. She could feel the tip of him pressing insistently between her thighs. Ava paused to hold him there, her thighs quivering, and her... her pussy, he'd called it, begging to take him all the way.

Kincaid's lip curled up. "Ava. Jaysus. Not here."

"Yes," she gasped, rubbing against him. She didn't want to give him a chance to say no. Not again. She wanted to fill herself with his body. To claim him, even as she surrendered herself to him. "Aren't you the one always telling me to be naughty?"

"I had a plan," he rasped, rocking her against him so his erection rode over the swell of her clitoris. "It did not include taking you in the carriage."

Sensation speared through her. Ava cupped the back of his broad neck and arched her spine, shamelessly riding him. "I would not... be averse to that."

After all, did she not want adventure? Did she not wish to take one trembling step outside her usual boundaries? And it didn't matter where she was, when she was with Kincaid, she was utterly, perfectly safe. This was her body. Her choice. And she wanted to be his.

"Damn you, kitten." He was breathing hard. His cock breached her, wet and slick and slippery, and impossibly wide.

Kincaid's hand rested on her waist, his breath coming harshly. "Fuck. *Ava.*" Their eyes met in the shadowy twilight, and then curling his fist in the gathering of fabric around her waist, he pushed her down, even as he thrust up.

Gone, her virginity, in a single thrust.

Gone, her innocence, and with it, a piece of her heart.

Ava froze, her body locking around him. It seemed too much for her; he was too wide, too long, a battering ram inside her. And the rocking of the carriage forced her to take *everything* in a single sharp glide.

"Ava, *Ava,*" he breathed, no, he begged, his hands urging her to stay there, his body still with pent-up violence, as if pressure wanted to burst through his skin. "I'm sorry, sweetheart."

"It had to hurt a little," she said, swallowing, and beginning to shift. "It's...." Fine was not the word. It was an intense feeling. Not quite pleasure. Not quite pain. Ava met his eyes and begged him to help her make sense of it.

He kissed her, and suddenly that was the answer she needed. Their mouths met, sloppy and heated. His tongue was pressing inside her mouth, a conqueror without mercy, and somehow he urged her to rock against him. To glide up and down, frozen inner muscles slowly unclenching as her body grew used to the stretch.

"You're beautiful," he breathed. "That's it. Ride me.

Rub yourself against me." He buried his face in her throat, grabbing a fistful of her chignon.

Ava moaned. Her thighs were quivering. "Please.... Oh." She was almost on that edge again, her body tightening, reaching for orgasm. Her fingers were clumsy in his shirt as she tried to keep the rhythm he was showing her, but couldn't quite manage. "Oh. My. *Goodness.*"

Kincaid laughed. "You make even the dirtiest fuck sound prim and proper. I love it." He licked her throat, teeth grating against her sensitive skin. "That's it, sweetheart. You're so close, aren't you? Take what you want.... That's it. Oh, Jaysus."

Hands tightened in her skirts, then his thumb was reaching between them, pressing indignantly against her clitoris. She felt hot all over, tingles erupting through her. Too much. Far too much. Ava's eyes widened, her hand squeezing the back of his neck as she tried to keep going, her body bucking under the force of that swirling pressure.

For once she didn't care where she was, or who could have heard them. She cried out as she came, silenced by the press of his mouth as he captured her scream with a ferocious kiss. His unrelenting thumb kept grinding against her, his hips thrusting up into her, forceful now, as if he'd lost all sense of himself, and then—

Wet heat spilled within her. Kincaid shuddered and groaned, his body stilling as he pressed into her, as if he could find himself within her skin.

And then it was over, Ava collapsing in his arms, her skin dewed with his sweat, and the heat of his body like a furnace beneath her, within her.

The stillness of the aftermath was almost as sweet. Ava's body clenched and unclenched in a dozen little aftershocks, his hand stroking the buttons down her spine, sweetly tender as sensation began flooding back in again.

Ava looked at him from beneath heavy lashes. Her mouth was wet and ravaged, her body too. No longer a maid. She felt the sudden urge to smile, and then he was smiling back at her and everything was perfect.

Utterly perfect.

"Thank you," she whispered, as he tried to shift her off him.

"It was my pleasure," Kincaid replied and then he gave her a boyish smile that stole her heart.

CHAPTER TWENTY-TWO

THE CARRIAGE ARRIVED at the Garden of Eden, and Kincaid helped her down. Ava stared up at the lush pleasure house. COR had celebrated a night out together to get used to each other, and the night had opened her eyes in a myriad of ways. It seemed like a year ago, and yet it was barely seven weeks.

Seven weeks since it all changed.

She looked down at the broad arm beneath her hand, and glanced up at Kincaid's shadowed jaw, feeling a flush of... *something*... squeeze in her chest.

There'd been shadow shows, with a man and two women behind a backlit sheet.

Fire-breathers. Jugglers wearing bright spangles and lurid makeup. More wine than she could ever drink, and men and women showing more skin than she'd ever seen.

But the pleasure house seemed quiet now, the lush gardens behind it whispering with only wind. Ava turned to him in surprise, and Kincaid smiled at her. "It's ours for the night. I asked Charlie to run ahead and pull some strings. He owed me a favor."

"A rather large favor."

Kincaid shrugged. "They were closed tonight anyway. They're always closed on a Monday."

She decided she didn't want to know how he knew that.

"This seems somehow anticlimactic," Kincaid said. He'd tucked his shirt back into his trousers, and his coat was on, but there was a rumpled air about him.

"Not for me." No man had ever tried to organize a surprise for her. "I want to see what you had planned."

"I'm fairly certain you've glimpsed a preview of it."

The pulsing throb between her thighs was still damp, though he'd helped clean her up in the carriage with his handkerchief. Ava blushed.

"Come," Kincaid said, capturing her fingers. He was carrying a heavy basket in his mech hand, and she kept peering at it, wondering what it contained. "I don't think you ever managed to view the gardens in detail. They're more exotic than you could realize. Full of flowers and plants. You can gush over them to your heart's delight."

The servants in the house wore livery this time, a bold luscious red. They averted their eyes as Kincaid guided her toward the back of the house.

"They have all manner of ferns back here, and lush foliage. There's a little waterfall in the back, with a beautiful clearing," he said, leading her through the winding paths in the garden, the lantern he'd taken from one of the servants casting a long shadow in front of him. His luxurious, fur-lined cloak made it look like his shadow had wings.

"It's lovely," she whispered, looking around. The place seemed completely different tonight. No capering jugglers or acrobats. No drunk men wandering around.

Just her. And Kincaid.

And the twitter of birds, settling in for the night.

Moss carpeted the ground, and little lanterns were strung through the trees. Not bright enough to light the garden, but it felt like she was following a mysterious trail. A rush of water whispered ahead of them. His waterfall.

Ava saw it and rushed to investigate, her soft-soled boots crushing the grass. Someone had set a string of lanterns over the waterfall, and light gleamed on the churning foam.

She had not expected a fairy tale, but she felt almost as if she stood in one.

Ava's breath caught.

"Come here," Kincaid murmured, holding out his hand to her as he stood on the gaping precipice of a clearing. "There's a reason I brought you here."

From the top of the small ridge, she could see London spread out in front of her, the Ivory Tower where the queen ruled pointing like a pale finger into the sky. There were no stars over the city—the smog probably obscured them—but thousands of little lights twinkled in the velvety darkness, reminding her of just how alone the two of them felt. Lawn stretched out in front of her until it reached the far wall that circled the Gardens. A cool breeze stirred her skirts, and Kincaid slid his arms around her, his heat sinking into her body.

"You were right," she said. "I barely managed to explore that night. This is lovely." Turning to wrap her arms around him, she lifted on her toes to kiss him. "Thank you."

When she drew back with a smile, he frowned. "What?"

"It's just"—Ava gestured to the clearing, and the picnic someone had set out for them—"I was expecting lurid art, or sumptuous red velvet throws and a bed covered in furs. This is almost"—*dare she say it*—

"romantic."

Kincaid rolled his eyes. He swirled his cloak off his shoulders and laid it down upon a bed of moss, and suddenly she realized why he'd worn such a luxurious cloak. "I'm not so much of a boor as to fuck you in some bordello."

The word was typical Kincaid. But she suddenly wondered if he used such a word to distance himself. Ava hid another smile. She had called him romantic, after all, which was probably the worst thing anyone had ever accused him of.

"Stop it," he growled, glaring at her.

"I didn't say anything!"

"You're thinking it." He gestured around them. "I left all of the details up to Charlie. The lad's clearly a closet poet."

"You took me to the place where it all began *for you*," she teased. "A garden, which you know I love. And I can smell strawberries in that basket. My favorite."

"I hadn't even noticed," he scoffed.

"Strawberry jam," she pointed out, because he'd made such a big deal of it at breakfast the first time she'd eaten it on toast, as though he'd only expected her to consume blood.

Kincaid clasped his hands behind his head, a small smile playing across his mouth. "All right, I admit it. I wanted you to have your fairy tale, even if it was just for one night. Instead, you corrupted me in the carriage."

"Corrupted *you*?"

Kincaid snagged a handful of her skirts, dragging her into his arms. "Had your way with me, tempted me into the most ungainly loss of virginity known to man...."

"Fucked you," she said, and watched heat fill his eyes.

Kincaid curled her closer, his hands on her bottom as

his glazed eyes locked on her lips. "Now who's the one with the dirty mouth?"

"I swear you're rubbing off on me," she told him, but she swayed into his touch. Thirty minutes ago she would have said she needed a day to recover. But the craving virus did heal *everything*, after all.

"Miss McLaren, are you propositioning me with those eyes?"

"Yes," she whispered, sliding her hands up his chest and stretching onto her toes. Confidence bloomed within her. She'd always wistfully wished she was a little more like Gemma, but had she mistaken the other woman's sauciness for confidence? Now she could be just herself, just Ava, but an Ava who felt like she could take on the whole world in this moment.

She kissed him, tasting the sweetness of his mouth.

It wasn't enough. Every encounter between them had been rushed and hurried, a mad scramble in the darkness. This time she wanted to take her time.

She pushed his coat off his shoulders, and found the buttons of his shirt. Kincaid made a growling sound deep in his throat as he helped her remove it. "Miss McLaren," he breathed, dancing her backward as she slid a hand up his bare chest. "I like this side of you. But I think we're unfairly positioned."

Gentle hands found the buttons on the back of her dress, and he turned her around, kissing the slope of her shoulder as he began to tug them free.

"It's cold," she whispered.

"I'll warm you up." The dress slipped from her arms and shoulders, curling around her feet. "And if you're thinking about the cold, then I'm clearly not doing my job correctly."

Helping her to step out of the discarded dress, he

turned her around with an appreciative little twirl. "Mmm. This needs to go." Crinoline and petticoats both fell prey to his deft fingers. Ava shivered as he captured her waist and kissed the smooth slope of her upper breasts. Her corset clasped at the front, and he laid waste to it, tossing it aside and running his hands up to cup her unbound breasts.

Finally, all that remained were her chemise and stockings. Ava could feel chill fingers of wind sliding straight through her chemise, but the look in Kincaid's eyes heated her within. Her nipples were cool, hard pebbles behind the fabric. He circled her slowly, fingertips trailing across the back of her hip. "Strip," he told her.

A thousand doubts sprang to mind; her scar, her small breasts, the way she'd be completely vulnerable to his gaze. What if he found her lacking?

"I believe I gave you an order," he whispered, moving behind her and tugging the pins from her hair.

Ava slowly slid her chemise off one shoulder, trembling a little. This was Kincaid. He never made her feel doubt, but her breath caught. "Are you certain?"

"I want to touch you all over," Kincaid breathed, capturing her waist and pressing against her so she could feel the steel of his erection. "I want to taste every inch of you. So yes, Ava. I want you naked. I want all of you. I want you to be mine, and I intend to claim you."

Her chemise ghosted down her body, and Kincaid sucked in a sharp breath. His hand slid up her stomach, capturing her breast. Ava moaned a little, and then he was pressing a kiss to the back of her neck, biting her there.

Suddenly she was no longer so shy. All she felt was need, her vision going dark as the hunger roused.

Kincaid gathered her in his arms and laid her upon his fur-lined cloak. Lantern light gilded his shoulders, and Ava ran her hands up his chest as he knelt over her, pressing a kiss to her collarbone, then her breast, then her nipple. The shock of his mouth made her cry out, and he made good on his promise to taste her all over, spreading her thighs and dipping down to spear his tongue into the thatch of blonde hair there, until she was no longer thinking about her nakedness or vulnerability, lost to sensation as he lapped and teased at her until she screamed.

"How do you do that to me?" she gasped, running her hands through his hair as he kissed his way back up her body, tracing his tongue over the long scar between her breasts. It was so unbearably sensitive, she had to pull his face away.

"I love hearing you cry out," he whispered.

Cool air kissed her skin. Ava dragged her fingertips along the hard line of his jaw, tracing that familiar stubble. She could see the stars over his shoulders, though most of Kincaid was a shadowy outline now. One of the lanterns nearby had faded. Without his expression, she was limited to communication through touch, or whispered words.

But she didn't feel like speaking right now.

"You frightened me," he whispered, nipping at her fingertips. "I've been trying not to think about it, but seeing you like that... coming so close to losing you—"

"You didn't lose me." Ava captured his face in both hands, a glint of light turning his eyes silver. She couldn't read his thoughts in them. "But it frightened me too. There's so much I haven't done. So much I haven't seen, or felt." Ava brushed her lips against his, a sweet caress. "And thank you, I needed this. I wanted it to be you. I wanted you to be my first."

She didn't dare say, *and last.*

He wouldn't like that, and she didn't want to complicate things—*they'd agreed, damn it*—but there was a little part of her that could imagine a life with Kincaid by her side.

Long, slow kisses every morning when they woke; a man who championed her at all times, encouraging her to speak her mind and step outside the laboratories where she felt her safest; seeing his face light up in a smile when she first stepped into a room; having him tease her and whisper naughty words in her ears.

Silence greeted her words, a drawn-out silence in which she thought they were both holding back.

"Don't ever forget me, Ava," he finally whispered, and there was the answer to her unspoken question.

This wasn't going to go any further, and a part of her grieved.

"I don't think I ever could," she admitted. *I never expected you to come into my life like this. I never....* Her heart felt like it was in her throat. *I never realized how much I want you to stay.*

His face slowly lowered, his breath stirring over her lips. And then he kissed her.

Gently.

So softly the ache of denial made her moan and arch up into him. She'd asked for fleshly pleasure, for him to make her a woman, but what she hadn't expected in this moment was connection or tenderness.

Kincaid was charming, and brash, and loud. Everything about him was physical, from the way he flung his arms wide when they argued, to the way he pushed her against a wall and claimed her mouth when he kissed her.

But this... there was a hesitancy here. As though he wanted to say something, and yet couldn't quite bring himself to do it.

"*Liam.*" A sigh of surrender on her lips.

She grew bold, reaching for his trousers and capturing the tented arch of his cock. Kincaid groaned, bracing himself on his hips over her and thrusting into her hand. He held her hand there, forcing her fingers to close over his thick length. "That's it, Ava."

She brushed his hand aside, fumbling with his buttons, desperate to feel his heated flesh upon hers, helping him tug his trousers down around his hips, finding the leather belt of the girdle around his hips, and pausing—

But he captured her hand, pushing it aside, and she could see his head shaking. "No," he whispered. "I can fuck you like this," he whispered, undoing the placket on his trousers and capturing her hand, pressing it against the swollen erection that spilled into her hands.

"But—" She wanted him naked.

"I can't get the brace off, not easily. It's fine." A hint of frustration came into his voice. "I hate it, but it gives my legs strength."

"You're perfect, Kincaid." This time she threw his own words back at him. "Strong, and brave, and always at my side. My very own knight in shining armor, if you believed in fairy tales."

A faint laugh exploded through his chest. "You never give up, do you?"

"Sometimes the fairy tale comes true." Ava smiled sadly.

Silence. He was thinking. Then his body pressed into hers, and she could feel his hardening erection hot against her belly, the buttons on his trousers pressing into her naked skin. "Then let's pretend we believe in fairy tales."

Even though she knew it roused him when she used his dirty words, she stroked the hair off his temples. "Make love to me. Give me a memory I'll never forget." She kissed his jaw, then his cheek, tracing the sharp lines of his face with her lips. "Just this one night, and then we can pretend the fairy tale is over, and you can fuck me as often as you like."

"As you wish," he breathed, and kissed her again.

This time Ava pushed everything but the feel of his body out of her mind, and set about making love to the man she... was falling for.

Kincaid lay there beside her, staring at the faint stars in the sky as Ava's head rested on his shoulder and her body curled against him, leg thrown carelessly over his. Soft breaths stirred the hair on his chest, and he glanced down at the blonde curls strewn across his shoulder. Moonlight turned them silver, and he couldn't make out her sleeping expression, but he could imagine peace there.

The trust she placed in him shattered him.

The emotion in her eyes, the thoughts she could never quite hide....

The way she looked at him destroyed him. Because there was something there tonight that hinted at more, something he desperately wanted to see.

He'd never been in love before. He'd seen the way Maggie looked at Xander, the way Byrnes looked at Ingrid, and thought it such a foreign experience he hadn't quite noticed it creeping up upon him.

He'd never asked for this feeling of unsolicited tenderness. It scared the hell out of him at times.

The future stretched in front of him, a future where Ava accepted what he could offer her, and it was the most tempting dream he'd ever had.

The thought of losing her had terrified him yesterday; the thought of a future with her, however, was infinitely worse. He didn't want to depend upon her. He didn't want her to see his body deteriorate until his heart finally stopped working. It was her heart, she held it in her hands, and she didn't even know it, but he couldn't... *he couldn't....*

His breath caught, his stomach knotting, and the muscles in his left calf launched into a painful cramp that made him grit his teeth as he silently tried to straighten his foot to alleviate it, and finally succeeded.

Kincaid stroked the pale curve of her back, dragging her cloak over them. Her body was cool, the result of being a blue blood, but he didn't complain. This moment was precious in a way he had never expected. Ava nuzzled into his throat as he shifted, a quiet, reflexive move that made him freeze.

They were so different. He'd never seen it coming. The hot flame of his temper to the cool logic of hers; the sweetness of Ava's smile, to the seductive quality of his own. His humanity versus her blue blood nature.

Complete opposites in every way, and yet she complemented him, fitted so perfectly against him. She gave him hope, and laughter, and a lightness that had been missing from his life for years, and he drove her to stand up for herself, and to see how perfect she was despite her own misgivings.

I could love you, he finally admitted to himself, twining one of her curls around his finger. *I could wake every day like this, and smile every time I saw your face. I could spend the rest of my life with you, and make something of my life. Something more than this, something that could last forever.*

But the problem was, he knew he didn't have forever.
And she did.

CHAPTER
TWENTY-THREE

AVA SET OUT the next day with renewed vigor, leading Kincaid on a merry chase through the streets of the East End and the docks. Malloryn had provided her with a list of potential importers who had connections to the Orient, and she was determined to track down some of the caterpillar mushroom.

It was the key to finding Ulbricht. Or the *dhampir*. Or whoever had killed Major Winthrop.

It was during their fifth visit they finally struck gold. Kincaid had decided to ride his velococycle again, insisting she cling to the back of him in a set of split skirts Gemma provided. He pulled up out the front of an importer near the docks, eyeing the huge warehouse, and Ava scrambled off the velococycle in a mad rush. She still wasn't used to it.

"Relax," he told her. "I barely shifted out of second gear."

"You are utterly mad! You— That thing— We nearly hit a carriage." And as far as carriage-driven collisions went, she felt like she'd had her fair share of *almosts*.

He turned the engine off, eyes twinkling as he lifted

his goggles. "They're the latest rage in the streets, Ava. Every man will be riding one soon."

She growled deep in her throat, and then faced the building. "Mr. Leicester and Sons. He imports rare items from the White Court, India, and Nepal. Furniture, rare books, decorative hangings, timberwork. Malloryn suspects the furniture covers an opium smuggling operation."

Kincaid dragged off his leather gloves, examining the place. "One guard by the look of it. Shall we go in?"

"What?" she challenged, swinging her parasol. "No questions about me getting hurt?"

"I've seen that parasol in action," he pointed out. "And while I would like to keep you safe from harm, Ava, leaving you behind would be counterintuitive to our case. I need that big, intelligent brain of yours to pick apart the truth." He glanced around. "There's a feeling in the streets today, as if one catastrophic spark will unleash a torrent of fury. I just.... We're running out of time. I want to stop this war before it begins."

He looked so earnest. But those would be his friends out there in the streets, all the humanists he'd once known and led.

"I want to stop it too," she said quietly, for *everyone's* sake, not just the humans.

"Then let's find our murderous mushroom." Kincaid led the way. "I can't believe I just said that."

Ava smiled.

Inside the factory, several men used cranes to manipulate large crates. The noise was enormous, and one fellow directed them toward the office. "Mr. Leicester will know if we've imported any of the items you want to buy."

They changed direction.

A man caught her eye, quickly looking away from her.

"Do the men seem to be staring a little more than

usual?" Ava murmured, clutching her parasol.

Kincaid looked around, moving closer to her. "Do you have your pistol on you?"

She blinked up at him. "Yes." But the idea of firing it at someone was completely different from trying to hit a target. She wasn't certain she had it in her.

"Keep moving," he told her. "You're right. They are watching us."

All the hairs on the back of her neck lifted. Ava swallowed, and marched behind him. Behind the glass windows of the office, a man was leaning over a desk, marking things off on a sheet of paper. He saw them coming and froze, his weedy little mustache quivering.

Ava swept ahead of Kincaid with a pleasant smile. "Good morning, sir. Mr. Leicester, I presume?"

Mr. Leicester was sweating in his beige cardigan. "Ah, good morning, ma'am. How may I help you?"

"We're looking for something," Kincaid said, moving around the desk and glancing at the papers strewn all over it. "Perhaps you could help us?"

Ava tugged her Nighthawks badge out from inside her reticule, showing it to the man. "Do you know what this is?"

His face paled, and then he took off running.

Ava stepped back in surprise. *What on—* "After him!"

Kincaid took two steps, ripped the lid off a nearby crate, and threw it discus-style toward the fleeing man. He went down, and Kincaid hurried after him, stomping a foot in the middle of his back when the fellow tried to flee. "I'm not much for speed," he told her, reaching down and flipping Mr. Leicester over. "Why'd you run?"

"P-pardon," the man said. "I didn't... I panicked. I just.... I meant no harm by it."

Kincaid circled him slowly, and with his leather coat

clinging to those broad shoulders and his thick brows drawn together, he looked quite menacing. "In my experience, innocent men don't run. Ava?"

"We're looking for something you might have imported," she said, withdrawing her notebook from her pocket so she could show him a sketch of the mushroom they were after.

"No! No! I won't say anything." The man cowered. "I can't! He'll kill me."

He?

"Who will kill you?" Kincaid demanded, shaking him a little.

Leicester kicked and scraped at the floor, trying to escape. Kincaid picked him up and slammed him back on the desk, both of his fists curled in Leicester's cardigan. "I won't ask again."

"You, unfortunately, have a choice to make," she told Mr. Leicester, trying to restrain Kincaid with a gentle touch. "You clearly have information we require, and we're running out of time to get it."

"Fucking craver," Leicester said, and spat in her face.

Ava didn't see what happened next. Kincaid's fist blurred past her in a savage blow, and blood spattered across the desk. Ava wiped her face clean with her handkerchief as he punched the man again and again, driving him onto the floor. "Kincaid!" she yelled, grabbing his raised arm.

Those blue Celtic eyes were wild with rage as he looked at her. "Are you all right?"

"I'm fine." She eased his arm down. "We need him to talk to us, Liam."

Kincaid let the man go with muttered curse, raking his hands through his hair as he turned away from her. The man curled into a ball on the floor, sniveling and clutching at his broken nose. Blood streamed from it, and for a second she felt like she wanted to cast up her accounts.

"If you even look at her less than politely," Kincaid snarled, "then next time I won't stop."

"As you can see, you're facing quite the predicament," she said, shaking a little. She'd never been spat upon before. "My friend here is not quite as civilized as I am. And if you don't answer my questions—"

"You're not going to kill me," the man blustered. "You can't. You're a Nighthawk."

"No, we're not going to hurt you." At least some people in this city still knew what the Nighthawks stood for. "But I think we're going to take you to see a friend. He's not quite as nice as we are, and unfortunately, he's willing to do whatever it takes for the greater good."

"Malloryn?" Kincaid asked.

"Malloryn," she confirmed. "Pick him up and I'll go through the shipping statements."

"There's no need for that," a child's voice called.

Both she and Kincaid spun around.

A young man, barely a lad, stepped hesitantly toward them, his hands raised in front of him, and a cap on his head. "Please don't hurt him," he called, his nervous eyes flickering to the man on the ground. "I can show you what you're looking for."

"What we're looking for?" Ava questioned, standing a little straighter. Neither she nor Kincaid had mentioned anything in particular.

"Edward! No!" the man on the ground bellowed.

"You're going to get us all killed," the boy shouted back. "You're going to get yourself killed. They're Nighthawks! They can help us."

"You have my word," Ava told him. "If you tell us what we want to know, I'll use any influence I have to see you and your family are safe."

"You're here for the serum, aren't you?" the boy piped.

Ava shot Kincaid a look. The serum? "You have the serum here?" They'd been looking for the mushroom, and instead struck gold.

The boy nodded. "Just promise you won't hurt my father, and I'll show you where it is."

Edward Leicester was most helpful.

"All of what we have on hand is in that crate," he said, gesturing to a small picnic-basket-shaped box.

Kincaid used a crowbar to pry it open. Inside, dozens of small vials rested neatly, filled with a bright green liquid. "There's more than enough serum here to kill hundreds of blue bloods."

Ava flashed before his eyes, curled in a heap on the floor and bleeding from her eyes, with black veins pulsing behind her pale skin. He felt sick. Blue blood or not, this was a crate full of murder, and he couldn't risk her again.

He needed to find the rest of this bloody serum and destroy it.

"That's only the last crate, sir," Edward said. "They took the rest of them. This one was misplaced in the rush."

"The rush?" Ava asked.

Kincaid slowly lowered the crowbar. "How many crates? Where are they coming from? Who's taking them?"

Edward took a step back, his freckles showing starkly against his pale face. "It's.... We're just shipping them."

"Smuggling, you mean?"

The boy swallowed. "There's a manufacturing facility near Brighton," Edward said. "I don't know what Da's been promised, but the men who came here weren't very nice. All we had to do was smuggle the crates in, hide them in the warehouse, and then hand them over when men with the right codes and tattoos appeared."

"Brighton." He exchanged a look with Ava.

"That seems awfully convenient," she replied. "Considering one of our suspects was supposedly seen in the area."

Lord Ulbricht. "Was it a tattoo of a rising sun?"

Edward's face brightened. "Aye, sir." He revealed his wrist. "One of them had it right here."

"And they were blue bloods?" Ava questioned. "Pale skin, pale hair?"

Edward shook his head. "I don't know, ma'am. I don't think Da would deal with blue bloods, but then he kept me and my brother out of all of this. I... I wasn't supposed to be watching."

"Describe them," she said, taking out her little notebook as Edward ran through the details.

Kincaid paced. Three different men, at least two blond, which could mean blue bloods. Rich clothes, a posh accent, one of them wearing well-shined shoes, so that indicated some money.

"They needed the shipments by tonight at the latest," she repeated, when Edward had finished. "Over three thousand vials of serum to be collected in the last few days." Her breath caught in her throat at the number. "Do you know what they're planning to do with all the serum?"

Edward looked pale now. "I don't really know. We were only the smugglers, ma'am. But... I heard one of them laughing. He said, 'flick the match and watch London burn,' and his friend said, 'they're not going to burn, they're going to die, kicking and clutching their chests.'"

Chests... that could mean hearts. What did this all

mean?

Edward swallowed. "And then the first one said, "Nighthawks first.""

"They're going to attack the Nighthawks," Ava said, the words spilling out of her in a rush as she filled in the rest of COR. Three *thousand* vials of serum. She squeezed her eyes shut and swallowed when she finished, waiting for the others to comment.

"Blood and ashes," Malloryn whispered.

"They could kill the entire Echelon with that amount of serum," Gemma added, in a sickened tone. "As well as the Nighthawks, and any other blue bloods in the general population."

No more blue bloods.

All of her friends, her newfound family.... Ava swayed, and then suddenly there was a warmth against her back, a presence there supporting her. Kincaid's hand rested on the small of her back.

"I won't let it happen, Ava," he told her. "I promise."

And she nodded up at him, letting everything she felt for him fill her eyes. He'd come so far in such a short time. Ava patted his arm, still feeling sickened, and it was only then she realized everyone in the room was looking at the pair of them.

Especially Malloryn.

The duke looked away, standing and pacing the room. "Ulbricht's an antihumanist but surely he wouldn't go this far. He believes in blue blood rights to power, and that humans are nothing but cattle. I can hardly see him spearheading a... a murder spree against blue bloods, and if this gets out of hand, then the very people he's fighting for will die."

"You're right," Kincaid breathed, "but what you're not taking into consideration is the fact none of these deaths are blue bloods of *any importance*. He doesn't care about the Nighthawks. He never has. He wants to protect the Echelon, and the past. Is Ulbricht arrogant enough to think he could use it and control it?"

The look on Malloryn's face was answer enough. "Yes," he said, closing his eyes briefly, as though he could see his world going up in flames.

"They were tests," Charlie said, as if the penny dropped for him too. "Mr. Thomas, and Mr. Long and the others. They're all new blue bloods no one suspected were even infected. Ulbricht must have had them tracked, and tested his serum to make sure it worked."

"The attack was always two-pronged." Malloryn waved a hand. "A poison that afflicts only blue bloods, a spate of murders, and the loss of the vaccine clinics. He's using fear tactics against both races. The humanists have no way to protect themselves from succumbing to the craving without the vaccine, and many of them will be wondering if they've already been stricken with a contaminated vaccine. And the blue bloods of the Echelon will be frightened about a disease that can kill them, thinking the humanists are trying to destroy them.... Blood and ashes, this is madness."

"Ulbricht wants a war," Kincaid said darkly, "no matter what the cost."

A chill ran through her. Of course. She'd said it herself. *How can we have a future when you hold such prejudices against me?*

"They're using our own tactics during the revolution against us—using riots to create fear in the Echelon, and stirring up that disgruntled memory within the human ranks until it spills over. This is all about dividing the races. About destroying our newly minted peace," Kincaid continued.

You could have heard a pin drop in the room.

"For three years," Kincaid said, "humans, mechs, verwulfen, and blue bloods have held equal rights." He stabbed his finger toward the map on Malloryn's wall, pointing to the first scene of riots. "During the revolution, the only thing the blue bloods feared was the might of a human mob storming the Ivory Tower. So they crushed the riots before they even began. We have peace now, but it's an uneasy peace, and nobody seems to quite know where they stand."

"That's what Ulbricht's trying to provoke," Ava blurted. "He wants the blue bloods who are left to feel frightened. He wants humans and blue bloods to see each other as enemies again. All of this is to frighten blue bloods into joining his cause, and setting them against the human ranks again."

Kincaid shot her a look, and nodded. "So far the riots have been subdued peacefully, but one flick of the match and all of a sudden London will burn. Trouble's brewing among the human population. I've heard it with my own ears, from friends. It's been a quiet grumble in the past year, but all it will take will be one clash gone wrong."

"The Nighthawks," Ava said, and swallowed. "They're on the front lines, and Garrett said during the last riot one of his men was shot. He's going to come down hard on the next mob. And if he does...." Ava felt like her breath punched out of her.

"There's your tinder strike," Gemma said grimly. "There's your match to an oily puddle."

"Blood and ashes," Malloryn swore. "How the hell did I not see this?"

Ava exchanged a glance with Gemma, who grinned unrepentantly. It was rare one got one over on Malloryn.

"Well, you were distracted, Your Grace, what with your upcoming marriage, and frosty relations between you and your soon-to-be wife," Gemma replied.

"I can't afford to be distracted." Malloryn paced shortly, rubbing his hand across his mouth. "Fear means there'll be blue bloods from the Echelon swarming to Ulbricht's ranks, and from there they'll start muttering against the queen. I thought we cut the head off the snake of the SOG when Zero died, but Ulbricht's... cleverer than I suspected." He looked genuinely baffled. "He's never been this patient or thoughtful before, and I should know."

"Unless he's not the one behind the plan," Ava suggested. She felt emboldened by the sudden belief in her theories. "You said you suspected someone was pulling *dhampir* and SOG strings last month. Some hidden mastermind we don't know about. Maybe whoever that mastermind is, he's set this plan in motion? Maybe Ulbricht's still a puppet?"

"But what we do know," Malloryn said grimly, "is that London is one riot away from going up in flames. And Ulbricht has the most dangerous weapon I've ever heard of in his hands, and is mad enough to use it."

"But how?" Kincaid demanded. "He needs to inject the poison, doesn't he? Which means getting close to a Nighthawk, and they're highly trained. None of his SOG are fighters, not like the Nighthawks."

"Get moving, everybody," Malloryn snapped. "Gemma, I want you to make a move on the SOG suspect we think we have. Break him if you have to, but make sure he tells you everything. We need to know what Ulbricht is planning. Charlie, go with her to watch her back.

"And you two"—Malloryn pointed a finger at both

him and Ava—"make your way to the Nighthawks guild as swiftly as possible and alert the guild master. Our first priority is stopping the Nighthawks from making a dangerous mistake. Then we can figure out how Ulbricht's going to use the serum."

CHAPTER
TWENTY-FOUR

THE RUMBLE OF a steam engine thrummed beneath her, and Ava clung to Kincaid's broad back as he wove in and out of the stream of traffic in a deft line, maneuvering his velococycle as though he had some wish to die a fiery death.

"Slow down!" she yelled, burying her face against his broad back, the wind whipping past her ears, and her split skirts flapping against her calves and thighs. She wasn't human, and could probably survive a fall, but he wouldn't. Not at this speed.

"Can you hear that?" he yelled over his shoulder, indicating the rumble that undercut the velococycle's noise.

It sounded like a roll of thunder on the horizon... or a whisper of mutiny echoing through the streets.

And it was getting louder.

"It's already happening," Ava breathed, her goggles pressing tightly against her cheeks as she bumped into his back.

Kincaid zipped around a steam cab, and slid to a halt in the middle of the next intersection. The velococycle quivered beneath them like some enraged beast, ready to bolt. All around them people stared curiously. They'd probably never seen its like before.

Plumes of smoke rose from the East, darkening the already murky afternoon light. "If that's a riot," Kincaid said, "then there'll be Nighthawks on the scene."

"Malloryn said we need to get to the guild."

"Malloryn said we need to stop any altercation between the Nighthawks and potential rioters," he corrected. "What do you think?"

Ava bit her lip. From the sounds of it, there would be Nighthawks gathering. Little garrisons of them were stationed all over London, ready to deploy at a moment's notice. "Go," she said, making a swift decision. "There's no point in us alerting Garrett if a riot's already being crushed."

The back wheels of the velocycle slid out behind them, and Ava squealed as Kincaid gunned the engine, heading directly toward the smoke column.

He gunned it through the streets, up onto the cobbled footpath when he needed to, and in and around slower moving vehicles. Ava clung to the barrel of his chest for dear life.

"There's the Nighthawks garrison!" Ava cried, spotting the first burning tower. St. Marcus's Garrison was built into the old walls the Romans had built around Londinium centuries ago—the Echelon had built onto the wall in the past, separating the inner city and their territory from the sprawling boroughs that held only humans. "They've fired it."

The gateway beneath the arch linked both towers, and allowed Nighthawks easy access. She hoped whoever had been on duty had escaped before all this began.

Nighthawks guarded the arch, riot shields at the ready

by the look of it. There were dozens of them packed into the narrow space, and she could barely see the crowd beyond thanks to the oily smoke. Another crew of Nighthawks powered the water cannon nearby, hosing down the West Tower of St. Marcus's.

Kincaid skidded to a halt, powering down the velococycle's boiler. A fierce line of Nighthawks glared at them, gesturing them to turn back. Anger lit their faces— no doubt they all knew of the Nighthawk who'd been shot several days ago, and retaliation would be brewing in the backs of their minds.

Ava swung off the velococycle, coughing as the smoke drifted past them. "I'll go through. Most of them should know me, and they'll listen to me. I think it best they don't set eyes on a mech just this moment."

She took one step, but Kincaid grabbed her wrist. "You bloody fool—you're running headlong into a riot!"

Screams started echoing ahead. There was no time for this. Ava stroked his hand, imploring him to let her go. "Trust me," she said. "Please. They'll listen to me."

"Here, now!" a Nighthawk bellowed, withdrawing a small truncheon and starting toward them. "What's going on here? Let the lady go, you bastard!"

She shot Kincaid one last look. Emotion warred on his face, a volatile mix of rage and fear, but he let her wrist go. "Don't get hurt. I'll wait for you back here."

"Thank you." She knew how much it cost him to allow her to do this.

"It's me!" she called, hurrying toward the Nighthawk and flashing her guild credentials. The embossed silver hawk came in handy sometimes. Ava breathed a sigh of relief when she recognized him. "Kennewick, thank heavens. I need to speak to the leader of the garrison. Immediately. You can't retaliate."

Ahead of them a roar of fury went up.

"Stand back!" someone bellowed, but a missile was launched over the crowded Nighthawks and smashed onto the cobbles among them. A bottle perhaps, one filled with oil. Flames whooshed out of the midst of the Nighthawks, and one of them screamed as they all parted.

The shield wall began to fail and howling rioters plunged through the gap, swallowed whole by Nighthawks. Truncheons went up and down, and she heard the crunch of breaking bones mingled with unearthly screams.

"Guild master's here himself!" Kennewick replied, wiping sweat from his face. His eyes were wild. "You can't go through, Miss McLaren. It's too dangerous."

Garrett is here? That could only be a good sign. The guild master was experienced in handling confrontations, and he knew how to control his Nighthawks. Ava grabbed Kennewick by the arm, forcing him to look at her. "Get me to Garrett now. I don't care how dangerous it is. If I don't talk to him, things are only going to get worse."

Maybe it was the intensity in her expression, or the firmness of her tone, but Kennewick nodded.

"He's just behind the shield wall." Kennewick took her hand and escorted her through the back ranks of Nighthawks, using his body to protect her. "Make way! Make way!" he yelled. "Important message for the guild master."

The smoke was thicker here, and she flinched as one of the men dragged a burning Nighthawk out of the legion. The scent of burning flesh made bile crawl up her throat, and she clasped her lace gloves over her mouth and nose.

Men pressed around her, bodies threatening to trample her at a moment's notice. It was so damned hot too. Barely any oxygen in the press. That hollow roaring sensation she knew so well dulled her hearing. *Not now.* Ava pressed onwards, her breathing coming a little faster, and a gasp catching in her throat.

"Message for the guild master!" Kennewick bellowed. "Make way! Make way!"

"Garrett!" Ava screamed, pushing against a man who stepped back and nearly knocked her over. "Garrett!"

"Jesus, lass." Doyle, Garrett's second-in-command, appeared out of nowhere and caught her by the arm. "What are you doing here? Get yourself well away. This crowd's about to go up like Guy Fawkes night. We've got nearly two legions of Nighthawks on the scene."

"I know!" She caught his forearm, her breath coming short and sharp. "I need to speak to Garrett. He can't let the Nighthawks retaliate! This is all planned. Someone wants to set the Nighthawks against the mob, and if we retaliate then we're playing into their plans!"

Thought flickered behind Doyle's rheumy eyes. He was the only human within Nighthawks ranks, and tended to be a touch old-fashioned. "Aye, well, they just shot Tommy Henderson—straight through the head. He's dead."

Straight through...? "What type of bullet did they use?"

Doyle paused. "A firebolt."

Firebolts had been designed by the humanist faction before they overthrew the Echelon. Each bullet was filled with a mix of dangerous chemicals separated by a thin metallic layer. Upon impact the chemicals mixed, and the bullet exploded.

They'd been designed to kill blue bloods.

And maybe it was happenstance, but maybe it wasn't.

"Where'd the bullet come from?" she demanded, her mind racing. "From the mob?"

"I don't see why—"

"Just bloody tell me," she snarled.

"We don't know," Doyle replied abruptly, as though

years of discipline inclined him to agree with a commanding tone. "Up high, Garrett thinks. Maybe one of them climbed a statue and used the height to pick off one of our own." A horrified expression crossed his face, and she realized he'd been there. He'd seen it happen.

A single bullet designed to set off a chain reaction. She'd been naïve once—before she started working for the Duke of Malloryn—but she wasn't anymore.

"I need to see Garrett." What were the odds the bullet hadn't come from the mob itself, but from some strategic vantage point?

Garrett was a patient man, and he had years of experience under his belt. The Nighthawks were trained to deal with combative forces, and had settled riots for years. They knew not to retaliate.

Unless they had reason to.

Unless emotion overruled them in the moment, and what better way to pit two forces against each other than to make one think the other had murdered one of their own?

"Hold the line!" someone bellowed, and it sounded like Charles Finch, the enormous weapons master of the guild.

"Please lay down your weapons," a voice said through a speaking trumpet, a desperate plea. "Disperse peacefully, or we will be *forced* to disband you."

Firelight reflected off the coppery hair in front of her—just a split-second glimpse she caught through the crowd of black-clad blue bloods. Garrett.

There.

If she was just fast enough to get to him....

"Let me through!" Nighthawks jostled her on all sides. Ava pushed and shoved, earning startled looks before they saw whom it was and let her through.

Garrett gestured men into place, clad head to toe in

strict black leather. Runnels of sweat slid through the sooty layer of grime on his handsome face. Every command came from him in a sharp staccato, as if he was holding the Nighthawks together by sheer force of will.

He saw her and paused, momentarily torn out of the melee around him. "Ava, what are you doing here?" he yelled.

"Don't suppress the mob!" she called back, staggering as the shield wall was pummeled by a wave of angry protesters and the horde of Nighthawks, in general, were forced body-to-body, crushing her a little. "Don't retaliate!"

Some instinct made her look past him, as if her peripheral vision caught sight of something moving across the street. A curtain twitching in an upper story window. Something long and hollow staring directly at them, no, at *him*—

It clicked into place far too slowly in her mind.

"Garrett!" she screamed, and made a last frantic scramble to get to him.

Maybe he saw it in her face. Maybe it was the tone of voice she used, but Garrett frowned and twisted back to look at what had caught her eye—

—and it was possibly the only reason the bullet that ripped through him took him in the shoulder, rather than the middle of the back.

Blood sprayed across her face as he jerked forward in surprise and began to fall, his left arm a bloody stump just below the shoulder.

Garrett. Charming, handsome Garrett who loved his wife, and had two sweet daughters who adored their father.

Garrett who'd been there for Ava at every moment during her recovery, after he and Perry rescued her from Hague's laboratory.

Gone beneath the feet of his Nighthawks.

CHAPTER TWENTY-FIVE

THE WORLD NARROWED to a very small bubble around her.

Ava blinked, and then she was at his side, her mouth babbling soundlessly as she saw the damage. "It's all right," she thought she said. "It's all right."

But it was not all right.

Too much blood. Bone. The gaping mush of burned flesh. Garrett gasped, his eyes so very wide, but it was Hague's face swimming through her mind as he shined the lamp in her eyes. Hague's hand lifting a scalpel as he said, *"This won't hurt at all, mijn lien."*

Suddenly she was in a distant world, where she was the one screaming—

—Blink—

Screams echoed. She looked up, nostrils flaring and her stomach in revolt. Found the streets a melee of Nighthawks fighting against the crowd. Not in Hague's laboratory. Not the one screaming.

And Garrett was bleeding to death beneath her hesitant hands.

Horror filled Ava, but it was a distant hollow ache as she stared at everything she'd tried to prevent. All she could do was babble to Garrett that he was going to survive, as she tried to stem the bleeding with a piece of torn skirt.

"Stay with me!" she cried desperately, but the pressure in her ears and around her forehead was getting tighter, and the world dulled around her.

—*Blink*—

A man at her side, asking if she was okay. No. Demanding it. Shaking her. "Ava? *Ava?*"

She looked up into Kincaid's face, and stupidly enough, the first thing that went through her head was his words from last night: *we have no future.*

"They shot him," she whispered. She saw it again. The rifle. The curtains moving. Garrett turning to look at what caught her eye. Ava looked down, to where her hands were covered in blood. "He's bleeding."

"Aye. I know." Kincaid stripped out of his coat. "Is there a doctor here?" He lifted his head to bellow, "The guild master's down! Is there a doctor here?"

Garrett's chest heaved and he tried to clutch her fingers with his remaining hand. His face was so, so pale. "Ava...." An exhale as he shivered. He tried to look at the ruined stump of his arm. "*Jesus*. Jesus, my arm—"

"You're going to be all right," Kincaid said sternly, ripping his shirt off over his head and pushing Ava's bloodied hands out of the way as he swiftly wrapped his shirt around the stump. "You've lost the arm, but you're a blue blood. You'll heal." He shot Ava a glance as he gently used his shirt to try and stem the bleeding. "He'll heal, yes?"

"Yes." *Maybe.* Her ears were ringing. The blood loss would be crucial.

"Get my belt off," Kincaid told her.

"What?"

"Get my belt off," he ground out, applying pressure to the wound and looking up at her with such vibrant blue eyes. "We need a tourniquet. At least until we can slow the bleeding down."

All she could do was focus on the blue. There was a rushing sound in her ears that sounded like it was going to swallow her whole. A cold band seemed to squeeze her head in a vise.

—Blink—

Garrett's teeth started chattering, and her stomach took a dive. Ava found Kincaid's coat in her hands and wrapped it around Garrett, trying to keep him warm.

"No other injuries?" Kincaid asked.

She checked him over, just as Garrett's eyes rolled back in his head. "None."

Someone screamed, and Ava flinched. *She could hear herself screaming, banging on the glass of the aquarium Hague had trapped her in, an oxygen mask over her face, and warm liquid caressing her naked body.*

But nobody heard her screaming.

"Ava?" someone barked, and a hand curled around hers, slick with blood. Kincaid's face swam into view. "Why are you friends with Garrett?"

"What?" She swam out of the nothing, jarred by the strange question. Forced to think.

"C'mon, kitten. Tell me a memory. One of you and Garrett." Even as he said the words, his hands worked constantly, doing what she could not—saving Garrett's life. Kincaid slashed a nick in the vein at his wrist, and held it to Garrett's mouth, cradling Garrett's head in his lap.

What a fool she was. Of course. Ava watched helplessly as Kincaid tried to get Garrett conscious enough to drink. Garrett's eyes flickered open, black with the hunger as the craving awoke within him at the scent of the blood.

"When was the first time you met him?" Kincaid crooned. "That's it. Drink it down."

She had to think. "He saved my life. He and Perry. They rescued me from Hague's laboratory."

Blue eyes seared her own. "When did you start working for the Nighthawks?"

It was all starting to come back to her. "It was Garrett." Heat flushed her eyes, but no tears, damn it. "He suggested if I wanted a career, then Fitz—the crime scene investigator—needed another set of hands at his side, and I'd shown an interest." She swallowed the lump in her throat, and held Garrett's cold fingers. "I think he knew I needed something."

I think he knew going home had torn the blindfold from her eyes—there was no home there in Edinburgh for her anymore, no fiancé, nothing but a cold barren hall where her father didn't know quite what to say to her anymore.

—Blink—

Dr. Gibson was there, pushing her aside. He had his medical bag, but the first thing he grabbed was a flask of blood. "Out of the way, lass. We need to get more blood into him."

Then there was a gurney, and worried Nighthawks helping to lift the guild master onto it.

A coat around her shoulders she couldn't remember acquiring.

Hands resting on those very same shoulders, drawing her back against a hard body.

Blood.

Ava tore her face away from Kincaid's bandaged wrist, shivering with need. "Don't touch me."

"All right. I'll stand here beside you then," he replied.

Dr. Gibson instructed the Nighthawks to lift the

gurney into the medical wagon. The streets were eerily quiet. People groaned on the cobbles, crushed by the retreating mob, or perhaps beaten down by Nighthawks' truncheons. A burned Nighthawk was rushed to Gibson's medical wagon, his leather body armor still smoldering, the stink of it making her retch.

Nighthawks crowded around. Some were bloodied. Others hung their heads as the doors were closed behind Garrett.

Ava clung to the lapels of Kincaid's coat, staring desolately at the smoky streets. "We failed," she whispered.

Nobody had won. Not the human mob. Not the Nighthawks. Not the Company of Rogues.

Only Ulbricht and his unseen master.

For she had the feeling this was just the start.

CHAPTER
TWENTY-SIX

IT WAS A nightmare, an utter nightmare.

Ava pressed her hands to her lips, letting Kincaid rub her back as they waited to hear word. He'd been particularly quiet since they arrived at the guild, letting her process what was happening around her without pushing her to make conversation, or trying to hug her or overwhelm her.

She was grateful for that. She needed the small touch of his hand in the middle of her back, but she didn't think she could cope with more. Not right now. Perry had stridden into the courtyard when they arrived, and Ava couldn't stop seeing the look on the other woman's face when Ava breathlessly tried to explain what had all gone so horribly wrong. Perry had known. The second she saw the medic van her face lost every trace of expression, and then she was barking orders, sending Doyle off with the twins, who desperately wanted to see their papa.

Ava nearly vomited in that moment.

The doors to Garrett's office slammed open, and Jasper Lynch, the Duke of Bleight, strode inside, his jaw firm and his nostrils thinned. Once upon a time he'd been the guild master, before he challenged his uncle for the duchy and took his uncle's place on the Council of Dukes that ruled the city.

It had been before her time with the guild, but Ava knew him well. Garrett and Byrnes considered him akin to a mentor, and he'd always been kind to her.

"How is he?" Lynch demanded, striding toward her and the door to Garrett's bedchamber.

"Alive," she whispered, choking on the sudden lump in her throat. She could see it all over again, feel Garrett's blood spraying across her face. "Though we haven't heard anything in the last half hour. Perry's with him."

"Who's this?" Lynch's gaze slid over Kincaid, and she had a funny feeling in her chest—almost as though she wanted to step between them, to protect Kincaid. But that was ridiculous.

"Liam Kincaid," the mech said. "I work with Ava for the Duke of Malloryn."

"The Duchess of Casavian's pet mech," Lynch said. "I remember you. From the night we stormed the Ivory Tower."

"I'm nobody's pet," Kincaid replied coolly.

Lynch's gaze flickered, very mildly, to her. "No?" Then he was heading for the door to Garrett's bedchamber. "Keep an eye on her. I should think a hot cup of tea laced with some blood wouldn't go astray."

"She's got her formula," Kincaid replied, lacing his arms across his chest, as though to prove he knew her better than the duke.

She hadn't told him she'd been taking blood.

"Sir." She caught Lynch's sleeve, and Lynch shot her a hawkish gaze that almost made her tremble. She'd been horribly out of sorts when it all happened, but now she needed to start thinking again. "I know you're aware I've been working with Malloryn on his *special* project."

"Yes, I recommended you to him."

He had? Ava pushed the thought aside. "This was planned, sir. Someone is behind these riots, stirring them up. We suspect it's Ulbricht, and he has enough of a certain type of poison to kill thousands of blue bloods, but the full depth of the plan is unknown." The words came out of her in a rush. "What I do know is this is a two-pronged attack. We don't know what they're planning with the poison, but they wanted to pit the Nighthawks against the humanists. If I hadn't called out to Garrett when I did, that bullet would have taken him right through the chest. It was deliberate, sir. There was a sniper, one who wasn't involved with the riot."

Lynch's face paled, but it wasn't a look of fear—but one of rage. "Why?"

"We think they meant to push this riot over the edge. If they assassinated the guild master, then nothing could hold the Nighthawks back from retaliation." She squeezed her eyes shut. "And it didn't hold them back. They crushed the mob. Forced them back. Beat them down. I've never...." She faltered. "These men are my friends, but I've never seen them like that before."

As if the loss of their leader drove half of them mad, their primal natures overrunning the strict control each Nighthawk was taught upon entry to the guild. Every blue blood knew what they were capable of, but she'd never seen it in such devastating detail.

"It felt like before," she whispered, "when the prince consort sent the Trojan cavalry through the streets crushing people, only this time, *we* were the prince consort and his automatons. We *were* the enemy."

Lynch's lips thinned at her assessment. "So they want

war?"

"It's a ploy, Your Grace," Kincaid added. "Something designed to take us back into the past, when it was humans against blue bloods, and murder in the streets. Humans have always been wary of the Nighthawks, but they trusted them more than the rest of the Echelon. Nighthawks worked to solve their murders, and kept the worst of the crime down. All of that vanishes after today. And that's exactly what Ulbricht wants—fear, terror, people too frightened to go to the Nighthawks who might protect them. Even unrest."

She could practically see Lynch absorbing the information. "Who's in charge of the Nighthawks cleaning up after the riot?"

"Charles Finch." She hastened to add, "I tried to warn him not to retaliate and to keep order."

Lynch swore under his breath. "Give me a moment to see Garrett, then I'll head out to the scene. Finch's a good man, but he prefers to receive orders, not to give them, and they'll listen to me." Lynch rapped on the door. "Perry? Gibson?"

Thank God. Lynch was going to handle it.

"Time to go home, I think," Kincaid murmured, his hand sliding over the small of her back again.

Agreed. Anything to get out of the ruin of her bloodstained clothes.

There was nothing for it but to return to Malloryn's. The duke needed to be told—though Kincaid quite suspected news of it would be all over the city—and Ava needed seeing to. He'd wiped the blood from her face, but it was all over her clothes, and she was oddly quiet and contained, startling every time he spoke to her, as if her mind had been elsewhere.

She felt cold too.

And far too pale.

He liked none of it.

"We're home," he murmured, helping her down from the steam cab they'd hired back to Malloryn's.

Ava stumbled along at his side, leaning heavily upon him. "I never thanked you."

Kincaid swept her up into his arms and carried her up the stairs. "For?"

"For saving Garrett's life." Those green eyes held self-recrimination. "I'm a trained professional, and for the life of me I could barely move. I don't know what happened. I just sat there, like a lump of—"

"It happens sometimes, luv." He shouldered the door open to the safe house.

Herbert, the butler, took one look at them. "Miss Ava, is everything all right?"

"She needs a warm bath, her formula, maybe a pot of tea," Kincaid said, heading for the stairs to her room. His braces strained around his legs as he took the first step. He hated stairs. "I'll run her bath if you'll fetch the rest. And send word to Malloryn. Tell him it's an emergency, and we'd appreciate his presence as soon as possible."

"Yes, sir."

Kincaid pushed open the door to the bathing chamber, thankful for Herbert's competence. He didn't quite know what the man did for Malloryn—Herbert had dangerous talents, he suspected—but he wasn't just using his butler role to be undercover.

"Here we are, sweetheart," Kincaid said, starting the bath running. One benefit of working for Malloryn was the plumbing.

Ava stood there, staring down at the steaming bath water, her tangled curls hanging bedraggled from the remnants of her chignon.

Kincaid plucked a pin from her hair. Then another, and another until finally the heavy mass fell down her back, almost to her waist. Ava glanced over her shoulder at him, her blonde lashes framing her green eyes, and the look in them made his heart clench in his chest.

She never could hide her thoughts. They were there, painted across her delicate features; want, fear, the urge to ask for his hands upon her, but doubt too... doubt *he'd* put there, with his careless words the other night.

Kincaid slid his palms up her bare arms, feeling the gooseflesh pebble beneath his real hand. He wanted to take back everything he'd said to her. To give her what she wanted—a fairy tale, a future, a dreamlike reality. But the words curdled on his tongue, unable to spill freely.

He couldn't lie to her. Not her.

"I wish we could have forever," he whispered hoarsely, and before she could turn to him, he swept her hair over her shoulder and kissed her nape. "You are so perfect, Ava—" The second she started to protest, he captured her chin and turned her face to his, shaking his head. "Perhaps you don't see it, but I do. Despite everything you've been through, you still see so much hope in the world and that's such an awe-inspiring thing to behold. You give *me* hope, and that's something I haven't felt since I was a lad. Don't ever change. Don't ever wish to be someone else, because to do so would be to deny the world the gift of yourself. You're the most beautiful woman I've ever seen."

Her lips parted in shock, and her green eyes gleamed. "Liam—"

"You are strong." He kissed the smooth patch of skin

where her neck met her shoulder. "You are brave." His fingers started on the buttons down her spine. "And you are so damned perfect I almost can't believe you'd let me lay hands upon you."

"When I'm with you, I feel like I don't have to be anyone else. You make me believe I'm perfect, just the way I am." A troubled look filled her gaze. "I've never felt this way before."

And there they were, the words neither of them dared utter. Kincaid slid the gown down her shoulders. Silence fell between them, but it wasn't uncomfortable, and it was filled with the rasp of her dress as it fell from her hips and pooled on the floor, and then the gentle rustle of hooks as he removed the press of her corset.

Piece by piece, he stripped her bare, kneeling behind her as he slid her chemise down over her bottom, revealing her pale skin. Golden curls brushed the dimples at the small of her back, and he couldn't stop himself from capturing her hips and kissing her there, a man of reverence though it was no god he served, but *her*.

"Liam," she whispered, and glanced down at him in shock.

Just one more night.

He closed his eyes, and rested his forehead against her bottom, cursing himself under his breath. He should have ended this last night. He should never have followed her in here.

But like a moth to the flame, he was drawn into her sphere, helpless against the look in her eyes.

Ava. It would always be Ava. And maybe the Kincaid curse would strike him down, but at least he'd know what it felt like to know love, just this once.

Ava turned, sliding a hand through his hair and tilting his head up so he could see her blushing. "What are you thinking?"

His gaze slid down over her small breasts and the smooth plane of her abdomen, toward the golden down between her thighs. "I'm thinking I don't want to waste another damned minute," he replied hoarsely, pressing his face into that hair and breathing in her sweet musk. Running his hands up the backs of her thighs, he cupped her ass and pushed his face against her.

Ava moaned, throwing her head back, and sliding her hand through his hair. "You are so wicked."

"And you love me for it."

The second the words were said, he wished he could take them back, but Ava merely looked down at him, her eyes wide and startled. "Yes," she whispered, "But that's not the only reason I love you." She dragged him up to her to kiss him before he could reply.

His ribs squeezed tight around his heart as Kincaid captured her mouth. He couldn't stop touching her, breathless with a feeling he didn't dare give name to.

I can't give you forever.

He crushed her close to him, capturing her slim form in his arms as he kissed her, pouring everything he couldn't find the courage to say into that kiss.

But I can give you my heart, poor, pathetic thing it is.

Taking her hand, he slid it through the gap in his shirt buttons, pressing her palm flat against his chest. His pulse hammered through his veins as he traced her tongue in a hot caress. *It's beating for you.* Then her hands were tugging at his buttons, her mouth breaking from his just long enough for him to see the determined look in her eye.

Nothing more needed to be said. Both of them could pretend last night never happened, and this was just pleasure between them.

"Off," Ava demanded, stripping his shirt from his

broad shoulders and tugging his sleeves from his wrists, taking care not to rip it on the bare spars of his mech hand.

"And these?" He slid a thumb behind his waistband, his cock pressing hard against his buttons.

"Off," Ava whispered, her eyes pure black with need as she took a step back toward the bath, and then another.

Kincaid watched her with lazy eyes as he stripped down to nothing, making short work of the leather straps that kept his braces in place. He'd never been naked in front of her before. Hell, he hadn't been naked in front of a woman for a long time. He saw her gaze slide down his body, taking in the jut of his erection, his strong thighs, his abnormally enlarged calves....

There was a lump in his throat as he waited for her to ask, but she merely held a hand out to him. "Come and love me, Liam. Just this once."

Ava stepped into the bath, sinking into the luxurious bubbles and capturing a handful of hair in a way that lifted her breasts. His mouth went dry. "We're not going to fit."

She went under, water pouring off her hair as she sat back up, rubbing her eyes. Then she smiled. "Yes, we are. Get in this bath with me right now, Liam Kincaid. I'm cold, and I just want to sink into your arms for a while and soak up all of that delicious heat."

The first step without his supportive braces always made him nervous. He managed to get into the bath, his cock rampant between them, as he settled in behind her. Ava surrendered herself back into his arms, as if she needed to be held. Water sloshed over the sides, and he was right: they barely fit. Yet somehow it was perfect.

"Today was horrible," she whispered. "And I thought I was going to become hysterical."

"But you didn't."

"It was close," she whispered, and rested her head on

his chest. "I can never control whether it will take me over, but it was easier there, with you by my side. Just knowing you're there makes me feel safe, though I don't think that will ever stop it."

They stayed there for long moments, absorbing the heat of the bath. Kincaid kissed the top of her head. He liked being able to share the troubles of the day with her, to assuage hers. They were two broken souls who became infinitely stronger together. Maybe he'd never be whole; maybe she never would be. But when she was in his arms, he felt like all the ruined cracks in his psyche were patched.

He could be happy with her.

Ava turned in his arms, looking up at him, her wet lashes clumping together. "Thank you."

"For what?"

"For what you said in Malloryn's study about trying to save the blue bloods. I know that can't have been easy for you."

He sighed, toying with one of her wet curls. "Ava... you were right. I have prejudices, and they're hard to overcome. That hate's been ingrained in me for so many years, and sometimes it was the only thing that kept me going in dark days, but... you're right. Not every blue blood is a bad person. Maybe it's time to look at the world again, and see it for what it is now, what it has the potential to be. A new London, one that works for everyone. One I'd give my life to see. The one Malloryn sees when he looks around him, the one you see. You opened my eyes to a future I never dreamed of, made me realize they're worth saving. We're worth saving."

"What are you saying?"

"Maybe there's hope," he breathed, "if we just believe in it hard enough." A shudder ran through him. "You were right. I'm not afraid of needles. I'm not afraid of the vaccine. Something stopped me from taking that step. I'm not saying I... I would take the step you suggested. I'm not sure yet. But... I'm willing to consider it."

Anything would be worth a lifetime in her arms.

Her whole face lit up. "And us?"

"Where would I be without you?" He kissed her upturned nose. "You're my hope, kitten."

"And you're my strength. My belief in myself." Happiness made her glow with some inner beauty that almost struck him dumb. How had no man seen it before? "I love you."

He kissed her, past the point of words. And she slid into his lap, straddling his thighs, a new eagerness swimming through her as she ravished him with her mouth, her hands.

Bath oil gleamed on her bare breasts when they broke apart just enough to catch their breaths. He tongued her nipple, tasting the lemon and chemical of the oil. His stubble grazed her tender flesh, but she'd grown used to his advances by now, and merely moaned, arching her back and clutching his head.

Kincaid stroked between her thighs, feeling a shiver run through her. He drove a finger into her wet, silken sheath, working her, stretching her. Added another until she was rocking in his grasp, making desperate, pleading noises. Somehow it wasn't enough. He needed to be inside her. Now. To give himself to her, and seal their future in one blazing act.

"Bend over the bath," he breathed.

Ava gave him a shy glance, but there was also a hint of the devil in her gaze. And *that* look felt like a hand stroking his cock. Slowly, she rose up onto her knees, glancing back over her shoulder at him, her hair dripping. "Just what are you planning to do?"

"I plan to take you," he told her, putting a hand between her shoulder blades and pushing her forward, until she was bent over the rim of the bath. Water sloshed on the floor as he reached for the bath oil. "Just like this."

"I know this trick."

Oiling his fingers, he rose up onto his knees behind her. "I think there's still a few things I could teach you."

She glanced back over her shoulder with a shy smile, one that stole his breath. "Really?"

He smiled. "Oh, yes."

Tracing her bottom, he slid his hand between her thighs, fucking his fingers into her in a slow, insistent drive. Ava grasped the edge of the bath with a soft shudder. The oil made his passage easy, for the water had stolen her natural wetness. He needed to work her a little, to make her wet again.

Every thrust of his fingers made her shiver, her body clenching around him.

Taking his cock in his hand, he pumped it a few times, biting his lip against the urge to plunge within her. "Are you ready?"

"For you? Always."

Kincaid eased the broad head of his cock inside her, swiveling his hips, but not letting her take any more of him. Fuck, she felt good. He breached her a little further, and Ava wilted over the bath in silent entreaty. "Do it."

"What do you say?" he breathed, running his mech fingers up her spine.

"Please." She arched her back upwards. "Please."

"Please what?"

A shudder ran through her. "Please *fuck* me."

He drove himself inside her, earning a moan, as he slid his mech hand across her tits and drew her back against him so he could bite her earlobe. "I love hearing your sweet mouth say dirty things."

"I think you like... corrupting me."

He thrust again, the angle a little shallower thanks to the position. "Maybe I do?" *And maybe you're the one corrupting me?* "Look at you, my dirty little angel." He slid his oiled fingers up her throat and brushed them over her lips. "Lick them, sweetness. Taste yourself."

Ava's wet mouth slid over his fingers, her tongue darting over them as she suckled. He thrust deeper, moaning himself. Fuck. Not so innocent now....

"That's it." Jaysus, she was so perfect. And he wasn't going to last long. Not tonight, with her silken passage milking his cock in teasing little clenches. His gaze dropped to the little bottle again. "Pour more oil on my fingers."

She let him go with a wet pop of her mouth, and then bent to retrieve the bottle. "Why?"

It lubricated his touch again, and he kissed her shoulder, and then bent her forward insistently. "Because I want to do dirty things to you."

Tracing teasing circles around the puckered rosebud between her crease, he pressed, oil easing just the tip of his finger inside her to show her what he intended. Ava froze, as though shocked. "What are you doing?"

"Do you like it?" He withdrew, and rubbed her there, making her whole body clench.

"I don't—" She gasped. "—know. Maybe. Yes."

"Do you trust me, Ava?" he whispered, breaching her again and waiting, waiting for her to say it.

"Yes," she whispered, and he felt her body surrender, felt her quiver at this new sensation as he slowly finger-fucked his way inside her. Everything in her body tightened. Everything. But she cried out softly, and he knew it wasn't in denial.

"Good," he rasped, and thrust a little harder, sheathing

both cock and finger inside her. He felt a little wild tonight. As though seeing her lost in the swarm of Nighthawks had unleashed something wild and primitive within him. He wanted to mark her, to fuck her hard enough she'd feel this possession on the morrow, and blush in remembrance.

Ava cried out, her inner passage milking him. "Oh, God. *Please....*"

And then the shockwave of pleasure vibrated through her, gripping him tight. Heat flashed through his balls, and he ground his teeth together, trying to last long enough to extend her pleasure, trying not to.... Too late. He came with a hard thrust, spilling within her and folding over the top of her.

Harsh breaths shuddered through them. Kincaid drew back, dragging her back into his arms. His hips were aching, the muscles protesting so much strenuous action. He'd probably pushed his body too far today.

But it was worth it.

"I could stay here forever," he murmured, kissing the top of her head, and enjoying the sensation of having her in his arms.

Green eyes flashed to his, and he realized he'd used the *f* word. But she nodded, and rested her head on his chest, her fingers toying with his shoulder.

"So could I," Ava whispered.

Malloryn sent word. He was aware of what happened, thanks to Lynch, and would be with them sometime that afternoon.

Ava contacted the guild for news on Garrett, but as yet, there was no reply and she couldn't afford to miss Malloryn. She spent the morning pacing, before voices echoed downstairs. There were two very familiar faces in the hallway when she hurried to the top of the stairs.

"Byrnes! Ingrid!" Ava said delightedly, hurrying down the stairs and giving Byrnes a swift hug, before turning to where Ingrid was stripping off her coat. Ava kissed her verwulfen friend on the cheek, squeezing Ingrid for long seconds. "What are you both doing here? I thought you were enjoying some time off for your honeymoon?"

"We were." Byrnes looked cold and focused, which meant his mind was on some task. The paleness of his hair was still a shock to her. "We heard what happened, and stopped by to see how Garrett is recovering."

"Is he all right?" Ava blurted.

"He'll heal," Ingrid said quietly, watching her husband's expression, and easing a hand over his forearm. "He's a little shocked to lose the arm though, and Perry's hovering over him fiercely." A warm smile softened Ingrid's face. "How have you been, Ava? Garrett was worried about you, he said you saw it happen."

A lump of sadness clogged her throat. Of course Garrett would worry about her, when he was the one who'd lost his arm. "I'm fine. I was a little rattled yesterday, but Kincaid took care of me and—"

"Kincaid?" Byrnes arched a pale brow. "Big, angry mech with a rather strong dislike for blue bloods? Would probably prefer to see the Nighthawks burn, rather than helping them? Are we speaking of the same fellow?"

"He's not like that," she said sharply, and Byrnes blinked in surprise. "He's been working with me since the two of you went away, and he's been very protective. He's brave, and gentle when he's alone with me.... He even saved Garrett's life! Without him...." She couldn't say it. Coming so close to losing Garrett was still painful.

"Ava—"

"Prejudice works both ways, Byrnes," she snapped.

There was silence in the hallway.

Ava realized she'd raised her voice, and she never dared to do so around the Nighthawks. "Oh, I'm so sorry."

"Don't be," Ingrid said, and the smile she gave Ava had a knowing edge to it, before she shot her husband an arched brow. "Byrnes needs to mind his own business. Kincaid helped rescue *you*, my love, and you're a Nighthawk."

Byrnes held both hands up in surrender. "I spoke out of turn, Ava. I'm sorry." But he gave her the queerest sort of look.

"Someone say my name?" Kincaid said loudly, appearing at the top of the stairs.

Oh, no. How long had he been there?

Long enough, clearly, for he gave Byrnes a cool look as he used the bannister to ease down the stairs. "You've both been gone. You missed a great many changes around here. I'm willing to concede blue bloods aren't all that bad. Present company excluded, of course." He coughed under his breath. "Asshole."

"Prick." Byrnes shot him a smile. "I think I've almost missed you."

"There are other changes too." Kincaid's hands settled gently on Ava's shoulders with careful deliberation, squeezing gently. "All good, kitten?"

Ava froze. What was he doing? This was supposed to be.... Everyone would know.

Perhaps that was precisely the point.

She knew he still saw Byrnes as competition for her feelings; he'd practically shouted it at her the other day. And although the matter had been settled in her mind—and heart—she hadn't realized it perhaps wasn't settled in his, despite what she'd told him last night.

You fool. Ava slowly reached up and caressed his hand. "I'm fine, thank you for asking." Then she smiled at him.

A tiny declaration, but she might as well have grown fangs and hissed at the others. Both Byrnes and Ingrid stared at her as if she had.

Then Ingrid stepped forward and kissed Ava on the cheek. "Congratulations."

And Ava panicked a little again, because they were presuming Kincaid had declared his intentions, when the pair of them hadn't quite worked everything out. Kincaid was the one holding back, but if he asked her for... forever... then she'd give it to him.

Her heart squeezed. She'd give him every part of herself if he only opened himself up to the possibility.

Byrnes wasn't quite as sanguine. "Do I need to—"

"No, you do not. I am not an idiot, and although you all treat me like a child, I can make my own decisions." Ava sucked in a slow breath, trying to fight her sudden anger. "I want this... whatever is between us, I want it with every part of my heart."

And God help her, but her mouth had said the words before she could edit them, and now her feelings were on the table, and they were all looking at her, and—

Kincaid squeezed her shoulders again, and stepped around her to take her hand. "We haven't worked out the specifics," he told the pair of them, "but frankly, it's none of your business."

"Or mine apparently," Malloryn said, startling all of them. He looked frustrated as he strode out of the shadows behind the stairs. "I think I'm going to make a company policy of pairing members of the same sex together to avoid this nonsense."

"Because that's working so well for Jack and my brother, Debney." Byrnes snorted. He drifted into the parlor and sank into a chair. "Now I've been told quite firmly to mind my own business, I think we should get to the crux of the matter. I want whoever shot Garrett." He clasped his hands between his knees, looking deadly serious. "And I want his head. I would advise all of you to stay out of my way."

That was... it?

Ava's shoulders relaxed. Everything was out in the open right now, and it felt like they'd all accepted it. It felt like Kincaid had even accepted it.

He brushed his knuckles against her back. "You can breathe now, luv."

"The sniper's yours," Malloryn said, "but *after* you bring me Ulbricht." He handed Ingrid the folder he carried. "I want the pair of you up-to-date on developments. Ava and Kincaid have discovered a poison that can kill blue bloods...."

Byrnes looked horrified as Malloryn swiftly filled the pair of them in on developments. "Sniper can wait," he finally agreed.

"The thing I don't understand, Your Grace, is the threat against the Nighthawks," Ava said thoughtfully. "Where was the serum? We all thought the SOG were going to fire poisoned darts at them. But they didn't. Just a single sniper to take Garrett down and spur the Nighthawks into a head-on collision with the mob. Why didn't they use the serum? It would have been the perfect opportunity."

"You mean, what are they saving it for?" Kincaid said, cracking his knuckles with his mech hand.

Precisely. Ava clenched both hands around the back of a chair as she stared at all of them. "Edward Leicester said they needed all the crates of serum by last night. So whatever they're planning, it must be soon, and I think there's something else going on here we haven't seen before. I think they plan to use the serum elsewhere."

Malloryn placed his fingers together, looking grim. "You're right." He met all their eyes in turn. "My spy networks turned up nothing. You're the investigators, where do we go from here?"

"Ingrid and I can try and track Ulbricht," Byrnes said, running a hand through his pale hair. The color had faded from it completely now, ever since he'd been turned into a *dhampir* against his will. "We were on his trail last month and know his hidey-holes, and his scent. My senses are better than ever, we might as well use them."

"And you two?" Malloryn asked, turning to her.

Ava sighed. "We have several leads to chase up. I think the vaccine issue has trailed off, and this is more important anyway. We need to find out who can manufacture dart guns, or guns with hollow bullets that might be filled with Black Vein, much the way the Firebolt bullets are filled with chemicals. And Kincaid has ties among the humanist population." She paused, glancing at him. "Do you think any of your friends would know anything?"

Kincaid nodded slowly. "They might."

CHAPTER TWENTY-SEVEN

AVA AND KINCAID spent another restless afternoon traipsing halfway across London.

Exhaustion rode her hard, but she couldn't give in. Not while Garrett was lying there, trying to recover. Not while her friends—all the Nighthawks she'd ever worked with—were under a cloud of danger.

Ava finally stumped out of the last warehouse they'd been checking. The two main manufacturers on her list had never heard of any strange shipments or requests. Both of them supplied the Nighthawks and the Coldrush Guards who guarded the queen with a standard-issue dart gun, though they used hemlock darts, and not Black Vein. Neither of them knew anything.

"Three thousand vials of serum," she said, wearily rubbing her face. "No dart guns. How are they planning on attacking blue bloods? Individually? With a one-on-one injection?" It made no sense. Ulbricht and his SOG were sons of the Echelon. Pampered fops who thought dueling was the limit of violence. There could only be a hundred or so SOG members at most, hardly enough to take on a force like the Nighthawks. "Think, Ava," she told herself. "How do you kill over four hundred blue bloods in a single hit?"

Kincaid slung his leg over the back of his velocycle. "You'll work it out. I believe in you."

"But what if I'm too late?" she cried. "These are my friends, Kincaid. I can't afford to waste time."

"Then we need to talk to *my* friends. See what they know." He helped her onto the seat behind him. Ava sat sideways, hampered by her skirts today, but she gladly clasped her hands around his waist.

She was almost starting to enjoy riding through the streets behind him. "Are you going to return me to Malloryn's?"

Kincaid started the boiler pack, letting it heat. "No." He let loose a loud sigh. "They're good people, Ava, just misguided. The same way I was. And I think—if we want peace in London—then it's about time both races started getting to know each other a little."

"Do you think they'll like me?" She swallowed nervously.

He laughed. "Not at first. But nobody who ever knew you could dislike you, kitten."

Xander and Maggie were setting up for the night when Kincaid rapped on the door of the inn, and called out, "Anybody home?"

"Good grief," Maggie called. "Twice in one week. One would almost think you'd remembered who you were, K!"

"Either that or he wants something," Xander added, and then he turned from his seat at the bar. Xander's smile slowly died when he saw Ava hiding in Kincaid's shadow.

He'd never brought a woman home. Nor had he ever introduced one to his friends.

"Ava, luv," he said, gesturing her forward, "this is my friend Xander McGraw, and his lovely wife, Maggie. Xander and Maggie, this is Miss Ava McLaren."

"How do you do?" He could tell Ava was nervous. She was pressing her hair into place, fidgeting.

"The blue blood?" Xander said bluntly.

Kincaid shot him an icy glare, but Maggie gave Xander a nudge with her elbow and smiled warmly. "A pleasure to meet you. I must say, I've been very curious about the woman who finally stole Kincaid's heart."

"Oh, we're just... we're—"

He slid a hand over the small of Ava's back. "We're negotiating where we are in this relationship," he told them, "but we haven't had much of a chance to sit down and discuss it yet."

All three of them blinked at him. Then Xander arched a brow. "No wedding bells then?"

Yet.

Ava choked on something, and Kincaid shot her a look. She looked horrified, but not at the notion, he thought. More the idea of even mentioning it when things between them were so unsettled.

Maggie slapped the back of Xander's head. "Why did I marry you again?"

"What did *I* do?" Xander protested.

"Maggie, want to see if you can boil a pot of tea for Ava?" Kincaid suggested, gritting his teeth. "We've been running all over London today, and I haven't taken very good care of her."

"Tea?" Maggie looked momentarily stumped, though she was clever enough to realize when he wanted to talk to Xander alone.

"Ava doesn't drink blood," he replied. "She's working on a formula to sustain herself, and she prefers tea."

"That's not technically true," Ava said, meeting his eyes. "I had... a little blood in my tea the other day."

He looked at her sharply.

"Someone once asked me how I could expect him to accept me, when I couldn't even accept myself," she told him a little proudly, and it felt like she kicked him in the ballocks.

He'd driven her to that? He felt a little ill.

"Well, I'm not going to lie to your friends," Ava pointed out, noticing the uneasy looks they gave her. "Or you."

Maggie arched a brow, but nodded. "I can do tea. If you want blood you'll have to go elsewhere."

"Oh, no, I really don't prefer it—" Ava babbled as she scurried after Maggie.

And then he was alone with Xander, still feeling like Ava had pulled the rug from under his feet.

"Bloody hell," Xander said, sitting on a barstool and crossing his arms over his chest. "I honestly don't know what to say."

"All I'm going to do is suggest you treat Ava as you'd expect me to treat Maggie." There was a hint of growl in his voice. She'd defended him against Byrnes this morning, after all.

Which was a hell of a thought.

Xander held his hands up. "I'm not saying I dislike her. She's... not what I imagined, is all. She's your complete opposite in every way." He looked disgusted all of a sudden. "She looks like she'd faint at the sight of blood."

"She's a crime scene investigator for the Nighthawks, and sometimes performs their autopsies. She won't faint, but she'd probably screw her nose up." He drummed his mech fingers on the bar. This wasn't an easy question to ask. Before he started working with COR, he'd not have flinched. These were his people; his friends. But he suddenly felt the distance between them, as though he was no longer that man.

What would he do if Xander knew something about what the humanists were up to and wouldn't tell him?

Or worse, lied to him?

"Spit it out," Xander said. "You've clearly got something on your mind."

"What would you do," he asked Xander, "if you saw Maggie almost dying in front of you, and there wasn't a damned thing you could do about it?"

Xander flinched. "I don't know. Jaysus, K. That's a brutal thought."

"Because I do know what that feels like. A couple of days ago, I watched Ava come so close to dying it was a thin line. And it tore me to pieces. I can't let that happen ever again, do you understand?"

Xander nodded.

Kincaid rested his elbows on the bar, swallowing hard. "I hinted at a weapon that could destroy blue bloods the other night. Someone used it on Ava. And I'm wondering if I can trust you with information that could get the woman I love killed. I need to know you've got my back on this."

There was a long moment of silence. "You're starting to worry me. Why does it feel like you want answers from me I might not want to tell you?"

"Because I do. I need to know what's going on in the humanist circles these days. I know you and Maggie are in the inner circles still. She mentioned the riots, and I warned her to stay out of them."

"What's this got to do with your weapon?"

"Because I think the people who have their hands on

the weapon are using humanists to stir a war."

"I might have heard something...." Xander swore under his breath. "But you're asking me to betray my men to the blue bloods, K. Jaysus. I don't know if I can do that."

Since when have we been on opposite sides?

Since the moment Ava smiled at him that night in the Garden of Eden.

"You believed in me when I had a dream," he told Xander, "a dream to escape the enclaves and gain the right for a man or woman to live life freely. And I led you to that freedom. Well, I have another dream now. A London where it doesn't matter if you are man, mech, verwulfen or blue blood. A London where all four races can survive side by side with equal rights, and forge their own futures. Peace, Xander. And not this wary mockery of it, but a true peace.

"And someone wants to take that peace away. There's an Echelon lord who's formed this... this bloody secret society of blue bloods who want the old ways back. They call themselves the SOG, and they're the ones who created this weapon against blue bloods—their own race. They're planning on killing the Nighthawks, or any blue bloods that don't agree with them, in order to drive the remaining blue bloods who aren't quite sure which side of the fence they're on into a war against humans."

Xander paled, shaking his head.

"You're a tool, Xander, that's all you and the rest of the humanists are to them. They're the ones stirring up the riots. They don't care how many humans or Nighthawks die in the streets. And I'm trying to stop it. We're on the same side here."

"Fuck." Xander scraped his hands over his face.

"Can you help me?"

"What do you want to know?" Xander asked hoarsely.

Relief flooded through him—he hadn't been certain if his oldest friend would do this. "Tell me about the humanists, tell me what they're planning, what they're up to, what the latest rallying cries are."

And Xander did, spilling about riots, and people getting together and muttering, and the odd theft. Nothing he needed to hear.

"What are they complaining about the most?"

"It's the blood taxes, K," Xander said. "Those cursed draining factories looming in the East End, churning with blood—our blood—to feed those pasty-faced vultures. That's the bone of contention. Some said we should blow them up, but then the taxes will go up again to refill them, and the Echelon guards them like hawks these days."

"That's not very helpful. How could this weapon—" Kincaid froze. He'd been phrasing it carefully, to keep Xander in the dark about Black Vein, but if he called it what it really was... it all made a horrible sort of sense. Poison. Black Vein was poisonous to blue bloods, and how better to poison the whole bloody lot of them than to contaminate their food source? "Jaysus, that's it. The draining factories." He shoved to his feet. "Ava?"

She and Maggie appeared in a flurry of skirts. Ava looked to him. "What is it?"

"Ulbricht's not looking for dart guns, or pistols. He's going to poison the blood supplies at the draining factories."

CHAPTER TWENTY-EIGHT

"LET'S NOT WASTE any more time," Malloryn commanded, slipping inside his steel-plated armor vest. "We're looking for humanists, or Ulbricht and his SOG, but don't forget the *dhampir*. They've seemingly gone to ground, but we cannot afford to presume they won't resurface at some point."

They were gathered near the outer edge of the factories, and smoke billowed into the moonlit skies as the factory furnaces burned coal. Ava breathed into her cupped hands. Nerves skittered in her belly. They needed to shut down this attack before it began, but she hoped they wouldn't be clashing with humanists tonight. For Kincaid's sake.

Maggie had given another hint before they left: some of the humanists had been talking about bombing the factories. Hopefully those plans hadn't amounted to much.

And it might be a hunch—Ulbricht wanting to poison the blood supply—but she hoped it paid out. She wanted this done, case or no case. She'd proven to herself what she needed to.

"Hold still," Byrnes muttered nearby, tugging the laces on Ingrid's armored corset tight.

"I'm not the one who can be poisoned," Ingrid muttered, and their eyes met.

Kincaid checked his pistol, shooting Ava a look as if to say he knew exactly how Ingrid felt. Ava had insisted upon coming, and Gemma was fitting her out in split skirts, with an armored corset, and a set of pistols.

A hiss of rope whirred past her as Charlie rappelled off the top of a building, landing in the street beside them and unhooking his grappling device. "There's definitely some suspicious movement near the factories. Lynch is coordinating the Nighthawks at factories one, two and three, and he's content to leave four and five to us. I couldn't afford to get too close, but there are dozens of shadows slipping into the factory."

"Ulbricht?" she demanded.

"Can't say."

A sudden noise rattled her to the core. Ava flinched.

"Just a cat," Kincaid murmured, stroking her back. He did that often.

She couldn't quite explain to him why she was so nervous. He'd insist she stay behind.

"Move out," Malloryn said, slipping the auditory device into his ear so he'd be able to communicate with them. "And keep your eyes open. If it is Ulbricht, then I want him alive."

"And if it's the humanists, then we use minimum force," Kincaid insisted.

"Indeed," Malloryn murmured. "Unless we're backed into a corner."

Ava slid the small brass communicator in her own ear, hearing the crackle of someone's harsh breathing. She wanted to be brave. She wanted to help the others, and she hated the idea of seeing Kincaid head in there without her to watch his back, but factory five loomed ahead of her.

Sending her right back into the past.

"Draining factory five," she whispered, staring up at the factory Hague's laboratory had once hidden beneath, as they finished arming themselves.

Kincaid looked at her sharply. "Are you all right? You've gone quite pale."

There was a tremor in her hands. "This is where Hague kept me for several months. There was a secret laboratory beneath the main floors, and he locked me in a tank of some sort of liquid, with a breathing mask over my face, and I could see everything—everything he did to those girls. To me...." Ava swallowed. Fear buzzed along her nerves, a warning tingle. "I don't think I-I can go in there."

"Look at me." Kincaid squeezed her arm. "Look at me, Ava."

She did, drawn by the heat in his voice.

"Nothing is going to happen to you. I promise. Hague is dead. And I would move hell and high water to keep you safe." He pressed a kiss to her forehead. "You're safe. You're always safe with me."

"But what if you're not always there?" she whispered, and if she could have shed a tear, she would have.

Kincaid froze, a storm cloud of expression darkening his face. "Ava."

But he was the one who'd said they had no future.

"I—"

"Don't make me any promises you cannot keep," she whispered. "I love you, and I won't hide that. I can't. And I could bear it if you'd let me love you for a little while, something to cherish, a time I could look back on fondly. But if you give me hope, and then dash my heart—that I could not bear."

"We need to talk about this," he said, "but now's not the time." Hesitation filled him. "I could love you too, kitten. It would be the easiest thing in the world, and I want to. I do. But... now is not the time to speak of this."

I could love you too.

He was right. Ava turned away, watching as the rest of the Rogues armed themselves. "Do you need any help with your mech-suit?"

"I can manage, but Ava?"

She looked back.

"Always," he told her sternly. "I will always be there for you, no matter what happens between us. If you ever need me... *ever*, do you understand? And that's a promise I can keep. For as long as I'm still breathing."

Ava released a shuddering breath. She felt a little better now, a little more herself. "I understand."

"Then let's go hunt down Ulbricht—so we can have a moment to ourselves to talk about where this is going." Then he turned to strap himself into his Achilles armor.

"Sure you know how to shoot a pistol?"

"Perry's been teaching me." Ava opened her pistol and loaded it, before reholstering it at her waist.

Tension slid through Kincaid's chest, but there wasn't much to say. "I know you're capable," he said roughly. "I'm just worried."

"I'm a blue blood," she said. "You're human. One could say the same."

Kincaid rapped his knuckles on his mech-suit. "They've got to get through this first." And he'd been killing before Ava even knew what the craving was. He glanced to where Byrnes was checking Ingrid's armored corset. The pair of them looked at each other and he saw the same concern on both their faces; a moment where sentiment reflected.

Clearly this did not get any easier, regardless of whether the woman you loved could rip a vampire to pieces with her bare hands, or not.

Gemma silently handed Ava a flask. "Drink it."

"What is it?"

"Blood." Gemma checked the weapons strapped to Ava's hips. "And don't argue. It will prime the predator within you so you're faster and stronger, and can see and hear a little better."

He let Gemma's competence distract him from his nerves about Ava. Gemma was dressed to kill in an armored corset that covered her clothes, and an under-dress that was split at the sides to allow her freedom of movement. Gauntlets protected her hands, and wicked little spikes drove out from her knuckles. One punch and they'd pierce a man's body. He suspected they were laced with hemlock, and she had little hemlock bombs hanging from her belt, beside at least four holstered pistols.

"You're looking particularly deadly today," he noted.

Gemma smiled as Ava hesitantly tipped the flask to her lips. "Only today? I must be slipping."

"I pity the poor bastard who crosses your path."

She rapped her knuckles on his breastplate, and the spikes squealed against the metal. "One could say the same."

His glance brushed over Ava's blonde curls, and Gemma saw the direction of his gaze. She nodded, almost imperceptibly, and relief filled him. They'd all keep an eye on her.

Ava's chest rose and fell breathlessly as she lowered

the flask from her lips. Her eyes gleamed black. Ava patted his cheek, and he captured her hand there, turning the move into a kiss to her palm.

"What was that for?" she asked.

"For being you," he said, stroking his thumb down her palm. "For being brave, and kind, and absolutely fucking perfect."

Heat pinkened her cheeks. "Hardly poetic, but appreciated, all the same."

"Here are the rules," he continued, capturing her face in both hands. His mech fingers dug into her cheek a little. "Survive at all costs. Watch your back. And stay with one of us at all times."

"Only if you promise to focus on your own task—and not on whether I'm safe or not. You're at risk too, you know."

His heart swelled in his chest. She was one hell of a woman. Kincaid reached over and cupped the back of her nape, dragging her up onto her toes so he could kiss her. He captured her mouth, devouring the taste of her. A kiss full of fire and passion, and something else. Something he couldn't quite put into words.

"Anytime you're ready," Malloryn said tartly, and Kincaid heard the sound of a pistol being loaded.

"You're just jealous because neither the baroness nor your future wife are offering to kiss *you* at the moment," Gemma shot back.

"I don't *want* to kiss Miss Hamilton," Malloryn growled, "and Isabella will come around. Are we ready? I for one would like to bury Ulbricht alive."

Kincaid broke away from Ava, breathing hard. The others could damn well wait.

"Let's go," Malloryn called. "Be wary. We don't know what Ulbricht is planning. He wants to destroy the draining factory and lay the blame at the feet of humanists, thus starting another war. We're about to stop him. At any cost. I will not see my city go up in flames again."

"Let's show the Sons of Gilead what the Company of Rogues can do!" Charlie called, darting ahead.

"Bloody hell," Malloryn muttered, and then they converged on the factory.

Gemma picked the lock at the back of the factory, using a glimmer ball to see what she was doing. Kincaid guarded her back, his enormous mech-suit blocking the light from any guards that might have been posted. Byrnes, Jack, Ingrid, and Ava were out there, removing any of said guards, but they couldn't be too careful.

He didn't like Ava being separated from him, but he couldn't argue against Malloryn's splitting of the teams. His group would be heading into danger first, which meant they'd draw the heavier fire. Better for her to be out there at this moment, rather than inside. And Ingrid had promised to kill anything that went near her.

Verwulfen had a protective instinct a mile wide.

"Got it," Gemma whispered, and then she turned the door handle so slowly sweat dripped down his spine.

Malloryn and Charlie slipped inside behind her. Inside the draining factory, the dull throb and roar of the steam engines that ran the machinery covered the hiss of the pistons in his suit as he brought up the rear.

He'd never been inside one of the factories before. The four of them fanned out, shadows in the night.

A grunt echoed. "Hey—"

Faint moonlight gleamed through the windows, highlighting a lithe dark shape that fought in a swift flurry of blows. A guard. And one of the Rogues. Kincaid held his pistol low. He could feel his blood rushing through his veins, but he kept his flickering gaze on the room, and not on whoever had attacked the guard.

"He's down," Gemma whispered through the communication device. And he could just make her out, lowering an unconscious—or dead—body to the ground.

"Humanist?" Kincaid asked.

Gemma knelt over the body. "Blue blood."

They looked at each other.

"Ulbricht," Malloryn breathed, with the tone of a man who would dearly love to get his hands on the vicious lordling.

Malloryn flickered through a patch of moonlight, gesturing them forward with his fingers. Kincaid brought up the rear once again as they all paused in the doorway that led onto the factory floor.

The noise here was much louder. Blood churned in enormous glass vats that lined the room. The swish of liquid danced through brass tubes like the rush of a river, and the enormous filtration devices thundered beneath the vats, their engines vibrating. How much blood was there? Kincaid's gaze slid up the nearest vat. What did that represent in terms of blood taxes, and people who were still forced to donate four times a year?

A hand slid over his armored forearm. Malloryn. A swift glare told him to focus, and he nodded.

The first glimpse of their adversary flickered between brass pipes. A man strode through the room, calling out to others. Excitement licked through Kincaid. Here they were. The Sons of Gilead. The bastards who'd tried to murder Ava.

Malloryn gestured to him and they peeled off, leaving Charlie and Gemma to head in the other direction. Byrnes and his team should be entering shortly, coming in via the front entrance. Sweat slid down his temple. It was hot as hell in here, steam from the filtration devices misting the air.

"Let's find Ulbricht," Malloryn breathed in his ear, before scurrying along the far side of the filtration vats.

Kincaid followed. Cut the head off the snake, and they'd shut down the Sons of Gilead for good.

Half a dozen red-robed figures slipped through the main floor of the factory, kneeling at certain places, and carrying crates. Some of them wore faceless silver masks with only eye slits for expression.

But one of them wore a black robe, and he left his face bare.

"That's him," Malloryn said, his glittering eyes locked on the lord. He smiled. "Got the son of a bitch."

Lord Ulbricht was a big man, almost as tall as Kincaid himself. His hair swept back from his face in distinguished silver wings, and he carried himself as though he were a king.

Ulbricht yelled at one of his followers, and Kincaid wanted to plant his fist in the bastard's face. While he might have reconsidered his stance on most blue bloods, Ulbricht was exactly the type he hated. Pompous, arrogant, and so certain of his superiority and his right to crush everyone else beneath his heel.

"Move out," Malloryn said through the communicator, and then the duke was crossing behind the simmering blood vats, his pistol held low as he pressed his back to the metal base of the enormous filtration device below the glass vat.

Kincaid followed. Every step of his Achilles suit made him confident. Pistons hissed, leaving him lighter on his feet than he'd been in ages.

A faint grunt sounded through the communicator. Kincaid looked at Malloryn, and then they both looked up as a body sailed from the mesh walkway above, slamming into the heavy floorboards.

"Sorry," Gemma muttered.

"We're not alone!" Ulbricht bellowed, and a dozen of the red robes scrambled to form a circle, back to back.

"Who's there?" Ulbricht called, brandishing a pistol.

"It's over, Ulbricht!" Malloryn yelled. "I've got the factory surrounded by Nighthawks, and none of you are making it out of here. If you throw your weapons down and surrender, I'll take that into consideration."

"Malloryn," Ulbricht spat. "Of course you'd be here to ruin the party."

"Destroying your petty schemes is the highlight of my life," the duke riposted, stepping out and pointing a pistol at him. "Step away from the gathering vats before I'm forced to shoot you."

There was a faint flicker of movement behind them, and Ulbricht's eyes shifted in that direction, just as all the hairs down the back of Kincaid's neck rose. "Look out!" he shouted, slamming into Malloryn and crushing the duke to the ground beneath his heavy mech-suit.

Bullets ricocheted off his back armor, and Kincaid swore under his breath, rolling them out of the way beneath one of the enormous vats of blood. More of Ulbricht's men appeared in the shadows at the back of the factory. *Ava!* Jaysus, where was Ava? He caught a glimpse of Charlie sprinting across the factory floor with Ava in hand, shoving her behind the filtration system in the corner.

Their eyes met, and Kincaid ducked his head back down as more bullets rained toward him and Malloryn. Safe. For now. Charlie would keep her out of the way, and it was clear Ulbricht's focus was on Malloryn.

"Son of a... bitch." Malloryn sucked in breath as though he was winded. He pushed at Kincaid's breastplate, but lacked the strength to shove him away.

"You hit?" Kincaid demanded, easing off him.

"By a small freight train by the feel of it," the duke rasped, sitting up and swaying.

"Better that than a Firebolt bullet."

Malloryn pressed tentative fingerprints to a dimple in the back plate of Kincaid's mech-suit. "They're not using Firebolts."

"Aye," Kincaid panted, as gunfire sparked above them on the walkways that circled the factory. "Not yet." The filtration device under the vat was keeping them safe, but he could feel the metal of the suit pressing uncomfortably against his skin where bullets had impacted. "They're using those new armor-piercers." Designed to send shrapnel through a blue blood's body so they caused as much damage as possible, clearly the bullets weren't quite strong enough to penetrate sheet metal.

Or maybe he'd been lucky.

"You saved my life," Malloryn blurted, and it was the first time Kincaid had ever seen the duke look close to ruffled.

Kincaid hauled the duke onto his knees. "I'm going to hold it over your head forever too."

There was the duke again, that icy gaze locking on him. "I might just let you, if we get out of this alive."

Holding his hands out, Malloryn ejected the pistols that were hidden inside his sleeves, and they swiveled into his palms. "Ulbricht's mine."

"That's the sort of thinking that gets people killed," Kincaid pointed out. "This isn't a duel, Your Grace, and we've got ladies in here. If I see him, I'll shoot him."

"Fair call." The duke pressed a pair of fingers to the auditory device in his ear. "Status, please."

Static buzzed in Kincaid's matching earpiece.

"I've got Ava," Charlie replied. *"We're hiding under the filtration device opposite you. There's a gunman pinning us down."*

Pistol fire bloomed above them, then Gemma strode along the mesh walkway, firing dramatically from two pistols. A man in black cried out, then tumbled off the walkway, slamming into the middle of the factory floor. *"One sniper down,"* Gemma said, and then sprinted into the shadows above as return fire pinged off the mesh under her feet.

"Jack here," growled the taciturn man. *"I'm hit."*

"Ingrid and I are keeping an eye on him," Byrnes echoed. *"Flesh wound only, but it will keep one of us out of action. He's not a blue blood, and Debney will wring my neck if he dies."*

Kincaid frowned, looking around. "What's that sound?"

"What sound?" Malloryn murmured, focusing on the rest of the group.

What the hell was it? "It's almost like a... a clock—"

"Anytime you want to join my party, Malloryn," Ulbricht called, his voice echoing through the factory. Laughter followed his words. "I'm told the fireworks display is going to be the *event of the year.*"

Fireworks—?

Shit.

"Move!" Malloryn screamed at him, shoving him out into the open.

Muscles ached in Kincaid's thighs as he pushed himself into a sprint, following Malloryn. Every second stretched out—

—and then a massive roar went up behind him, the force punching him in the back and sending him head over heels. His knees jarred against his mech-suit as he hit the ground, heat searing across his back and something wet splattering all over him. His lungs sucked in dry air. Jaysus. He was frigging boiling inside the suit.

Malloryn slapped at his back, and some part of Kincaid's mind distantly realized he'd been on fire.

"Looks like we're even," Malloryn said, dragging him to his feet. "Can you move?"

"I'll have to," he croaked.

There was blood spattered all over the duke's face, and ash darkened his coppery brown hair. Kincaid threw a glance over his shoulder. The vat was gone. Just gone. Smoke and flames boiled out from the ruined filtration device, and blood steamed in patches on the floor.

"He must have some sort of remote detonator," Malloryn observed. "He's blowing them up, not poisoning them."

But how many charges had Ulbricht set?

Pistol fire pinged off Kincaid's shoulder armor.

"Keep moving!" the duke barked, and then they were running through black clouds of smoke.

Starfire bursts in the darkness indicated pistols firing at them. Something hit Kincaid, throwing him off balance. Another bullet ripped into the chest-plate, hammering a punch into his ribs. His mech hand shattered as he flung it up to protect his face, and Kincaid had the sudden sensation someone had *actually shot him*, as Malloryn drove him under cover with Ava and Charlie.

"Covering you!" Charlie called, firing over his shoulder and momentarily silencing their opponents.

Kincaid slumped on his back, sucking in lungfuls of air.

"Are you all right?" Ava demanded, touching his shoulder.

He held up his ruined hand. Fifteen years with this steel fused into his flesh. fifteen years of blood and sweat in order to pay for it; his brother's life; his sister's suicide; it had seen him through all of it. "Hell."

It felt like losing the bloody hand all over again, and his forearm ached from the impact.

"I'll buy you a new one," Malloryn barked, returning fire.

"All good," he breathed, meeting Ava's eyes. "Just winded me, and shattered my hand."

Her face was so pale. "I couldn't see you! When the vat exploded, you and Malloryn vanished and—"

"I'm here. I promise, luv," he said.

She sucked in a shaky breath, and then helped him sit up.

"Gemma?" Malloryn snapped. "Byrnes? Are we all alive?"

"Get out of there!" Byrnes's voice echoed in all their ears. *"Ulbricht's rigged all the vats. We're too late."*

Not only too late—they'd walked into a frigging trap.

"Where's Ulbricht?" Malloryn demanded.

"Evacu—"

Another whoosh of hot air, and the second vat went up, a fireball of heat blossoming out from its base. Shards of metal hammered into the tanks on either side of it, and glass shattered, spewing waves of blood across the floor.

Ava screamed. Kincaid hauled her to her feet, using his body and mech-suit to protect her. "We've got to get out of here!"

"Working on it!" Malloryn yelled back.

"Kincaid!" Ava cried, as he scanned the room.

"What?"

"I think there's a bomb under here," she said in a very quiet voice.

Both he and Charlie looked at each other, and then knelt where she'd been to see. A small case was attached to the base of the filtration device, and it was ticking.

"Come out, come out, wherever you are, Malloryn," a voice called.

"Above us!" Kincaid croaked. And there on the mesh walkway was a figure wearing a black cloak. Ulbricht.

"We're pinned down." Malloryn shot a look at the door.

"The bloody bomb's ticking down! We have to get out of here!" Kincaid eyed the distance. "How good a marksman are you?"

"Tolerably good," Malloryn replied, "though I'm better with knives."

"Can you shoot him from here?"

Malloryn eyed the distance. "Perhaps."

"Charlie?"

The lad shook his head. "I'm out of bullets too."

Kincaid sighed. "I have an idea, but you're not going to like it. I can make that shot, but I need a moment to take it. I need his mind on something else."

"I want him alive," Malloryn snapped.

"I want to get out of here alive," Kincaid snarled. "That bomb's about to go off any moment now."

"It's got a minute on the clock," Ava called, kneeling in front of the case.

Malloryn's lips pursed. "Blood and bloody ashes! Fine."

"Come out, Malloryn. Let's settle this once and for all."

They looked at each other.

"I'll distract him," Malloryn said tersely. "You kill him." Then he bolted across the open floor. He aimed a scattered shot toward Ulbricht, and the lord ducked, then strode across the walkway, tracking Malloryn with his pistol.

Kincaid eased out of the shadows. He was packing Firebolt bullets. Ulbricht rained bullets down upon Malloryn, forcing the duke under cover.

Come on. Turn this way just a little bit. Sweat dripped down his face, and Kincaid focused on the lord's head, the rest of the world vanishing around him.

"Hurry!" Ava called.

He eased out a slow breath, squeezing the trigger. The shot exploded out of his pistol.

Ulbricht's head burst like a ripe melon. The headless body stiffened, and then slumped forward onto its knees and hit the walkway.

"Got him!" Kincaid screamed. The other SOG members seemed to have vanished.

Malloryn sprinted to his side. "Let's get out of here! Ava, how much time?"

"Twenty seconds!"

Kincaid grabbed her by the hand and hauled her to her feet. "Run!" he said, shoving Charlie ahead of him.

Hell bloomed around them, fiery with rage. Ava's eyes stung, and she couldn't suck in enough air to breathe. The oxygen in her lungs was hot and thick.

"Keep low," Kincaid bellowed, shoving her through the smoke.

"This way!"

A hand yanked her forward. Malloryn. She had no idea where Charlie and the others were. Behind her another explosion rocked the factory. Then another, like some sort of chain reaction.

The force drove them all into the nearest wall. There was a hand pushing her, a huge shape behind her that yelled in her ear, "Run!"

A doorway loomed ahead of them.

The second she was through it, the heat and light cut down, leaving her in the relative darkness of the back room. So much... smoke. Ava coughed.

Something loomed in front of her; something falling. Ava screamed, and then a hand on her back sent her sprawling. A heavy weight hit her in the back. Part of the roof? A timber support?

"Kincaid!" She pushed herself off the floor, dislodging several timber struts.

Kincaid strained beneath a heavy roof beam, the steel in his armor buckling, and his knees shaking as he ground his teeth together. "Get out of here!"

No! "Not without you!" She tripped on her skirt as she leaped to his side, trying vainly to help him shift the beam. The stupid fool! He'd tried to protect her from the worst of it. "You're not invincible, not even in your bloody suit!"

His arms shook. His ruined hand was peeling in on itself, unable to support the weight.

"Ava!" She saw the whites of his eyes starkly against his sooty face—the look in them. "Get out. Get out before it's too late."

And suddenly she knew what he was telling her.

The heat drained out of her face, a shiver of horror trailing cold fingers down her spine.

"No," she sobbed. This wasn't happening. "I love you. I'm not going to leave you here all alone!"

"Don't let me die here knowing I've brought you down with me. You've got a whole life to live."

"Malloryn!" she screamed. "Malloryn, help!"

"Curse you!" Kincaid ground his teeth together,

forcing his knees to straighten.

She could see the strain in his face. Flames licked up the wall nearby, the heat drying her eyeballs. There was no hope, no matter where she looked. Kincaid was trapped, and if he moved then this part of the roof would collapse upon them.

If he didn't... then they'd burn alive.

Ava's head spun. There was another beam nearby. One that might be able to support the one that was threatening to crush him. She darted for it, grabbing hold of the hot end and burning her hands. Withdrawing them with a flinch, she looked around. Nothing to protect them. No time to worry about it. Ava ripped shreds off the bottom of her dress and wrapped them around her palms, then grabbed hold of the beam again.

She put her back into it, all of her weight. It barely shifted. "Damn you!" Her hands were blistering hot. Pushing and shoving, she tried everything she could to get it to move.

"Ava, go! For the love of God, get out of here!" He started coughing.

"I. Am. *Not*. Leaving. You. Here!"

Another explosion ripped through the factory, the hot rush of wind sweeping her skirts out behind them. Balls of flame whizzed past her ear.

"No!" Ava screamed, as the ceiling fell down upon him.

CHAPTER TWENTY-NINE

"KINCAID! KINCAID!" SHE screamed, staggering through the murky dark as the dust finally stopped raining down.

He'd been there one second. Gone the next.

Ava coughed, fighting her way over rubble. "Liam!"

Then the duke was there, materializing so suddenly she almost screamed. "We've got to get out of here," Malloryn said grimly. "That explosion took out the support beams in the roof here. They missed some of the blood vats, but I don't like our chances that the rest of the roof won't come down."

"Malloryn?" Gemma called through the listening device in Ava's ear.

"Alive! I've got Ava. We'll meet you out the front," he called.

Ava dug her heels in. "No! Not without Kincaid."

"Ava." The duke grabbed her by the arms, shaking his head apologetically. "Ava, sweetheart, I'm sorry—"

She didn't want to hear it, and fought him until he was forced to let her go. "He wouldn't leave me behind. Please.

Please. He saved *your life*."

Emotion fought logic on his expression. Then his resolve firmed. "One minute. That's all I'll give you, Ava. Then we leave, with or without him."

Relief flooded through her. "He was just here."

The smoke obscured the mess of the wall where it had fallen upon them. She saw the end of the bloody beam Kincaid had been trapped under, crushing a metal workbench along the wall, but not quite all the way. Suddenly hope went through her. "He was under this when the wall fell! He won't be crushed! It's holding the weight of the wall and roof off him."

Ava started flinging pieces of metal and timber off the pile of rubble. Fire licked at the edges of the mess, and she started coughing. "Kincaid? Kincaid!"

Malloryn produced the tracking beacon. Orange light gleamed across his pale skin, and the heat of the fire was tremendous. The compass hand swiveled steadily, leading him to a certain spot. "He's under here!"

Then they were both tearing at the pile. It suddenly heaved beneath them, and Ava's heart soared. "He's alive! Kincaid?"

She pulled aside one last piece of timber, revealing the man she loved. Ava gave a sob of relief. "Liam!"

Kincaid's chest heaved. The mech-suit was dented, the carapace that protected his chest caved in and bloodied.

"A-va," he gasped, seeing her.

She slid to her knees, hauling wreckage out of the way.

Malloryn kept kicking pieces of rubble aside. "Not much time, Ava."

Ava tried to lift the beam. It shook, but despite her blue blood strength she couldn't shift it. Then Malloryn was there, his smooth aristocrat hands sliding under both sides of it. "I've got it. On the count of three you need to pull him out from under it."

The duke gave her confidence and hope. Ava scrambled to Kincaid's ankles, latching on to each foot. "Got him," she called.

"Make it quick." The duke met her gaze. "One. Two. And *three*!"

He lifted the beam several inches, straining under the weight. Ava wrenched hard, dragging Kincaid out from beneath it. "Clear!"

Malloryn dropped the beam, but she was on her knees, capturing Kincaid's face in her hands. His eyes rolled up in his head, then he blinked, his breath coming in wet rasps. Her heart fell.

"He's bleeding," she whispered. "Inside, I think."

And she, with her cursed anatomical knowledge, knew what that meant. She'd done enough autopsies in her time. She'd always kept her feelings locked away inside her as she played investigator with the body, but this time it was Kincaid's body she saw lying there on the mortuary slab in her imagination. "No."

"He's still breathing. Ava," Malloryn warned, taking her hand. Streaks of soot stained his face as he glanced around. "The entire building's going to come down."

"Get her... out..." Kincaid rasped.

There was a certain look on the duke's face. "Lead me out of here, Ava. I'll carry him."

She helped Malloryn draw Kincaid up over his shoulder. Kincaid moaned in pain, but there was no time to lose. "This way!"

She could barely see. At least the smoke was funneling up through the hole in the roof, though her skin felt blistered from the heat coming from the main floor of the factory. Ava coughed and staggered, her searching fingers finally finding the door. Then they were through it.

Cold, pure air seared her lungs. It hurt so much, but she kept moving, leading Malloryn as far away from the burning factory as she could.

They finally collapsed a hundred feet away, and Malloryn shuddered as he gently laid Kincaid flat on his back.

"Kincaid? Liam?" She slapped his face gently, her breath catching in her lungs for one heart-stopping moment as she tried to see whether his chest still rose and fell—*no, no*—before Kincaid blinked at her, his lashes stirring weakly.

"There's only one way to save him," Malloryn murmured, "though he won't like it."

Ava looked up, through raw smoke-burned eyes. "The craving virus."

Hope and dread wove her into knots. He'd mentioned his reasons in not accepting the vaccination, but was that enough?

Kincaid groaned, and shifted beneath her touch. Malloryn looked down. "It's his only hope, and even then I don't like his chances. He's bleeding inside. Kincaid, can you hear me?"

Those very blue eyes looked even bluer against his smoke-stained face. "You're gonna... infect me?"

"Only with your permission," Malloryn replied.

There was a long, drawn-out moment as her future revealed itself in her imagination, barren and lifeless, and lacking the one person she needed....

"Please! Please don't leave me. I've lost everything, and I've survived it all... but I don't think I could survive losing you. Not when I've just found you. Not when I've just realized *you* were what I've always been looking for." Collapsing over Kincaid's chest, she buried her face in his throat, sobbing tearlessly. "I love you. And I know you don't want this, but please... please stay with me. Please say yes."

His human hand curled around her, catching roughly in her hair. "Ava...."

"Now or never, Kincaid," Malloryn warned.

Ava clung to him breathlessly, begging him silently to give her the answer she so desperately needed.

Kincaid shuddered. "Do it."

CHAPTER THIRTY

THE WORLD BLINKED in and out of focus. Shadows, smoke, pain.... Voices echoing as people he knew barked orders.

His head swam. Then his body was moving, jolting slightly as something shifted beneath him. A carriage? A woman settling onto the seat beside him? Kincaid coughed up blood, and then he was struggling to breathe, his lungs flooded, his heart hammering weakly in his chest....

He could still taste Malloryn's blood.

"We're losing him!" Ava cried.

"Be patient." Malloryn. The prick. Cool and commanding even now. *"Give the virus time to work its way through him."*

Kincaid's chest heaved. Then he was rolling—or being rolled—and he choked up the blood in his lungs, his throat working desperately for oxygen. He couldn't breathe. Pressure flooded his head, pounding through the veins at his temples.... His ears rang, and his eyeballs bulged in their sockets.

The world went black, sensation fading.

Everything was warm, and dark. A cocoon devoid of sound. Silence. Nothingness.

Peace.

Then... a single voice intruded. *"...keep him breathing...."*

Pressure on his chest forced pain back through his lax muscles, and a mouth hovered over his own, forcing air into his lungs. Kincaid swam up through the nothingness, crying out silently as he fell back into his body with a heavy feeling. Sensation hammered back into him, twice as agonizing as before as all the nerve endings in his body fired to life again. He wanted that peace again. No pain there in the warm dark, but there was something holding him back.

Something....

"I'll never forgive myself," Ava whispered, and distantly he thought he felt a cool hand in his. *"He tried to save me."*

Don't cry, luv. But she was, and there wasn't a damned thing he could do about it.

He wanted to kiss away her sadness. To curl her in his arms and let her feel safe there forever. To hold her one more time... that was worth the pain and the fear and all the complicated emotions that roared through him.

What would you do if you had a future? Orla had once asked, and he couldn't answer her then.

But he could now.

I would love Ava. Forever.

Someone breathed into his lungs, and Kincaid started to thrash. There was something happening deep in his chest, a pain, an agony, but also a kindling, as though someone stoked the fires on a steam engine. Hot little sparks fired along his nerve endings. The world went dark, but this time it was his vision, rather than his senses fading.

"He's back, he's breathing!" That sounded like the duke.

Jaysus. Was Malloryn resuscitating him?

Kincaid thrust upward. "*G'away....*"

"*There he is. Get some more blood into him!*" Malloryn yelled. It was all so very distant, as though there was a bubble around Kincaid, keeping their voices at bay. "*Or he'll start convulsing.*"

A hot coppery scent washed past his nose, and his mouth watered.

More. I want.... The urge to strike and take what he wanted was blinding.

"*Drink,*" someone urged, and then there was a woman's wrist against his lips, and the sweet scent of Ava's perfume. Her wrist. Her blood welling in his mouth, hot and salty, and both disgusting and yet insanely seductive, for some reason.

"*Drink and live,*" someone else murmured. "*The more of the virus we can get into him, the better his chances of surviving.*"

Byrnes?

Then sound rushed in with a snap that made his ears pop.

Kincaid came to, cradled in Ava's lap, his mouth wrapped around her wrist as he swallowed her blood. He wanted it. Wanted more. Maybe it was his body hungering for heat after the chill of his near death, or maybe it was the predator awakening inside him. He didn't know, but his chest hurt like a bastard, and he'd never been so aware of all the aches and pains in his body.

"That's it," Ava whispered, stroking his hair.

Malloryn loomed over her shoulder, helping to hold Kincaid up.

He caught a glimpse of Ava, her blonde curls frizzing around her worried face like a halo. And it was everything, in that moment, to see her; his reason to live. The light in his dark world. He tried to capture her wrist, but his fingers barely worked. Somehow she sensed it, and he felt her take his hand.

"I love you," Ava whispered. "And I'll be waiting for you when you wake."

Kincaid groaned. "Too much... light."

His eyes ached. He pressed his palm into them, but something held his other hand back.

"You've lost your mech hand," Ava said gently, and he realized she was pinning his left arm to the bed so he couldn't use it. "We've bound it up, but you might hurt yourself with the stump."

His mouth watered again, every scent that spoke of Ava dominating his senses. She felt warm. So warm.

The light dimmed as she turned the gas lamp down as low as it could go.

"How do you feel?" Ava murmured, and her pale face swam into view.

Insanely hungry. How the hell had she managed to abstain from drinking blood for so long?

Ava saw it in his face and tipped the flask of blood to his lips. It wasn't disgusting anymore, and maybe that was what frightened him the most. Had he become what he despised? Or was this... new territory to be explored, a new life to begin, just a sidestep of the man he'd truly been.

"I'm sorry," Ava whispered, and something pricked his arm. "Malloryn insisted I sedate you, or I wasn't allowed to be in here with you alone."

"Won't hurt you...." He was feeling sleepy again.

"You're newly made. You don't understand the full extent of the changes to your body." Ava hesitated. "You wouldn't mean to do it, but the craving... it's quite powerful when you're freshly made, and you were injured so badly your craving virus levels spiked immediately. You're already sitting at 12 percent, which is rather high after only three days."

Three days?

The spike of anxiety faded as warmth flooded through him. Somehow he captured her hand, sinking into the soft pillows. He blinked sleepily.

"Promise you'll stay?" he whispered.

Ava rested her elbows on the bed, giving him a tremulous smile as she kissed his hand. "Not even Malloryn could drag me out. I'll be here when you wake again. I promise."

Another three days passed.

Ava grew restless, pacing the small room when Kincaid slept, and tucking up beside his broad body when she needed rest. Every time he opened his eyes, she poured blood into him, and sedated him afterwards as soon as she could.

Sometimes she cried, though of course, no tears formed. And it was silly to cry, because he'd lived, but she'd been so certain in those blackest moments she was losing him. Perhaps that was what brought on the sobs—her mind's struggle to realize he'd *actually* survived.

It was during one such moment Kincaid woke. The first Ava knew of it, his hand was stroking through her hair as she knelt beside the bed and stifled the sobs in the mattress.

"Come here, kitten," he whispered.

So Ava slid into his warm blankets and the wide-open arms that greeted her. "I'm sorry. I didn't mean to wake you."

"Just don't sedate me yet," he murmured, dragging her against his chest. "Why are you crying, Ava?"

"I thought you were dead. It was so close. You stopped breathing, and I didn't know what to do, and I know this isn't what you wanted—"

"Isn't it?" He pressed a kiss to her hair. "Ava, there was a reason I never got the craving virus vaccination."

She looked up into his scruff-jawed face.

Kincaid released a heavy breath. "You're right. A part of me didn't want this to happen, even as a part of me knew it might be my only hope. But I don't think I would have taken that step, not until I met you and realized we could have forever together."

"Forever?" she breathed.

"Forever," he insisted, and then rolled onto his side so they were sharing the pillow and staring into each other's eyes. Kincaid stroked her thick hair off her face. "I'm an idiot, Ava. But I don't look a gift horse in the mouth. You and I have been given a miracle. And... I have a new proposition for you."

"What sort of proposition?"

Kincaid captured her face and turned it up to his. "The kind I think you'll like. Marry me, Ava. Marry me and spend all our years at my side. Let me love you every day."

Happiness spilled within her. "I didn't think you were the marrying type."

"Nor do I mess with virgins, women who have their hearts in their eyes, or blue bloods," he said solemnly, and then smiled. "You've ruined all my rules, made me throw them straight out the window. I'm head over heels for you, kitten. And I don't like the way the Major Winthrops of the world look at you. You're mine, and I want everyone to know it." He leaned forward to brush his lips against hers. "Especially you. I want *you* to know you're mine, Ava, because you have this terrible habit of doubting yourself, and I won't have that. Be my wife. Let me love you. We can sort out all the rest."

Ava threw her arms around him, capturing his mouth in a blistering kiss.

"Was that a yes?" Kincaid drawled, rolling her onto her back and settling between her thighs.

"Yes!" she cried, so deliriously happy she wished she could capture this moment and freeze it somehow, so she could look back on it and smile every day. There were still many things to work out, but she felt like they could compromise. She'd always wanted children, but there was no reason they couldn't adopt, if he wished not to have his own.

"Excellent," he purred, and kissed her again, this time setting her ablaze. "Because I'm having a hard time concentrating right now. Is it always like this?"

"Like what?"

"An overwhelming, relentless urge to fuck, to mark your skin a little, as if I can put my own brand there."

"No." She captured his face and kissed him. "Not until I met you, anyway."

Kincaid groaned, his hand restless down her side, and his hips insistent. He drove her down into the sheets, his hard body pressing over her, rubbing against her clitoris in little half thrusts.

The others had warned her about this. Blood wasn't the only hunger that would have awoken within him. Yes, he'd always been virile, but this was an almost mating intensity. Blue bloods were territorial with those they considered their own, and all his lusts—for blood or for flesh—would be stirred to an almost virulent fever pitch.

"Ava," he breathed as he shoved her nightgown up between them.

She pulled him down to her, letting her thighs cradle his hips. *Yes.* She wanted this man, wanted to claim him herself. Heat rose within her, primal urges demanding she let him take her.

Then his mouth was on hers, and his erection was pressing inside her, filling her in one hard thrust. She wasn't quite ready, and gasped, catching hold of his nightshirt.

"Gentle," she whispered, feeling him still inside her.

Kincaid groaned, and buried his face in the pillow beside her throat. His hips rocked a little, his hand capturing hers, fingers webbing together as he pinned her left hand to the bed. She could feel him trying to be ever so careful with her, fighting the urge to claim her. And she didn't want to wait.

Ava slid her fingers between them, finding that sensitive area between her thighs. The first touch sent need spiraling through her, and Kincaid lifted his hips just enough to allow her access.

"That's it," he whispered. "Make yourself wet for me."

Her body clenched around him, her fingers pushing her closer to the edge. "Fuck me," she whispered, earning a startled thrust from him. "And don't stop, my love."

His ruined mech stump caught in her nightgown. Kincaid growled under his breath, and Ava decided enough was enough. Thrusting a hand against his shoulder, she shoved him flat onto his back, rolling as he went. Her nightgown fell around her legs, and she settled herself over those powerful thighs, the hard thrust of his erection slipping free from her body and rasping against her hip.

Kincaid blinked up at her, then his mouth softened into a rusty smile. "Well now, kitten. Are you going to ride me?"

"Perhaps. Soon." Ava leaned down, nuzzling his jaw. "But I seem to recall some unfulfilled experiments. Some paintings we never quite got around to emulating. And you're hurt. Let me take care of you."

His eyes smoldered. "What precisely did you have in mind?"

A thrill ran through her. In all their previous encounters, he'd been firmly in control, and while she enjoyed him taking her in hand, she was also curious. Ava slid her palms up his bare chest, running her fingers over the heavy slabs of his pectoral muscles. "Perhaps... a little practical experimentation to align with my theory."

He caressed her hair, wrapping one of her blonde curls around his finger. "Say it."

Ava bent and kissed his chest, never taking her eyes off him. "I would like to... cuddle."

He frowned, and then recognition dawned. Kincaid tugged on the strand of hair. "Tease."

She laughed breathlessly, heat curling through her abdomen. "I believe the word I'm searching for is 'fellatio.'"

That hand grabbed a fistful of her hair. "Suck my cock, Ava." His hips gave a small flex beneath her. "Before you torture me too much. I feel a little... restless."

That would be the craving virus driving him to claim her. A muscle ticked in his jaw.

"Does it hurt?" She kissed her way lower, playing along. She'd never felt like this before, curiously free to explore her own sexuality. Powerful in a way.

"A little." His abdomen tensed, and a slow breath poured out of him. "Kiss it better, sweetheart."

Ava bent and pressed her lips to the tip of his erection. He sucked in a sharp breath, freezing beneath her. How curious. One touch, one caress, and he was like putty in her hands.

"More," he groaned.

Ava licked him, capturing the base of his cock with

both hands and then tentatively opening her mouth around the purple, glistening head of him. Salt wept in her mouth, a hint of how close he was to the edge, and so she swallowed him down, testing to see how this worked, before coming back up.

The wet pop of her mouth was loud, and then he was thrusting into her throat, deeper than she'd expected. Deeper perhaps than she was prepared to take. Kincaid groaned, and reached up behind him to grip the timber slats on the bedhead with his one hand. "Fuck. Sorry. Just let me hold on, and try and behave."

"I like seeing you so undone," she whispered, bending back to her task and swallowing him again, the head of his cock sliding smoothly into her throat, as far as she could take him before her throat rebelled. Ava bobbed up and down, watching the way he moaned, the way his fist flexed tighter around the bedhead, his hips thrusting. Helpless gestures, as if he simply couldn't control himself.

She did this to him.

Took a man noted for his iron control, and obliterated it.

"Ava." The word exploded out of him, and he caught a fistful of her hair with his good hand, the other bumping uselessly against her. "Up. I want to be inside you."

Ava straddled his lap as he sat up, sliding into the V of his hips. His cock brushed against the curls between her thighs, and then he slid one hand down her hips, capturing her bottom and pressing her hard against him. She gasped. Fucking him with her mouth had made her wet, and the slick ache between her thighs demanded fulfillment.

"That's it," he rasped, the blunt head of his cock finding her. "Ride me."

He thrust up just as she slid down, and suddenly they were locked together again, two beings forming into one.

Ava moaned, capturing his mouth as her hips rocked, taking in his thick length. He'd always been a big man, but it was easier to manage how much of him she took in this way.

Kincaid kissed her breasts, shoving her nightgown down over her shoulder to reveal them, and tearing it a little. She didn't care. She was wild with need, desperate to stake her own claim on his flesh.

"I love you," she cried softly, as her body began to tighten and he suckled on her nipple. "Oh *my goodness*."

And he laughed at the prim tone of her words, riding her through her orgasm, his hand more insistent upon her hip as he bared his teeth in a wordless snarl and came inside her with a spill of heat.

Kincaid collapsed back on the pillow, and Ava wilted over him, the thick mass of her golden curls spilling over them. He pushed some of it out of his face with a laugh, then rubbed her back, his cock softening inside her. "Stay like this."

She burrowed her face into his throat, feeling like she'd finally found a home for herself. Kincaid stroked her hair, twining each curl around his finger, the relentless urge to mark her clearly softening into affection as they cuddled each other and slowly caught their breaths.

His abdominal muscles flexed as he curled so he could look down into her eyes. An intimate confession turned his own gaze molten. "Perfect, Ava. You and I are perfect. I love you."

And Ava smiled with pure happiness, and fell asleep in his arms.

CHAPTER THIRTY-ONE

THERE WAS SOMEONE in his room.

Someone who was not Ava.

Kincaid woke with a growl, his vision sliding through shades of gray. Every sense was alive in a way he'd never known before, when he was human. Malloryn came into focus, standing by the window and looking out, his hands clasped behind him and his face awash in the cool afternoon light. Kincaid automatically winced as that very same light stabbed his eyes.

"Good afternoon," the duke said. "You're looking better."

"Where's Ava?"

"Definitely better, if one is to judge by the surliness in your tone," Malloryn said, with no small amount of amusement, dragging the chair out beside Kincaid's bed and sinking into it. "Ava has gone to visit her friends at the guild, to make sure the guild master is all right."

"And is he?" He owed Garrett and Perry a debt, after all, for taking care of Ava for all those years.

"Garrett's wound has healed," Malloryn said, "though

the next stage is to fit him with a biomech arm. Lynch and I pushed the Council to pay for it, considering all he's done for the city."

"Takes a bit of getting used to," he said, looking down at the ruined stump of his own hand. "I can show him how it all works."

"Ava would be appreciative of that, I think. How are you feeling?"

He considered the question. Every day he felt better than he ever had. There was a strength in his legs and arms he'd not realized was lacking. Every step he took was stronger, and he no longer feared falling.

The craving virus had worked. He'd not be 100 percent certain his illness had abated, until he had a chance to test his limits—or perhaps until years passed and he could be certain he wasn't getting worse—but hope filled him.

"As fit as a bull," he confessed.

"And mentally? The craving's not easy to get used to."

Heat flushed through Kincaid's cheeks. "Insanely irrational," he admitted. "Territorial. All my emotions seem heightened, and I have... strong urges at times." The last few days ran through his head in a sudden series of vignettes; of fucking Ava over and over, interspersed with moments where he drained a flask of blood dry, before he took her again.

The duke couldn't be referring to that, but all the same....

"Is it always like this?" he growled. The others seemed to be able to control themselves in polite company, but at just the thought of her, his cock was stiffening again.

"Not... always. You're facing a dilemma few blue bloods encounter. Not only are you newly changed, but it seems you're also claiming a female."

"*Claiming* her?"

"I'm told it's a phenomenon that occurs when blue bloods give themselves over to the primal nature of the blue blood within whenever they meet their match."

Kincaid scraped a hand through his unruly black hair. He needed a shave by the feel of it too. "Jaysus."

"Indeed." Malloryn shuddered, as if the thought horrified him a little. No doubt it did, for the duke lived and breathed control. "What do you remember?"

The memory of the duke breathing into his mouth sprang to mind. "Were you fuckin' resuscitating me?"

Malloryn paused, his knuckles whitening on the hilt of his cane, an odd look on his face. "That is one of those moments we shall never speak of again."

Fine with him. "Right. It never happened." He could remember other things too, and none of it made sense. "You came back for us. *And* you carried me out of there."

Malloryn arched a brow. "I only wear my monster-who-crushes-humans-beneath-his-heel face on Mondays, Wednesdays, and Fridays. You were in luck. It was Thursday. Hero day. Besides, you saved my life in that factory. I'm a duke. We never allow ourselves to fall into debt to others."

Kincaid grimaced. "I think I owe you one now."

"Who's counting?" Malloryn asked, but his smile was evil.

"Thank you."

"Wonders never cease," Malloryn said, in a tone that mocked both of them.

Kincaid slumped back onto the pillows. He didn't want to like this man, but perhaps they had more in common than they'd expected. "What happened to the girl? The one you loved."

Silence was his only answer. He didn't think Malloryn

was going to reply, until—

"It's the sort of thing I share only with my nearest and dearest."

"Aren't we friends now?" Kincaid drew his arm up to rest behind his head and smiled at the duke.

Who stared at him flatly.

"I got her killed," the duke said, very softly. "She belonged to someone else, and in my youthful infatuation, I believed I was invincible. That I could take what was his and walk away unscathed. The man she belonged to shot her, right in front of me. Straight through the heart."

Kincaid rolled his head on the pillow to look at the duke. If that was Ava, he would have burned the world to ashes to get revenge. "What happened to him?"

Malloryn's smile was chilling. "I spent the next ten years searching for a way to destroy him."

"Did you succeed?"

"Oh, yes." Malloryn's tone could have frozen an entire sea. "I ruined his every scheme. I destroyed his puppet prince consort, burned his little kingdom to the ground, set his tower ablaze, and then I cut his throat from ear to ear the night the revolution occurred. He managed to escape at the time, but I found his body later in the yard with a bullet to the chest. I wanted to burn his corpse, but the queen insisted he be buried. She wanted Lord Balfour to rot instead, and it seemed fitting."

This was why Malloryn joined the revolution to bring the prince consort undone, and restore human rights to England? "You're a dangerous man."

"I can be." Malloryn relaxed back into his chair. "As Ulbricht and his friends discovered. I have no intention of seeing London destroyed after I sacrificed years of my life to build it."

"What happened to the serum? The SOG?"

"It seems we entered the wrong factory. Ulbricht and the SOG set three of them to blow, and they planned on blaming the humanists. The remaining two factories are in perfect working order. If one doesn't consider the fact all the blood was poisoned."

Kincaid scraped his hands over his face. "So they blame the humanists, and set off a war, and with so little blood remaining, everyone rushes to get what's left."

"That was the plan, yes." Malloryn sighed. "And of course, the only blue bloods who keep enough thralls to feed themselves—and therefore don't require the blood—are the Echelon. Some of them might have died, but it was a risk Ulbricht seemed content to take. I must have pissed him off last month."

"It's your winning charm," Kincaid muttered.

Malloryn barked a laugh. "Perhaps. Ulbricht used to fawn at Balfour's feet, so I was never his favorite person. I wish I'd gotten a chance to question him before he died, to ask him why he suddenly decided to launch this foolish scheme to destroy London. What stirred him up after three years of kissing the queen's hand and pretending he was on board with her plans?"

"That's the problem with dead enemies. You can't question them afterwards," Kincaid replied sleepily. "If I had my time again, I'd have tried not to shoot him for you."

"No matter." Malloryn shrugged and stood, his shadow falling over the bed. "I just wish I knew where those bloody *dhampir* were now. They can't have just vanished, and I suspect they're up to something. Hurry up and get better. Now we've got Byrnes and Ingrid back, I want all hands on deck. Ulbricht and his Sons of Gilead have been vanquished, but now we need to work on the real mission: discovering just *who* has been pulling the strings behind the SOG and the *dhampir*. The mastermind behind all of this nonsense."

"Sounds good." Kincaid yawned. "But you'd better get me a new hand first."

EPILOGUE

"WHAT HAVE YOU got to tell me?" the Master asked.

Obsidian bent his head as he knelt upon the rotted timber floor, and stared at the hem of the Master's velvet robe. It was so bloody cold and dank in here, and he hated it, but the subterfuge was necessary for the next stage of the Master's plans. If anyone found them before they could complete phase two, then everything would be ruined.

And he did not want to be the one to tell the Master or Ghost their little plan had been destroyed.

"Everything's going according to plan," Ghost replied, tugging off his gloves, finger by finger. The tall *dhampir* was ghostly pale in the dark confines of Undertown, faint light highlighting the stark slope of his cheekbones. "The clinical trials of the control chip work. We can move forward with that plan once our pet mech's created enough of them."

"Casualties?"

"It has a success rate of 50 percent."

"Hmm," the Master murmured.

"We can't get close to the queen, as expected," Obsidian stated emotionlessly. "We've been testing the defenses of the Ivory Tower, and it's too tight."

"You'll figure it out, I assume?"

"Yes, Master," they both echoed.

"We just need time," Ghost added. "Ulbricht's little scheme has been a distraction, as we cleaned up after him."

"It was actually rather clever, for Ulbricht," the Master replied. "Poisoning the Echelon's entire drinking supply. Imagine the uproar."

Obsidian froze. Sometimes it felt like the man was testing them. He shouldn't have known that.

"It failed," Ghost said. "And now Malloryn knows what the caterpillar mushroom does. His little company interrupted Ulbricht halfway through completion, and Ulbricht tried to detonate the charges with them inside the factory. Malloryn had brought the Nighthawks in on the scheme, and they managed to capture the remaining Sons of Gilead before they could destroy the other factories."

"So only one factory burned? Obsidian?" the Master demanded.

Obsidian couldn't tell if the Master was displeased. "Yes."

"You watched and did nothing?"

A frisson of alarm went along his nerves. Obsidian looked up, meeting Ghost's eyes where the leader of the *dhampir* stood on the underground train platform at the Master's side. "As instructed, Master," Obsidian replied. "I was told not to interfere. Not to be sighted. We wanted to know what Ulbricht was up to, now he was off Zero's leash."

He held his breath. Ghost brooked no challenges to his leadership, and any infringement was punished cruelly—but the Master... he'd saved them, and brought them together. They owed him everything.

"And Ulbricht?" the Master continued. "Where is he now?"

"Dead. Malloryn must have killed him."

"Any witnesses?"

"The Nighthawks got their hands on a couple of SOG members. I killed a few with the serum when they tried to flee."

"The serum worked?"

"Within minutes," he replied, and then hesitated.

"What is it?" Ghost asked. He never could fool that bastard.

Obsidian swallowed. "There was one anomaly. Corbyn died in the assassination attempt upon Miss McLaren, but to all extents she seems to have survived an injection of the serum."

They looked at each other.

"All of the blue blood test subjects have died," Ghost said slowly. "How did she survive?"

"I don't know, sir."

"Yet," Ghost said, and it wasn't a question.

"Yet," he conceded.

"So Ulbricht failed, and the Sons of Gilead are dead, my lord," Ghost continued. "Most of their higher-ranking members were killed in the explosion, and the rest captured by the Nighthawks."

"It's not important," the Master stated. "Ulbricht was a puppet, and his loss means little to the cause. What *is* important is blue bloods are being killed all across London—at the hands of humans and mechs. The aristocrats of the Echelon are running scared, and bleating to the queen and the Council of Dukes that the people want them dead. Three of their precious draining factories have been burned, and they'll blame the humans for it. The humanists have clashed with the Nighthawks in a catastrophic manner. London's ripe for dissent. Now is the time to divide the classes. I want war in the streets."

"The Nighthawks are claiming blue bloods were

involved with the draining factory explosion. It's all through the papers, my lord," Obsidian said.

Ghost cut him a sharp glance. They'd agreed not to mention that.

The Master's lips thinned. "Malloryn's doing, no doubt. He's starting to truly irritate me."

"I could deal with him," Ghost offered. "Slowly."

"*No.*" The word was hard and emphatic. "Malloryn must be the last to die. I want to take everything away from him first: his precious queen; the city he loves and fought to protect; I want to destroy his ancestral home; to kill every single person around him, including all the agents he's surrounded himself with...."

Obsidian watched as the man paused. He recognized hate when he saw it—the same emotion bound him to the past.

"Then what do you want us to do? This draining factory scheme was a defeat. Malloryn won, despite Ulbricht's maverick plans. That can't be tolerated, despite the desire for secrecy while we enact the next phase of the plan," Ghost argued.

Obsidian waited breathlessly.

"It's not a complete loss. The blue bloods are running scared. Spread some whispers the Nighthawks are covering up the truth about the explosions. Paint a few humanist symbols around the site, or on one of the remaining factories." The Master paused, rubbing at the blackened scar across his throat he usually hid. Its edge was puckered, and it looked as though it had never truly healed. "And then kill one of Malloryn's little company as punishment for ruining my little scheme with Ulbricht. One of the women."

"Which one should we kill?" Ghost asked.

"What do they look like?"

Obsidian and Ghost exchanged glances. "Why?" Obsidian chanced.

"I want to send Malloryn a message," the Master said. "I want to remind him of the past, and let him start to wonder who he's dealing with." He laughed suddenly, a rusty noise, as though this was a great joke.

Obsidian had spent the most time observing Malloryn's Company of Rogues. "Miss McLaren is a blonde with a slim build; Isabella Rouchard has dark hair and voluptuous curves; Ingrid Byrnes has brown hair, amber eyes, and an Amazonian figure typical of her verwulfen race; and... the woman who calls herself Gemma Townsend has dyed black hair."

And an even blacker heart.

Pale eyes seared him as the Master clearly heard something in Obsidian's voice he hadn't been aware of. "Gemma Townsend?"

The name echoed through the abandoned underground train station.

"Hollis Beechworth," Obsidian stated coldly, hiding a flinch. His fist clenched. *Not her.* He wasn't done with her yet. "Emma Rusden. Alice Clayton. Or Gemma Townsend, as she goes by now. She's been Malloryn's right hand for years."

"The spy in Malloryn's party in Saint Petersburg seven years ago," Ghost added quietly, and both he and the master exchanged a significant look.

"Black hair," the Master repeated, reaching into his pocket. "Her. She's the one. The perfect candidate. Have her killed. Put her in a white gown, like something a debutante—or a thrall—would wear. Then shoot straight through the heart. And leave her on Malloryn's doorstep."

Obsidian's chest tightened, as though a metal fist

gripped his heart. *No.* Blood began to rush through his ears as the darker half of him rose to the surface, picturing her death.

Violence rose in his throat, threatening to choke him. A demanding rage he fought, locking it down deep inside him. He could almost feel the electric lash of the whip across his back, the leather gag between his teeth as Ghost put him through his conditioning after he'd failed to kill her the first time.

"Do you still love her?" Ghost had asked, as Obsidian fought to breathe around the gag. Ghost held up the electric wire. *"Do you have any feelings for that lying little bitch still within you?"*

No. He'd shaken his head. And that *no* had echoed in the place his heart used to lie. Before she ripped it out of his chest.

Ghost straightened. "Yes, Lord Balfour. I'll get one of the new recruits to do it. Perhaps Langley. He needs to prove he's ready to be initiated into the Brotherhood."

Langley was a dead man. Obsidian kept all signs of it off his face, however.

The Master removed his hand from his pocket, fingering something with a certain kind of careful grace. He stared at it for a long moment, as though it meant something to him. Then his lips thinned, and he thrust the thing at Ghost. "And have him put this around her neck."

"A locket?" Ghost sounded surprised.

"Malloryn will know who it belongs to." The Master finally smiled. "Make sure you watch when he finds the locket. I want you to describe the look on his face to me, in perfect, exquisite detail."

"And you, my lord?" Ghost dared to ask, the words echoing distantly in Obsidian's ears.

Control it, he told himself, staying utterly still.

The Master swung a fur-lined cape over his shoulders, the sable color highlighting the gray in his coppery hair. "I'm going to take care of the Russian problem. You have a month until I return. Initiate phase two of our plan. I'll expect to see the blood splashed all across Europe's newspapers."

"Yes, my lord," they both echoed, though only Obsidian felt the crushing heat of fury ignite in his heart as Lord Balfour vanished through the blackened tunnels of Undertown.

Gemma's death belonged to him.

And no one else.

Is that why you saved her life last month when Ghost sent one of the recruits to kill her?

He pushed to his feet. He'd had his chance then to repay the debt she owed.

It was just the shock of seeing her again that stayed my hand.

The sight of her pale, heart-shaped face as she lay unconscious and bleeding had thrust him years into the past, when she'd whispered love words in his ears and almost swayed him to her side. Gemma—or Hollis, as he'd known her—had been the one person who'd threatened the foundation upon which he'd placed his trust, and made him question exactly who he owed his loyalty to.

Just another of her pretty lies.

But he'd had time to think past the shock of seeing her. Time to reassess what she meant to him, and the damage she'd done him.

Next time... next time it wouldn't be as difficult.

But first, he had to keep her alive long enough to exact his revenge.

Skoro moya yadovitaya lyubov....

Soon.

If you enjoyed *The Mech Who Loved me*, then get ready for *You Only Love Twice*! Book three in the *Blue Blood Conspiracy* series, it will be available early 2018, so make sure you sign up for my newsletter at www.becmcmaster.com to receive news and excerpts about this release!

Thank you for reading *The Mech Who Loved Me*! I hope you enjoyed it. Please consider leaving a review online, to help others find my books.

Not ready to leave steampunk London? Read on for a preview of what's next for the Company of Rogues...

YOU ONLY LOVE TWICE

THE BLUE BLOOD CONSPIRACY, BOOK THREE

With the clock ticking down, the Company of Rogues must find a deadly killer and stop them from assassinating the Queen... before London burns.

Gemma Townsend failed her mission once, and knows love is a weakness she can never afford again. When offered a chance at redemption, the seductive spy is determined to complete her assigned task: to track down a dangerous assassin known as the Chameleon, a mysterious killer whose identity seems to constantly change. As her investigation leads Gemma into a trap, she's rescued by a shadowy figure she thought was dead—the double agent who stole her heart five years ago, before he put a bullet in her chest.

Born in fire. Brainwashed. Betrayed.

A man with few memories thanks to the harsh conditioning he was put through, all Obsidian knows is that Gemma betrayed him, and he wants revenge. But one kiss ignites the forbidden passion between them, and he can't bring himself to kill her. As they find themselves on opposite sides of a war, they must question everything they believed to be true. Because it soon becomes clear someone is lying and the Chameleon might be closer than either of them realized. Can Obsidian break the ties of his allegiance? Before his only chance at redemption—and love—is lost forever?

ACKNOWLEDGMENTS

Writing fast-paced, sexy, paranormal romance is the best fun imaginable, but as with every project I take on, I couldn't have done it without a lot of help from these amazing people:

I owe huge thanks to my editor Olivia from Hot Tree Editing for her work on this manuscript; to Mandy from Hot Tree Edits for the proofread; my wonderful cover artists from Damonza.com; and Marisa Shor from Cover Me Darling and Allyson Gottlieb for the print formatting.

To the CVW Group, thanks for keeping me sane, and being my support group! Special thanks also go to my beta readers, Kylie Griffin and Jennie Kew—who ask me all of the hard questions, and support me on every step of this journey. And to my family for always supporting me on this journey. But the most thanks go to Byron, who has been my rock from the very beginning. I couldn't do what I do without his help.

Last, not certainly not least, to all of my readers who support me on this journey, and have been crazy vocal about their love for the London Steampunk series, and anything else I write! I hope you enjoy the next phase of London Steampunk, and yes... Charlie is still coming.

ABOUT THE AUTHOR

Bec McMaster grew up on a steady diet of 80's fantasy movies like Ladyhawke, Labyrinth and The Princess Bride, and loves creating epic, fantasy-based worlds with heroes and heroines who must defeat all the odds to have their HEA. If you like sexy, dark, paranormal romance, try her Dark Arts series; for some kick-bustle ladies-saving-the-day steampunk romance then check out London Steampunk; and for rocket-fuelled post-apocalyptic romance with a twist on the werewolf theme, then see her Burned Lands series.

Bec has won a PRISM Award for Historical Fantasy with Hexbound (2016), been nominated for RT Reviews Best Steampunk Romance for Heart of Iron (2013), won RT Reviews Best Steampunk Romance with Of Silk And Steam (2015), and Forged By Desire was nominated for an RWA RITA award in 2015. The London Steampunk series has received starred reviews from Booklist, Publishers Weekly, and Library Journal, with Heart of Iron named one of their Best Romances of 2013.

She's also a dreamer. A travel addict. And an enthusiastic baker. If she's not sitting in front of the computer, she's probably plotting her next world trip. Bec lives in Australia, with her very own hero, Byron; a dog who will eat anything (even used teabags); and demanding chickens, Siggy and Lagertha.

For news on new releases, cover reveals, contests, and special promotions, join her mailing list at www.becmcmaster.com, or follow her on Twitter @BecMcMaster, or www.facebook.com/BecMcMaster

31041975R00244

Printed in Poland
by Amazon Fulfillment
Poland Sp. z o.o., Wrocław